ALSO BY CATHRYN GRANT

THE WOMAN IN THE CASTLE

A PSYCHOLOGICAL SUSPENSE NOVEL

ALEXANDRA MALLORY
BOOK FIFTEEN

CATHRYN GRANT

Perspectives

ISBN: 978-1-943142-78-1

This book is a work of fiction. References to real people, events, establishments, organizations, or locales are intended only to provide a sense of authenticity, and are used fictitiously. All other characters, and incidents and dialogue, are drawn from the author's imagination and are not to be construed as real.

Visit Cathryn online at CathrynGrant.com

Cover design by Lydia Mullins Copyright © 2024

CHAPTER 1

NAPA VALLEY, CALIFORNIA

*T*ess was waiting for Damien and me. She stood on the front patio of her palatial Mediterranean home wearing a pale green dress that fell to mid-calf.

As I slid out of the Uber, she took off her sunglasses and stared at me, shaking her head ever so slightly.

I had no doubt the head-shaking was over my new hair color.

The evening before my flight, I'd had my hair dyed a stunning strawberry blonde with streaks of copper. It was longer now, reaching to the center of my back. Every morning, I used a fat curling iron to give it wild, luscious waves. It attracted more attention than I was used to, so I wasn't sure how long I would leave it that color, but I was enjoying it. The colors felt summery and perfect for my temporary new life in California.

I didn't know if I'd done it for California, or for Tess, or because I needed to see someone different when I looked in the mirror every morning.

I reached back into the car and removed Damien's travel cage. When I emerged holding him, Tess dropped her sunglasses onto a small table and came running toward me. She began talking to Damien a mile a minute. He squawked back, clearly not happy with what he'd experienced during his nearly six-hour flight, not to mention all the shuffling around he'd had to endure before and after his time in the air.

"Wait until he sees his aviary," Tess said. "He'll never shriek like this again."

She picked up his cage and started toward the house. I followed, pulling two large suitcases, two zippered carryalls and my everyday bag slung over my shoulders.

The entryway was magnificent. It opened to the second story, with a landing that looked down onto the tile floor below. To the left was a bench with a potted palm on each side. To the right was a recessed wall displaying framed photographs of Tess and her fiancé, Marcus, many of them taken in Australia. There was also a sixteen-by-twenty photograph of Tess and me. We were sitting on the patio in the backyard of the house where we'd lived in Australia, sipping martinis. Both of us were laughing. Tess was gazing at me, almost as if she were in love with me. Both of us looked blissfully happy.

Directly across from the front door was the aviary. It stood at a towering twelve feet and was almost the size of a small bedroom. Inside were potted eucalyptus branches and several live plants. There were three perches at varying heights from which Damien could survey his surroundings. There was a large dish of water and another bowl containing mango, and some of the seed mix that provided him with a balanced diet.

Tess unlatched the door, stepped inside, and placed his travel cage on the floor, which was covered with fine gravel. She opened his cage door and stepped back.

Damien wasted no time stepping out of his cage. He strutted directly to the bowl of mango and took a piece without comment. His crown was lowered, and he bobbed slightly as he gobbled the fruit. If a bird could smile, if he could look as blissfully happy as Tess and I did in that oversized photograph, that was how Damien appeared when he swallowed the first piece of mango. He cocked his head to the side and looked directly into Tess's eyes.

Delicious mango, he said.

We watched him eat every piece of fruit in the bowl, then we stepped out of the aviary, leaving him alone to get comfortable in his new home.

As I followed Tess through to a living room lined with bifold doors that opened onto a huge patio and a lush garden beyond, I felt my shoulders relax. It was a relief to no longer be responsible for her charming, opinionated cockatoo. It had been a lot of fun listening to him speak. I was constantly entertained as I imagined him carrying on conversations with me. I liked pretending I could tell him my secrets, that he was listening and keeping them safe, but I had not liked dragging him around New York City. I had not liked being responsible for his wellbeing. I had not liked keeping him locked in my small bedroom to ensure my roommate's fiancé didn't harass him, or worse.

"Do you want a cappuccino or iced latte?" Tess asked. "Water? A glass of wine?"

"Water, for now."

She disappeared from the living room and I settled onto her enormous sectional, looking out at more greenery and blue sky than I'd seen in over a year, almost two. All that endless blue sky seemed to promise a peaceful existence. I felt a thousand miles from the grit of New York City, from the gray skyscrapers, the nearly constant noise of traffic, and a tremendous number of people navigating a very small area.

Lingering back there in the shadows of those skyscrapers was Ned Carter. I'd pointed a shadowy finger at him in the death of Carolina Scott. It was unlikely he would connect me to her and the trouble I'd caused him. Almost impossible. Still, I longed to know the outcome of my finger-pointing. I didn't like not knowing the outcome because even though he couldn't connect me to Carolina, he definitely blamed me for the loss of his fiancée. I had no idea how deep his anger went, knowing that my recording of him hitting on me had cut Eileen cleanly out of his life.

I hadn't been able to resist punishing him. But I wanted both the satisfaction of knowing I'd caused trouble, and the assurance that he hadn't tied it to me.

It was a curiosity I would have to live with, so I tried to put it out of my mind. So far, it wasn't cooperating as well as I'd hoped. I stood and walked to the glass doors to get a better view of the garden.

I wondered where Marcus was and how long it would be until I met him—the man who had transformed Tess into a woman who had chosen to sideline her successful and lucrative career in order to stomp grapes and, soon, start making babies. I was beyond curious.

A guy who had made millions with his cyber security start-up. I knew the type. A techie with so much money he'd come to believe he was always the smartest guy in the room. The most deserving guy in the room. The Man. Anyone who didn't speak his language was stupid by default.

Maybe he wasn't. But a lot of them were, and even though my experience was limited, I wasn't predisposed to assume he and I were going to click.

CHAPTER 2

*N*early ten minutes passed before Tess returned, balancing a tray with two tall glasses of iced water. Lemon wedges that looked like they'd been plucked out of the sun, they were such a perfect yellow, were perched on the edges of the glasses. She placed the tray on the coffee table and handed a glass to me.

"I hope you didn't change your mind and decide you wanted something else after all this time." She picked up her own glass of water and took a sip.

I laughed. "Where were you?"

"I needed to check on Damien."

"And how is he?"

"He seems very happy."

"Are you planning to add more cockatoos to the aviary? Or other birds?"

She shrugged. "We'll see. I'll let Marcus get used to Damien first."

Dangerous woman! Damien's comment was loud enough to carry into the living room. I laughed. Tess rolled her eyes and took a few more sips of water. "I'll show you your room and you can get settled. Take a shower. There's a pool, if you want to …"

Her voice trailed off as she must have remembered I wasn't a fan of water. Although I'd learned to swim, it still wasn't something I was going to spend my free time doing.

"There's a workout room too," she said. "And a yoga studio."

"The house looks amazing. I can't wait to see it."

"I love it." She placed her glass on the tray. "Lots of room for babies." She gave me a smile that had a whisper of a madonna quality to it. I couldn't figure out if she'd manufactured the suggestion of a glow, or it had emerged on its own.

I recalled how she'd shown up at my apartment door with Damien in his travel cage, asking me to care for him indefinitely, and wondered how she would handle a child or two tied to her hip for eighteen years. I definitely would not be able to help her out in that situation. I hoped she was aware of that. Maybe I would need to make that clear the moment she announced one was on its way.

"And we can't wait to entertain, of course."

"Your wedding?"

"It won't be here after all. I changed my mind."

I finished my water and placed the glass beside hers. "Why?"

"You'll find out." She gave me a sly smile. "I'll show you around. You can try some of our wine, and you can meet Marcus."

Instructing me to leave my suitcases in the entryway until my tour was finished, she took me through the rooms on the ground floor, showing me a formal dining room with a long table surrounded by sixteen chairs, a massive kitchen that was all silver and white, a breakfast room, a study, a workout room, the yoga studio that looked out on a small garden with a koi pond, and a library. On the second floor was a suite of rooms that could have been its own apartment, occupied by Tess and Marcus. The suite had a small kitchenette, a sitting room, a walk-in closet, and a palatial bathroom. The bed faced a semi-circle of tall windows that were ringed by a window seat. The windows opened out into a thick grove of trees, making it feel as if we were standing in a tree house.

There were five other bedrooms, each with their own bathroom.

On the floor above were three more bedrooms and a games room with a pool table. There was an entertainment room with theater chairs and an enormous TV that was almost like a small movie screen.

After my bags were unpacked, my clothes hung in a closet filled with wood hangers, and my makeup arranged in a spacious bathroom, it seemed as if I'd moved in for a two-month stay. There was something about the bedroom suite that felt as if it belonged to me. Tess had hung photographs from the house we'd shared with Gavin and Seth in Australia. There were also two framed photos of Damien and another of Tess and me.

The drawers and closet were empty, so I didn't feel as if I were squeezing into someone else's space. The king-sized bed looked palatial compared to anything I'd slept in before. It almost made me want to take a nap right that minute. There were candles on the nightstand and a beautiful pottery bowl of polished stones on a desk equipped with all the things I needed for charging my phone and tablet.

After a shower, I changed into jeans and a white tank top and white sweater. I slipped on a pair of black flip-flops and went downstairs, losing my way when I reached the ground floor, then getting distracted as I stumbled upon the yoga studio again and spent time looking at the bolsters and blocks and mats in the cabinet. It had been a long time since I'd had space to do yoga properly. In the apartment I'd shared with Eileen, once Ned started invading our space, I lost the desire to do yoga in the living room and found myself banging my forearms and ankles on my bedroom furniture as I tried to move into poses in the tiny floor space.

I could get used to staying here. Already my mind was searching for ways to extend my visit, to convince Diana I needed more time for my fabricated family emergency. But if Marcus and I took an instant dislike to each other, maybe I wouldn't be enjoying my incredible king-sized bed for very long, or stretching into more challenging yoga positions after all.

Instead, I'd be back in New York city battling Diana. I'd lose the chance to figure out how I would get out of my smothering apartment where Eileen wanted to know what I was doing every minute of the day. I would miss my chance to figure out how to escape from a job that was turning sour. It had started out as a fabulous smorgasbord of human beings I could photograph in luscious settings, talking to them until I slithered my way into their minds and enticed them to expose their deepest selves so that Trystan could do his job.

Now, Trystan was dead, and Diana was sucking the life out of the work that had made my blood pump eagerly through my veins. She'd turned it into something bland. I felt as if I was taking photographs, wearing handcuffs and shackles.

Maybe I was having a midlife crisis in my thirties. Lately, I'd seen myself drifting endlessly through the years, never owning property, living in someone else's apartment, always working for a boss who controlled everything I did, grabbing what little fun I could in the evenings and on the weekends.

Staying in Tess's house, getting lost in her excessive number of rooms or out in her acres of vineyards, drinking her wine, and listening to her wedding plans would put my mind in a completely different state. I was absolutely sure of it.

Somehow, this was going to change everything and I would figure out a new direction for my life. I would figure out a direction for the first time, because I'd never considered having a *direction*. Every morning of my life, I'd gotten out of bed and followed my instincts. I still liked doing that, but now I needed to give a little more thought to what my instincts might be telling me beyond the next twelve hours.

CHAPTER 3

*I*n the living room, two of the bifold doors had been opened onto the flagstone patio. Tess and Marcus stood near a table shaded by a forest-green umbrella. On the table was a bottle of wine and three glasses. I stepped outside. I placed my sunglasses over my eyes while I placed a gracious smile across the bottom of my face and walked toward Tess and her fiancé.

"Alexandra! This is Marcus."

He turned and held out his hand. His grip was warm and firm and his smile was as gracious as mine. His eyes were also concealed, so everything was equal in the first instant of our meeting.

"The infamous Alex," he said.

And I knew from the tone of his voice that he might be alright. "The mysterious Marcus."

It's the animal instinct, that half second when you viscerally *know* everything about a person. Maybe not even half a second. It might be a scent you're not even aware of, a sense of the way a person stands and the way they arrange their facial features, even when their eyes are concealed. And yes, the tone of voice, the words, even a word like *infamous*. In a different tone, with a slightly different smile, with a changed posture, it might have put me on my guard, it might have made my skin crawl.

"This is a Chardonnay from our vines," Tess said. "Marcus and I didn't make it, of course. It was produced by the previous owners, but you can get a sense of what we'll be up to over the next few years." She poured a splash of wine into each of the three glasses, handed them around, and held hers up so we could tap our glasses against each other.

"To making wine and new friends," she said.

It was a charming blend of words. Marcus was obviously charmed because he kissed her cheek, that looked quite seductive, before he sipped his wine. Both of Tess's cheeks turned pink. She ducked her head slightly, then took a quick sip of wine.

"Tell me all about yourself, Alex," Marcus said.

Even that obnoxious statement didn't slither down my spine as it might have coming from some people. Especially because he immediately poked fun at the absurdity of his request.

"Everything there is to tell that you can manage to cover in the next three to four minutes before we talk casually about growing grapes and the California weather and Tess's plans for our wedding cake, of course." He held up his glass in a mock toast, then took a sip.

"I grew up in Oregon. I met Tess in California. We worked together in Australia, and now I live in New York."

"A geography lesson," he said.

"Did you learn anything?" Tess asked.

Marcus laughed. "I learned Alex is succinct. So I'm impressed."

"Your wine is very nice." It seemed like the right thing to say at that point, since we were gazing out across acres of vineyards, and Tess had made a big deal out of displaying the label to me.

"We can't take credit, yet," Tess said.

"Will yours taste different?"

"I really don't know." She laughed. "Part of me hopes not. But we also want to be distinctive. To raise the bar. And, of course, every year has a different character, so from that perspective, it will."

"Are you artfully changing the subject, Alex?" Marcus asked.

"No. I'm drinking your wine and looking at your grapes."

"I want to know more about you," Marcus said. "Tess wants you front and center at our wedding. She thinks you're a remarkable human being. Or are you someone who doesn't like to talk about herself?"

I smiled.

"A listener," he said.

Tess laughed.

"She's not?" Marcus asked.

"She listens when she feels like it. But she has *opinions*, and she is never shy about handing them around. But yes, she's also a good listener. It's just not the first thing I think of when her name comes to mind." She gave me a conspiratorial smile.

Marcus nodded. "You've mentioned that."

I wondered how many conversations they'd had about me. I wondered if Marcus wanted to know why Tess had promoted me from bridal attendant to maid of honor. I wasn't sure if it had been a promotion or if she'd intended that role for me all along and hadn't been clear about it at first because she thought I might say no, so she'd decided to reel me in slowly.

Maybe she'd had to justify her choice. It was possible she'd asked Marcus to do the same. Or maybe it wasn't like that at all. Married people did all kinds of things I wasn't familiar with. One of those things seemed to be analyzing and discussing the people they knew.

After someone was married, their friends moved into an outer ring. Now, anything I said to Tess would make its way to Marcus. But I would probably know quite a bit less about him. The imbalance of it was strange. It made me curious whether things would start winding down between Tess and me just as we were starting to get reacquainted.

"How do you like New York?" Marcus asked.

"It's great. I like eating out and I like having endless restaurant choices, and really amazing food. I like the excitement. The noise is annoying sometimes. I'd probably like it better if I lived in a penthouse."

Marcus laughed so hard, wine splashed out of his glass. He placed the glass on the table and wiped the back of his hand on his jeans. He picked up his glass, and just as he was about to take a sip, he started laughing again. "That's too much."

"Why?" I asked.

"You're very candid."

"I told you," Tess said.

He took a sip of wine. "We would all love to live in a penthouse."

I was certain he was someone who could afford to do exactly that, so I wasn't sure why he was acting as if he and I had the same obstacles to our theoretical enjoyment of New York, but I didn't point that out. I wanted to, but Tess would be annoyed. More than annoyed.

"Anyway, I like all the people. I like the anonymity of it. I like Central Park and the nightlife, although I didn't go out as much as I thought I would when I first moved there."

"Why not?" he asked.

I shrugged. It probably had something to do with Eileen, but I'd never really thought about it until that moment. Or maybe it had everything to do with me and my avocation.

Marcus refilled our glasses, and we moved away from the table to an arrangement of wood patio furniture with thick, cornflower blue cushions. We sat down and Marcus continued asking detailed questions about my life. He wanted to know all about my job, and then he wanted to know about Trystan's death.

He didn't seem at all like the CEO of a cyber security company and he didn't seem like a tech guy that was full of himself and thought he knew more than everyone else. He didn't seem like the kind of man who believed everyone who didn't understand how the internet and artificial intelligence worked deep inside their mysterious chips and software wasn't worth the brain cells they did have.

He asked about my running and wanted me to explain why I liked it. He was fascinated by the fact that I lifted weights, *for a woman*, and insisted I outline my workout regimen to him.

When I said I lifted weights because I liked feeling strong, he asked, "Why do you need to feel strong?"

"Don't you like feeling strong?"

"I'm a guy. It's a given we want to feel strong. Most women don't think that's important."

"I do."

"Why?"

"Does everything have to have a reason?"

"Do you have a reason?"

"It's the same as yours."

"It can't be. My reason is because I'm male."

"That's not a reason. It's an excuse. It's not your reason, it's only your assumption."

He stared at me. He pushed his sunglasses onto the top of his head and squinted. He took a sip of wine. He smiled slowly, then started laughing. "You're funny."

"It wasn't meant as a joke."

"You're still funny. And I still don't know why you lift heavy weights."

I glanced toward the side of the patio, past the large wood table surrounded by eight sturdy chairs, past the outdoor kitchen, past the half wall filled with flowering plants that draped themselves over the stone sides.

A man stood a few yards away on the path that led to the garden beyond us. He wore dark brown slacks and a white button-down shirt. The sleeves were rolled up to reveal muscled, lightly tanned forearms. He had walnut brown hair cut short, and a tightly trimmed beard. He wore aviator sunglasses and appeared to be looking at us.

As I watched him, he didn't turn away, uncomfortable with being caught staring. He didn't move toward us as if he'd come to speak to Tess or Marcus. He stood like a marble statue, watching.

"Who's that?" I asked.

Marcus turned his head slightly. "Silas Birch. He's head of our wine tasting, marketing, and PR."

"He was with the winery before we bought it," Tess said. "He's one of the best in the field. I don't know how we would get this place up and running without him. He's been our savior."

I took a sip of wine. I doubted that. Most people who position themselves as saviors are anything but that.

CHAPTER 4

*M*arcus stood. "I have a few calls to make before dinner. Why don't you introduce Alexandra to our savior?" He laughed, a sound that could have been interpreted as sarcastic, but also could have been playful. I wasn't sure.

He went into the house and I turned my attention back to the guy in the aviator glasses, who still appeared to be absolutely motionless.

Tess put down her wineglass and stood. "Come on."

"To bow in front of your savior?"

She laughed. "Seriously. He is. We had the option to buy out the contracts for all our staff. It was a great deal and as much as I want to get my hands in the clay here, we would not have been able to keep this place running without the experts."

"I'm sure not." I remained seated and took a sip of wine.

"I really want to introduce you to him. You can finish your wine later."

"Just one more sip. There's no rush." I took a sip, then lowered my voice. "I don't want to tell you how to run your business, since I know nothing about wine. But I do know a little about people, and I know you do too, after all the teams you've managed. But it's really not a great idea to let him think he's your *savior*. He'll—"

"I get it," Tess said. "But it's also important to let your employees know you value them. And I would have been lost without Silas." She held out her hand. "Let's go. I don't want to keep him waiting. He's probably ready to leave for the day."

"Then why doesn't he walk over here instead of standing there like a stalker?"

Tess didn't laugh. I thought she might, but she pressed her lips together, and not as if she were suppressing a laugh, but with a definite look of annoyance. She turned and crossed the patio, leaving me on the sofa, sipping my wine.

A moment later, she and Silas were standing in front of me, blocking the sun that was sinking toward the foothills.

"Alex, this is Silas. Our Sommelier and CMO. The voice of Black Mask Wines."

"Hi," I said.

"Good to meet you." He didn't extend his hand. "I've heard a lot about you."

I took a sip of wine, sorry to see only a small dribble remained in my glass. "I've heard almost nothing about you."

He touched the frame of his glasses as if he were about to lift them away from his face and give me a wink, but he lowered his hand and made an abrupt change of course. "I love your hair," he said. "It's eye-catching."

"It comes from a bottle, but thank you."

"It's absolutely breathtaking. I thought it was natural."

I laughed. "No, you didn't. If you've heard a lot about me, and you've been in Tess's home, you've seen the larger-than-life photo of me and Tess in the entryway."

"I hadn't noticed," he said.

"It's a sixteen-by-twenty photograph in a huge frame hanging in the entryway. You can't miss it."

He shrugged and gave me a slightly vacant smile.

I finished my wine.

Now, he held out his hand for me to shake it. I tipped the wine-glass to my lips again, ignoring his hand. He let it fall to his side, then slid it into his pocket.

"I hear you know everything there is to know about wine," I said.

"Probably not everything."

"Don't be modest."

"I'm not," he said. "Just truthful."

He gave me a smile that would have been charming if he hadn't lied to my face about thinking my hair color was natural, and about not having noticed the ridiculously large picture in the entryway.

"It must be fun to have a job that's just day drinking," I said.

"I don't drink when I'm working."

"How do you taste the wine?"

"I don't taste wine. I oversee the tasting room."

I nodded. "And you're never tempted to have a few sips? Who makes sure it's a good bottle, before you serve it to people who come in expecting a stunning taste? People who want a little taste before they decide to buy a case to take home?"

"I don't drink while I'm working. I'm a professional."

"I'm sure Tess is relieved to hear that."

"She was already aware."

"But someone must taste the wine."

"A pro can tell by the bouquet. Tasting isn't necessary."

"Then why all the ceremonial tasting in restaurants?"

"To give the customer every opportunity to ensure they like what they're buying."

I wondered if he was telling the truth. After his blatant lie about my hair, everything he said from here on out would be suspect. I supposed the same could be said about me. Like him, I said what was convenient. But I didn't lie about things that could be disproven by opening the front door to someone's home. Did he think Tess and I were stupid? Easily duped? She didn't seem bothered by his obvious lie. Maybe it was a marketing thing. A certain number of half-truths were to be expected and, therefore, were taken in stride. But still … it was absurd. And pointless. Why did he need to pretend my hair color was natural? I didn't, so it wasn't a point of flattery.

"How long have you worked at Black Mask?" I asked.

"Fifteen years."

He hardly looked old enough. I would have guessed he was about thirty. Maybe thirty-two. Was that also a lie? Or was I off on my estimate? I longed to ask his age, but I wouldn't get an accurate answer, so it didn't seemed worth it.

"What's the best thing about wine?" I asked.

"The variety."

It was a good answer. It made me think he wasn't as superficial as he'd seemed.

But then he had to spoil it by spelling it out. "No two years are ever the same, even if we keep the grapes on the vines, the identical number of days. We can use the same process, the same equipment, and the wines will change as if they have their own unique personalities, as if they want to be recognized as individuals. It's endlessly, eternally fascinating." He stopped, taking a deep breath, as if the passionate explanation of wine personalities had exhausted him.

"I guess the weather—"

"It's much more complex than weather," he sneered. "So much more. The soil, the timing of the rain, the pruning … everything. There are an infinite number of details to be aware of. It's more complex than anyone who doesn't work with wine can ever understand."

"That's why you're the expert," I said.

He gave me a half smile. "I'll let you ladies get back to relaxing with your afternoon wine. It was a pleasure to meet you, Alexandra. Enjoy your visit, and I'm sure I'll see you again." He left quickly.

Tess drifted over to the wine chiller and brought it to where we were sitting. She poured a splash of wine into our glasses and settled on the couch across from me. "Isn't he great?"

"A bit of a liar, so I hope you keep a close eye on him."

"He's not a liar."

"He said he thought my hair was natural. He couldn't possibly think that after seeing that tribute to us in your entryway."

"Don't be petty."

"I'm not. I'm just pointing out that he's a liar. A clumsy liar."

"He likes to flatter people. He's young. He might be a little rough around the edges, but so great at what he does. He's still learning."

"He's been in the wine business fifteen years."

"He worked in his family business as a teenager. And he needs to develop some maturity, that's all."

I nodded. So not really in the wine business. More that he was *around* wine. Two lies in less than twenty minutes. And as I'd said to Tess, clumsy lies. A savior and a liar. I hoped I didn't have an opportunity to see him again. I also hoped that Tess wasn't too blinded by her need for wine experts and too focused on weddings and babies to pay close attention to what was going on around her.

CHAPTER 5

When Marcus served the duck with risotto and a side dish of grilled artichokes, Tess could see that Alex was impressed. It was rare that Tess could decipher what Alex was thinking or feeling, but her delight in the meal was painted across her face as if she were enjoying one of the most rapturous moments of her life.

Of course, Alex often looked rapturous when she was eating good food, but this was clearly something that was a cut above.

The first time Marcus had cooked dinner for Tess, she'd felt as if she'd clawed her way to the heart of a diamond mine and plucked out the most brilliant specimen the planet had to offer. Of course, she'd also known that the moment they met. For so many years, she'd thought lifelong love or the idea of a soul mate was something that either probably didn't truly exist, or might not be possible for her. Then, without warning, there he was.

And then it turned out he was an amazing cook. It was, as they said, too good to be true.

Was it her imagination that Alex looked impressed, possibly the first time Tess had ever observed that expression on her face, when

Marcus carried his chocolate tart into the room and placed it on the table beside the coffee press?

Then, just as she thought their evening, and the introduction of the only woman Tess had ever come close to calling a best friend and her fiancé were really clicking, Marcus received a call from a customer that he had to take.

She was disappointed. But at the same time, she had a few questions for Alex and time alone with her might be a good thing. With all the charm Alex had poured out on Marcus, all her distrustful opinions about Silas, all her updates about how Damien had fared in New York, she'd been deliberately silent about the new guy in her life.

Tess leaned across the table, gazing at Alex with an intense look that she hoped would force Alex to maintain eye contact. "You've been here for six and a half hours and I haven't heard a word about Hunter. You haven't even spoken his name."

"Why would I mention his name?"

"Isn't that what couples do?"

Alex cut the piece of tart on her plate with the side of her fork. She carefully placed the piece of pastry and chocolate into her mouth. She chewed slowly. She took a sip of coffee. She broke eye contact, looking around the room, noting the artwork, gazing up at the chandelier.

"Why are you going quiet on me?" Tess asked.

"I'm enjoying this incredible dessert."

"No, you're not. You're avoiding my question." Tess smiled, keeping her eyes fixed on Alex, waiting.

"You don't know what I'm doing," Alex said. "I'm lost in this tart. It's delicious. Where did Marcus learn to cook?"

"His dad taught him. And he loves it, so he picked things up from doing it all the time. Don't change the subject. I want to hear about your new boyfriend. Is that too much to ask when I haven't seen you for ages? For more than ages?"

"I don't have anything to say about him."

"I thought he would come with you," Tess said.

"Why?"

"I just assumed."

"I wouldn't show up with an uninvited guest."

"You should have known he was welcome."

"You probably should have said he was invited, but I still wouldn't have brought him. I thought we were doing wedding stuff."

"We are. But not all day, every day. Not even every day. Just cake tasting. Champagne tasting, and we might go dress shopping, but we might not. I still have to narrow it down more."

Alex took another bite of tart. "Hunter and I don't have that kind of relationship."

"What kind?"

"The vacation together kind."

Tess laughed. "Are you serious?"

Alex took another bite of tart. "This is so good. I can't find enough words to tell you how amazing it is."

"I'm glad to hear that. But I'm trying to have a conversation about a delicious guy, not chocolate and pastry."

Alex smiled. Her tongue slid out of her mouth, flicking at the corners of her lips for stray flecks of chocolate before it disappeared inside.

"So what kind of relationship is it where you don't take trips together?" Tess asked.

Alex shrugged. She took another bite of the tart. Soon, it would be gone. Maybe then she would be able to focus and Tess might be able to get a straight answer out of her. Although, it wasn't likely. Alex was very good at avoiding questions and making it seem perfectly normal, retaining a pleasant demeanor as if it were absolutely polite and pleasant to stubbornly refuse to participate in a conversation.

"Have you gone anywhere together?" Tess asked.

"We spent the weekend in a five-star hotel."

"Where?"

"In New York."

"That's not traveling."

"Lots of people travel to New York. We were already there." Alex grinned.

"Come on, Alex. Are you and Hunter even together, or are you just having sex with him?"

Alex shrugged.

"Just having sex? I thought it was more than that. You seemed …"

"Why do I have to define it?"

"Why do you make it sound like that's a bad thing—to define a relationship? It's normal." Tess looked past her, out at the garden where the shadows had fallen across the flowers, and turned the trees into dark shapes that looked either protective or threatening. Right now, she wasn't sure which.

She shivered and returned her attention to Alex's relaxed, smiling face. Alex looked utterly unconcerned, and possibly oblivious to the fact that she was driving Tess insane with her non-answers.

"Do you have an issue with making a commitment? You've been with a lot of guys and it seems like—"

"So have you."

"But I'm engaged now."

"Does that mean everyone you know has to get engaged? You don't feel comfortable unless everyone else is doing exactly what you are?"

"No. But I realized you've never been with anyone for more than two months. If that."

"Have you? Before Marcus?"

"Yes."

"Really? For how long?"

"That's not the point."

"What is the point? May I have another piece of tart? It's really amazing."

Tess stood and cut another slice. She placed it on Alex's plate. "Do you want more coffee?"

"Yes, please." Alex nudged her cup and saucer closer to where Tess stood.

"Are you afraid of being in a committed relationship?"

"I'm not afraid of anything," Alex said.

Tess laughed. "I doubt that."

"It's the truth."

"Then what's going on? Tell me about Hunter."

"He's hot. He's fun to talk to, easy to be with. We get along. He liked Damien." She took a bite of tart. "I can't tell you how good this is. It melts in my mouth. I wonder if I should learn how to bake. It never looked that much fun to me, but—"

"God, Alex. Do you like the tart more than Hunter?"

Alex laughed.

Tess pushed her own half-eaten tart away from her. It was truly delicious, but she was so frustrated, she'd lost her appetite. Alex was clearly hiding something. She didn't think Alex was afraid of making a commitment. She'd never been flakey about her job, and she'd taken great care of Damien. Their friendship had had gaps, but that happened with all friendships. Work and geography created those, but they'd stayed in touch and kept their connection for years now.

Whatever was going on with Alex and Hunter didn't look like a commitment phobia on Alex's part. The only answer was there must be a significant red flag that Alex was hiding from her. If Alex revealed more than the basics about this guy, the red flag would become immediately obvious, and so she was refusing to say anything. She'd refused to allow Hunter to join her on this mini vacation for the same reason.

CHAPTER 6

*W*hen I was in my spacious guest bedroom, away from Tess's relentless questions, I found myself thinking about Hunter. How could I not think about him? She'd done nothing for the past ninety minutes but repeat his name and try to find out more about him and why I liked him and what was wrong with me for not talking about him and not inviting him to tag along with me to Napa Valley.

I'd come to Napa Valley because I could see that my life was starting to disintegrate. Eileen's fabulous apartment and furnishings came with Eileen, who was smothering me. My fabulous job had turned into a prison, and it was about to get a whole lot worse.

I needed the endless views of rolling hills and vineyards and limitless blue skies to help me figure out what I was going to do. At every other point in my life until now, there hadn't been a need to figure out anything. Life had risen up and handed something to me and I'd stepped off into a new adventure.

Until now, life had offered me jobs I was curious about or places I'd never been. Now, I looked around me and saw nothing but a boss trying to chain me to rules and procedures, co-workers and my desk. I saw four walls that were far too close and days that had become more and more the same. Diana had sucked the thrill and excitement out of every client engagement.

I wasn't about to apply for a job taking photographs of children or pets, or assisting someone who photographed couples getting married. There were jobs photographing food, but those weren't positions you just walked into. And as much as I loved food, I liked eating it, not taking pictures of it looking intensely desirable and then being told I couldn't have a taste.

Every technology company needed photographers to fill their web pages with images of machinery they deemed sexy and alluring. But taking pictures of hunks of metal and wires would be like enclosing myself in a steel box, spending twelve hours a day breathing metallic air. I think I would rather be dead, and find out what death was like.

The fun of photography was the entertainment of getting people to tell me things they didn't want to say. It was the fun of watching their faces and their eyes, trying to guess what they were thinking. It was the thrill of capturing them and realizing I'd seen expressions and vulnerabilities and fears that no one else had. It was the victory of getting inside their heads, if only for the briefest moment in time.

I needed a new job. I needed a job without a boss trying to break me, and ultimately, I needed money flowing into my life without having to answer to anyone. It was such a dream that it made me laugh. It was what every woman, and every man, on the planet wanted, and very few had. But it never stopped anyone from dreaming about it. And here I was, a woman with very few so-called *marketable* skills.

I'd landed the job with Trystan based solely on my personality. He believed I could learn to take the kind of photographs he wanted, and I had. It was a fluke. I couldn't make a plan to meet someone like him again, offering a lucrative job doing something I'd never done before but would fascinate me endlessly.

It was a lot to think about while I gazed at vineyards and saw mansions in the distance that were homes to families and corporations that grew grapes, transforming them into beverages they'd made famous around the world.

I was also close to homeless. I only had an apartment because I'd hooked up with a woman who had four million dollars to keep her life secure and comfortable. And even with that, it was a modest, unremarkable apartment. An apartment that I couldn't call mine by any stretch of the imagination. An apartment where even having a part-time pet bird had put my security at risk. An apartment where a man was able to move in and force me out the door.

Marching through a parade of roommates was not how I wanted to live. Picking up random people who passed by and moving in with them simply because they had beautiful homes, like Sean's in Australia, or because they were secluded and the guy was someone I liked in my bed, like Jared in our creek side home, was not the contentment and peace of mind that I dreamed of. Even though I hadn't fully realized until recently that I'd been dreaming of it, maybe all my life. Even when I was a tiny prisoner in my parents' three-story Victorian home.

How long would it be until I had the money to afford a home that I could call my own? Where I decided who came through the front door and who spent the night and what every single piece of furniture and artwork looked like?

It was too much.

I didn't need Hunter there whispering in my ear, asking me questions. As much fun as he was, I needed time inside my own head without any intruders.

So I'd come alone. It had nothing to do with what kind of relationship Hunter and I did or didn't have. I didn't have time to consider how I wanted to define my connection to him. The other things were too huge.

But hearing Tess talk about him made me want to hear his voice.

I stripped off my clothes, put on a camisole top and silky short-shorts, and slid into bed. I propped three of the four long, fat pillows behind me and looked out the picture window across from the bed at the stars glittering over the vineyard. I tapped Hunter's number, knowing it was after one in the morning in New York, knowing he would be awake and ready for my call.

Instead, his phone rang several times, and I heard him telling me to leave a message.

I told him to call if he was awake and placed my phone beside me. The dark screen stared at me accusingly, reminding me the phone belonged to Fly Higher, the bill paid by Diana. I was suddenly hyper-aware that if she really wanted to, Diana could probably access all my text messages with Hunter.

Hunter's face filled the phone screen. I slid the virtual button to answer.

"Hey. You missed me already," he said.

"I haven't had a lot of time for missing anything."

He was quiet for a moment. I heard the hiss of a bottle cap coming off a beer. "What's the winery like?"

"I haven't had a tour yet. But the house is amazing. It's so quiet. I forgot what living outside a city is like."

"You haven't been in New York for even three years," he said.

"I have a short memory."

"I've noticed."

I laughed.

"I miss you, even if you don't miss me," he said.

"I didn't say that."

"It sounded like you wanted to give me that impression," he said.

"I wasn't trying to give any impression. It's really great here. So quiet. I'm already relaxed. Tess's wine is really good. And she's not going on about the wedding all the time, so that's nice."

"What else are you doing?"

I laughed. "I just got here. I was on the plane most of the day. We got Damien settled, had some wine, met the head of their tasting room, talked to Marcus, ate dinner, and that's it."

"What are you doing tomorrow?"

"I have no idea."

"Wine tasting?"

"Maybe."

"I could still join you. It's easy to get time off. I'm due for—"

"No. Bad idea."

"Why?"

"Because it is." I didn't want to explain that I was re-designing my life. And I didn't want his help doing that. Trying to explain any of that was too much work. Besides, it had nothing to do with him.

"I thought we were planning a trip with the ridiculous amount of cash Carolina gave you for watching her kid," he said.

"This isn't that." I climbed out of bed and walked to the windows. There were so many stars, I felt like the Napa Valley was on a different planet from Manhattan.

"It could be."

"It's not. This involves wedding planning." I put my phone on speaker and placed it on the window seat. I did a few stretches, still gazing out the window.

"Wedding planning takes all day, every day for three weeks or however long you're there?"

"I don't know."

He was quiet for a few minutes.

"Are we breaking up?" he asked.

"Why would you think that?"

"Because you don't want me there."

"Those are two entirely different things."

"Are they?" he asked.

"Yes."

"*Are* you coming back?"

That was a trickier question. Obviously, I had possessions in New York, but aside from Hunter, I didn't have much else. I was crazy about the city. But I wasn't crazy about the noise and the grit and the claustrophobia.

"Yes."

"It took you a long time to answer."

"I don't think it did."

He didn't ask if I was returning to stay, which seemed like an oversight on his part. I wondered if he would realize that later.

We talked about other things after that, unimportant things. When he hung up, I wondered if he would call me again. He seemed to want me to prove how I felt about him, or something.

I didn't want to prove anything to anyone.

CHAPTER 7

There was a note on the kitchen counter when I went downstairs at seven thirty. The aroma of freshly brewed coffee filled the room, so I poured some into a mug before I picked up the note. It was from Tess, telling me she had a doctor's appointment she'd forgotten about. Marcus had gone to San Francisco for meetings, so I was on my own.

The note went on to list all the foods in the fridge and the various breakfasts I could make for myself. She ended with a suggestion that if I ran into Silas, I should be nice to him. It was more than a suggestion, actually, it was a directive. Maybe she'd forgotten I hadn't been her employee for several years.

I shoved the note into the pocket of my robe, grabbed a cup of yogurt, and mixed in some granola. I grabbed a banana, tucked it into the other pocket of my robe, and went out to the patio. It was cold to be sitting outside with bare feet and legs that were also bare because the robe kept sliding off. But I ate quickly and my coffee cooled quickly, allowing me to drink it fast.

By a few minutes past eight, I was dressed in running clothes, stretching on the front patio.

I was completely unfamiliar with the area, but I had an app on my phone that allowed me to trace a route with my fingertip. The GPS dot that was me could follow the roads I'd identified.

Leaving the long driveway from Tess's house to the gate at the entrance to her property was like entering another world. I hadn't run on an uneven surface in ages. It had been all paved pathways and concrete sidewalks. I'd breathed in exhaust from cars and buses and dodged hundreds of pedestrians at a time, pausing for traffic lights, making quick pivots around people stopping suddenly to look at their phones veering abruptly to the curb to fling open taxi doors.

I didn't even need to put my earbuds in to drown out the sounds with classical piano music playing at top volume. Even though the music got my blood pumping, I decided to let songbirds and the distant hum of cars on Highway 29 carry me.

Jogging slowly, I turned onto the main road and ran on the shoulder, still keeping a careful pace even though my legs longed to stretch farther, flying at top speed with nothing to impede my course.

I ran for about a mile and a half, then saw a side road about a quarter mile ahead. It was a single lane but didn't have entrance gates or a sign. It had unusually wide, flat shoulders where I would be able to run faster without worrying about twisting my ankle.

As I turned, I could feel a slight incline, but I pushed myself to increase my speed, enjoying the feel of my heart pumping harder, the air moving in and out of my lungs.

After another mile, I was considering turning back when I heard the faint buzz of a motorcycle. A moment later, I saw a motorcycle headed toward me, moving quickly. As it approached, it swerved to its right, almost as if it might be moving onto the shoulder, coming directly at me.

I slowed, but my heart rate continued at the same pace. Surely the rider saw me by now, but it wasn't slowing and it was definitely coming very close to the side of the road. I had no plans to play chicken with a motorcycle, even a small one. But this wasn't small.

Now that it was getting close, I saw that it was a Harley, and the buzz had grown to a roar.

It was only fifty yards away, right on the edge of the shoulder.

A sane person would move off the shoulder, as close to the razor wire fence running along the boundary of the open field dotted with small fruit trees. But I'm not always sane. He was on the wrong side of the road and he appeared to be trying to scare me. I didn't like it. I increased my speed.

He revved his engine, causing the bike to release a menacing sound, then turned with a screech of his tires and stopped only a car's length from where I was. He flipped up the shade on his helmet. It didn't allow me to see much of his face—only a pair of dark eyes and the bridge of a thin nose. "You shouldn't be running here."

"It's a public road."

"That's where you're wrong. This is a private road, so I need to ask you to turn around right now."

"There wasn't a sign."

"You must have missed it."

"There was no sign."

"Who are you? I've never seen you before."

"Who are *you*?"

"I'm a landowner."

"Where?"

"That's not important. This is a private road and you don't belong here."

"There was no sign, no fence, no gate. There wasn't even a street sign."

"Maybe that should have told you something."

"I'm just going for a run."

"Not here."

"Are you a security guard or something? Can I see a badge?"

"I told you, I'm a landowner and I need to ask you to leave. Now."

"There's nothing here that says I'm on private property." I gestured toward the fence. "That's clearly private property. This is the shoulder of a road that has no gate and no signs." I took a few steps back and started jogging away from him, headed in the same direction I'd been going before he tried to scare me.

"Hey. I asked you nicely to leave."

I continued running. I heard the rumble of the bike as he backed it up, then a low, thrumming purr as it followed behind me for ten or twenty yards. "You don't belong here and you obviously don't live around here or you would know that. Where are you staying?"

I ignored him.

"I asked where you're staying. If you're at a hotel or B&B, they should have provided you with suggestions for appropriate running paths."

I wanted to laugh. Tess had listed all the items in her fridge, which were clearly visible, but she hadn't said a word about private roads or suggested I might be threatened if I went for a run in the beautiful countryside.

"I've asked you several times and I don't want to ask again."

I stopped and faced him. "You won't say who you are or why you have the right to tell me not to run here. So …" I shrugged. "It sounds like you're just over-protective. I'm not eating grapes or peeking into someone's wine cellar trying to find out their secrets. I'm just going for a run."

"You're not funny."

"Not trying to be. I'm just stating the obvious. I'm not hurting anyone or damaging anyone's property. It's still not even clear to me that I'm actually on anyone's property. It looks like the shoulder of a side road, like a hundred other side roads around here."

He revved his engine. "Don't say you haven't been warned."

"I won't."

He flipped down the sunscreen on his helmet, revved the bike, much louder this time, then took off with a light spray of gravel, headed back in the same direction he'd come from. After a moment,

THE WOMAN IN THE CASTLE

he disappeared from sight, and a few minutes later, the silence returned, followed shortly by the tentative songs of the birds who had gone silent in his roaring presence.

I ran for another quarter of a mile, then turned back toward the main road. When I reached the intersection, I paused, looking for signs indicating a private road. There were none.

CHAPTER 8

Tess arrived home from her medical appointment full of plans, actually a single plan, for the afternoon. We were going to see her chosen wedding venue.

"Why did you decide not to have it here? Your place is enormous. The patio and gardens are gorgeous. And I thought that was the whole idea—your own vineyard, your marriage, your partnership, setting down roots, all the symbolism." I wasn't sure about that last part, but I thought I remembered something like that. She'd been very dreamy and romantic-sounding when she'd flipped through all the pictures of her Mediterranean home surrounded by acres of grapevines. It looked as if it had been custom-designed for luscious parties.

"This is better. Wait until you see it."

"But it's not yours."

"That doesn't matter. It's better."

She made me dress up. High heels, makeup, a fancy dress.

"Why is that important?" I asked.

"It's a hard place to book. And the owners are very particular. They like to get your vibe and they like to feel the romance of the couple and the mood. It's important to show them how serious I am about this and how I feel about my wedding."

"Then why are you going with me and not Marcus?"

"He's working, and I need to get it booked. They'll get a sense of who I am. And since you're my maid of honor … you'll see. It's a mystique they like to convey for their venue."

"It sounds like a game." Other words came to mind, but I didn't speak them.

"Maybe. A little." She laughed. "But it's fun. It's an honor to be chosen as one of their couples. Today is almost like an audition. And they will absolutely want to meet me and Marcus together, but often the first meeting is only the bride. Because let's face it, even in the twenty-first century, the bride is usually the one with the vision, the one who has the dream. They know that and they can feel it. You'll see." She smiled as if she knew a secret that I didn't. She obviously did.

After a lunch of chicken salad nestled inside half an avocado, sprinkled with a spicy vinaigrette dressing that was still biting pleasantly at my tastebuds, we slid into Tess's BMW. We sped along Highway 29 to a road that could hardly be seen from the highway if you didn't know it was there, then up a curving single lane road toward the top of a hill. As we rounded the final curve, we came face-to-face with a bona fide castle.

There were two towers that rose above the rest of the structure, all of it stone, as if the building had been lifted out of the European countryside and dropped into the Napa Valley by helicopter.

The entrance had an enormous, arched wooden door with iron fittings that could surely be a drawbridge if it wanted to, although the building lacked a moat. The windows were deep, giving no hint of what might be inside.

A forest surrounded the castle, covering the hillside. Through the trees ,I could see a few cottages, also made of stone.

"Is it a winery?" I asked.

Tess pulled into the curved drive and off to the side where there was space for ten or twelve cars under covered parking.

"It was, but now it's only used for weddings. The grapevines were removed years ago. You'll see in the area behind the castle, the trees are much smaller."

"How old is it?"

"It was built in the late fifties."

"Have you ever been inside?"

"No."

"Then how do you know you want your wedding here?"

"Because it's a castle! It's like a fairy tale. Besides, I've seen photos."

I turned to look at her. She was staring through the windshield, gazing at the stone walls in front of us. Her face looked like that of a child, staring enraptured at her first fairy-tale film on the big screen.

Everything was stone. It seemed like a risky design in a state prone to earthquakes, constantly poised for the *big one*, something always at the back of residents' minds, rarely talked about, but definitely planned for in building construction and emergency preparedness.

"I guess earthquake consciousness wasn't the same in the fifties," I said.

"Don't be so practical. And negative. It's survived."

"It's probably good in wildfires." I opened the car door.

"It's magical. A fairy-tale wedding in a castle." She laughed softly. "I can't wait until Marcus sees it."

"He doesn't know you're getting married in a castle?"

"It's not definite yet. They have to accept us. And we have to find out if there's a date available."

"I'm sure if you wait long enough, there's always a date available."

"We'll see." She got out of the car and closed the door.

I followed her across the drive and up to the massive front doors.

As we approached, the doors opened. They turned out not to be a drawbridge, but two halves that opened to the sides like normal double doors. Because we had an appointment, they must have been watching our arrival on concealed cameras. The opening of the doors was timed so perfectly to our proximity to the entrance.

A woman appeared just inside the doorway.

I wasn't sure if it was the towers and all that stone, or Tess's obvious desire to live out her vision of a fairy tale in a misplaced castle, but the woman who greeted us looked like she could have been Cinderella before she was swept off to the ball in a converted pumpkin. She wore a calf-length brown dress with a white bib apron. The sleeves of the dress were puffy, and she had black ballet-slipper shoes on her feet. Her hair was light brown, coiled into a bun at the nape of her neck, her thick bangs emphasized by a black headband.

"Hello, Tess. Welcome. And this is your maid of honor, Alexandra?"

I held out my hand. Instead of taking it, she curtsied, first toward Tess, then, with less of a dip, toward me.

I wanted to laugh, but I could feel the intensity emanating from Tess. I could feel her disappearing into a fantasy I never would have dreamed was hers. That made me want to laugh as well, but it also made me curious. How could a woman who had proven herself as a fierce and dominant force in the world of technology, managing teams of over a hundred people, going toe-to-toe with powerful, and sometimes aggressive and scornful men, still be so caught up in the little-girl dream of being a princess?

I was baffled.

And yet ... doesn't everyone like a little bit of magic and doesn't everyone grow up missing the world of make believe? Isn't that why Halloween is so popular?

"I'm Sara," the Cinderella look-a-like said. "Let me take you inside. Ella will be with you shortly." Sara turned and walked into the castle.

Tess and I followed her, past a stone gargoyle that was easily eight feet tall, through a long, dark hallway. Torches with live flames were mounted on the stone walls, providing the only light. The floor was also stone, fortunately not the same round stones that formed the structure or it would have been impossible to walk in our high heels. Our footsteps echoed off the stone walls until we emerged into a room the size of a basketball arena, the ceiling rising more than two stories above us.

Across from us were long narrow windows that looked out on a terrace and a massive lawn surrounded by rose bushes. The room had a few sofas and chairs in the corners with small tables between them, but otherwise it was empty, clearly designed to be set up for a banquet, with plenty of room for dancing. At one end was a platform for musicians, backed by a black velvet curtain and flanked by more torches, although these were unlit.

Sarah led us to one of the sitting areas and gestured toward the sofas without speaking.

When we were seated, she smiled and took a few steps back. "What would you like to drink? Tea? Coffee? Sparkling water? Wine? Or a cocktail?"

"I'll have tea, thank you," Tess said.

"I'll have the same."

Sarah left, and we were alone in the massive hall, silence weighing down on us.

"Isn't it amazing?" Tess spoke softly, as if we were seated in a cathedral and speaking louder might be an affront to the being who claimed to live there.

"It's very big," I said. "How many guests are you having?"

She narrowed her eyes slightly. "We haven't gotten that far. A castle. Can you believe it? I would have thought I'd have to go to Europe to find a real castle."

"What makes it a *real* castle?"

She laughed softly, as if she were afraid that her laughter might fill the enormous space and turn into something loud and garish. "I don't know, but this is it. I can't wait to show Marcus. He will absolutely love it."

"How do you know?"

She smiled with a certain degree of smugness. "Because he loves me." The note of triumph in her voice was perfect because it seemed an introduction to the woman who had appeared in the center of the room.

She was slender and tall with blonde hair that hung to her waist. She wore a pink dress with a plunging neckline, revealing large breasts. As she drew closer, I saw a ruby the size of a quarter hanging from a gold chain between them. She also had a narrow black ribbon around her neck, but whatever was on the end of it was hidden inside her dress.

She stopped several feet away. A shocked, almost frightened look spasmed across her face. "And who are you?" She was looking directly at me, ignoring Tess as if she hadn't even noticed she was there.

CHAPTER 9

The look Ella gave me was one that shot daggers into my eyes, clichéd as that thought was, especially in the castle setting. I had the strong impression she thought she'd met me before, and yet her question clearly stated that she had no idea who I was. It was a strange, unsettling sensation.

"I'm Tess's maid of honor, Alexandra."

"I know that."

Now I was more confused.

She continued giving me a hard, icy stare, as if she wanted to wrap her hands around my throat and strangle the life out of me. Her eyes were dark blue, and she hardly blinked. She kept them locked onto my face, the fear in them seeming to grow, spreading across every feature, draining the color from her cheeks.

After several minutes, she recovered her composure somewhat. She turned slightly. "Hello, Tess. I'm Ella."

She moved around us and took the armchair that faced the sofa where Tess and I were seated. She crossed her legs and arranged the flowing skirt of her dress. She wore black ballet flats that were identical to those of the woman who had ushered us into the castle.

Maybe they were the most comfortable shoes for navigating the stone floors. Maybe they had padding to keep their feet warm against the chill of all that stone.

Sara returned with a tray holding three cups of tea. She placed it on the table and left.

"Welcome to the Windy Hills Castle," Ella said in a slightly unwelcoming voice. "I really regret that Nolan can't be here. We love telling our story together. Part of the charm of a wedding in the Windy Hills Castle is the stories of the couples who seal their lives together here. For eternity."

I glanced at Tess. Most people getting married tend to have the general idea that they're going into it for the rest of their lives. But eternity? That seemed like the stuff of fairy tales. Or horror stories. Maybe they're the same thing.

The way Ella spoke the words, they sounded especially fraught, threatening. Almost as if someone might come to extract a body part from Tess and Marcus if they dared to break their vows before the end of eternity, which was an oxymoron in itself.

Tess smiled as if it were the best thing she'd heard all month, maybe the best thing she'd heard since Marcus popped the question, if that's what he'd done. She hadn't given me any of the details, only that she was getting married, before displaying her lavish ring.

"Even though he's not here, I'll still tell you our story. It sets the mood for what we're about and how we feel about our little castle." She laughed softly. "It's not so little, but compared to some, it probably is. We want all the marriages that begin here to have the same romance and undying love that Nolan and I share with each other. A bond that so many people now fail to value. Don't you agree?"

Tess grinned in a way that made me think she wasn't quite so sure, but she added a little nod of her head to emphasize her desire to agree.

"Nolan and I have, and we cherish, the kind of love that is the marriage of two hearts, two bodies, and two minds ... especially two minds. One in which everything is intertwined, so that two are truly one being. So that the two lives become one, with a single purpose, with a single focus. A single heartbeat without rancor."

Her idea of two people dissolving into a single creature sounded not only boring, but somewhat frightening, as if one would need to devour the other for that to realistically take place. Maybe that was the point of the gargoyle in the entryway. Beware those who enter. Only one would emerge. A horror story indeed.

"Is that how you and Marcus view the marriage relationship, Tess?"

"I think so?"

"You do?" The words were out of my mouth before I realized I'd spoken.

Tess looked at me blankly. She tipped her head slightly, as if letting the thought roll to one side like a marble in a jar. "I think so, yes. Marriage is about unity."

I didn't think she'd heard correctly, but I let it go. This was her wedding, her marriage, her castle, her fantasy. All I had to do was host the bachelorette party, hold the flowers while she spoke her vows, and sign the piece of paper. Whatever happened after that was none of my business.

And maybe she was just saying what this strange woman wanted to hear. Because all Tess wanted was her castle.

As if to prove me right, Tess gave me a large, winning smile.

Ella furrowed her brow. She lifted her hand to the ruby necklace and rubbed it several times before returning her hand to her lap. "Nolan swept me off my feet. I was walking along the road, headed to the Farmer's Market, and I saw him standing in the vineyard. He looked like a Greek god."

I laughed softly.

Ella shot me an angry look.

I composed my expression and gave her my full attention, although I was now eager to meet Nolan, the Greek god. Despite her long wavy golden hair and her curvy figure that might capture the eye of a sculptor, I wasn't sure I would describe her as a Greek goddess. I wondered whether Nolan would.

"It was a cloudy day and a ray of sunlight had broken through the thick clouds. It circled him and made his hair shimmer. I couldn't stop looking at him. When he saw me, I could see that he'd instantly fallen in love with me, the same as I had with him." Ella sighed. She covered the ruby with her hand and closed her eyes for a moment.

"He walked toward me and opened the gate. I stepped into the vineyard, and he lifted me into his arms. He carried me to a grove of trees where there was a pond with a small waterfall tumbling into it. We sat there for hours. He fed me grapes and stroked my hair. He looked into my eyes and I knew that he could read my thoughts. I could feel that he understood everything about me. That he was devoted to me and would put my concerns and needs above his for the rest of his life. I was his queen."

"That's quite a story," I said.

"Shh!" Tess's voice was sharp. "You're breaking the spell."

Ella lowered her chin and smiled gently at Tess. "That's a lovely way to express it. The story casts a spell. Our love casts a spell. That's how I felt the moment I saw Nolan. That's how I felt as he carried me to our secret place. And that's how I've felt every moment since."

"Remarkable," I said. "How long have you been married?"

"We're together until the stars fall from the sky."

"Oh." Tess pressed her hands to her breastbone. "I love that. It's so romantic. Like poetry."

I thought it came from a song. It probably came from a hundred songs, a thousand poems. I was sure Google would help me identify a few if I bothered to look.

"Thank you," Ella said. "I look forward to hearing you and Marcus tell us your love story. When he's available." She stood. "I'll give you a tour now, if you've finished your tea."

This was the part I was looking forward to. I wondered if Ella would take her eyes off me long enough to allow me to slip away by myself.

CHAPTER 10

*E*lla ushered us through all the rooms on the ground floor of the castle. It was awkward because she walked behind us, herding us like a flock of sheep. It seemed as if she'd read my mind and was aware of my desire to slip off to explore the castle on my own.

We saw a kitchen large enough to prepare a banquet for several hundred people, a dining hall with four long tables surrounded by regal high-back chairs that could accommodate a more *intimate* dinner of about sixty. We saw two large sitting rooms, an entertainment room, and elegantly decorated dressing rooms for the bride and groom and their attendants.

There were a multitude of other small rooms—a library filled with ancient-looking books on shelves that covered the walls nearly to the ceiling, accessed by rolling ladders, tiny sitting rooms comfortable for only two or three people, a few bedrooms, three powder rooms, two full bathrooms, a pantry that was the size of a small market, and a staircase leading down to a wine cellar that she didn't invite us to descend. Neither did she invite us to ascend to the second floor to see the bedrooms and more sitting rooms. Access to both towers was also off limits.

Way off limits.

As best I could tell, the entrances to both towers appeared to be accessed via long, narrow corridors. The corridors were lined with burning torches, the walls draped with white chiffon that hung from iron bars clustered between the torches, the same as what covered many of the doorways.

"May we see the towers?" I asked.

Ella ignored my question, talking about their lavish rehearsal dinners prior to the weddings and their plentiful bedrooms that allowed bridal parties to stay the night before the wedding in the castle.

"As you probably saw when you drove up, we also have cottages on the property for your guests. It truly can be a destination wedding. And if your guest list is large, there are several boutique hotels where we have group packages arranged so that guests can be close by. With limo transportation included, of course."

Tess began firing questions at her, and as Ella grew more animated, I began taking steps away from them, glancing over my shoulder for a chance to slip away. We'd returned to the kitchen and Ella stood with her hip pressed against the center island, describing the various menus available for rehearsal dinners. Tess was turned away from her, looking out the window at the vegetable garden. I was near the doorway, pleased by my good fortune that both of them were so captivated by their discussion of food that even Ella, who was determined to keep us under her watchful eye, seemed to have forgotten about me for a moment.

I slipped out the door and a moment later was walking as fast as I could back toward the great hall. The corridors leading to the towers were on opposite sides of the entryway. I turned right and started down the dimly lit hallway, eager to find out if I could access the tower or would be greeted by a locked door. I was curious to find out what rooms were inside. I wanted to see what it was like to climb to the top. I wanted to look out over the property and see how far the view extended.

It was disappointing that they would host wedding parties overnight, offering bedrooms that Ella hadn't wanted to show Tess until Marcus joined her, but they kept the towers off limits. Those were the most fascinating part of the castle. They were the features that *made* it a castle. Otherwise, it was simply a large stone house. But they weren't available to the couples craving and kowtowing before Ella and Nolan for a chance to seal their vows for eternity in this magnificent building.

It didn't make sense. Tess's lack of curiosity about them didn't make sense to me either. It was possible she was so intent upon pleasing Ella and being agreeable, she refused to do anything that would disqualify her from being a candidate. Anything that would upset the clearly dictatorial Ella. The woman seemed to relish her power, as if she felt the castle had crowned her the queen of something—perhaps the queen of weddings. She would rule over the brides and determine who was worthy of marriage in her fantasyland.

Little girls want to be princesses. It's a strange phenomenon. It's unclear whether it's fed by fantastical movies, animated or not, or there's some universal desire to be powerful and also dressed in lavish clothes. If Carl Jung were still around, perhaps he could explain the need that seems to take hold of such a significant number of small girls. It fades as they grow older, then erupts when they begin to plan weddings.

And those who have built businesses in the wedding industry have capitalized on the desire. But Ella, and possibly Nolan as well, had taken it to an entirely new level.

As I moved along the corridor, the light grew more dim, the torches spaced farther apart, so I had to place my hand on the stone wall, running my fingers over the rocks and mortar to feel my way. I pulled my phone out of my pocket and turned on the flashlight.

"Where are you going?" Ella's voice was loud, almost a scream, echoing down the stone passageway behind me.

"I wanted to see the tower." I spoke without turning, still walking, hoping to reach the door to the tower before she caught up with me. As I heard my voice carry through the narrow space, I realized Ella had also spoken in a fairly normal tone, if somewhat shrill in her impatience with me. The closeness of the walls, the low ceiling, and all that stone amplified the sound.

A moment later, I felt her hand on my back, and then she grabbed my arm just above my elbow. "I told you not to come in here."

I turned to face her. The light from my phone was directed toward the floor, but shot up and cast an eery glow across her pink dress, which looked almost white, and her blonde hair, which now had a pink hue.

"The towers are the best part of the castle," I said. "The wedding would be more exciting if the guests could stay in the towers."

"They aren't open to the public, and no one asked your opinion."

"You're missing a huge opportunity. You could even charge more for the chance to stay there. Are the rooms round?"

"I need you to come out of here right now." She tugged on my arm.

I allowed her to pull me back the way I'd come.

Tess was standing at the mouth of the corridor. She glared at me. I smiled, but it did nothing to soften her expression. Together, the three of us walked back to the castle entrance and stood awkwardly, staring at each other. For several minutes, no one spoke.

Finally, Ella took a few steps away from us, moving closer to the gargoyle and the passage leading to the great hall, leaving us alone as if she expected the doors to open and spit us out into the front garden.

"Is that your natural hair color?" Ella asked.

The question was so out of context, I wondered if she had been brooding about it the entire time. Was that the reason she'd studied me so intensely from the moment she'd first seen me? Most women would consider the question rude. I didn't care, but I was curious why she would leap that hurdle over convention to pose it to a stranger, the associate of a potential client. Maybe she didn't care. She'd made it clear the Windy Hills Castle was in such demand she didn't have to concern herself with pleasing her clients. She was in the power position and could do whatever she pleased.

"What do you think?" I asked.

"I don't think it is."

I smiled. "A lady never tells."

The look on her face was almost a snarl that matched the gargoyle standing beside her. She grabbed the ruby hanging around her neck. "We're not going to be able to accommodate your wedding, Ms. Turner."

"Why not?" Tess's voice was laced with panic. "You haven't met my fiancé. Our wedding isn't until—"

"Surely you've heard we're booked years in advance. It's a scheduling nightmare."

"I understand, but I haven't given you the ... we're super flexible on our dates," Tess said. "Can you tell us what dates are available? We're absolutely flexible."

Ella shook her head. "No."

"But you haven't met ..."

Ella turned and walked out of the entryway, disappearing through a doorway that was covered by green chiffon hanging from one of the ubiquitous iron rods.

We stood without speaking, aware of the gargoyle watching over us. The only sound was the slight gasp of air as Tess tried to absorb the senseless, crushing news.

I turned to face the gargoyle with his snarling face and massive wings. I vowed, perhaps to him, that I would find a way for Tess to have her fantasy wedding in that castle. I was also going to find a way to get into those towers.

CHAPTER 11

$\mathcal{T}$ess didn't speak to Alex until they were in the car headed down the long curving road away from the Windy Hills Castle. It was easy not to say anything. She'd been shocked into silence. She'd known it was difficult to get accepted as one of the brides privileged enough to be married at the castle. But she'd assumed she would be one of them. She'd known she and Marcus, especially Marcus, would charm them with their love story, with their shared vision to become vintners.

There hadn't been a moment of doubt. And she was willing to wait. Yes, her biological clock was ticking, but it wasn't so loud it was drowning out everything else. Not yet. There was time.

She hadn't expected the cold rejection before she and Marcus even had a chance to meet with Ella and Nolan as a couple. Had it been a mistake to take Alex? To not have her initial meeting as a couple? And to add Alex and her aggressive, sometimes anti-social behavior into the mix? Alex could be so charming and such an asset at times. When she wanted to. But she could also derail social situations with her unfiltered comments. And wandering off had probably not endeared her to Ella. But it had also been clear that Ella had some sort of negative reaction the moment she'd seen Alex.

What was that about?

She had no idea. Ella acted as if she'd encountered Alex in a previous situation.

"Have you met Ella before?" Tess asked as she turned on to the highway.

"No."

"She looked shocked when she saw you. And what was that weird comment about your hair?"

"I have no clue," Alex said.

"I can't believe she rejected us."

"She'll change her mind."

Tess laughed. "She's not going to change her mind. That's it. Marcus and I won't get an appointment together."

"How do you know?"

"You heard what she said. That's how it works."

"What kind of power trip is she on?"

"That's how it is when you have a coveted property."

"Maybe. But they can't be booked every weekend forever."

"I don't have forever."

Alex laughed. "No, but I don't believe it that they're booked every single weekend for the next two years."

"It's possible."

"Then why did she agree to meet with you at all?"

Tess considered this question as she pressed down more firmly on the accelerator, feeling the roar of the BMW's engine beneath her as it raced along the straight, well-paved road.

She wanted that castle.

Since the day she'd first heard about it, then when she'd driven up the hill and admired it from a distance, and when she'd talked to Silas and heard the stories of magical weddings and the lore of having to tell your love story in order to be accepted. She'd been fascinated. She loved the exclusivity of it. She loved the uniqueness of it. But most of all, she loved the feeling of something she and Marcus could have fun with.

CATHRYN GRANT

One of her favorite things about Marcus was that he'd brought so much playfulness into her life. For a man who was seriously driven and consumed by technology, he loved to play. He liked video games, he liked board games. He liked to play in bed. He liked kicking a soccer ball around their lawn and he liked playing practical jokes on her.

At least once a month, he hid something fun inside one of the meals he cooked. She would swipe at a forkful of rice and the tine would catch on the chain of a bracelet. She would dig into one of his scrumptious desserts and the spoon would have a tiny ceramic cat sitting on it. She was lucky she hadn't choked to death. But she absolutely adored that about him.

She'd known he was the one since the moment he'd shaken her hand, saying, "I've heard that your marketing magic will set my company apart even if we were the least technically capable product in the top three. Which we're not."

She'd said, "It's not magic. It's data."

He'd said, "The fact that you're clear about that proves you have magic."

She smiled, thinking about it now, as she did every time she recalled that moment. Sometimes, she wasn't even sure why she found it so clever and appealing. She was certain she'd fallen in love with him in that moment. And maybe that's why it was so appealing. Because she was already in love. Being in love colored everything, and what appeared mundane to others shimmered with magic to the ones in love.

"Do you think Hunter is The *One*?" she asked.

"What?"

"Is Hunter your one and only? Your other half?"

"There's no such thing."

"I think there is. Marcus is the one for me."

"Out of approximately three and a half billion men on the planet, the only one you could ever be happy with is Marcus?"

"Yes."

"So if he dies someday ... *when* he dies, you'll be a widow forever?"

Tess sighed. Of course, Alex would leap to the most horrific scenario. She was planning her wedding, not a funeral. "I'm not thinking about him dying. We're young. Like Ella said, we're committed for life."

"That's great."

"And he's the one for me."

"Also great," Alex said.

"But I knew it right away. And I wondered if you got that feeling with Hunter."

"No."

"Oh. So you're ... does that make you feel like you're wasting your time?"

Alex laughed. "Wasting my time?"

"Since he won't be the one ... maybe you should cut your losses."

"That's weird. I like being with him. It works for now."

"Are you even in love?"

"Why do I have to describe everything and define it? Hunter and I are having a great time. It's all good."

"Not that great. He's not here."

"When we're together, it's great."

"Is there something ..." Tess sighed. She didn't want to ask about red flags. She couldn't figure out what was going on with Alex and Hunter. When Alex first mentioned him, she'd seemed excited.

For Tess, she'd thought she'd been in love with every man she dated. Otherwise, why keep going out with any man? Just to pass the time of day? Once she'd met Marcus, she understood the difference, but until then, she had thought she'd been in love. Quite a few times. If Alex didn't think she was in love, how could it be *great*?

"You really don't think there's one person who's perfect for you?" Tess asked.

"No."

"Why not?"

"Because that's absurd."

"Why is it absurd?"

"Because you haven't met more than a few thousand men in your entire life. If that. You can't possibly know if he's the only one that you're attracted to and that you would have a lot of fun with. It's just not possible."

"I can feel it."

Alex said nothing.

"Is there something that bothers you about Hunter? A red flag or something?"

"Nope."

"Are you sure? You can tell me if—"

"There are no red flags. Whatever that means."

"Commitment phobia?"

Alex laughed.

They were silent for the rest of the trip back to Tess and Marcus's place. As Tess turned into the driveway, Alex pulled out her phone and began tapping furiously.

"What are you doing?" Tess asked.

"I'm researching the castle. There has to be a way for you to get married there. Ella is on a power trip, but you haven't met Nolan. Maybe they aren't really one mind. Maybe he has different opinions. If we can get in touch with him, maybe there's a second chance."

CHAPTER 12

BEFORE: AMELIA

This castle is the only home I've ever known. My parents told me we moved here when I was three, but I have no memory of that and there are no photographs telling me where I lived before.

Of course, I have a few pictures of myself as a baby and a toddler. Pictures of myself in my mother's arms, photos of myself taking my first steps, my hair in red fluffy curls, backlit by the sun. There are a few shots of me in a bucket swing with an indistinguishable background, and two of me sitting in a red wagon, smiling.

When I asked my parents where those pictures were taken, they told me it wasn't important. The only thing that matters is where we are now. In the castle. We're happy here. We're safe here. Nothing can ever hurt me here.

The stone walls will keep me safe from everything.

When I was small, I thought the stone walls were to keep me safe from dragons and men wearing armored suits, their faces covered by metal, carrying deadly lances, riding on the backs of galloping horses toward the castle, ready to impale us all.

As I got older, I understood there were no dragons. I realized men going to battle were no longer clothed in steel. I also learned that battles were far, far more deadly in modern times, but that I was lucky enough to live in a place where wars weren't being fought in my town, or in any place close to me.

My mother and father told me I could ask all the questions I pleased. And when my questions are related to biology or astronomy, literature or history or math, they eagerly provide information, or help me research the answer in books and on the sleek computer that sits on the desk in my private schoolroom. The computer has so much information stored in it. I can find almost anything I want. But sometimes I try to search for answers to my questions when my parents aren't in the room, and there are no answers. The computer screen turns blank and tells me the web page can't be found because there's no internet connection. I'm not really sure what that means. My parents said that means it's not time to be studying.

When I ask questions about leaving our castle, they ignore me. They pretend they didn't hear me. Or they tell me to think about things that are worthwhile. They tell me not to wish for things that will cause me enormous, endless, eternal pain. They tell me that some things, like leaving the castle, aren't worth the risk.

The tower I live in is so beautiful. I love it. No princess ever had a more beautiful place to live. I know because my parents have shown me so many pictures of the rooms where other girls my age sleep. They look small and dull. My room was designed for a princess.

My bedroom is the top room in the tower. I have a perfectly round bedroom with a large, soft bed. There's a canopy made of pink chiffon that I can see through. My ceiling is painted midnight blue with tiny stars all around. The stars only show when the lights are turned off at night. My room has a large oval mirror and a chest of drawers painted shimmery gold. It's filled with beautiful clothes. My closet is filled with gowns that are silk and chiffon—in all the colors of the rainbow.

There are other rooms in my tower, and they all belong to me.

Just below my bedroom is my classroom, with its sleek computer and a desk. There's a globe. There are charts on the wall for chemistry and astronomy and math. There are books and notebooks for me to use for my schoolwork.

The other rooms in the tower are a dance room where I practice ballet, an entertainment room where I play video games and watch movies, a library filled with books, a playroom with games and toys. I didn't use the playroom much after I turned twelve. Ever since, my dolls have sat alone on the shelves, and the block tower I built when I was thirteen has been standing there untouched now for six years.

The last room is an art room. I have an easel and acrylic paints, a beautiful set of colored pencils. I have modeling clay and supplies for knitting and crocheting and making beaded bracelets and necklaces. Whenever I get interested in any kind of craft project, my mother buys me all the supplies I need.

Outside the tower is a walled garden. It belongs entirely to me. When I was younger, my father helped me plant roses. He showed me how to care for them, and I've done that ever since. I have a bench shaded by an apple tree. When I'm reading a book, I can grab an apple whenever I like and enjoy a juicy, sweet snack.

There's a swing hanging from another tree, and even though I'm nineteen now, I still love sitting on it and gliding back and forth on hot afternoons, feeling the air moving across my skin and through my hair.

It's the most beautiful home anyone could ever ask for. I know that in my heart.

But I feel like a prisoner in my tower.

I've read all the fairy tales. My library has so many books, and there are hundreds of fairy tales included in its shelves. I know about Rapunzel. I think about her all the time. My hair is also long, although not nearly long enough for a prince to climb up my braid as if it were a rope, rescuing me from the window of my tower.

CHAPTER 13

NOW: ALEX

*L*istening to Tess talk about one man on the planet for her, for me, and, I assume, one person for every person, made my head hurt. It made no logical sense. It sounded as if she thought there was a massive spreadsheet wrapped around the globe with each human being plugged into a cell, mapping who lived where and who should be linked up with the person in the adjacent cells. Or, perhaps a cell on another sheet, not adjacent at all, but connected by a complex macro.

At the same time, mixed in with her illogical logic, was a fairy tale gone awry. A story like the unbelievable vignette Ella had told, suggesting that a chance sighting on the side of the road had caused two people to connect in a ridiculous way, creating a bond which sealed them together for eternity, magically compatible in every way imaginable.

And then I thought of Hunter. The moment he'd crossed my field of vision, I'd been captivated. I suppose I'd lied to Tess about that.

Still, I didn't believe in fairy tales. And I didn't believe in magic. I didn't believe in the astronomical odds of only one person being a good candidate for a long-term relationship. It was laughable. It made it sound as if people were born and lived in proximity to people who were perfect for them and the rest of the billions of people were irrelevant. You couldn't possibly know that. And no one had ever bothered to study or thoroughly test it.

But mostly, I wasn't that interested in her theory. It wasn't important. If she wanted to immerse herself in romantic stories floating through her mind, she could have all the fun she wanted with that. I was more interested in the castle.

She wanted the man. I wanted the mansion.

I'd never known I had such strong feelings about castles, but after walking through the hallways and rooms of stone, gazing up at those forbidden towers, I wanted that castle more than I'd wanted anything in a very long time. It almost felt as if I'd been dreaming of it my entire life.

As much as I wanted Tess to have her fairy-tale wedding in the castle, I wanted to return so I could explore it further. I wanted to wander around the rooms we'd been allowed to spend only a moment or two peeking into. I wanted to see the bedrooms on the second and third floors. And most of all, I wanted to climb the stairs of those towers. I wanted to look out through the thick glass at the acres of forest surrounding the castle and the valley and vineyards beyond.

If Tess and Marcus were accepted as one of the elite couples allowed to hold their wedding celebration in the castle, we would soon be invited to a welcoming champagne reception with other brides. We would have her cake tasting there. I would dine at the castle on the evening of their wedding rehearsal and I would spend the night in one of its luxurious bedrooms. I would definitely invite Hunter to that.

I wondered, knowing how Ella believed she and Nolan were the queen and king of their castle, if they planned to live there forever. Would there come a time it was put up for sale? Was it possible to buy land and build my own castle?

I'd always known I wanted a lot of property and a large home where I could breathe, where I could stretch out my arms and move and never again feel cramped and crowded and hunkered into a dark corner like a rat in a cardboard box.

A castle. It was too amazing to think about.

Was that what I wanted?

I loved Tess's house too, with its red tile Spanish roof, picture windows and tiled floors, every room filled with light. I was equally enthralled by ultra modern designs—all angles and straight lines, also with lots of glass.

The castle was dark. But with white furniture instead of the dark brown wood and black leather that currently filled its rooms, it would be different. Better lighting would transform the place. Besides, I didn't mind some quiet shadows when I was indoors. In California, there was plenty of sunlight to splash around in outdoors almost year-round. I wouldn't necessarily need it flooding my house every hour of the day.

Alone in the guest room, sipping the sparkling water Tess had in plentiful supply in her fridge, I browsed through the photos on the website for the Windy Hills Castle. Most of them featured weddings with brides in flowing white gowns, flowers and ribbons woven through their hair. One even pictured a bride and groom riding through an arch of flowers, approaching the castle doors on the backs of white horses.

It was all too much.

There were no photographs showing the inside of the towers.

I wondered if the towers lived up to their promise. Were they simply small rooms, the round spaces carved up like slices of pie? Were they crammed with furniture and desks and space for the large staff that it took to put on these fabulous weddings, working on scheduling and menu planning, ensuring wine and champagne orders were set to be delivered on time? Buried in mundane tasks like ordering fertilizer for the vegetable garden and making sure the laundry delivered one hundred pink linen napkins in a particular shade on a particular day for a particular bride?

Why was Ella so concerned that I not even set foot in the corridor leading to one of the towers? Why were those corridors so dark, the torches hardly providing enough light to find your way to the end? That suggested there was not any normal work being done there. Surely their employees weren't traipsing down dark stone hallways with flashlights to get to their desks.

What was inside those magnificent towers?

CHAPTER 14

PORTLAND, OREGON

*T*here was a new youth minister at Pure Truth Tabernacle church. Pastor Jim had been well-received and the church elders were thrilled that he'd increased attendance at all the youth events. Because he had so much goodwill from scooping up new, unchurched kids and bringing them into the fold, he got away with some things that previous youth ministers hadn't been allowed.

They let him plan more events with boys and girls together, trusting he knew what he was doing when he said too much forbidden fruit could stir up unanticipated rebellion. They even allowed him to play some secular music, as long as the elders pre-approved it. This was also done under the forbidden fruit theory umbrella. He pointed out that we heard this music at school and coming from the houses in the neighborhoods where we lived. If we weren't allowed to listen, and we didn't have righteous people explaining why some lyrics were offensive to god, we would be lured into worshipping it in our ignorance.

The elders were fidgety, but they saw his point.

Then he wanted to have a harvest festival. This was something many churches did to put out their own, stripped-down, devil-free version of Halloween. All the fun of candy and costumes without the connotation of death and the occult. No dancing with the devil, but plenty of bobbing for apples and carving friendly-looking pumpkins. Menacing jack-o'-lanterns were forbidden.

The elders said no.

Pastor Jim persisted—*forbidden fruit.*

The elders had heard that one too many times. Handing out all the forbidden fruit was going to create a trail of breadcrumbs straight to hell.

Pastor Jim pointed out that wearing costumes inspired healthy, admirable emulation of godly heroes. He explained kids could try on heroic roles and see how it felt. They could dress up as first responders and physicians and nurses. They could come as biblical figures or wear costumes depicting the careers they hoped to have serving their communities in the future—missionaries and preachers, school teachers and farmers and mothers carrying plastic infants.

The music would be limited to religious pop songs. The games would teach the traits we were all aiming to develop, helping us become lifelong servants of mankind. We would eat home-baked treats and yes, there would be candy. We would carve crosses and suns into our pumpkins. We would clean off the seeds for roasting and package them up as treats to take to the senior center in November.

Finally, the elders relented. We could have our harvest festival on October 27. It absolutely would not be held on the wicked date of the thirty-first.

I knew immediately what I wanted to be. The idea had come from a book at the school library. I hadn't checked it out to bring home because it was unrelated to my schoolwork. This was a large, thick book about the middle ages. I hadn't read much of it. I mostly liked looking at the pictures. They were dark, mysterious paintings of castles and scenes of battles in the woods. There were kings and queens, fairies and children. There were all kinds of animals that interacted with the humans as if they were house pets—deer who allowed the people to stroke their fur, and lions who curled up next to young girls as they read books in the exposed, curved roots of ancient, gnarled trees.

The images fascinated me with their intricate details. The eery atmosphere of them suggested they not only came from another time, but possibly from another world that hadn't really existed.

One of the pictures was of a girl who was about fifteen. She looked like a princess. She wore a long yellow dress that hid her feet except for the bare toes of her left foot poking out, the folds of the dress lying on the soft, tender grass of the forest floor. She had bracelets circling her arms up to her elbows. Gems surrounded the waist of the dress, from her hipbones up to the bottom of her ribcage. The edges of the cap sleeves sparkled with diamonds. On her head was a gold crown studded with rubies and emeralds.

"No," my father said. "I'll allow the harvest festival because the church has agreed it will have a worthwhile purpose. But you're not dressing up as a princess."

"Why not?" I asked.

"Because it's not appropriate."

"The only rule is that our costume has to be a positive role model. Nothing that offends god."

"A princess costume is offensive to god."

"Why?"

"Because royalty has become a reality TV show. It's turned into fodder for gossip and slander. People are fascinated by royalty only when they can whisper about ungodly behavior that's taking place. It's disgusting. Royalty is all about power and prestige and decadence. Hoarding money that doesn't belong to you."

"There were queens and kings in the bible."

"That's different."

"How is it different?"

He pushed his coffee cup away from him and pushed his chair away from the table. He stood, towering over me. "God ordained those rulers to lead his people. In most cases. When he didn't, they were examples of wickedness. And there were no princesses."

"If the kings and queens had children, there had to be princesses."

I heard my brother snort with laughter from the other room.

My father raised his voice. "Stop eavesdropping, Tom." He walked away from the table, headed toward the living room. "You're not dressing up as a princess. Even if there were princesses, they would not be like the kind you're thinking of. You're not getting a fancy, outrageous dress that calls attention to yourself. And you're certainly not wearing a crown. The idea is to choose a heroic role model. You can dress up as a nurse."

"I hate blood. I would never be a nurse. Not ever."

He glared at me. I knew that he knew I was thinking about Lexy. I knew he was also thinking about Lexy, and he knew I was aware of that. We held each other's gaze for a very long time. I heard Tom moving around in the living room. He was probably waiting for an explosion of some kind. It sounded as if he were trapped in a cage, trying to escape a coming attack. I heard thuds as he bumped into furniture in his anxious anticipation of my father's expected outburst.

"If you're going to be a princess, it has to be biblical. With a simple, modest gown. Nothing lavish and no display of wealth. Get out your old picture bible for some ideas. Your mother will make your costume. And no crown. Absolutely no makeup."

That was not the kind of princess in the book I loved at my school library.

If he was this worked up about fancy princesses, I couldn't imagine what he would have to say about some of the other ideas I'd gathered at the library.

CHAPTER 15

NAPA VALLEY, CALIFORNIA

*I*t hadn't taken me long to figure out how to get another chance for Tess to achieve her castle wedding. I didn't believe for a single minute that Ella's mind had melded into a single brain with her husband's. He was a different person with different thoughts, and maybe not quite so fairy tale oriented. And then there was Marcus.

I told Tess that Marcus needed to find a way to get in touch with Nolan directly, set up an appointment, and book their wedding. Even if he had to tell an elaborate fairy tale to Nolan, Marcus was a good storyteller. He wouldn't have a problem wrapping his first meeting with Tess in something shimmery and imaginative.

Tess gave me a look that suggested I was the only one who believed in fairy tales. "Ella said no, Alex. I'll figure out something else amazing."

"But you wanted the castle."

"And Ella took the castle off the table."

"You're giving in, just like that?"

She shrugged. "There's not much I can do."

"Marcus. He's very charming. And he knows how to sell."

She smiled. "He does."

"It would take him ten minutes to get Nolan checking their date book. He could sell your love story better than any groom-to-be in the state of California."

"I'm glad you're so impressed with him."

"He sells his company to investors and customers every day of the week and half the night."

"True."

"Besides, I think it was me she didn't like."

"Don't be paranoid." She laughed. "And narcissistic, for that matter."

"You saw how she reacted when she saw me. And I'm sure it didn't help when I took my own tour after she told me not to."

"I doubt it was anything that petty. She has her fantastical idea, and somehow, I didn't fit her vision. It's arbitrary."

"The whole set-up is petty. So I absolutely think it was that petty."

She shrugged.

"Marcus should at least give it a try."

"How would he get to Nolan without her knowing? She said it's usually both of them."

"He could emphasize that he has some guy questions or whatever. I'm sure he could come up with something."

"It sounds complicated," Tess said. "And once Ella realizes it's me—"

"Do you want your wedding in the castle or not?"

"I do."

"Then you should at least try."

She gave me a tiny smile. "I did give up too easily."

Two days later, Marcus was driving their SUV up the winding road to the castle. He parked at the side of the curved drive, got out of the car, hit the fob to lock it, and walked toward the massive front doors. A moment later, he disappeared into the castle.

It hadn't been necessary for Tess and me to tag along, but we'd decided there was a chance Nolan might want Tess to join Marcus.

Although I'd pointed out it was decidedly unromantic that he'd left her sitting in the car, so did he really want to let them know she was available to meet on a whim like that? Tess still wanted to go, and Marcus wanted her there. And I, as always, was too curious to sit at their house, ignorant of what was happening moment-by-moment. Besides, I couldn't get enough of that castle, and simply sitting in the car, gazing up at the stone facade, looking at the towers flanking the drawbridge-like front door, sounded like a great way to spend an hour on a late summer afternoon.

Tess and I passed the time on our phones, checking email and playing games. We talked about her winery, and she talked about their plans for the wedding.

After a while, I put my phone on my lap and looked out the window. I studied the wall surrounding the tower nearest to where we were parked. I wondered what was behind it. The space between the wall and the sides of the tower looked to be at least thirty or forty feet, and the wall extended back along the side of the castle. I tried to orient myself to where the kitchen had been located, wondering if I was looking at the outside walls of the vegetable garden. I hadn't recalled seeing such high stone walls surrounding the plants, but neither had I glanced out the window for more than a moment or two.

As I studied the structure, a man appeared near the spot where the wall curved around the side of the castle. He began walking toward the two other cars and a motorcycle which were parked a few yards away. I glanced at his tall, lithe body, his short red hair, his pointed ankle boots, and back at the motorcycle—a Harley, I now realized.

It was the man who had tried to intimidate me when I was running. A landowner indeed. He owned an unbelievably large piece of land, not to mention a castle. I wanted to laugh, but I swallowed it, preferring to watch him before I said anything to Tess.

This had to be Nolan. He was dressed in light colored slacks and a white shirt and walked as if he knew his way around. When he stopped, he stood near the wall of the castle with a proprietary air, not someone who came there for eight or nine hours a day to prepare wedding feasts or perform clerical tasks.

The windows in the back of the SUV were partially lowered. I put my arm out, and waved at him, leaning my head toward the window so he could see my face, and especially my hair, which everyone kept telling me was so distinctive.

He looked at me as he continued walking toward the parked cars. He turned his head without acknowledging me. He unlocked one of the cars, opened the passenger door, and reached inside. He removed something I couldn't see and closed the door. He glanced again in my direction and stared at me for a moment. Long enough for me to know that he definitely saw me, that he absolutely recognized me. But he didn't wave or nod, didn't acknowledge at all that he was aware that he'd seen me before and that he'd told me I had no right to run on a public road.

It seemed fitting that the husband of the woman who wanted to dictate how people conducted their married lives wanted to determine where people could go running on roads that gave every indication they were paved and managed by the state of California.

As I ducked my head back into the car, I hoped I hadn't double-jinxed Tess. If Nolan was as touchy as his wife, maybe he would decide Marcus wasn't fit to be married in the castle since he was associated with a lawless woman who ran wherever she pleased rather than respecting the tender grapes of the Napa Valley, or whatever it was he was so concerned about.

"Why were you waving at him?" Tess asked.

"I saw him when I was running."

"Seriously?"

"Yes. He told me I was on a private road and I needed to leave."

She laughed. "Great. So you sabotaged us again."

"I hope not. I'm still counting on Marcus convincing them you and he are the perfect queen and king for their castle fantasy."

"We'll see."

We sat in the car for over an hour before the doors opened and Marcus strolled out onto the walkway, heading toward us. He was grinning as if he'd just slain his own personal dragon. I could sense Tess's excitement building as she wriggled in the passenger seat, waiting for him to get into the car.

He started the engine and rolled up the windows before he spoke.

"The castle is ours. May of next year."

Tess leaned across the center console and kissed his jaw. He turned to her and they engaged in a serious, extended kiss.

After a moment or two, she pulled away. "How did you manage?"

"I told them how we met. I told them about our vineyard. I told them—"

"She was there?" Tess asked.

"Yes. She came in toward the end, after he and I had had a really good chat."

"Did she realize you were my fiancé, that she'd already turned us down?" Tess asked.

"She absolutely did. After I told them our story, he left. She had a lot of questions about Alex—where she'd lived, how old she was. Once I answered them, she calmed down and everything was fine. She'd mistaken Alex for someone else."

A chill ran up my spine and across my scalp. I hoped that was the truth. That she had mistaken me, not that she still thought she knew me and I was the one who had failed to recognize her. I didn't like it that Marcus had told a woman who had clearly reacted badly to me, the places I'd lived, that he'd given her my full name and my age. It wasn't much, but I didn't like it.

CHAPTER 16

*B*efore dinner, I spent an hour staring at the website for the Windy Hills Castle. Primarily, I was staring at the face of Ella Monroe, trying to figure out if I'd seen her before. If she was so certain she knew me, and had reacted so violently to that thought, where had that feeling come from? Was it only my hair color? She'd asked about it so bluntly, maybe it was only that. Maybe my frivolous decision to change it had struck a chord, and it had nothing to do with anything else about me.

Still, I couldn't be sure. I enlarged the photograph as much as I could without losing the resolution. I searched my memory, flipping back through hundreds of people who had crossed my path, thinking about the men I'd killed, considering all the women associated with them, straining with every nerve running through my skull to make a connection.

Nothing clicked.

It *must* have been my hair color. Did she react that way to every woman with red hair and copper highlights? It made me uneasy. But there was nothing about her that felt familiar, and there was nothing I could find in her biographical information whispering in my subconscious that we might have come face-to-face at some point in time.

All through dinner, I tried to put it out of my mind. When Tess suggested martinis on the patio after our meal, I finally succeeded in turning my attention away from Ella. We sipped our drinks slowly. I sat quietly while Tess and Marcus made plans for what they would do when they took over the castle for a weekend.

I let my mind drift back to the castle towers. I watched the sun go down and felt pleased with myself that I'd pushed Tess to refuse to take no for an answer.

She had her castle. Would I ever have mine?

The next morning, I went for a run at dawn. I took the same route as I had the previous time. Since I was earlier, I figured I was less likely to run into Nolan on his Harley. Even if I did, I wondered if he would be less territorial now that he'd accepted Tess and Marcus as one of their valued couples. Maybe now that he knew they were also *landowners*, and since he'd seen me in the car with Tess, it would give me some kind of pass.

I ran the entire three and a half miles without seeing any motor-cycles, and only a few cars zipping past on the highway as the sun began to spread its light across the sky, turning it a pale yellowish blue. Being outside with my feet hitting the earth rather than concrete, and my lungs breathing fresh air, made me feel like a different person. I vowed to run every day during the rest of my time in California.

I had no idea how long that might be, although Diana had only agreed to three weeks, so it was either three weeks or an indefinite period without a paycheck at the end. Hopefully, running every day would bring some clarity to that situation. However, I might need to extend the distance beyond three miles. Maybe before I knew it, I would be running a half marathon every morning. I certainly had the time.

As I headed up Tess's long driveway, I slowed to a jog. I stopped near the building that housed the tasting room and gift shop that sold coasters and hats and other promotional items bearing the name of the Black Mask Winery and its distinctive logo—a slim black mask with three tiny rubies in the upper left corner.

I used the posts on the portico covering the outdoor tasting area to stretch my legs.

Just as I was finishing up, the tasting room door opened, and Silas stepped out. "This isn't a gym."

I smiled and turned toward the house.

"Don't be in such a hurry to run away," he said.

"I don't want to sully your tasting area with my sweat."

"I'm sure your sweat is as sweet and tasty as you are."

I turned and started walking toward the house. He was worse than my gut had suggested when I'd first felt my skin crawl in his presence. I shouldn't have been surprised. Maybe he wasn't worse, he was just bolder than I'd realized at exposing what he was.

"Don't be mad."

I kept walking.

"Hey, Alexan-*dra*. I'm talking to you. We should be friends."

"Not necessarily," I said.

I heard his footsteps close behind me. "I'm Tess and Marcus's most valued employee. And you're Tess's best friend. It's imperative that we get along."

It wasn't. I didn't think we would have much contact at all. I couldn't see any reason why I would ever have to spend another moment anywhere in his vicinity.

"I'm talking to you. Don't be so fucking rude."

I was almost at Tess's front patio. The chirps of the songbirds, really letting loose now that the sun was over the horizon, was a startling contrast to the aggressive voice of Silas as his footsteps continued to thud on the ground behind me, growing louder as I increased my pace.

He grabbed my arm, yanking so hard, I felt my shoulder wrench and was forced to stop. "Let go of me." I twisted away from him.

"I'm trying to have a conversation with you. It's rude to walk away."

"It's not a conversation. Let go of my arm. Right now."

"Or what?"

"Let go."

He released his grip, and I started toward the house.

"This isn't going to go down well with Marcus," he said. "He knows the success of this little wine-making adventure depends upon me. He and his bride-to-be don't know the first thing about the wine industry, growing grapes, or making wine. Without me, they're doomed to failure."

"I doubt that."

"You know less than they do about any of this."

"You're right. But I know a lot more about Tess and Marcus than you do."

"I'm telling you, it's to your advantage, and the success of your friends, that you and I have a harmonious relationship."

I folded my arms across my ribs. "I don't need to have any kind of relationship with you. I'm only a guest here. And saying crude things to me is not the way to have even a superficially polite relationship. So back off and don't ever speak to me like that again. *If* we happen to run into each other."

"Oh, we'll be running into each other. I guarantee it."

I didn't like giving him the last word, but I also didn't like giving him any more of my thoughts. There was no reason for me to see him again. I wouldn't be doing any wine tasting except when a bottle from their winery was served with a meal. And I definitely didn't need coasters or a ball cap with the winery name. If I needed a souvenir for Hunter, or Eileen, I would find something at the castle.

I'd never bought anyone a souvenir in my life, but now that the idea flitted across my mind, I thought it might be something fun to consider. I wondered if the castle had a gift shop. I pictured miniature ceramic and metal castles as I walked back to the house without turning to see what had happened to Silas.

CHAPTER 17

*T*ess spent most of the day in her office hoping that Alex wasn't getting herself into trouble. When they'd met briefly at the coffeepot, Alex sweaty from her run, Alex had bragged that she'd taken the same route, the same so-called private road, but hadn't encountered Nolan, so apparently patrolling the side roads surrounding the castle wasn't *a full-time gig for him.*

Her attitude made Tess nervous. Alex had been certain that Marcus could persuade Nolan to open the doors to the castle for their wedding, but she was utterly unconcerned about disrupting the relationship. Sometimes, Alex was impossible to figure out. She'd taken responsibility for Ella's initial rejection, but now that they'd secured a date, she'd re-assumed her combative attitude.

Every twenty minutes, Tess found herself peering out the window, wondering if she'd catch a glimpse of Alex. When the patio and pool area, the garden and every piece of the property she could see from the bay window of her office remained deserted, she opened the door, listening for sounds of Alex moving about the house. What was she up to?

Tess didn't feel any obligation to keep Alex entertained while she was visiting, but it had slowly dawned on her that without transportation, and being used to the constant stimulation of New York city, Alex might get bored, left on her own all day. She was the kind of person who liked a continuous flow of new experiences. She didn't spend a lot of time reading or relaxing, or even watching TV, as far as Tess could tell. She didn't seem to pay much attention to the news. She wasn't uninformed, but she didn't devour it and analyze it and discuss her reactions like Tess and Marcus enjoyed doing.

Thinking about Alex made it difficult to concentrate on her work. It didn't help that after they'd filled their coffee mugs that morning, moments before she left the kitchen, Alex had said she wanted to discuss something serious. When Tess asked what it was, Alex said it wasn't a good time since Tess needed to get to work. When Tess pushed for more details, Alex assured her it was nothing about Hunter, no disastrous fallout from taking extended time off from her job, no family emergency. But the comment nagged at the back of Tess's mind and kept her concentration from functioning at one hundred percent.

Getting up to speed on the day-to-day operations of a winery the size of Black Mask had been more challenging than she'd anticipated. Understanding the finances had been a full-time job in itself. The previous owners had arranged several meetings with their accountants. After interviewing a few other firms, Tess had made the decision to stay with them. The continuity helped, and they'd given her a fast and first-class education.

Now, there were a thousand things she needed to learn about agriculture and health standards, government regulations and distribution, bottling and sales. And the list went on. It wasn't as if she had to do it all herself, but she had to know enough to understand what the staff was talking about when they reported to her in their daily updates and weekly staff meetings.

At four-thirty, Alex's seemingly low-key but targeted bait got the best of her. She locked the screen on her desktop computer, turned off the wireless mouse and keyboard, and left her office. She changed into yoga clothes, went downstairs to the yoga studio where she worked out the kinks in her neck and back for fifteen minutes, then set off in search of Alex.

She found her on the back patio. She wore cut-off denim shorts and a black bikini top. She was stretched out on the lounge chair with a straw hat over her face. The black ribbon around the hat was shaped into a flat bow with tails that draped across Alex's shoulder. The ribbons fluttered in the breeze.

Tess scratched her arm, watching the satin drift across Alex's bare skin. It would drive her insane, feeling something so soft tickling her skin. She scratched harder, fighting the urge to yank the hat off Alex's face. Was Alex actually asleep, or was she lying there enjoying the torment? Possibly playing a game with herself to see how long she could endure it?

"Do you want a martini?" Tess asked, her voice tense with the imagined touch of the ribbon on her skin.

"Do you have to ask?"

The hat remained motionless when Alex spoke, the ribbon continuing to slither across her skin.

Tess turned quickly and went into the house.

When she returned with two drinks on a tray, Alex was sitting up, the hat in its proper place on her head, large sunglasses covering her eyes.

"Did you have a good nap?"

"I wasn't sleeping. I was thinking."

"About what?"

"About what you should do with Silas."

Tess sighed. She placed the tray on the table, and Alex picked up her drink.

"Cheers." Tess took a sip from her own glass and settled in one of the Adirondack chairs. "I shouldn't even respond to that, but first of all, you don't need to worry about any of our employees. And second, we're not *doing anything* with Silas. He's—"

"I don't think he's going to be the savior you think he is."

"He already has been. And as I said, you don't need to—"

"He was really crude to me."

Tess sipped her drink and waited. After a dramatic pause, Alex recounted the interaction she'd had with Silas.

Alex was right. It had been crude. Tess felt her stomach lurch. It was one thing to manage employees when you had the backing of an HR department and you could follow procedure and hand off harassment issues to others, expecting company-trained experts and attorneys to deal with it smoothly and without financial fallout.

But now she and Marcus were the company. They hired the lawyers. She set the policies. And there was no HR department. Her hand felt clammy holding the martini glass. She brought the fingers of her other hand to the rim of the glass for extra support. "That's disgusting, I agree," she said.

"Are you going to fire him?"

Tess laughed, aware that she sounded less than confident. "No."

"Why not?"

Tess took another sip of her drink. "I don't need advice on running my business, so let's talk about something else."

"It was creepy." Alex shuddered dramatically.

"I get that. And I already explained how critical he is. You don't understand the situation we're in, just now ramping up. If we fire him, he could destroy our business before we even get started."

"Aren't you upset by what he said? That he grabbed me? It's unacceptable. Why aren't you angry?"

"I am. I'm furious. But I can't … Marcus will see it differently. He'll see it as a guy crossing a line. He'll think one of us needs to have a word with him. But he'll also say you're tough and you know the score. He'd say you should ignore him."

"Typical."

"Yes, it is typical. And often, it works."

"It shouldn't have to be that way. It doesn't have to be that way."

"You can't bend everything to your liking. That's how things break."

Alex sipped her drink. She wiggled her toes, appearing to study them as if they were the most fascinating things she'd ever seen. "Is Marcus in charge of everything?"

"We're a partnership. For the most part, I'm—"

"So you agree with him on this?"

"Not necessarily. But partnerships require compromise."

"Of course. But he doesn't even know about this."

"I know how he thinks."

"Always? On every topic?"

"No. But I know how he's likely to react to this. We need Silas. And overall, he's—"

"Yes, your savior."

"Okay, that might not have been the best way to describe him. But he's critical to our success."

"So you said."

Alex was quiet for several minutes.

Tess felt her shoulders relax. She ate one of her olives and gazed across the garden, enjoying the breeze that was cooling the air on the patio. The longer the silence stretched between them, the more at ease she felt. It seemed as if Alex was finally ready to stop fixating on something that was probably a one-off misstep. Tess would speak to him and they could move on. Tess had empathized with what had happened, and that was enough. But Silas wasn't going anywhere. She couldn't get rid of him, not right now.

"What if he does something like that to one of your customers?"

"He won't."

Alex sat up, swinging her legs over the side of the lounge chair. The liquid in her glass swayed with the sudden movement. "How do you know?"

"Because you provoke people."

Alex adjusted her hat. She took a long swallow of her drink.

"I know you don't think you do," Tess said. "And I'm sure you think I'm victim-blaming or something, but—"

"Is that what I think?"

"He's never said anything inappropriate to any of our customers," Tess said. "I told you he's rough around the edges. He's a sales guy. I know how sales guys can be, and so do you. But he's never done anything to tarnish our brand."

"That you know of."

Tess stood. "I'll get some snacks."

"Good idea. And I'll have another martini if you're up for one." Alex grinned.

"Absolutely," Tess said.

In the kitchen, she fixed a charcuterie board and mixed two more drinks. A second martini would take the edge off the conversation. And the pause would allow them to shift their thoughts to something more pleasant. She was confident Silas would never do anything like that to one of their customers or vendors.

She'd meant it when she said Alex provoked people. And she was equally certain that Alex was aware of that fact.

CHAPTER 18

*L*istening to Tess defend the Neanderthal who worked for her, and then imply that Marcus might adhere to the *boys will be boys'* mentality was unsettling. But two martinis and another fabulous dinner prepared by Marcus, followed by a hilarious movie, and then the three of us dancing to 1980s tunes in the living room, turned my thoughts away from it.

The following morning, I decided that staying away from the snake in the tasting room wasn't all that hard. Managing the winery was Tess and Marcus's business. It wasn't my dream that was being threatened by a man who let his repulsive desire slide off his tongue so easily. It was difficult for me to believe Tess was so naïve to think Silas would behave that way toward me, but he would never do something similar to a woman who came for a wine tasting. I *knew* she wasn't that naïve. She'd made a calculated decision that his perceived value was greater than the risk.

Or she believed he was a decent guy, and I'd aroused some dark side of him that had never shown its face before. Of course I provoked people. But only those who were easily provoked. A man who isn't inclined to say disgusting things, or grab a woman's arm when she tries to walk away, isn't going to be *provoked* into doing either.

That had been my experience. I wondered what Tess's experience had been.

I could be a snake, too. I would lie hidden in the grass and keep a distant eye on Silas. There was a reason his first words to me had been a bald-faced, easily disproven lie. But for now, I could avoid him. I would go out of my way to avoid him, but it might not be enough because my gut was whispering that he objected to my very presence at the winery and he was going to make an equal effort to go out of his way to put himself in my path.

After my run, I went into the house and did my stretching in the yoga room. I showered, drank coffee, and ate a sliced apple with cheddar cheese. I was done with Silas. I was ready to turn my attention back to the castle and figuring out how to gain access to those magnificent towers.

I went looking for Marcus's office. His door was partially opened, and he looked up from his computer with an expression that said he wasn't bothered by my interruption.

"Do you have any free time today?" I asked.

"For what?"

"When I toured the castle with Tess, we didn't spend much time in any of the rooms. Since I'm the maid of honor, I really need a better sense of the layout so I can help advise her on decorations."

He laughed. "I don't know if Tess will want a lot of advice."

"She'll definitely want to bounce ideas off me."

"Maybe."

"Trust me, she will. She has brilliant ideas, but she sometimes gets ..." I hesitated, hoping he would fill in the empty space so I wasn't criticizing his fiancée to him. I wasn't sure how he would take that. I didn't want to provoke him. "She changes her mind a lot. Not that it's a bad thing. She's a perfectionist."

He laughed. "Isn't that the truth."

"That's how she ended up with you—looking for perfection."

"Your manipulation is showing."

I smiled. "I know Ella got over thinking I was someone she didn't want to see, but she probably isn't going to let me in there without one of you. And I wanted to take some time to get familiar with the layout. I just think it might be better without Tess so I can absorb it on my own."

He shook his head slowly. "You're too much."

"Possibly. But if you have time, I'd be so appreciative. When you call to make the appointment, it might be a good idea to avoid mentioning I'm coming."

"In your mind, this is a done deal."

"The entire reason I'm in California is to help Tess plan her wedding."

"I thought you were here for tasting—champagne and cake—and for shopping."

"And other things."

"If you say so."

"You'll call?"

He picked up his phone and tapped the screen. "I have ninety minutes this afternoon. But that means working through dinner. You and Tess can go out. I'll make a reservation."

"I'll take care of that."

"You don't know any of the restaurants here."

"I'll figure it out."

He grinned. "I'm sure you will."

Later that afternoon, as Marcus and I approached the castle doors, he informed me he'd been completely up front in letting Ella know I was joining him. "We already had a rocky start booking this place. I'm not playing games with them. And I'm not sure why you want to."

"I wasn't playing games."

"You were."

"I didn't want her to refuse to let me inside," I said.

"You didn't strike me as a game player, but now, I'm not sure."

"I'm not." I was. At least a lot of people would see it that way. I didn't see myself that way. I just didn't think I needed to explain every single thing I did. I'm also aware that the things I like to do aren't normal, so I suppose they come across as games. But games are fun. Life should be fun. So if people want to characterize them as games, that's fine with me. I know Marcus thought that was a mark against me.

The doors swung open as they had the first time. It was eery that someone watched their security cameras so closely the doors opened with perfect timing. I suppose it wasn't required around the clock. There was an electronically operated gate at the entrance to the property, so if no visitors were expected and that gate was secured, there would be no need for supervision of the front doors.

We stepped inside, welcomed by the same woman who had ushered Tess and me inside during our first visit. A moment later, Ella appeared in the entryway. Her smile and greeting were warm to the point of gushing affection. Now that Marcus and Tess had been transformed into one of her beloved fairy tales, there wasn't a hint of animosity on her face or in her tone of voice. Even her handshake felt gentle and accepting when she took my hand in hers.

Marcus was definitely not up to playing any so-called games. "Alexandra wanted to get a better look at the space. I'm sure Tess mentioned she's the maid of honor. She thinks she needs a good sense of the layout and flow so she can advise Tess on décor and planning for the event."

I expected Ella to recoil, remembering me slinking down the forbidden corridor to her secret tower. Instead, her welcoming smile grew even warmer. "Of course. I'm so glad Tess has such a wonderful support person. How many attendants are there?"

Marcus shrugged.

"Have you chosen the men who are standing with you?"

"We're in the early stages," Marcus said.

"I see. Well, plenty of time."

She turned toward me. "Do you have any specific questions or concerns?"

"I'd just like to spend more time in the rooms, get a feel for them."

"Absolutely."

Now, I realized her warm smile was manufactured, like hot wax that had been molded onto her face.

CHAPTER 19

*W*e followed Ella and her waxen smile into the great hall. Words flowed out of her mouth as she walked. The phrases sounded like the stories and sales copy on their website, but there was something to them that struck me as false. It sounded as if she wanted to captivate Marcus with stories that she was making up as she went along. I had the sense that if we returned the following week, the stories would be entirely different and she wouldn't remember a single word she'd spoken. Her eyes had a glazed quality, and she talked without stopping, hardly seeming to breathe.

A similar glazed look came over Marcus's eyes. He began shifting from one foot to the other as if he were eager to escape. After a few minutes, he took several steps away from her, looking as if he wanted to run for his life.

I didn't like that he seemed to be glancing over his shoulder, as if he were plotting his escape. Was he thinking he might slip out of the room and leave me alone with her? Wasn't that what I'd told him I wanted? But it wasn't what I wanted. I wanted to find a way to get closer to the tower entrance. I wanted to find Nolan.

She regaled us with story after story of gorgeous grooms and beautiful brides. She described gowns in breathless tones, outlining every detail of the necklines and beadwork, the trains and buttons and laces up the back. She named famous designers and discussed shoes and garters before moving on to wedding bands and engagement rings, growing teary-eyed over the cut of flawless stones.

I longed to challenge her stories. When she said the stones on her brides' fingers—yes, *her* brides—were flawless, I knew she was lying. Truly flawless diamonds were so rare, it was a statistical impossibility that all her brides would have displayed one on their ring fingers. It was funny and frightening at the same time.

Was this woman mentally unstable? Had she been locked up alone in her castle for so long, she'd lost her mind? It gave me another reason, besides wanting to know why he'd been so determined not to let me know who he was, to find Nolan and speak to him without Ella, or Marcus, overhearing.

I asked her about the dimensions of the hall, hoping to prove my intentions were bona fide. Also hoping she might have to leave the room to get me a fact sheet or to check her records. She didn't. She quoted the number without missing a beat. I asked her how many tables fit in the room and whether bands could have access to the castle when we auditioned them. She assured me that was acceptable as long as we gave them a list of the members' names and two weeks' notice.

She had a ready answer for every question I could come up with.

Each time I spoke, I sensed Marcus moving farther away from me. He was no longer in my range of vision and I began to wonder if he was even in the room, although I imagined Ella would chase him down if she lost sight of him.

Despite the soaring ceiling and the arena size of the hall, I felt claustrophobic. I couldn't escape her staring eyes, her constant chatter. The towers felt as if they were moving farther away from me every moment we stood there.

"Will Nolan be joining us?" I asked.

"Why?"

"I've never met him."

"There's no need."

I nodded.

"Why the sudden interest in Nolan?"

"It's not sudden. You told such a compelling love story ... I had the impression you worked side-by-side on all your weddings."

"We do."

She didn't elaborate. Now, I'd shown my hand. Escaping her watchful eye had become that much more difficult because I'd stirred her curiosity about what I really wanted. "Can we see the kitchen? I also wanted to see the bedrooms. So we can plan—"

"It's premature for that. Let's wait until we're closer to the nuptials."

I laughed softly.

"You think that's funny?"

"It's such an old-fashioned word. I'm not used to hearing it."

"That doesn't make it funny."

I needed to breathe some fresh air. I wanted Marcus to talk to this woman so I could escape, even if I never found the entrance to the towers or Nolan.

I turned. "Marcus, do you have any questions?"

"This is your gig." He said it so fast, it seemed as if he'd planned it, in case I tried to toss her off onto his shoulders. He turned quickly and wandered back toward the doorway, peering out into the entry as if he, too, was curious about finding his way to one of the towers.

"I was really hoping to look at the bedrooms."

"There's plenty of time." Her waxen smile stiffened. "Will that be all?"

It couldn't be all. I didn't think I would easily get another chance. "I'd like to see the other rooms. I don't have a good sense of the overall layout. I'd also like to spend more time in the kitchen."

"Of course." She began walking toward the spacious rooms that were designated for the bride and groom to get ready for their big day.

"You'll want to see this, Marcus." My voice echoed slightly as it carried across the great hall.

He turned and walked toward us.

We followed Ella through all the rooms. Marcus hadn't had a full tour on his visit, and now he seemed more relaxed, eager to see how all the pieces of the castle fit together.

As we stood in the library, I saw Nolan pass by the doorway, headed in the direction we'd just come. "There's Nolan. Maybe he can—"

"He's busy today." Ella gave me a firm smile. "You seem very interested in him. Is there a reason for that?"

"No, but I—"

"Good." She walked to the shelves and ran her fingers along the spines of the books. "Aren't they beautiful?" She took her hand away and kissed her fingertips.

Marcus frowned. "Were you involved in the design?"

"Sadly, no," Ella said. "It was built before our time."

"What's in the towers?" Marcus asked.

I wasn't sure if I was pleased with his question or annoyed.

"They're off-limits to our guests."

"Too bad," Marcus said.

We left the library and made our way down a long hallway, ending up in the kitchen. I looked out at the vegetable garden and saw Nolan.

"There's Nolan again. I'd just like to meet him, since I haven't." Before she could stop me, I headed toward the door.

"I told you, he's busy."

"He doesn't look busy." I touched the door handle. "He's just wandering around." I pressed down on the handle, but before I could pull it open, Ella was beside me, her hand gripping my wrist. "Why are you so pushy? I told you he's busy. You'll meet him eventually, but he doesn't have time today. If there's something you want to know about our story, or the castle, you can ask me. As I told you quite clearly, Nolan and I are one. There's nothing he can tell you that I can't."

"Please take your hand off me," I said.

"When you let go of the handle."

I glanced at Marcus. He looked amused.

Ella and I were frozen in place, both of us refusing to be the first to yield. I loosened my grip on the door handle and she released her fingers slightly, easing the pressure on my wrist. I let go of the handle and she dropped her hand to her side.

"Is that all?" she asked.

Clearly I was not going to speak to Nolan and there was no way I was going to get anywhere near either one of the towers.

CHAPTER 20

$\mathcal{E}$lla gestured toward the kitchen doorway in a decidedly unsubtle directive that it was time for us to go. As she'd done before, she hung back, herding us toward the door to be sure she had us in her sights and there was no way for us to do so much as touch an object without her being aware of what we were up to.

We turned out of the kitchen and walked down a long hallway. Despite the more leisurely tour, I still felt somewhat disoriented about the layout of the castle. Part of that sensation came from the fact that all the hallways were interior. As we walked along dimly lit passageways, the walls hung with chiffon draperies that flowed like grass moving in the wind as we passed, and torches that cast garish light on the others' faces, there was no way to get a fix on which direction we were heading.

Once we were inside a room, there wasn't always a clear view of the outside landscape. All the windows were nearly two feet deep, cut through the thick stone walls. The glass was also thick in many of the windows, giving a distorted, almost watery view of the outdoors. Chiffon draperies hung from iron bars over windows and doorways, making everything feel somewhat like a dream—a building that existed beyond the realm of a normal setting, as if it were floating among the clouds.

We ended up in the great hall, where Ella turned to face us. A warm, slightly more genuine smile returned to her face. She held out her hand. "Thank you very much for coming to visit us again."

Marcus shook her hand. As she slowly released his grip, a piercing scream shot through the room, quick and sharp. The sound was so sudden, ending abruptly, it resembled a clap of thunder.

The sound of it tore through my body, causing me to jerk my head to the side in time to see Marcus pull his head back, startled.

"Who is that?" I asked.

Ella smiled. "If you have any more questions, when you need to set up time with your flower person, or your wedding coordinator, please let me know and I'll make arrangements. We always—"

"What was that scream?" I asked.

She stared at me.

"It sounded like someone is in a lot of pain," I said.

"Or scared out of their mind," Marcus added.

"Pardon?" Ella said.

I tilted my head slightly. "That horrible scream."

"What are you talking about?" Ella smiled. "As I was saying, two weeks' notice is preferable. I was able to accommodate you today, but I ... we get quite busy. The castle is in huge demand, and we're booked nearly every weekend. It was unusual that—"

"Ella. Someone just screamed bloody murder," Marcus said. "Are you just ignoring it?"

"I didn't hear anything," she said.

"You must have. It shattered my eardrums." I cupped my hands over my ears.

"Sometimes the wind can cause strange sound effects because of all the stone. I'm used to it, so I didn't even notice."

"This wasn't the wind," I said. "Someone screamed. It was—"

"No one screamed," she said.

"I heard a scream. It was piercing," I said.

"I explained what you might have heard. As I said, I'm used to the unusual sounds that emanate from a structure made entirely of stone."

"I suppose that's possible," Marcus said. "The towers. And all these narrow hallways. I saw that some of them have very low ceilings. I lived in a high rise that was glass on two sides and—"

"This was not the wind," I said. "It's not building materials settling or making unusual sound effects. Someone just screamed their head off as if they were about to be stabbed to death, or they'd sliced off their left hand."

"Oh, that's so gruesome." Ella shuddered. "Why would you say something like that, Alexandra? Do you always have such morbid thoughts?"

"My thought was prompted by hearing someone scream as if their life were about to end."

Ella laughed. "No one's life is ending today. I can assure you of that. In fact, the only people here today are Nolan, our accountant, and a few others on the staff. So don't get yourself all worked up."

I moved closer to her. I stared into her eyes, waiting for her to look away, to collapse under the pressure of her ridiculous story.

She stared back at me with clear, guileless eyes, a peaceful smile on her lips. The waxen quality had evaporated as if it had never existed.

"I'm not worked up," I said. "I'm wondering why you're so undisturbed by a loud, horrifying scream. I'm wondering why you would lie about something like that."

She laughed. Finally, I heard it—a faint hint of nerves in her laughter. "I'm not lying. I've lived her for decades. Stone walls provide a different kind of atmosphere. If you don't believe me, that's not my problem. Shall we?" She gestured toward the entryway.

I remained rooted to the spot, but Marcus and I were not on the same page. He began walking, rather quickly, I thought, toward the arched opening that led to the entryway. A moment later, he disappeared from view.

"Let's go. I really do have a lot of work to catch up on," Ella said. "I've been more than generous with my time. And at the last minute. Please show a little respect."

She nudged me slightly, causing me to stumble.

"Alexandra, please. You're testing my patience."

Another scream echoed somewhere in the castle. It wasn't as piercing this time, and also less shocking. It sounded as if it came from above us, far away. I knew in my gut it had come from one of the towers.

CHAPTER 21

BEFORE: AMELIA

*W*hen I was five years old, I was happy in the castle, alone with my parents. We played games and read stories. My mother made delicious dinners, and we ate together every night at a large table with a candelabra in the center. With my father's help, I was allowed to hold the long matchstick to light the candles. After we'd finished, I used the pewter cup on the end of a stick to extinguish the flame on each candle while my father kept my hand steady.

The three of us went for long walks in the forest, and my father began teaching me how to ride a horse.

My first lessons were on the back of a pony. I learned how to direct the pony to turn, how to make her stop and start when I wanted, and how to make her trot. Once I was comfortable with the pony, he took me up onto the back of one of the mares, sitting in front of him. We rode together and I fell in love with the large, quiet, gentle animals.

He taught me how to groom the horses and how to feed them chunks of apple in a way that wouldn't startle them.

I didn't know yet that other people had larger families. I heard about big families in the stories they read to me, but they told me those were make believe, they weren't like real life. And of course, that was the truth. I think I was aware that there were other people in the world. Sometimes, from my tower windows, I saw cars on the road and people picking grapes or sitting in gardens.

People came to our house to deliver the food we didn't grow in our garden. I knew that sometimes my mother or father went out when I was in my classroom with the other parent. They would appear with things that had come from outside our castle—new clothes, books, or things for our castle.

On Christmas there was always a new ornament for our tree. It needed a lot of ornaments because it stood in the great hall and was so big my father needed a ladder to decorate the branches up high and to put the star on the top. On Christmas and on my birthday, new toys appeared.

So I knew there were places outside the castle. They weren't just make believe in books. Not all of them. But I didn't think about them very much.

I was happy. I never felt sad or angry or alone, like some of the children in the stories we read. Of course, in the end, things worked out happily for children in the stories, and even for the grown-ups. But they were sad and angry and had fights and battles and experienced difficulties getting to their happiness.

My mother said I would never endure any of that. Because we lived in our castle, we would always be safe and happy there.

Then, after Christmas one year, but before I turned six, my father went away for a very long time.

My mother told me not to cry. She wouldn't say why he was gone. She wouldn't tell me where he'd gone. She wouldn't tell me when he was coming home. All she would say was that I shouldn't cry. I should be happy because my life was still perfect. I was safe. I had everything I needed.

I had her love. I had my books and healthy food. I wasn't abandoned and no one could ever hurt me. In another year or two, I would be able to ride my father's horse. As soon as I was a little bigger. I cried because I liked riding his horse with my father. She begged me not to cry. She said that over and over until I wanted to slap her face.

"Please don't cry, Amelia. Please don't cry. Please, please *don't cry!*"

I still cried.

"You're safe here with me, and that's the most important thing."

Because I still cried, she got impatient with me. She told me if I didn't stop, I wouldn't get any desserts. So I cried when I was alone in bed at night. In the morning, she asked if I'd been crying. I said I hadn't. She said, "Your pillow is stained."

There were no desserts for a while.

One day, after weeks and weeks, maybe more, someone came to the door with a package. My mother took it to her room in the other tower. When she came up to my room that afternoon, she had a small box wrapped in white paper with a blue satin ribbon around it. She handed it to me. "Open it."

I pulled the ribbon and tore off the paper. I opened the box. Inside was a gold heart-shaped locket on a chain. My mother used her fingernail to open it. Inside were two pictures—one of my mother and one of my father.

"This will remind you of how much we love you and how much we love each other. You can wear it every day."

"I don't want it," I said. "I want Daddy."

"But he's here with you. See." She pointed to the picture.

I could hardly tell it was him. The picture was so tiny. Part of their faces were cut off. I could only see my father's red hair and my mother's blonde hair. I could see their eyes and noses and part of their mouths.

"I can hardly tell it's Daddy."

"But you know it's him. You can see that. And you can see me."

She unhooked the clasp and put it around my neck. I looked in the mirror. It was pretty, but it made me want to start crying all over again. I wondered if she really thought a necklace was the same as having my father with me.

It was worse. Every time I looked in the mirror, every time I felt the locket against my skin, I remembered he was gone, and I remembered how it used to be.

CHAPTER 22

NOW: ALEX

*M*arcus and I discussed Ella's strange behavior during our drive back to their home. Mostly, we debated the reality of the screams.

"She's an unusual woman," Marcus said. "Definitely eccentric, but that's part of the charm. The fixation on their love story, her interest in emphasizing the love stories of people who get married there ... it's charming."

"It's controlling."

"Don't turn it into something dark."

"I'm not. But she's creepy."

"Eccentric, like I said. One person's creep is another person's eccentric. Let her be. The castle is unique, and Tess loves it. So do I. Her eccentricities have nothing to do with our wedding. If she wants to hear how we met and make a big deal out if it, that's fine with me."

"But she has such a weird view of marriage."

"So what? A lot of people do. That has nothing to do with Tess and me."

"And the screaming didn't shock you?"

"Yes. But she had a reasonable explanation."

I laughed. "That was not reasonable."

"Okay. I agree, they sounded blood curdling. But I've never lived in a stone house. And I've never lived in a house with towers, or with all those long narrow hallways. What do I know?"

"Someone was screaming. She's trying to gaslight us."

He laughed so hard I thought he might lose control of the SUV. "She's not *gaslighting* us. It makes perfect sense that it could be a natural phenomenon."

"It's not."

"You sound very sure of yourself."

"Because I know a scream when I hear one. And so do you."

"It did sound like a scream. The first time. But the second one? Who knows?"

"Maybe she has someone locked in one of those towers."

"Come on, Alex. You have a wild imagination. Tess never mentioned that about you."

I thought about how it sounded. I knew I was obsessed with the towers. I'd started to believe there was something sinister about them. When someone is trying that hard to be secretive, it almost compels you to think there's something unpleasant they're trying to hide. But I suppose I sounded a little unbalanced myself. Still, I know a scream when I hear one. "Someone screamed," I said.

"She seemed unconcerned, so I'm guessing she knows what she's talking about."

"What if ..."

"What if, what?"

I didn't even know what I'd planned to say, because I didn't know what I was thinking. It was not a pleasant scream and the fact that Ella had no reaction at all was eery. It was not possible that she hadn't heard it. I didn't believe it was the wind, and she was so used to it she hadn't noticed. She hadn't wanted to talk about it with us, hadn't wanted to acknowledge it. Why?

Marcus and I batted it back and forth a few more times, but we got nowhere, and by the time we were half a mile from their winery,

I could tell from his tone that he'd lost interest and his thoughts were moving back to his work. In twenty minutes, all of it would be wiped from his mind and he would be thinking about threats to online banks and individuals' personal data.

I went to my room and changed into yoga clothes, but instead of going to their yoga room, I went looking for Tess. The screams were burning their way through my skull and I wouldn't be able to focus on my breath. I could still hear those screams echoing inside my skull.

I knocked on Tess's office door and opened it without waiting for an answer. She wasn't on the phone, so I walked in and plopped myself down on the love seat adjacent to her desk.

"Make yourself at home," she said.

"Did Marcus tell you what happened?"

"I've been working, not chatting with Marcus. So has he, I assume."

"I convinced him to take some time off to visit the castle."

She laughed. "I think I've left you with too much time on your hands. Do I need to plan some activities for you? I thought you'd do some sightseeing when I was busy. The cake tasting is—"

"You need to hear this. And I don't have too much time on my hands. I came here to relax and to get some time to think."

"It sounds like you have too *much* time to think."

"But not about the things I need to be thinking about." I told her what had happened at the castle.

She looked alarmed when I got to the part about the screams.

"What did Marcus say?"

"He agrees with her. He was shocked at first. But now he's pivoted to thinking it's a weather phenomenon never before discovered by modern humankind."

"Maybe he's right."

"Someone was screaming."

"Marcus is good at finding the simple, logical explanation."

"So am I."

"Not always."

"I think I am."

"Sometimes, often, yes. Other times, not so much. If he thinks it makes sense, then maybe that's all it was."

"You didn't hear it. You would have had chills. You would have been freaked out. I guarantee it."

"But he heard it. And he wasn't. And he thinks it's possible, even likely, it was the wind," she said.

"It's not like all the windows and doors are standing open. Marcus needs to be more curious."

"You mean he needs to be more intrusive and nosey?"

"That's not what this is about. When you hear someone scream, isn't it a good idea to find out why?"

"Well, I didn't hear it, so I can't know. I agree it sounds weird, but it was probably a onetime thing. Even if it was someone screaming, maybe their chef cut her finger or burned herself or something."

"We were in the kitchen seconds before this happened. There was no chef. No meal preparation in progress."

Tess glanced over her shoulder at her computer screen. "I'm kind of in the middle of something here. We'll be spending lots of time at the castle. We have our cake tasting there tomorrow. And there's a champagne reception the week after next for all the recently accepted brides who are getting married next spring."

"You've been busy."

She smiled. "I have. So if there was an incident today, I'm sure it will be resolved. It won't impact our wedding, which is ages away." She glanced at her computer screen. She clicked her mouse and was quiet for a moment or two. Without turning back to me, she said, "Do you want me to figure out some things for you to do while you're here? Are you bored? If you want Hunter to come out, he's more than welcome."

"No thanks."

I stood and went out of her office. I had plenty to keep me busy.

I could figure out a way into the castle. Maybe. It seemed impossible, but things could change. There was the cake tasting.

And I absolutely needed to decide what I was going to do about my job. And my living situation. And my life.

Maybe that's why the castle was so appealing.

Maybe I wanted to escape to a fantasy world of my own.

CHAPTER 23

I called Hunter for a video chat to get his take on the bizarre woman who had ordained herself the queen of the Windy Hills Castle. And the screams.

He started walking into his bedroom as I told him about Marcus and Tess's willingness to believe the story about wind, coming from no source that I was aware of, causing a sound like a terrified human scream.

"I'm looking that up," he said.

I heard the soft tap of keys on his laptop. He was quiet for several minutes.

I waited impatiently.

Finally, he spoke. "The only thing I can find suggesting that it could happen says there would have to be open doors or windows at both ends of the building. If a strong wind was passing through, and was split around an object, with the currents pushing against each other, it can make eery sounds. Still, that's more of a howling, the way this describes it. I'll send you a link to a recording of the sound. You can listen later."

I smiled at the screen.

"What's so funny?"

"It's not funny. Well, maybe it's funny. Tess went on and on about Marcus being logical, but no one bothered to look it up."

Hunter shrugged. "I don't know why not."

"The way Ella behaved was stranger than the scream itself, though. It makes me think she's heard it quite a few times. Because she didn't react at all. If that was the first time, her body would have reacted without her being able to control it. So I think she's used to the screaming."

"If you really want to know, you should talk to other people who have been married there, or will be soon."

"She would never give me their names."

"Tell her you want some references."

I shook my head. "She wouldn't. People get on their knees to get married in that castle. She holds all the cards. If you want references, you obviously don't want it badly enough. That's her mindset."

He laughed. "Okay. Whatever."

He talked about his work for a while, mostly about office politics, and a little about a big fall fashion show the Herrera Agency was getting ready for.

"What else have you been up to?" he asked

I thought about Silas. "I've been going for long runs. It's nice running without breathing exhaust and waiting for traffic lights."

"There aren't any traffic lights in Central Park," he said.

"True."

"Or exhaust. At least not right in your face."

"Also true. I enjoy running where there's a lot of space. I can go for miles."

"I thought you liked the city."

"It's awesome."

He laughed. "You're confusing, sometimes."

"Why is it confusing to like two things?"

He gave me a puzzled look, but said nothing. It was the truth. It was part of the reason I couldn't decide where I wanted to have my fantasy home, which at this point in time was absolutely a fantasy. It was the reason a castle seemed as viable an alternative as anything. I had a lot of money stashed away, especially because of the time I'd lived in Australia where sharing a house with the company owner was one of the perks and I'd saved nearly every dollar I'd earned. But I was still a very long way from buying property, and I didn't like that.

There was a part of me that didn't want to settle anywhere, to be tied down with furniture, data about my life spread all over the internet, fired around the globe, telling people what I'd bought and when and how much it was worth, with satellites pointing out where my house was, showing pictures of any car I might own and the patio furniture in my yard.

"Aside from hearing mysterious screamers and listening to a strange woman gaslight you, and dreaming about cake, what *else* have you been up to?"

"Running."

"You already *said* that."

"Right. I've missed going long distances. I'm hoping to work my way back up to ten miles a few times a week."

"So that's it? Running and scoping out the castle?"

"Pretty much."

"What about all the wedding prep?"

"We're going cake tasting tomorrow," I said.

"Sweet."

"Ha ha."

"I wouldn't mind tasting cake."

"It's not a party where she invites twenty people."

"Just saying."

"Okay. Good to know."

"Am I invited to the wedding?"

"I haven't asked."

"But you get a plus-one," he said.

"Probably."

"Isn't that how it usually works?"

"I don't know a lot about how weddings work."

"How can a woman your age not know how weddings work?"

I stared at him. I hadn't realized he'd given so much thought to weddings and my age, and, he seemed to be implying, doing couple-type things like going to weddings. What else had he been thinking about that I was completely unaware of? "I just don't."

"You don't want me to go to the wedding?"

I took a deep breath. I wondered if he noticed me doing it. I wasn't sure what he wanted from me. He seemed different, some-how, than he'd been in New York. Maybe because we weren't used to talking on the phone. Even though we could see each other, it wasn't the same. In fact, seeing each other on a screen forced us to look at each other more than we did under normal circumstances. Maybe that was it. Usually, we sat beside each other. We wouldn't notice every change of expression.

Video chats weren't unfamiliar to me, but I'd never done them with a guy I was seeing, and this wasn't turning out to be a lot of fun. I didn't like how he was looking at me.

"I didn't say that. I don't even have an invitation yet."

"Well, obviously, you don't really need an invitation because you're the maid of honor. The invitation is just a formality."

I stared at him. Probably, he would be attending the wedding with me, but why were we talking about it now? I wanted to talk about the screaming. It was interesting and unsettling. I liked that he'd researched the reality of Ella's explanation, but now he was acting like a little kid who wasn't getting his way.

"Never mind. It's not important." He moved the phone so I could only see the side of his face. He was standing up from his desk chair, walking into the kitchen. He disappeared for a moment as I heard his refrigerator open. Then I heard the sound of him prying the cap off a bottle of beer. He spoke, but I still only saw the side of his face. "I should let you go. I'm sure you have things to do."

"Not really."

"Wedding stuff."

"You seem bent out of shape," I said.

"I'm not. Just tired."

"I guess it's late there."

"Not sleepy. Just tired of the games."

"What games?"

"It's really unclear why you're in California. And I'm getting a weird vibe about whether you're actually planning to come back."

"A *vibe*?"

"Yes."

"There is no vibe. I just needed to get out of there. Things are not great at work. And I want to figure some stuff out."

"It's disappointing that you don't think you can talk to me about whatever it is you need to figure out."

"Maybe I will."

He was quiet for a moment or two. "Let me know when that happens. When, and if. I'm gonna hang up now." He ended the call.

I dropped my phone onto the bed. I had no idea what was bothering him. And no idea what he wanted from me. But I was sure about one thing—it was not the wind making a screaming sound inside the Windy Hills Castle.

CHAPTER 24

PORTLAND, OREGON

*M*y mother bought fabric and let me help choose a pattern for my princess dress. Of course, the pattern was nothing like I'd envisioned. Neither was the fabric.

In the library book, the princess dress I'd chosen had a full skirt with petticoats underneath to make it stand out. It was longer in the back, so it dragged along the ground in a display of careless decadence. The sleeves were puffy near the shoulders, barely touching the princess's clavicle, and long and fitted below, coming to points on the backs of her hands. It scooped low in the front to show the tops of her newly budding breasts, like it would for mine. It was even lower in the back, exposing her skin to the center of her spine.

My dress looked like it belonged to the virgin Mary. It also had long sleeves, but they went well over my shoulders, with a collar that stood in a tiny ridge around my neck. The only flashy aspect, revealing a thin sliver of skin, was a four-inch long teardrop opening in the back, held closed by a button. There was a wide ribbon around the waist that tied in a bow, the ends trailing down to the backs of my knees. The dress stopped at my ankles.

It was pale blue cotton, not the rich brocade I wanted. There would be no jewels attached to the dress.

At night, I lay in my bed and stared into the darkness, trying to think of what I could do to make it resemble something even close to a dress fit for a princess. Petticoats were out of the question. Even though my mother had made sure to instill adequate sewing skills in me, I didn't have access to the fabric to make them myself. I wasn't even sure there was enough room in the slim skirt to allow for layers of netting underneath. Unless I took my mother's deadly looking silver sewing sheers to the top of the dress, the neckline and back wouldn't have the dramatic sweeps exposing my skin. I had no crown.

I wasn't going to look like a princess at all. I would look like a girl who had stepped out of her prairie farmhouse to stack bales of hay at the harvest festival. My father would be thrilled. My mother would feel she'd done what was expected. The church elders would be pleased that I blended in with the other kids.

Closing my eyes, I imagined sparks flying from my fingertips, daggers flashing out of my eyes, swirls of magic stars circling my head. Maybe I was confusing a fantasy queen or a sorceress with a medieval princess. I didn't care. I wanted flash and dazzle and mystery.

This was my first costume party. It might be my last until I was eighteen, or older, and free from my parents' supervision.

For years, I'd watched other children traipse up and down our street in fabulous costumes, pretending to be pirates and witches, ballerinas and astronauts, cats and princesses. They wore masks that hid their identities. I wanted to live in a world of make believe. I wanted to pretend I was someone entirely different. Just for one night. It was so unfair that we were allowed to dress up and then the chance to invent a costume was turned into the most incredibly dull display imaginable.

Part of me wondered if I should tell my father I wanted to go as Moses, or some other powerful man from the bible. I wondered what he would think of that. There would be no flash or mystery. Nothing wild. The character was surely one he would be forced to approve intellectually, but I laughed inside to think what he would say about his daughter going as a male figure.

I turned onto my stomach and pressed my face into the pillow.

It was early October, and the stores were filled with displays of Halloween candy and costumes. As I followed my mother down the aisles, I slowed my pace.

"Hurry up," my mother said. "We already have your costume. Besides, most of these are focused on the occult. It's not something you should be entertaining thoughts about."

I hurried after her, but I had my idea. Right in the center of the display had been a rack of masks. Most of them were uncomfortable, disgusting looking rubber sacks that fit over two-thirds of a person's head, with small holes for the eyes. Others, for small children, were stiff plastic with either silly grinning faces or monstrous leers.

But at the top of the rack was a mask that I knew I had to have. It was black, designed to cover only the eyes and nose. At the sides were small black feathers, held in place with green and blue gems. It was perfect. It would match my dress. It would give me a mysterious air, and there was nothing ungodly or occult about it. There was nothing seductive, nothing that would be offensive to god.

My mother whisked me out of the store, her shopping bag filled with the sponges and cleaning spray she'd come for.

Still, a quiet voice inside whispered that my parents would find a reason. I would have to ask my brother to drive me back to the discount store. I had enough money saved up to buy that mask. I needed to do it immediately before someone else snatched it off the rack.

Tom drove me to the store on a Saturday morning without asking any questions. He probably figured I wanted to buy some early Halloween candy for a secret stash. Or maybe he thought I was experimenting with makeup. I don't know what he thought. He didn't ask, and I didn't tell. We talked about the little white lies we told our parents in order for him to get access to the car at all. This time, we'd said we were dropping off soda cans at the church for the recycling program they operated to raise money for the soup kitchen.

We laughed that our parents would definitely tell us we had a special room in hell for not only lying, but lying about something that was god's work. We were creative with our lies. Not all of them were about god's work. But I knew if I mentioned going to the store, there would be far too many questions.

When my mother told me it was time to try on the dress for hemming, I came downstairs wearing the mask. My father took one look and shook his head. "Absolutely not."

"It's a costume party," I said. "Costumes need masks."

"It's not a costume party. It's a harvest festival. The purpose is to show gratitude for god's bounty, for feeding us throughout the year."

"We're supposed to dress up to pretend we're someone we aspire to be like."

He laughed. "*Aspire*. That's a fancy word for a thirteen-year-old child. You should aspire to be like our role models in the scriptures. If you get carried away with the costume, you won't be going. A mask is out of the question. You should never try to hide who you are. Never. God sees through every mask we try to wear. Never forget that."

Something about the way he said it filled me with an even greater aspiration. I was fascinated with the idea of hiding who I was. Suddenly, that was all I wanted.

CHAPTER 25

NAPA VALLEY, CALIFORNIA

*T*ess loved getting dressed up and the cake tasting was a terrific reason for dressing up midday. Working from home, running the business, which often demanded her presence in the winery itself, didn't often invite opportunities for high heels and a dress.

As she descended the curving staircase to the ground floor, she saw Alex standing in front of their portrait in the entryway. She was flooded with appreciation that Alex had caught her enthusiasm, putting equal effort into what she was wearing. It made up, mostly, for her ridiculous obsession over the terrifying screams that Alex continued to insist she'd heard inside the castle.

Tess adored Alex. She truly did. Alex had brought more fun and excitement into her life than any woman she'd ever befriended. She never felt she had to watch what she said or apologize for any of her behavior around Alex. It was incredibly freeing to spend time with her. But Alex could be difficult. She absolutely provoked people. She seemed to enjoy it. And the way she fixated on certain situations and people was almost scary at times.

Alex wore electric blue shoes with four-inch heels. She had on a short dress of the same color. She wasn't wearing a necklace, which made the stunning color of the dress even more dramatic. There was a gold bracelet on each of her wrists, and gold earrings that were long, slender 3D rectangles.

Walking toward her, Tess felt a smile spread across her face. She'd made the right choice, asking Alex to be her maid of honor. Every moment from now until she began her walk down the aisle toward Marcus was going to be the time of her life, and she knew Alex would help make the entire experience memorable.

"You look amazing," Tess said.

"So do you."

Tess ran her hands down her white sheath dress. "Thank you. I feel very bridal."

"I should have bought you one of those mini veils."

"We're a little old for that kind of nonsense."

"Are we? Who says?"

Tess laughed.

When they arrived at the castle, the doors were standing open.

The entryway was filled with clear, round helium balloons. Inside the balloons were gold and silver foil disks, shimmering in the light from a few strategically placed candles. The balloons clung to the ceiling, their gold and silver ribbons trailing across Tess and Alex's faces as they passed through.

Tess gasped when she saw the great hall. It had been transformed into something that could only be described as magical.

Everything she'd heard about the perfection of having a wedding at the Windy Hills Castle was true. They went all out. Every detail was treated as if it were the most crucial part of the wedding. It appeared they viewed the cake tasting the same way.

Placed throughout the hall were small black metal trees with a few representative branches and leaves. Balloons matching those in the entryway were tied to the trees with varying lengths of ribbon, so they ascended high into the cavernous space. The rest of the room had been filled with white flowering plants. They were set up to create a series of pathways leading to a long table in the center, where three multi-tiered cakes were placed at one end. Dome-covered serving plates held pre-cut slices of cake.

A few yards from the long table was another table with a champagne bottle in a bucket of ice, two champagne flutes, a silver coffeepot, two cups and saucers, and a stack of cake plates. Set apart from the rest was a small round table with two chairs. A single white rose in a bud vase stood in the center of the table.

"Isn't it spectacular?" Tess asked.

"I'm impressed," Alex said.

Ella appeared beside them, having crossed the room without making a sound. "Please have a seat. Would you like champagne or coffee?"

They agreed on champagne. A moment later, they were clicking their glasses over their first serving of cake. The baker stood beside the table, telling them about the icing and the lemon zest in the white cake.

For the next hour, they tasted more cake than Tess had eaten in her entire adult life. She was sure of it. After a while, she wasn't sure she was going to be able to make a decision. There were a few she eliminated easily—the rich chocolates, although absolutely delicious, were too much for a wedding. And no one wanted to be smiling for photos with ridges of thick, dark goop wedged between their teeth, their lips stained as if they'd been drinking blood.

The textures were divine. Every single one tasted like it had been whipped up by angels they were so light, with just the right level of sweetness.

"Do you have any favorites?" she asked.

"All of them," Alex said.

"That's completely unhelpful."

"It's the truth. I've never tasted cake like this in my life. If I'd known cake could taste this good, I'd be eating it more often. I think of cake as something eaten at children's parties or left on your plate at office celebrations and weddings. I would choose any of these from a dessert bar after Sunday brunch."

"I know," Tess said. "So, which are your top three?"

"The chocolate with—"

"No chocolate," Tess said.

"Everyone will love you and remember your wedding forever if you serve chocolate."

"Not necessarily in a good way. They'll definitely remember the photos if they have chocolatey smiles."

Alex laughed.

"Crossing chocolate off the list—"

"Are you worried Marcus will smash it in your face and your dress will be stained? So you want to play it safe with white cake? Since he can't be trusted?"

"I trust him one hundred percent. We're not twenty-two-year-olds. We aren't going to be playing stupid games like food fights and garter tosses."

"No bouquet toss either?"

"No, so your chance to use superstition to snag Hunter is off the table."

"Not a problem." Alex took a sip of champagne.

"I'm waiting. Which are your top three?"

"You're the bride," Alex said.

Tess sighed. "I brought you here instead of Marcus because you're the most opinionated person I've ever met." She laughed. "Especially when it comes to food. And now you have nothing to say?"

"I told you—chocolate. But you're worried about photographs instead of serving the best dessert ever."

Tess took another bite of cake.

The baker was hovering several yards from the table. Her expression was the neutral epitome of professionalism, but her hovering sent off waves of pressure that Tess could feel undulating through her own body. The woman—Melody Mars—seemed eager for praise. Or a decision. Tess wasn't sure which, but she'd offered plenty of praise, so maybe it was a decision Melody was waiting for.

This was the pressure of planning their wedding. The expectation that every detail had to be not only perfect, but a cut above anything you'd experienced at the myriad of weddings you'd attended in your life, as well as the weddings all your guests had attended. It was too much. And yet, she found herself striving to reach that unattainable goal.

Somehow, it all became inextricably tangled up with demonstrating the strength and uniqueness of their love. How would the world know, in a tangible way, how deeply and profoundly she and Marcus loved each other, and were committing themselves to one another for a lifetime, that their love transcended *everything*, if their wedding wasn't breathtaking and beyond compare?

It was absurd. She wanted to scream with the increasing weight of it all.

Maybe that was the cause of the screams Alex had heard in the castle. The haunted echos of the brides who had come before Tess.

CHAPTER 26

*a*fter eating what amounted to an entire layer of one of the magnificent, towering cakes that had been displayed the day before in the center of that lavishly decorated castle hall, I felt the intense desire to go for a ten-mile run. It didn't matter that I hadn't run even two-thirds of that distance in almost two years.

I wanted to burn off the sugar and the thick icing that had settled in my veins, making my blood feel like it was moving like syrup through my body. I wanted to burn off the wedding pressure that I could see building in Tess's occasional panic-stricken expression. I wanted to sweep away my cluttered thoughts and push my body as hard as I could.

Living in New York, I'd missed that. Running had turned into something I did when the time of day and time of year promised marginally reduced crowds in Central Park. And that was assuming the muggy heat had eased off into something bearable by evening, which it often did not. Weight-lifting, even though I had easy access to a nice gym, had somehow become erratic as well. Maybe it was the constant hum of the city that had lulled me into believing I'd been more active than I was.

I stuck a power bar into the pocket of my running shorts,

mapped out a route, and sipped plenty of water while I did an extra long stretch.

As I started a slow jog down the driveway, my thoughts spun back over the previous day. I hadn't even reached the entrance gates before I found myself diverted from my ten-mile plan, my mind overrun with thoughts of the castle and those off-limits towers.

If Ella and Nolan's living quarters and their offices occupied one tower, what was in the other? In the midst of our cake tasting, after two glasses of champagne, I'd excused myself to use one of the powder rooms. Of course, I hadn't been allowed to go alone. Ella had sent the woman who was clearing our cake plates between samples to follow me down the twisting, turning hallways into a powder room decorated in fuchsia. I used the toilet and washed my hands repeatedly until the young woman started to look antsy about how long I was taking.

As I dried each finger with meticulous care, I turned to her. "What's inside the tower on the left?"

She shrugged.

"Does anyone ever go up there?"

"How should I know?"

"I thought since you work here every day, you might have noticed."

"I haven't. We should get back."

I smiled. "I need to digest some of the cake. It's a lot."

"You need to try them all before the time is up."

"Is there a time limit?"

"I think so. There are a lot of events here. It's always booked."

"Aren't you curious about the tower?"

"A little, but we can't go in there, so I don't think about it."

"Have you ever heard anyone screaming?"

"We need to go. You're taking too long and I'm supposed to be clearing the plates."

"I'm not there, which means Tess isn't tasting any cake right now, so there aren't any plates to clear."

"Your hands are dry." She'd turned and walked out.

I followed, curious about how someone who worked in that fascinating castle could be so disinterested in seeing all the rooms, in climbing up inside that tower, exploring its secrets, and gazing out across the valley.

After the memory of that conversation finished unspooling in my thoughts, I changed my plans.

I jogged back up and went inside to the library, where I'd seen a small pair of binoculars that Marcus used for bird watching. I took out my phone and mapped out a shorter route, one that led up the hill to the castle gates. I grabbed the binoculars and hurried out of the house, eager to avoid anyone who might ask what I wanted them for.

Running with a pair of binoculars in my hand was less than ideal, even though they were small and fit neatly inside my curled fist. It still threw me somewhat off balance. As the distance between me and the Black Mask Winery increased and I began to perspire a bit, the binoculars became more cumbersome, slipping around in my hand, forcing me to shift them frequently from one hand to the other while I wiped the sweat off my palm onto my shorts.

When I reached the road leading to the castle, I turned on a burst of speed and started up the incline. The shoulder of the road was gravel, more narrow than the shoulder of the main road, with a deep gully beside it, and a razor wire fence protecting the wooded area. Every so often I glimpsed one of the stone cottages peeking out from among the trees.

I considered trying to ease my way through the lines of razor wire, snaking my way around the trees to one of the cottages to see if any were unlocked. A few minutes later, I discarded the idea. The towers were what I wanted. And the risk of tearing my legs or arms, or worse, my face on razor wire, was too great.

The shoulder of the road had narrowed further, forcing me to keep my gaze fixed on the ground to be sure I didn't slide down into the gully. I slowed my pace to an easy jog.

Finally, I rounded a bend, and the castle came fully into view. I stopped and lifted the binoculars to my eyes, all my annoyance at juggling them for the past two and a half miles evaporating in an instant. I directed them toward the tower on the left. Although they brought the details of the stonework perfectly into view, and I could see the windows dotted up the sides, they still didn't allow me to see what lay beyond the thick glass. Not even the shadow of something, or someone, inside one of the rooms.

As I peered through the binoculars, I lost track of time, moving them a bit up and down so I could see the entire tower from the ground to the peaked roof, hoping to catch sight of someone moving close to a window. There wasn't a sign of life anywhere. The entire structure might be filled with the bones of former occupants for all I could see.

After a while, my arms grew tired, and I lowered them to my sides. The castle was a fortress. The only movement was the breeze passing through the trees on the hillside. I stood there for another fifteen minutes, wondering if I was driving myself insane, thinking there was any way I would ever gain access to either of the forbidden towers.

I turned and started a slow jog down the hill. Within a quarter of a mile, the downward slope and the force of momentum overtook me and I began running faster. It felt good not to be fighting the incline, to be sailing along with nothing to hold me back.

And then my foot skidded on the loose gravel. I felt myself sliding fast toward the gully. As I tried to regain my balance, my left foot shot out awkwardly. My right foot slid off the shoulder into empty space and my left ankle wrenched painfully, throwing me to the side. The next moment, I was down, gravel tearing at the palms of my hands and the undersides of my forearms, pain shooting through my left leg, the binoculars in the bottom of the gully.

CHAPTER 27

*C*arefully, I pushed myself into a sitting position, my left leg bent, my ankle throbbing. I pressed my fingers against it and winced. I rotated my foot and although the pain was awful, I could move my foot, which gave me confidence it wasn't broken. I eased myself onto my knees, and despite the gravel digging into my skin and biting at my kneecaps, I crawled down into the gully and picked up the binoculars. They were dusty but free of scratches. I wiped them clean on the edge of my shorts, stuffed them into my waistband, and crawled back up to the shoulder.

I gingerly eased myself into a standing position and tested my weight on my foot. Pain shot through my leg and my whole body tensed in response. It was going to be a long walk back to Tess's place. I pulled out my phone and stared at it. I could send her a text and ask her to pick me up, but the road I was currently standing on led only to the castle. I had to at least make my way back to the connecting road before I let her know where I was.

With careful, painful steps, I began walking down the hill. It was tedious going, making sure that my unsteady movements didn't cause my good foot to skid on the gravel.

After twenty or thirty yards, I noticed that some of the oak tree's branches hung over the razor wire fence. I eased myself down the side of the gully, half-sliding down to the bottom, then crawled on my hands and knees up the opposite side. Grabbing one of the fenceposts, I gripped a branch and tried to snap it off. It bent under the force but didn't break. I moved to the side and found a branch that looked dead.

Balancing on one foot, leaning my hip against a fence post, I wrapped both hands around the branch and bent it. After a few seconds of force, it cracked. I wiggled it back and forth, weakening the spot where it had splintered until it broke free.

My estimate of its length had been good. It was the perfect size to use as a walking stick. I tossed it across the gully, slid down again, and crawled back up to the shoulder of the road.

Walking was easier now. I limped down the incline holding my stick, putting as little weight on my left foot as possible. Forty minutes later, I was on the main road. Just as I pulled out my phone, ready to send a message to Tess, I heard a car behind me. I moved to the side, making sure I was well away from the pavement.

Instead of passing by, the black Mini Cooper slowed and pulled off the road. I turned. Sitting behind the wheel was Silas.

I turned and started walking, stabbing the ground a foot ahead of me with my stick, trying to pull myself along more quickly, knowing I couldn't escape him.

I heard the car door open.

"Alexandra!"

I stabbed my stick into the loose gravel and dirt, feeling it scrape the ground and move a few inches to the side, throwing me off balance. I hobbled to steady myself and kept going.

"Do you need a ride?"

I stabbed the ground again, gave a quick shake of my head, and continued walking.

A moment later, he was beside me. "What happened?"

I continued walking.

With two long strides, he was standing in front of me. "Obviously you're injured. Let me give you a lift."

"I'm fine."

He laughed. "You're far from fine. You can't walk all the way back to the winery like that. It's not safe."

"I said, I'm fine."

"You could fall again."

"Stop bothering me."

He raised both hands beside his face, palms facing me. "Whatever." He strode past me and a moment later, I heard the car door slam and the engine start.

His car sped past me and turned onto a side road. I pulled my phone from my pocket again. I was about to message Tess, but I paused with my finger touching the screen. If Silas told her he'd seen me after I'd interrupted her at work asking her to pick me up, she would be annoyed.

I pocketed my phone and continued hobbling.

I'd made it another half mile when I heard his car pull in behind me again. The tires crunched on the gravel as the car sluggishly moved closer to where I was walking, the engine a soft purr as it crept along, mildly respectful of my space, but threatening my sense of safety at the same time. It stopped, the engine turned off, and the door opened.

"Alexandraaaa! Have you dropped your stubborn charade?"

I kept walking. It was getting more difficult. My right foot was tired from the awkward stance I was taking trying to protect my other foot, and my hand was scraped raw from my fall and from gripping the walking stick.

"Don't be a moron," Silas called after me. "You could get hit by a car. You could fall again and wind up in the gully where no one will see you. It's possible you could die out here. Or get attacked by a coyote. Recently, there have been quite a few sightings. They would love to gnaw on the fresh meat of a woman like you."

"I asked you to stop bothering me."

"What a tasty treat you would be."

"I'm not going to be eaten by a coyote in broad daylight. Don't you have better things to do than drive around in circles?" I stabbed the ground with my stick. It was satisfying, stabbing it into the dirt, imagining the point of the stick going into various parts of his body, stabbing him with each word he spoke.

"They get so hungry this time of year when there hasn't been any rain for a while. You'd be surprised."

"And you'd be surprised how offensive your presence is to me."

"You're being really stupid. You're rather risk your health and your long-term healing than accept a ride with me? That is some world-class stubbornness."

"I'm not risking my healing. Leave me alone."

"I'd have you back to the winery in less than ten minutes. You've said more words to me arguing than you'd have said riding in the car. You could already be inside Tess's house, your foot up, icing that injury." He laughed. "You're too much."

What he'd said was accurate. I was probably damaging my ankle further, no matter how much I was trying to keep my weight off it. But I was not getting into a car with him. I was not sitting that close to him, feeling the heat of him, listening to him say more disgusting things, or watching his hand creep toward me, touching me when I had no place to escape his reach.

"Last chance," he said.

"No thanks." I kept walking.

"Your loss."

Eventually, he left me alone. I folded my hand around the top of my stick, and kept on, suddenly quite tired, almost wishing I'd accepted his offer. I slowed, tired and wishing there was a roadside bench where I could sit down.

It was probably good there wasn't. I needed to power through.

When Silas appeared a third time, I conceded. I endured his smugness. I endured his smirking and silent condescension for six and a half minutes from the moment I buckled the seatbelt until the moment I flung open the car door, hobbled to the patio, and into the house.

CHAPTER 28

The view from Tess's second floor sitting room was peaceful. More interesting than from the living room directly below, because from this room I could see over the top of the tasting room to the vineyards beyond and it gave me a greater sense of how large the Black Mask estate was.

My ankle was wrapped in two support bandages, propped up on a footstool, with a cushion beneath it. Every hour, I unwrapped the bandage and placed a fresh ice pack, thoughtfully delivered by Tess, on my ankle. I was taking Ibuprofen which I didn't like, but was required to reduce the swelling.

During dinner the night before, Marcus had tried to spin my complaints into something positive. "The sitting room has a fantastic view. We have a library full of books and subscriptions to more streaming services than you can possibly make use of. You can play games. You can do some early online Christmas shopping. You said you want to change careers. Now you can do some research into how you want to shape your future."

Nothing was a problem, in his view, there was something good to be found in every situation. It was admirable, I supposed. But I didn't want to be sitting inside when I'd been primed to enjoy the California summer weather.

I wanted to get my running back on track. Now I wouldn't even be running up the stairs.

He told me Tess would pamper me. I never minded pampering, but not by my friend, who was busy learning how to run a winery and planning the party of her life.

Marcus was right that I should relish the time to think about the slow implosion of my career and how I was going to put myself in a better situation. But Marcus didn't know me. I couldn't do that, and certainly not any of those other things, when my thoughts were consumed by what was inside the towers of that castle and the person who had screamed as if their life were about to end.

Besides that, I was now curled up in a virtual nest with a bird's eye view of Silas as he came and went from the tasting room. If I told Tess what had happened as I'd limped along the highway with my makeshift walking stick, she would say my pride was damaged and my ego wounded and I was lashing out at Silas, looking to punish him for getting the best of me. That would be her psychological take. But my thoughts about Silas were not any different than they had been the moment I'd first met him, or the moment he'd told me my sweat was tasty.

That nonsense on the side of the road was just more of the same.

Watching him from my second-floor perch stirred up all kinds of questions—new and old. I wanted to know why he was so eager to devote himself to the new owners of Black Mask Winery when he'd spent years devoting himself to the previous owners, the ones who had created the brand and the wine itself. It didn't usually work that way with loyalty. I still wanted to know why he'd told such an obvious lie right to my face. I wanted to know why he'd said such creepy things to me when he definitely would have known I would tell the story to his boss.

It seemed to me that Tess and Marcus had a viper in their garden, and he was all the more dangerous because they thought he was an exotic songbird, chirping the praise of their wine and drawing customers to sip from their barrels and bottles.

He didn't seem like a guy who was content to stand behind a bar pouring calibrated sips of wine, discussing the fruits and other tastes the drinkers would experience if their palates were attuned. He seemed like a guy who was smugly aware that he knew more than Tess and Marcus about wine.

All employees are certain of that fact to some extent. In a large company, they're held in check by the sheer weight of the infrastructure surrounding them. All they can do is complain about the blind spots and egos and inadequacies of those standing above them on the ladder. But in a smaller company, like the one where I'd been working, the idea of taking over was always within the realm of possibility. Or at least it appeared that way.

It was what gave Stephanie the hubris to claw her way into becoming a photographer, fighting with me to the death, literally, for what she thought was rightfully hers. That possibility was what allowed Diana to mentally develop her own plan for upending Trystan's brain child into something entirely different, poised to implement it the moment he'd stopped breathing.

Maybe having an injured foot wasn't such a bad thing. Even though I didn't have x-ray vision into the tasting room itself, or inside Silas's mind, for that matter, I could watch him coming and going which would tell me a little about how he managed his day. That was something. Not much, but something. It seemed like it was my obligation to protect Tess from this thing she couldn't seem to see.

So instead of considering my future, or entertaining myself as Marcus had cheerfully suggested, I let my thoughts spin around the impenetrable walls of the castle towers, and the impenetrable mind of Silas Birch. I iced my foot and used Tess's small dumbbells to keep my arms and shoulders from atrophying.

After two days, I'd made a detailed log of the times Silas arrived for work and every time he left and re-entered the tasting room. I'd noted the clothing he wore, and using the small set of binoculars, I'd studied the expressions on his face—always neutral.

I'd also realized I needed to contact Diana.

It had now been a week since I'd arrived in California. Diana had reluctantly agreed, if I could even call it an agreement, that I could take three weeks off work. Between the castle and Silas, and figuring out my future, there was no question I needed to stay longer.

Tess wouldn't mind. I could lose myself in her five thousand square foot house and she'd never know I was there.

But telling Diana I was staying would possibly mean her telling me I never needed to return. I wasn't sure I was ready for that. Even though I had plenty of money stashed away, I had absolutely no idea how I would replenish it once I started to drain it.

I was still paying rent to Eileen. We didn't have any formal agreement about how long I would continue doing that. She was the one who had signed the lease. She trusted me, which might not have been the wisest decision on her part. Did she understand who I really was? She'd listened to her mother rail against me. But I imagined she'd dismissed every critical word as something filtered through the extreme religious lens her mother placed over the world.

Eileen saw in me what she wanted to see and she'd tried to turn me into someone who fit the mold of what she wanted in her life—a role model and a confidante, someone who wanted all the same things she did. She failed to recognize that I was nothing like her. And so she was constantly confused and hurt by my behavior.

She could afford the apartment on her own. And she had plenty of friends in the modeling business who would be thrilled to share that beautiful apartment with her if she didn't want to live alone. Friends who wouldn't come dragging a huge bird and who definitely wouldn't be slipping out in the middle of the night to commit murder.

My thoughts were running off track—Diana was the person I

needed to deal with first. She was expecting me at my desk in two weeks and I was absolutely certain I could not leave the Napa Valley until I found a way to get inside the tower at the Windy Hills Castle and discovered who was screaming as if their life were about to end. Unless it already had.

CHAPTER 29

With my decision made, I picked up my tablet. It seemed important to tell Diana in an email that I was leaving, rather than pinging her with a text that might invite a string of back-and-forth messages.

It wasn't as if I thought I needed some kind of legal documentation. Legal protection wasn't something I could rely upon in my life. That was for people who followed the law. Still, an email seemed like the best choice. Maybe I was stalling and didn't want an immediate response and email was the surest bet for avoiding that, the easiest to dodge when a response arrived.

Diana—

I've decided it's time for me to leave Fly Higher.

I paused with my fingers still on the keypad. It should end with a professional-sounding phrase. Good wishes or something like that. I'd never written anything like this, and I wasn't sure what people normally said. I opened Google and looked for samples. I was given advice on departure dates and explaining my reasons and offering help with a transition. I wasn't inclined to do any of that, beyond giving a departure date, which had already passed. I had departed over a week ago. She didn't need me to transition because Dean, the photographer she'd hired behind my back, had clearly been ready to take over before I'd even shaken his hand.

I finished my rather brief email:

My resignation is effective immediately.

All the best in your future endeavors. May you and your team fly ever higher.

Regards, Alexandra Mallory

I thought the mention of the company name in my good wishes was a clever touch, if more than a little nauseating and contrived. But it made me laugh, and that was enough.

The sun had moved away from the window, making it easier for me to look out toward the tasting room. I hadn't seen Silas all morning, which was probably a good thing. Not seeing him had allowed me to focus long enough to write the email.

I thought about calling Hunter. It had been a few days since I'd talked to him. I had heard nothing, not even a text message with a kissing emoji. Not so much as a lone question mark, which he sometimes sent to ask how I was doing. Nothing. He was sulking because I hadn't invited him to California.

He would not like it that I was staying indefinitely. But not telling him wasn't an option. Because his boss, Pauline, was a former client of Fly Higher, there was still a thin connection. Even though we'd completed our work with her, it wasn't impossible he could somehow find out I'd resigned.

I wanted to keep Hunter in my life, but I had no idea how I was going to do that. It was starting to look like I might not return to New York for more than the day or two it would take to pack a few more suitcases with the rest of my belongings and to list my few pieces of furniture on Craig's List. I wasn't absolutely sure why I thought this. I just had a sense that I needed a change of scenery.

It was eleven—the middle of the afternoon in New York. Not an ideal time to pop up unexpectedly with a video call. I sent him a text message to ask if he had time to talk.

Tess came in with the coffee carafe and refilled my mug. She also had a plate with a croissant and a tiny bowl of whipped butter.

"I'm not incapable of walking down the stairs," I said.

"Marcus told me to pamper you."

"It's not necessary."

"You need to get that swelling resolved so you can slip that foot into a high-heeled shoe when we go to the champagne reception."

I was more interested in getting my foot back into a running shoe, but I smiled and began buttering the croissant.

I played a few games on my tablet. I looked at photographs on the Windy Hills Castle website, trying to see if I could find any I'd missed that showed different shots of the towers, hoping, even though I knew it was futile, I might catch a glimpse of someone in one of its windows.

Tess brought up lunch—clam chowder with an arugula and cranberry salad. We ate together, and she returned to work. Finally, when it was almost two o'clock, a text arrived from Hunter—*If you're still around, I can do a video call.*

I clicked the icon to call him, took a sip of sparkling water, and waited for him to answer.

It would be nice to have him in the same room with me. It would be nice to have him wrap the bandages around my ankle. I closed my eyes and imaged the sensation of his hands on my injured leg. Why *hadn't* I invited him? I wasn't completely sure. It seemed like a lot of extra baggage. Maybe.

I wasn't used to having another person to think about. I'd never even sat on an airplane beside someone I knew, comfortably sharing an armrest, standing beside them at baggage claim.

It was too much.

Maybe.

And I truly needed to spend time thinking about my future. Soon. But now, I'd quit my job simply because I'd sprained my ankle. I was faced with giving up on getting inside those towers or giving up my job. The towers seemed more important right now.

And letting go of the job now seemed inevitable. But there hadn't been any real thinking. Or maybe all the thinking had gone on below the surface. Maybe I'd known I was going to quit before I got on the plane to California. I might have known the moment I was introduced to Dean. I'd known when Diana kept telling me I was being difficult. Maybe I'd known the day Trystan died.

In some ways, I never actually thought about anything I did in my life. I just did it.

Hunter looked better than ever. I smiled and made a kissing face.

"What's going on?" Hunter asked.

"I sprained my ankle."

"That sucks. How did you do that?"

"Running."

"That doesn't seem like you."

"It was uphill, and there was a gully."

He nodded.

I turned my tablet so he could see my bandaged ankle and foot.

"Did you go to the ER?"

"No. They'll just say ice and Ibuprofen, so that's what I'm doing."

He nodded. "Do you have crutches?"

"Tess is waiting on me, so I hardly have to walk at all."

"Nice. Doesn't she have to work?"

"It's not like I require that much attention."

He smirked. "So what are you doing with yourself while you're being waited on?"

"Figuring out how I'm going to get inside those towers at the castle."

"Is that all?" Hunter asked.

"It's enough."

"How did you end up sliding into the gully?"

"There was loose gravel on the side of the road and the shoulder was narrow …" I shrugged. "Accidents happen."

"You don't seem like the accident-prone type."

I laughed. "Having one accident doesn't make me accident-prone."

"I just can't picture you with a sprained ankle."

"I showed it to you."

"I saw a bandage, but I'm having trouble imagining you sitting around all day. You must be driving them crazy."

"I'm not. I'm a very good patient."

He laughed. "Is that what they said, or is that *your* assessment?"

"I don't think they would disagree."

"Does it hurt when you put weight on it?"

"Are you a doctor or something?"

"Just asking."

"Why all the questions? Do you not believe me?"

"Should I not believe you?"

I stared at him.

"So, why did you call? I'm guessing your injury means you're extending your vacation."

He used air quotes when he said vacation. I'd never seen him use air quotes before, and just as getting injured didn't seem like me, the gesture seemed nothing like him. It was also eery that he'd guessed why I'd called.

"Maybe I just called to talk. It's been a few days."

"It has."

"So, what have you been up to?" I asked.

"That's not why you wanted to talk, is it?"

"Why do you think that?"

"Because if you wanted to talk, you wouldn't have texted me in the middle of the workday as if it was something that had to be taken care of immediately. You would have just called in the evening. Right?"

I smiled. "I guess you can read me."

"In this case, it's not difficult."

"You're right, I'm staying longer."

"How long?"

I shrugged.

"Because you can't fly with a bum foot?"

"Because I wanted to do more running here, and I can't run for a while."

"Are you serious?"

"Yes."

"So ... basically, indefinitely? Just so you can go running?"

"Not really."

"What the hell does that mean?"

"I don't know how long I'm staying. I just need some breathing room."

"From what?"

"From everything. My job. My apartment."

"From me?"

"No. I said, my job and my apartment."

"You said, from *everything*."

"Okay, not everything. But I don't like my job anymore. Diana sucked all the fun out of it. And my apartment feels like a prison."

"Then find a new apartment." He paused. "To be honest, for a while there, I thought you might want to move in with me."

I stared at him.

"But I guess that's off the table."

"I'm not sure I want to live in New York."

"So we *are* done."

"I didn't say that. Why do you jump right to that? I don't know what I want."

"That's clear."

"It's not clear to me. I'm trying to figure things out."

He said nothing.

"And I really do want to know what's going on inside that castle."

"Why? It has nothing to do with you."

"So? I'm curious."

"You're obsessed."

"You didn't hear those screams. They were chilling. Any normal person would want to know."

"Are you sure? *Any* normal person?"

"*I* want to know."

"That sounds more honest."

We stared at each other for a few minutes. He looked annoyed, and something else I couldn't figure out.

"I have to ask you again," he said. "Are you ever coming back?"

It probably wasn't a good idea to tell him I no longer had a job there. And soon, I wouldn't have an apartment. It was better to leave things as they were.

"Of course." And I meant it. I wasn't done with him, despite his sulking. And although it made me edgy that he could guess at my motive for calling, and some of my other motives from time to time, I was also enthralled that he could see things in me that other people couldn't seem to.

CHAPTER 30

BEFORE: AMELIA

I don't remember how old I was when my Daddy came back. I should remember. I've tried to remember, but no matter how hard I squeeze my eyes shut and no matter how hard I try to squeeze my brain, I can't remember. I close my eyes and squeeze everything, imagining my brain like a sponge, squishing it in my hand until every drop of my life oozes out, and I still can't remember anything that gives me a hint about how old I was.

Instead, I remember things that feel like they were only dreams.

I know I could read books by myself. Couldn't I? So why did Daddy sit beside my bed and read books to me until I fell asleep? Except I wasn't asleep. I closed my eyes and changed my breathing and let my head fall a little to the side. I even opened my mouth so he would think I was asleep. Then he closed the book and placed it on my nightstand. He turned out the light and kissed my cheek.

Finally, he walked out of my bedroom.

Then, I would ease the breath out between my open lips. Inside my head, so he couldn't hear me, in case he was standing just outside my door listening, I would whisper—*You're not my Daddy.*

I only said those words once out loud.

First, I said, "He doesn't read stories the same way Daddy used to."

My mother said, "Don't be silly. Of course he does."

I shook my head. "He doesn't. He doesn't use the same voices for girls. Daddy would always make a voice that sounded like a girl. And a voice that sounded like a boy."

My mother giggled. "You're misremembering."

"I'm not."

"Maybe he forgot."

"I asked him to read it right, and he said he was."

"Then stop worrying about it."

"I asked him to make a girl voice, but his voice sounded like a mouse."

My mother giggled again, but she sounded like she didn't think it was very funny. "You're making a mountain out of a molehill."

"I'm not. The voices aren't the same."

"No one stays the same. You're not the same either. You're taller. Your hair is longer. Your voice is different. It's not as high-pitched. He probably wants the voices to sound—"

"No. He makes them squeaky. Like a mouse."

"Stop it, Amelia. You're getting yourself all worked up."

"Where did he go?"

"He had to go away. To make sure things were safe for us here."

"What does that mean?"

"It's grown-up stuff. You'll understand when you're older."

"Why can't I know now?"

"It's complicated."

"He smells different."

"What?"

"He doesn't smell like Daddy."

"Don't be ridiculous."

"I'm not. He smells different."

"Different, how?"

"He just does. I can't explain it."

"If you can't explain it, then it's not true."

"Yes, it is. I can smell it. He's not the same."

"Stop saying that. Of course he's the same."

My mother and I were baking cookies. Chocolate chip, which were my favorites. I ate a chocolate chip. She didn't tell me not to, which meant she wasn't paying attention, because usually she said not to. I ate another one. She switched on the mixer, turning it to a higher speed than she usually did for mixing the eggs and sugar and butter. A bit of egg splashed out, and she turned it down.

I could tell she was annoyed, and she wanted it to be loud so she couldn't hear my questions, and didn't have to answer them. But I wasn't going to stop. I didn't like that man. I especially didn't like him in my bedroom at night, sitting so close to my bed, kissing my cheek. It was so disgusting.

Making noise with the mixer was fine with me. I could wait. I wasn't going to stop telling her I didn't like him.

After a few minutes, she had to give in and turn it off because if she kept it going forever, we would never have chocolate chip cookies.

"He doesn't read stories like Daddy. He doesn't smell like Daddy. He doesn't even walk like Daddy. He doesn't kiss me good night like Daddy."

My mother grabbed the bowl of chocolate chips and moved it to a spot on the counter where I couldn't reach it. "I don't even know what that means."

"It means I don't think he's Daddy."

A sound came out of her—a tiny screech. She turned toward me. I could see what was going to happen, but I didn't move. She lifted her hand and slapped me hard on my cheek. So hard, I could feel the bones of her fingers against my cheekbone, so hard it felt like bees stinging my skin.

Tears filled my eyes. I couldn't see her face because my eyes were so blurry.

"Take that back," she said.

"I can't take it back. I already said it."

"Take it back!"

"No."

"That's a terrible, terrible thing to say."

"But it's true. You said I should always tell the truth. And that's the truth. That man isn't my Daddy. He's trying to trick us. Why don't you know that?"

She lifted the top of the mixer and detached the blades. She threw them into the sink. They clattered against the measuring cups that were waiting to be washed. She took the mixing bowl and scraped the egg and sugar and butter into the garbage.

"Why are you throwing it away?" I was crying now, my eyes even more blurred by tears, but not so much that I couldn't see what she was doing to our cookies.

"You don't deserve cookies. You're saying evil things. Cookies are for sweet princesses. Not girls who have dark, wicked thoughts. Not for girls who say ugly things and make up hurtful lies."

She poured the bowl of chocolate chips into the garbage, pulled out the bag, and tied the handles into a snarl of knots.

"I want to make cookies!"

"Go to your room. And don't come down for dinner, either. You're banished."

I'd never been banished. She'd talked about it. She'd read stories to me about people who were banished, but it had never happened to me. I was sobbing now, trying to hug her, but she shoved me away. "Please don't. Please don't banish me."

"Go. And your father will not be coming into your room to read stories. Not tonight. Not for the rest of the week. Maybe ... maybe not ever again."

I didn't care about that. I really, truly didn't. That man was not my father. And I didn't understand why she thought he was. It was so confusing it made my chest hurt.

The next day, she didn't say anything about it. She never mentioned it again. I never said anything about it again either. The man who called himself my father never read stories to me again, and he never came close enough for me to smell him ever again. But they still kept saying he was my daddy.

I spent a lot of time sitting in my window seat, looking at the picture in my locket, trying to figure out if that tiny picture looked the same as the man who had come home. The picture was so little. And he didn't smell the same. But it had been a long time since he'd left. I really didn't know how long. I really couldn't say what my daddy smelled like. Just not like that man.

CHAPTER 31

BEFORE: TESS

*L*ooking back, it seemed as if it was all somehow … predestined.

Maybe that's why Tess had been so drawn to getting married in the castle. There was a fairy tale aspect to the way she and Marcus had become a couple. A fairy tale because it had been love at first sight for her. It wasn't just a physical attraction, but actual love. No one could convince her otherwise, not that she'd told that many people.

She didn't tell people because they would laugh at the idea of a woman in her mid-thirties insisting that she'd known true love the moment she laid eyes on that man. It hadn't been that he towered over her at six foot-three, which she didn't encounter often at her height. It wasn't his hair, almost as dark as hers, and his truly piercing blue eyes. That too, sounded clichéd, but there was no other word. They were ice blue and made her breath catch in her throat. And his smile was indescribable.

But it was none of that. She truly, honestly knew deep in her heart, this wasn't about physical attraction.

There was something beyond the ice-blue gaze, a sensation of feeling his heart connect to hers. In a single moment, she'd felt she knew him and that he knew her. She could imagine herself looking into those eyes every evening for the rest of her life, watching his eyelids close over them as he went to sleep at night, gazing into them over coffee in the morning. She was certain she and Marcus would spend their lives sharing their innermost thoughts, knowing they both loved every facet of the other.

No one would believe she'd seen all of that in a business meeting, felt it in a perfunctory handshake, when other hands were being shaken and names and job titles exchanged.

But like a fairy tale, there was also a darker side. She didn't like to think about that. And one of the things that she cherished most in their relationship was their ability to tell each other everything. There was nothing in her life before she'd met him that Marcus didn't know about. And based on the things he'd told her, she was confident there were no secrets lurking in the shadows of his life, either.

Still, there was this one thing, and that was the way she'd gotten closer to him. So he didn't, truthfully, know every single thing about her.

She wanted to believe he'd known there was something between them in that first glance. But she hadn't been sure. She'd hoped. She'd wished. She'd wondered. But he gave no indication that he'd felt that spark of awareness. What she'd felt, was a sense that they'd known each other all their lives. And even if it wasn't utterly ridiculous, which it was, that they'd known each other in a different life.

He'd treated her with the utmost professionalism. They'd shaken hands. He'd offered a few complimentary words about her expertise, and released her grip. He'd looked away to the next person on her team and they'd seated themselves around the conference table.

They were a small group with a massive agenda—Marcus and one of his vice presidents, Tess and two members of the virtual marketing team she managed, the graphic designer, Lori, and the head of a small PR firm, Josh.

After two years, Tess had built a solid, well-functioning virtual network of marketing professionals who bid on projects as a team. With all of them working as independent contractors, they were able to pitch lower costs as one of their key differentiators compared to large marketing companies.

They trusted her, and she'd valued their trust. She'd built her reputation on that. But she hadn't achieved everything in her long and lucrative marketing career by always putting trust and loyalty above opportunity and a chance to take a step forward, especially a big step up the ladder.

But this move hadn't been about climbing higher on the ladder.

The meeting with Marcus's cyber security firm, that wasn't large enough yet to have its own marketing department, had gone extremely well. When Tess and the others went out for coffee after to talk about what size the team would need to be, the multi-year contract, and of course, the revenue potential over the next three to five years, Lori and Josh were salivating.

Then, Tess had done the unthinkable.

She'd asked for a second private meeting with Marcus. She'd given a new, much different pitch.

If Marcus's firm hired her as their chief marketing officer, she could accomplish everything they needed with a very small team. Using an outsourced network had much higher risks in terms of the loss of continuity that came with employee turnover and unexpected costs. Having worked in both roles, she also knew that the potential for finger-pointing was much greater when, and it was always *when*, not *if*, something went wrong. There was a greater risk of key pieces in a project being overlooked, things falling through the cracks. And with a company with such critical intellectual property, the sheer risk of leaks was something to seriously consider as well.

Her counter pitch had been so compelling, Marcus almost looked scared by the time she was finished. Tess didn't feel a shred of guilt. She felt triumphant when he agreed that even though it was more expensive in terms of fixed expenses, the soft costs and the risks of her original proposal were so unpredictable, this was the better, the only, choice.

Tess told her team they wouldn't be getting the contract. They were stunned. How had they misread the reaction so completely? Marcus and his VP had seemed ready to sign a contract that day. What had changed? They speculated and debated and tried to analyze where they might have gone wrong, what they'd missed. Tess didn't say much.

She waited almost a month before she told them, not like a coward via email, but in a face-to-face meeting, that she'd accepted a position as CMO with Marcus's firm. Truthfully, she might have been *slightly* cowardly, because she told them in a coffee shop so they had to control their vitriol to some degree.

"You fucking bitch." Lori didn't raise her voice. In fact, she almost spoke in a whisper, which was more sinister.

Tess took a sip of her coffee. She'd told herself not to react. To take their assault, to let them feel their feelings.

Josh's voice had been even more chilling in its utter calm, without the unoriginal, misogynistic gutter talk. "Was that already your strategy when you walked into our meeting with them?"

"Honestly, no," Tess said.

Josh looked at her. "That's an interesting choice of words. There's nothing honest about you. Every word you've spoken to us, every agreement we've made for the past three years, has been a lie. Your reputation is worthless. You'll never have a consulting business in the Sydney area again. I hope you realize that."

Tess held his gaze. She wasn't going to let him make her feel guilty. She was guilty, of course. What she'd done was underhanded and unethical. Probably. It depended on how you defined ethical. There were many people she knew who would have done the same for the money. And the money Marcus had offered was phenomenal.

What no one knew was that she hadn't done it for the money.

No one would ever know that. Her relationship with Marcus would appear to evolve naturally. It would seem as if it had developed from working closely together. Day after day they would have meetings in their offices, there would be occasional day-long strategy sessions. Those would sometimes flow into dinner meetings. Soon, their relationship would shift from employee and boss to that of colleagues. And then there would be whispers of friendship, maybe after a holiday party.

Eventually, they would cross that line, she would leave his company, if necessary. But she could afford not to work. She'd worked long enough and hard enough, and done well enough that she could manage to live quite well without working for several years.

"You don't give a shit," Lori said. "You don't care about us or what we think of you. I'm not even sure you care about your reputation with our clients."

Tess kept her gaze neutral. She'd vowed not to respond, not to get into an argument or to give them fuel for their anger and their understandable feelings of betrayal.

"Are you a sociopath?" Lori's voice rose. "You're just going to sit there and stare at us? You've stolen from us! You've stolen at least three years of income from us and the people on our teams. You know that. I know you're absolutely aware of that and you don't give a flying fuck!"

"Calm down," Tess said.

"Are you afraid people are staring at us? Are you ashamed? I doubt it. Sociopaths don't feel shame."

"You're the one attracting attention, not me," Tess said.

In a low voice, as if he were still trying to decide if his statement was viable, Josh said, "We could sue you."

"Doubtful," Tess said.

Tess had told herself to be prepared for anything. She was alert for them to make an aggressive move, both of them. Her senses were poised for violence. At least that's what she'd thought.

Josh pushed his chair away from the table. He stood and walked out of the coffee shop into the bright afternoon sun. She never saw him or heard from him again.

Lori sat there for another moment. Then she stood suddenly and walked toward the counter without speaking.

Tess took a few sips of her coffee. Despite her mental preparation, her heart was beating faster than normal. She thought it proved she was not a sociopath. Her hand trembled when she picked up her coffee cup for another sip. She returned the oversized cup to the saucer. Overall, it hadn't gone too badly.

Pushing her half finished coffee away from her, she turned a little to unhook the strap of her purse from the back of the chair. From the corner of her eye, she saw Lori walking toward her, carrying a cup of coffee. Tess straightened, trying to read the expression on Lori's face. She looked as if she'd calmed down, but there was something alarming about the set of her lips.

Lori came up close.

A moment later, Tess screamed as scalding coffee ran down her neck, soaking the back of her blouse, trickling down her spine. Tears blinded her as she plucked at her blouse and wiped her hand across the back of her neck, trying to ease the pain.

When her vision cleared, Lori was gone.

She looked around. Everyone in the shop was staring at her. A woman at the table nearest to her offered her some napkins. "Are you okay? Can I get you some ice? Or maybe some wet towels would be better?"

Tess nodded. "Thank you," she whispered.

Afterwards, she still felt as if it probably could have been worse.

She never felt the guilt she thought she should have. She felt victorious and excited. Eager. She was certain she'd met the man she would spend the rest of her life with. And if she hadn't gone after him in the only way that had presented itself, she might have lost her chance.

When opportunity knocks, you open the door. That's what she believed.

Guilt was relative and sometimes, it wasn't really guilt at all. Just an overblown fear of what other people might think of you. Who was to say Josh or Lori wouldn't have done the same if opportunity had knocked on their doors?

CHAPTER 32

NOW: ALEX

*A*fter three days of pampering, I'd had enough. Tess had served me massive breakfasts of bacon and eggs and the most delicious potatoes I'd ever tasted. This had been followed by delicately buttered croissants mid-morning with a third cup of coffee. I'd had several glasses of delicious Black Mask wine every evening. I'd eaten desserts, and we'd enjoyed buttered popcorn and martinis while we watched movies and comedy shows at night.

I could imagine what it was going to be like trying to lift my soggy muscles out of the chair if I remained there for another week.

I asked her to go to a medical supply store and buy me a pair of crutches.

As soon as she returned, I moved the footstool away from where I'd been sitting, cleaned up my little pile of supplies on the side table, and tidied the room so it looked as if I'd never camped out there. After a shower and another icing of my foot, I practiced a bit with the crutches, then made my way down the stairs, using the railing as a sort of third crutch to keep me from falling forward.

I stood by Damien's cage for a while and had a chat with him. Then I hobbled outside and blinked at the bright sunshine. I propelled myself around the side of the house to pathway leading to the tasting room. The same path forked and led farther to the back of the property, where the actual winemaking and bottling facility was located.

The pathway was paved and flat, both of which I appreciated as I placed my crutches firmly on the ground and swung my body forward. After a while, I developed a rhythm and began to enjoy it, feeling the muscles in my shoulders working in new places. I smiled at the thought that despite my disability, I was getting a good workout.

I breathed in the fresh air and listened to the bees humming around the Mexican sage, bursting with purple blossoms. As I drew closer to the enormous building that was the winery itself, I heard the voices of people working inside.

The path turned and ran along the side of the building, ending in a large paved area. The front of the building was open, as if an over-sized garage door had been pulled up.

I stood for a few minutes and watched people moving around inside the building, wondering if I should schedule a tour for myself at some point. For all the time I'd lived in California, and all the years I'd enjoyed hundreds of glasses of wine, I had only a sketchy idea of how it was made. I knew enough to know that people didn't actually stomp on grapes in their bare feet anymore. And I knew that some years produced better quality wine than others, that wine needed to age, and that climate affected the taste of the wine. But that was about it.

A man came up to me, having appeared from somewhere inside the dark recesses of the building. He wore a tan baseball cap with the Black Mask logo, a white T-shirt with the logo on the back, and blue jeans faded almost to white. I hadn't noticed him approaching, but suddenly he was only a few yards away.

"What can I do for you?"

"I'm a friend of Tess and Marcus."

He extended his hand. "Chuck Guryev."

I leaned on my crutch, released my grip on the handle, and

shook his hand. "Alexandra. I've known Tess for years. I'm her maid of honor."

"Good to meet you. I'd give you a tour, but we're not set up for that right now."

"It's fine. I just wanted to see what it looked like."

"Maybe Friday."

"It's okay. I don't need a private tour. I can join one of the regular groups on a weekend."

"We're happy to give you a private one. Just let me know."

"How long have you worked here?"

"'Bout ten years. Give or take."

"Did you grow up in a wine family?"

"How did you know?"

"It seems like a lot of people around here did."

"A lot?"

I laughed. "Silas."

His expression didn't change. He nodded. "That's not what I would call a *lot*."

"You meet one person and you start to form opinions."

"Or biases," he said.

I laughed. "Fair enough."

"But yeah, I did. And so did a lot of people. But not everyone. Not even most."

"Did the people who own Windy Hills Castle grow up in wine families?"

He shifted subtly. I couldn't tell if he was moving away from me, or just trying to alleviate the stiffness of standing in the same position for too long. Maybe it was simply the latter, but I read into it, because of the timing.

"Their story is on their website," he said.

"I know. But it seems a little ... it sounds like a fairy tale." I laughed.

He laughed with me, but there was a wariness in his expression. I couldn't see his eyes because when he'd moved away from me, he tilted his head so his ball cap now covered them. "Isn't that the point?" he asked.

"There's a lot left out of their story. It was vague about where they came from. It implied they were from around here, but it didn't quite say so, in a way that they have deniability if someone says they're not being truthful."

He laughed, more of a snort this time. "You're perceptive. Or maybe imaginative."

"A little of both," I said.

He nodded. "I guess you'll have to ask them if you want to know more. But you probably won't find out anything that's not on the website. They're very secretive. No one around here knows them beyond what they do."

"The fabulous weddings."

"The fairy-tale weddings," he said.

"Have you ever been inside the castle?"

"Nope. Only invited guests."

"So no one you know has been married there?"

He laughed. "That is so far out of the price range of anyone I know, aside from those I've worked for, it would never even enter their thoughts."

"Did they ever have a winery at the castle?"

"A long time ago. Now, they don't like people on their property."

"Except invited wedding guests," I said.

"And as I've heard it, even wedding guests have to follow strict rules."

"They aren't allowed in the towers," I said.

"What?"

"Tess and Marcus are getting married there."

"I didn't know."

"But when they gave us a tour, we weren't allowed to see the towers."

"Their castle, their rules."

Obviously. But in my mind, there was something they didn't want people to see.

"I guess Tess and Marcus are showing they're newbies around here," he said.

"Why is that?"

"Maybe they haven't heard the rumor. Or maybe they don't care. Tech people don't tend to have a lot of superstitions."

"What superstitions? And what rumor?"

"There's a story that someone was murdered there."

"Who?"

"No idea. That's not part of the story." He laughed. "Rumors are like that. Half a story. Less than half. A fraction of a story. Someone was murdered. Don't even know if it was male or female. A murder. And the body is buried there. Probably why they don't want a winery, don't want people walking on the property. Maybe that's why the towers are off-limits."

"You think there's a dead body stashed in one of the towers?" I clenched the handles on my crutches. My armpits were starting to ache, but there was no way I was moving an inch until I heard everything he had to say.

"Who knows? Never say never. There's a body somewhere up there, if the rumor is true. And it's a rumor that's stuck for a long time. But people from all over the country, heck from quite a few other countries from what I've heard, flock there like a bunch of swans to get married. Almost every weekend of the year."

"I guess I should mention that to Tess and Marcus."

"Maybe they know. They seemed to know a lot about the area when they bought the place. They were well-versed in the history of Black Mask. They knew what they were talking about, knew the issues with running a winery." He shrugged.

I told him about the screams.

"Maybe it's haunted. Maybe you heard the ghost of the person who was murdered."

"I don't believe in ghosts," I said.

"Neither do I."

"It was not a ghost."

"It's still something to consider."

I studied his expression. Was he playing a game? Did he believe in ghosts or not? Maybe he just didn't want to speculate about the screaming. A lot of people don't like speculating. Maybe he thought he'd given me enough time. He'd certainly given me more information than I'd expected to find. I couldn't complain.

I asked him about the wine and his job. When he said he needed to get back to it, I thanked him for talking to me. I wondered if he expected me to tell Tess and Marcus about the rumor.

CHAPTER 33

*T*ess had decided I needed a massage to ease my muscles from so much sitting and to get some blood flowing more vigorously through my ankle and foot. She booked us a spa day in Calistoga, thirty miles from the town of Napa.

It wasn't until we were relaxing on lounge chairs, sipping fruity cocktails on the shaded patio, our bodies like soft noodles, our skin glowing from oils and steam, and our stomachs filled with spinach salad and figs, exotic cheeses and flatbread, that I mentioned meeting Chuck.

"Such a brilliant winemaker," Tess said. "He runs the whole show for us. Without him, I don't know if we would have a single bottle of wine in our tasting room."

"I thought Silas was your savior. It sounds like Chuck is."

"Don't be snarky." Tess clicked the metal straw against her teeth.

"Don't do that, it sounds awful."

"Does it give you the chills?" She clicked the metal against her teeth again.

I closed my eyes and took a long, cooling sip from my drink. She would get bored with trying to irritate me soon enough. "I had an interesting conversation with him."

"Did he give you a tour?"

"He offered."

"You'll be so knowledgeable after a tour with him. There's nothing about wine that man doesn't know."

"I'm looking forward to it. But he did tell me something about the castle."

"What's that?" She clicked the straw against her teeth.

"He said someone was murdered there. And the body—"

"Who?"

"He didn't know. He said—"

"When was this?"

"He didn't know that either. But it's a well-known story among the locals."

"I'm a local and I've never heard it."

"Are you really? You've only been here a few months. It might be premature to call yourself a local."

"I think I would have heard that. Marcus and I have met a *lot* of people. We're members of the winemaker's association. We've met people through several other wine and business organizations, through the city council. In fact, I've mentioned quite a few times that we're hoping to get married at the castle, and no one said anything about a murder." She shoved the straw into her mouth and took a sip.

"Chuck has lived here a long time."

She put her drink on the table between us and leaned her head back. "Whatever. The story has all the traits of an urban legend that never died. No details about when it happened or who it was. Just some creepy story to scare people away. It almost sounds like slander."

"He said everyone knows."

"Not everyone. I would have heard something."

"You've been busy learning about wine. How many people have you really had an in-depth conversation with about the castle?"

"As I said, I've mentioned it several times, and if it was a true story, I would have been told. People can't shut up about stories like that. When they're true." She picked up her drink again and pulled out the stick holding several pieces of fruit. She slid the pineapple slice off the end and ate it.

"We should try to find out the details," I said.

"No." Tess crossed her ankles. She plucked at her bangs, rearranging them carefully across her brow. "It's just gossip. Even if it's true, it was probably decades ago. That's why there aren't any details. So it doesn't matter. It has nothing to do with Ella and Nolan. Their story is so romantic. They'll host a wedding that Marcus and I will cherish for the rest of our lives."

"What if their story is just a story? What if—"

"It doesn't matter. Hundreds of people have gotten married there. They've had fabulous, romantic weddings, and so will we."

"If it were me—"

"It's not you. It's me. The castle is incredible, and the weddings that are held there are out of this world. Between going on about thinking you heard someone screaming—"

"I don't *think* I heard someone screaming. I *know* I did."

"...and now this, it's feeling like you don't want me to have my castle fantasy."

"That's not true."

"Then why are you doing this?"

"Doing what?"

"Being so negative?"

"I'm not being negative. I'm telling you things I've heard. Don't you want to know the truth?"

"You're telling me ugly stories. You said Ella didn't react to this so-called scream, that she didn't even hear it. So you're hearing—"

"Is Marcus hearing things? Because he heard it."

"Are you going to support our wedding one hundred percent or not?"

"I—"

"Do you hate romance and true love so much you have to tell me awful things about my dream venue? Or are you jealous?"

I laughed. "I'm not jealous."

"Maybe that's why you didn't invite Hunter to come with you. He's the type that says he's never getting married and you couldn't stand having him around all the wedding planning. And now you're trying to spoil my fun."

I took a sip of my drink. I wondered how she had come up with that story. Apparently, my not inviting Hunter was really bothering her. So much so that she wrote an entire story about it in her head.

"I guess I hit a nerve," Tess said.

"No."

"Then why isn't he here?"

"Because I don't feel the need to drag him everywhere I go."

"He's that much of a burden?"

"He's not a burden at all."

"You said you need to drag him."

"It was a figure of speech. I like to travel by myself. I like to do things by myself. I don't need constant companionship like some people seem to. I enjoy my own company."

"That must be lonely."

"Absolutely not. It's the opposite." I took a sip of my drink. "But I guess we're agreed that if I find out anything more about the castle, you don't want to know."

"I didn't say that."

I managed not to laugh. Mainly because slushy cold fruit and vodka was sliding down my throat and I didn't want to choke and send it flowing into my lungs. But also because she did have a tiny bubble of curiosity hiding inside her chest.

She sighed. "A little more enthusiasm, and some romance would be nice."

"I was enthusiastic about the cake."

"You didn't help me choose."

"I said, chocolate. It was the clear winner."

She sighed more loudly this time. "We can't have chocolate cake. I'm wearing a white gown. And there will be photographs without the opportunity for brushing our teeth. Forget the chocolate. Okay?"

"Sure."

"And forget the dead body buried there. In fact, there are a lot of old buildings around the valley. It wouldn't surprise me if eighty percent of them have bodies buried on the property. For all I know, Black Mask has bodies buried in the vineyard. People did strange things back in the day."

People did strange things nowadays, too. But I didn't point that out to her.

CHAPTER 34

PORTLAND, OREGON

*M*y father had taken away my beautiful mask. I had no doubt it was buried in the bottom of the trash can. Not even the recycling, it would have gone straight into the garbage. It was now spoiling under bags where the seams had started to split, allowing chicken bones with bits of skin and grizzle clinging to them and the remains of egg scraped off plates to seep out.

It wasn't going to stop me. Now that I'd seen myself hidden behind that exotic, mysterious mask, nothing would prevent me from finding a new one. I hadn't spent all my money on it. There were other discount stores and every single one of them was filled with Halloween decorations, candy, and costumes. There was an entire store dedicated to Halloween supplies. Tom was still somewhat willing to offer transportation.

This time, I wouldn't be stupid enough to parade something as provocative as a mask in front of my father. I should have known. If he thought *aspire* was a fancy word for thirteen-year-old me, he would have a fainting spell like the ladies in old-fashioned novels if he heard me use the word *provocative*.

At school, I talked to the girls in my English class. Girls who didn't go to my church. Girls who were experts at Halloween, girls who pitied me when they heard about my life without the TV shows they lived for, the music that filled their souls, and the semi-provocative costumes they wore for Halloween, trying on the role of an older teenager for one night a year.

I didn't like their pity, so I rarely mentioned the shows I'd never seen, the songs I'd never heard. But I listened carefully when they talked and learned as much as I could. I didn't complain. Keeping my mouth shut worked out. They let me hang around despite my ignorance because sometimes I made them laugh. Sometimes I shocked them and sometimes I came up with ideas they hadn't thought of, and they liked that.

They all agreed. If I wanted a really good mask to cover my eyes, an exotic mask with gems and some black feathers or sequins, the store that devoted itself one hundred percent to Halloween night was the best place.

Getting Tom to take me there was a little trickier. I didn't want him to know I was buying the mask. He was fine with making plans behind our parents' backs, but my brothers and I had always walked a fine line between pushing the boundaries of our virtual prison and suffering the punishments that were deviously planned to fit the crimes when we were caught.

Tom wasn't going to the harvest festival. He thought it was stupid. "A fake Halloween party? I'm not dressing up like Moses. Or a cop. I have homework to do. AP classes pile on the extra work, just because they can. You'll find out."

I didn't think I would find out. Tom was determined to get into the best college he could. And he knew he had to get a scholarship because my parents were unlikely to pay for him to go to a top school on the East Coast. So he spent all his free time studying and doing other things that would make his college application *stand out*. He'd done a lot of research into how to make himself *stand out*. A *lot*.

I think my father was pleased. He saw Tom as serious-minded, refusing to put his foot too close to the line of sin like everyone else was with all this costume nonsense.

I stood in the doorway of Tom's bedroom. I'd had to knock four times before he told me it was okay to open the door. Knocking was a strict rule of Tom's. "Will you drive me to the Halloween store?"

"What for? Mom's making your costume."

"I need a cape."

"A cape? I don't think princesses wear capes."

"In this book I found about medieval kings and queens, the princess had a cape."

"I don't think you need a cape. Did Dad approve that?"

"What's wrong with a cape?"

"I don't know. If you need a cape, shouldn't you ask mom to make it?"

"It's too late. My dress is almost done. It's only four days. It's just a brown cape. There's nothing creepy about it."

He narrowed his eyes, as if he wasn't sure I was telling the truth. He glanced at his wristwatch. "What will you give me?"

"I'll buy you a Snickers bar."

"Sure. Give me five minutes." He turned back to his desk.

I closed the door.

Tom waited in the car while I went into the store. I'd known he would. He wasn't interested in traipsing around a costume store with me. All he wanted was the candy bar. I found a cape easily enough. The mask selection was much better than it had been at the first store. It took me a long time to make up my mind, which made me realize it would be safer to buy two candy bars for Tom.

Finally, I found a mask that was black with fake diamonds. It had small black feathers glued to both corners. The diamonds were nearly twice as large as the ones on the other mask, which made them catch the light and shimmer from a lot farther away. The entire edge of the mask was trimmed with tiny fake diamonds. I would look magical and glittery even if my dress looked like a prairie dress, although I was still thinking about ways to fix that.

For now, I was thrilled with my mask. As I walked out of the store, I slipped the mask into my jacket pocket. In the car, I hid the cape inside my jacket and zipped it closed. I wasn't taking any chances.

From now on, the only part of my costume my father would see was the part my mother had sewn.

CHAPTER 35

NAPA VALLEY, CALIFORNIA

ess was sitting at the bar in the kitchen drinking coffee with her tablet propped up in front of her when Alex came into the room. It was the first time she'd appeared without crutches.

"How's your foot?"

"Good. I'm thinking of going for a walk, testing it out for jogging."

Tess sipped her coffee. It would be better to make sure her ankle was completely healed, but Alex never wanted advice. Tess took another sip of coffee and closed her tablet. "I know it's early, with the wedding nine months away, but I'm meeting the wedding planner and designer at the castle today."

Alex filled a mug with coffee.

"I wouldn't mind if you came with me." Tess wanted her to come. It had been the entire point of inviting Alex to visit for a few weeks, but Alex's fixation on thinking there was some sinister story behind the castle was still grating on her. She hoped that keeping everything focused on planning would divert Alex's attention. But it was a big ask.

"Okay." Alex took a sip of coffee and opened the fridge.

"But ... I don't want any more talk about screaming. Or murder. Definitely not murder. I don't want you mentioning any of that to the wedding planner."

"I wouldn't—"

"You absolutely would."

Alex laughed. "Maybe."

"Do you promise?"

She turned and stared at Tess as if she couldn't quite process the meaning of the word *promise*.

"Do you?"

"I doubt it would come up," Alex said.

"I need you to promise."

"Please don't treat me like a little kid, Tess."

"Then don't act like one."

Alex smiled. "I won't."

"No murder. No screaming. No complaining about not being allowed inside the towers."

"Got it." Alex took a container of yogurt out of the fridge and closed the door.

"Are you sure? I don't want bad vibes around my wedding. And I don't want people associated with our wedding gossiping about rumors that have nothing to do with me or Marcus. I want all positive energy all the time."

"That's a lot to expect."

"I don't think it is. We can all make the effort."

"You can't expect perfection."

Tess felt her jaw tighten. This shouldn't be a debate. It was a simple and completely justified request. "I said, we can make the effort. Can you do that? Make an effort?"

"Absolutely." Alex took a sip of coffee.

"Do you *want* to be in my wedding?"

"Yes."

"You could show a little more enthusiasm."

"I'm not a giddy cheerleader. You know that."

Tess laughed, feeling a tad calmer, but only a tad. "You're right. I know that. We haven't spent much time together these past two years. Maybe I've forgotten. I just want positive energy, that's all."

"Then stop lecturing me."

"I'm not lecturing you. I'm asking for a simple favor. I want to be excited about my wedding and all you're talking about are rumors and dark stuff that you're making into something they aren't."

"Marcus heard the screaming too."

"Please, just stop. Not another word. I really think you have too much time on your hands. And your injury has made it worse. You really should have invited Hunter to come with you. Instead of sitting around brooding about murder and whatever else you have twisting through your brain, you could be out sightseeing and hiking and having fun."

"I sprained my ankle."

"Maybe that wouldn't have happened if you weren't trying to spy on the castle."

"What?"

"Don't play games. Silas said he saw you coming down the hill from the road that leads to Windy Hills."

Alex stared at her. She didn't look surprised. She also didn't look happy.

"So, we're agreed? And we're finished discussing this?" Tess asked.

"Absolutely." Alex returned to the refrigerator. She pulled out the bacon. "Mind if I cook the rest of this?"

"Help yourself."

"Do you want some?"

"No thanks. I already ate."

After she finished her coffee, Tess went to her office and didn't see Alex until that afternoon when they met in the entryway, ready for their drive to the castle.

Alex wore a short black dress and black vintage canvas high-tops. Tess wasn't thrilled about the high-tops, but it wasn't as if they were doing anything formal. It was a working meeting. The wedding planner would be viewing the rooms and asking Tess questions about her vision. She would be talking to Ella about working with the catering staff at the castle and discussing logistics and timelines. The designer would be taking measurements and considering color schemes. It was probably a good idea to wear comfortable shoes. Tess had done the same, but hers were conventional sandals to complement her dark green sundress.

Kate and Julia were waiting outside the castle doors when Tess and Alex pulled up. They made introductions. Then, as if on cue, the castle doors swung open.

Ella greeted them, and they entered.

Kate recoiled at the sight of the gargoyle leering at them. The creature gave the impression it wanted to block their way, as if he demanded a password or a drop of blood before they would be allowed to enter the main hall. It wasn't as if the entryway was small by any means, but with five people making their way past the oversized stone carving, the thing appeared more threatening.

Tess wasn't sure why she'd thought of blood. It might have been Kate's visceral reaction, it might have been the seeds planted by Alex's story about a murder at the castle. She felt a flicker of anger toward her friend. Why had Alex felt compelled to tell her that story? Tess wanted her wedding to be full of love and positive energy.

In one way, it was irrational to feel anger. Alex probably thought she was helping, giving her the information she would want to have in case it motivated her to change her mind. But didn't Alex understand how much she wanted to get married here? How unique and fun and exciting it was?

Tess did not want to think about murder. She wanted that vague, horrific, yet at the same time, nothing-story out of her head. It *was* nothing. No date, no name, not even a gender. It hardly constituted a rumor.

"Does this thing have to be here?" Julia asked.

"It's set into the stone," Ella said.

Julia laughed. "Literally?" She pushed her fingers through her short, blonde hair, making it stand up slightly. "It's literally set in stone?" She laughed again, somewhat sharply. "Why would you design a wedding venue with a hideous creature like that in the entrance?"

"It was part of the original building. Most people find it charming and in keeping with the atmosphere of a castle." Ella's tone was terse, ready to argue about the authenticity of her home.

"I don't," Julia said.

"It doesn't matter what you think," Ella said.

"Maybe we can drape it somehow. I'll give that some thought," Julia said.

"Don't be ridiculous," Ella said. "You're not draping him. Let's move on. This will take all day if you're going to let the actual features of a castle make you averse to a castle." She laughed, her voice shrill, the sound piercing as it echoed off the surrounding stone.

Tess shivered. "I don't mind it. He's kind of cute once you get used to him."

"That's the last word I would use," Julia said.

"He's more than *cute*," Ella said. "That's actually degrading. Clearly, none of you have any understanding of history or you would be pleased to see this creature standing here." She pulled her shoulders back as if she were about to give a lecture to a classroom of college students. "Gargoyles were used in Greece and Egypt to ward off evil spirits."

"I don't believe in evil spirits," Tess said. Why was Ella doing this? Tess wanted her to revert to her original instructions to move on. Talking about evil spirits was sure to wind Alex up with thoughts of screaming and murder.

As if Ella hadn't heard, she kept speaking. "They were used for the same purpose on buildings in medieval Europe. Not to mention the fact they also had a practical purpose. Rain water would flow through the mouth, draining water away from the structure. In some cultures, gargoyles are believed to keep out negative energy. That belief seems appropriate right this very minute." Ella gave them a knowing smile, turned, and continued along the passage into the main hall.

Tess felt triumphant. That should be the final warning to Alex. It couldn't have gone more perfectly if she'd planned it. Knowing Alex, she might think Tess had put Ella up to it. She suppressed a giggle and followed Ella into the passageway.

The others obediently fell in line.

While Julia walked around the hall snapping photographs with her phone, Kate took out her tablet and began firing questions at Tess and Ella about the overall plans for the day of the wedding. "This isn't set in stone," she paused, somewhat dramatically, "I just want to brainstorm and see where we'll need to come together. If there are any big gaps between Tess's vision and what Ella's guidelines are."

As Tess began cautiously answering a few of her questions, Julia interrupted. "Don't think too much about your answers. Just give me your initial thoughts, the things that have been in your mind since you became engaged, and of course, your girlhood dreams." She winked. "Anything that came up for you when you first saw the castle. This is all just brainstorming and creating a mood. We'll have plenty of time to adjust and fine tune. Nothing is set in stone."

Tess glanced at Alex, who was making no effort to hide her smirk. Alex turned away and walked toward the platform at the front of the hall. She stepped onto it and turned to face them. She cocked her hip to one side and mimed being the lead singer in a band. Tess smiled, then placed her attention on the flow of questions coming from Kate. "Could you repeat those last few, please?"

They spent about twenty minutes in the hall before taking a quick tour of the other rooms.

Everything went smoothly. Alex was quiet, only speaking when she was asked a direct question. She was friendly and went out of her way to try to warm up the relationship between herself and Ella.

Tess wondered why she was so anxiety-ridden toward Alex. She'd been acting as if Alex were a misbehaving child. Someone she was afraid might embarrass her at any moment. Alex was her maid of honor! Why did she have such a deep-seated concern that Alex was going to blow things up? If she was this worried, why had she asked her to be her maid of honor? It made no sense.

There was some sort of attraction-repulsion going on, she supposed. She was drawn to Alex's lack of restraint, to her brutal honesty. It was incredibly refreshing. Her refusal to bow to what anyone else wanted. At the same time, Tess felt a prick of fear that Alex, with her lack of impulse control, might do something that could seriously hurt her.

She needed to be less distrustful. Maybe she was projecting, thinking back to her own less than loyal behavior in the past and expecting some sort of karmic payback.

Kate, Julia, and Ella were now huddled near the side of the band platform, all of them studying their tablets. Alex had disappeared. That wasn't good. Once Ella looked up and discovered her missing, the goodwill Alex had managed to establish would evaporate in an instant.

Tess walked toward the four arched doors that opened onto the terrace and garden area. The center two had been left open when they'd returned from the terrace. She stepped out and glanced around the garden. It was deserted. She moved back inside and walked into the large dining room. It, too, was empty.

She passed out of the dining room and into a narrow hallway, one that she sensed might lead to the tower at the left side of the castle.

As she hurried down the hallway, her sandals tapping the stone floor, she felt cool air move around the bare skin of her arms. She rubbed her hands on her arms to warm herself and quickened her pace. The sound of something, she wasn't sure what, another pair of footsteps, maybe, caused her to turn.

No one was behind her.

As she turned back, she heard a faint scream. She cupped her hands over her ears. She'd imagined it. All Alex's talk about screaming had primed her for this. There was no scream. It was the echo of her footsteps, and the chill on her arms that stirred her imagination. There were three people waiting for her in the great hall. Nolan was somewhere else in the castle, as was Alex. There were probably other people working in various rooms as well. She'd seen a gardener when they arrived.

No one had screamed.

She started walking, letting her arms swing loosely at her sides, forcing herself to relax.

Another thin, distant scream drifted into the hallway. She shivered violently. The sound was shrill and unmistakably human. She felt her stomach clench and the muscles in her jaw tighten. She walked as fast as she could, feeling ridiculous, but also slightly scared. At the same time, she knew she was not going to say a word about this to Alex. No matter how clearly she'd heard it and how certain she was that it was most definitely not the wind. Someone had screamed. She was not breathing a word about it to anyone.

CHAPTER 36

$\mathcal{T}$hanks to the nonstop questions from Kate and Julia, I saw my chance to escape. There was hardly room for Tess or Ella to breathe between the questions. As a result, both were completely locked onto the wedding planner and designer and I had turned into a stone figure in the corner, as unimportant to their conversation as the gargoyle in the entryway.

It was the sole reason I'd worn my high-top sneakers. They would carry me softly and quickly anywhere in the castle.

A moment later, I was hurrying along the narrow corridor, lit only by torches, headed straight toward what I believed was the entrance to the tower at the left side of the castle. I'd decided to focus my attention on that one because this was the tower shrouded in mystery. For all I knew, it absolutely contained the bones of an unnamed murder victim. Maybe it was similar to the closet in Bluebeard's castle. Maybe I, like Bluebeard's final wife, was similarly obsessed with discovering what was behind a forbidden door.

As the corridor turned and the light from the anteroom was blotted out, I pressed my phone to turn on the flashlight. I moved more carefully now. Even with the bright light spreading across the stone floor ahead of me, and splashing up the walls, there was a lot I couldn't see. If nothing else, there might be rats crouched in the shadows, their razor-sharp teeth bared, ready to pounce. Spiders might be sitting on thin, invisible strands of webbing, poised to descend into my hair or simply land on my face, exploring my skin for something edible.

I moved the light up and down the walls every few steps, checking for protrusions that might block my way.

Without warning, a cold hand grabbed my arm just above my elbow.

I yelped and wrenched forward, trying to pull myself free. I turned my flashlight and directed it toward the person hanging onto my arm with such force I felt my hand growing numb.

Nolan.

"Let go of me."

"Where do you think you're going?"

"I'm looking for the entrance to the tower."

"You're supposed to stay with Ella."

"She's busy."

He tightened his grip and began pulling me back the way I'd come.

"Let go of my arm."

"I will when I'm sure you'll behave like a proper guest in our home."

"I'm just curious about the towers." I decided to opt for flattery. He must have some pride in his castle. "It must be so fantastic to be the owner of an actual castle. Don't you want to show the towers off to your guests? They're the best part."

"They're off limits."

"I know, but I don't understand why."

"If you're told they're off limits, why are you trying to go where you don't belong? Do you always break the law like this?"

"I didn't know it was a *law*."

"You go running on private property as if the entire Napa Valley belongs to you. Now I find you wandering around our home as if you think you have the right to intrude in our lives and make our things your own."

"That's not what I was doing."

"That's exactly what you were doing. I can see it in the entitled look on your face."

"I'm not entitled."

He tightened his grip and twisted his fingers, turning my skin so it felt like he might tear it right off my bones.

"You're hurting me."

"Good." He smiled.

What was wrong with him? Was he a sadist? Were the castle towers filled with the dead, mutilated bodies of his victims? Did he enjoy torturing people? Is that why I heard screams? If he twisted any harder, I would be screaming myself. I was biting my tongue to keep from letting him know how badly he was hurting me. My eyes burned with tears.

He continued dragging me along the corridor. I was scrambling to keep up, but found myself tripping as he took ever longer strides, forcing me to stumble after him, almost falling, except the grip he had on my arm kept me upright.

"You're going to wreck my shoulder. I already have a sprained ankle and if you don't let go of me, it's going to get—"

"You should have thought about that before you went prowling through our home, as if it belonged to you."

"My friends are getting married here. Ella said we'll be staying overnight, and I just wanted to see the rest of the—"

"Stop talking. You're supposed to stay with Ella. You don't go wandering around. And if I catch you on our property, or going into the private rooms of our home again, you won't be allowed back. Do you understand?"

"My friends are paying a lot of money for—"

"That doesn't give you the right of ownership. If I catch you prowling around again, you won't be welcome. Even for the wedding. Understood?"

We were at the entrance to the corridor. I looked at his face. He didn't look angry or fierce or particularly aggressive. His face was pleasant and calm. In fact, as I studied his expression, he smiled as if he'd just welcomed me inside for the first time.

"Understood?" he asked.

"Perfectly."

"Good. And keep this conversation to yourself. Your friend doesn't need to know what a little sneak you are, does she? And she doesn't need to know you have a warning. You behave yourself and everything will be fine. No need to go tattling and whining about things. You don't want to spoil her wedding, do you?"

I gave him a thin smile.

"Do you?"

"Of course not."

"Good. I think we're clear." He released his hold on my arm.

He was clear, but I was not. I was more determined than ever to find out what they were, so very, *very* determined to keep hidden.

CHAPTER 37

*A*s Tess and I drove down the winding road away from the castle, I wondered who would speak first.

I wasn't sure how to bring up the incident with Nolan. She had to know about it. She had to know what kind of people were hosting her wedding. Even though they weren't technically the hosts, they had a lot of control over what would happen while her guests were eating and sleeping, drinking and dancing at the castle.

She needed to know. Even if it changed nothing. Even if she told me I was stirring up more negative energy.

At the same time, it seemed as if there was something she was avoiding saying. I couldn't be sure why I thought that. Possibly because she was quiet, which wasn't like her. Tess was a talkative person, and she'd just spent over an hour and a half making plans for the event of a lifetime, if all the ads and cultural myths were to be believed.

Any other time, words would be spilling out of her mouth. Especially since I'd been out of the room for part of the time. I expected questions about where I'd gone. I expected a reprimand for wandering off. I expected to be asked my opinion about Kate and

Julia, my thoughts about the plans for the wedding weekend, food and music and table arrangements and how much she should rely upon Kate's expertise.

If she hadn't been navigating the car around sharp turns, I might have wondered if she was even breathing. She looked anxious.

"Is this the first time you met Kate and Julia?" I asked.

She nodded.

Even stranger. Why wasn't she speaking?

"Do you feel you clicked?" I asked.

"I think so, yes. They have lots of creative ideas, they're both highly recommended."

"That's good."

Silence. She pressed the brake, slowing more than necessary.

"How was Ella after her lecture on the history of gargoyles? You must have liked the idea of that creature keeping out negative energy."

"Hmm."

"It looks kind of cool. It's unique."

"It's definitely that," she said.

Finally, a few words. "Did you accomplish everything you wanted to?"

"It's hard to say. They got a sense of the place. They had an introduction to Ella, so I think so."

"That's good."

She nodded.

She obviously didn't want to talk about the wedding details or anything that had happened, so I figured I would get right to it. Maybe that would prime the pump. "I had a disturbing encounter with Nolan," I said.

"I hope you didn't say anything about the rumor."

"I told you I wouldn't."

"Did you tell me that?"

I sighed. "Not exactly."

"Why was it disturbing? Did you—"

"Did I, what?"

"Nothing. What happened?"

"What were you going to ask?"

"Nothing. Tell me what happened."

I didn't think it was nothing, but she'd clearly decided not to say any more. "I was checking out the passage that leads to one of the towers to see if—"

"God, Alex! Why? Why do you do stuff like this? Are you *trying* to sabotage my wedding?"

"No."

"It doesn't feel that way. Maybe it's your subconscious."

I laughed. "It's not my subconscious. I'm fully conscious of what I'm doing. I want to know what's in those towers. At first, I was just curious because they're so cool. I wanted to see what the rooms are like. And I wanted to look out the windows at the top. But after the way they've been acting. And the screaming—"

"Don't."

"It had to be said."

"I asked you not to."

Her voice was almost a whisper, almost hoarse, as if she didn't want to say the words, as if she was ... it almost sounded as if she was afraid of something. Maybe the gargoyle had freaked her out. I'd thought it would make her superstitious self happy, knowing that it was supposed to block the supposed bad energy, which was exactly what she'd said she wanted. Who knew? "I'm not trying to sabotage your wedding. I would never do that."

"Not deliberately. But subconsciously—"

"I'm not. I just think you should know, even if it was rude or whatever of me to sneak around where they didn't want me. But he grabbed me like he wanted to hurt me. He did hurt me. He almost dislocated my shoulder."

"Don't exaggerate."

"I'm not. And with my ankle still so fragile, I think it was damaged again."

"How would he know you had a sprained ankle? You can't blame that on him."

"He shouldn't have grabbed me. That's not how you talk to people."

"I'm aware."

"I just wanted you to know. He's aggressive. He tried to hurt me. He wanted to hurt me. And he threatened me. I'm not saying you shouldn't have your wedding there. The castle is amazing. But there's something not right about those two. I don't care how wildly romantic their fairy tale is. They're creepy."

"The castle is in huge demand, so they have to establish firm boundaries. That's all. And you're violating them all over the place. So stop. Okay?"

"Aren't you at all curious? Even a little? The towers are what *make* it a castle."

"We're not getting married in a tower."

"They're missing a great opportunity. The reception could be on multiple levels, different parts of the meal on each level. It would be very cool."

"Why don't you offer to advise them on how to run their business?"

"It's just a thought. It's a castle! And you can't use the towers. It's absurd. It's like having a winery and not allowing people to taste the wine."

"It's not at all the same."

I turned and looked out the window. We were nearing the gates leading to Tess and Marcus's winery. It seemed as if the conversation had run its course. She didn't care what Nolan had done, and she didn't care that she might never see inside the towers. I should probably let it go. A normal person would.

But I knew I wouldn't. Not with that rumor. Not with the

screams that I had heard as clearly as I heard the rapid breathing coming from Tess.

I wondered what was bothering her. It seemed to be more than just my refusal to follow her rules, the rules of the castle, all the rules.

CHAPTER 38

*T*he screams echoed inside Tess's mind. She heard them as she drove home, when the car was filled with lengthy silences. They even rang in her ears like tinnitus when Alex was talking, blathering on yet again about the towers, telling Tess she'd wandered off, gone exploring where she didn't belong, invading someone's private space. She had the hubris to complain that Nolan was rude to her when she'd been trying to sneak into an area of his home that she'd been explicitly told was off-limits.

What was wrong with her?

Tess was keeping her vow not to tell Alex she'd heard someone screaming. It had been distinct and memorable. There was no chance the sounds had been caused by the wind, but she wasn't telling Alex that. It would fuel her compulsion to peer into every nook and cranny of the castle until Ella and Nolan couldn't take it and canceled the contract for Tess's dream wedding.

The screams absolutely bothered her. And the fact that it had happened on more than one occasion worried her. But there had to be a logical explanation. Maybe someone on their staff was prone to temper tantrums if something didn't go according to plan. They had perfectionistic standards. It was one of the things Tess loved about the venue. She was confident her wedding would be spectacular because Ella kept her finger on the pulse of even the smallest details.

Perfectionists were high-strung, and it made sense that Ella hired other perfectionists to ensure her wishes were carried out.

She was going to put it out of her mind. What troubled her was Alex's stubborn refusal to let go of this pathological need to dig into something dark. Her compulsion to find out about a rumor that was nothing but gossip. Her obsession with those towers. What did it matter? The idea of holding the reception in the towers was absurd. It wouldn't be conducive to a lively party. Ella knew that. Tess knew that. Kate and Julia hadn't even asked about the towers. Any sane person could see that the great hall and the terrace and dining room would provide a lovely venue.

At home, she and Alex parted ways, Alex going up to her room and Tess going immediately to Marcus's office.

She unbuckled her sandals and let them fall off her feet. She half reclined on the sofa adjacent to his desk and waited for him to turn his chair to face her.

"How did it go?"

"Great. It feels a little like putting together one of the launch events I used to run."

He laughed. "So you don't need the wedding planner."

"But I do. I didn't plan everything myself for those events either."

She ran her fingers through her bangs, lifting them off her brow, leaving her hand on top of her head, her fingers laced through her hair.

"Headache?"

She moved her hand to her lap. "No. Just a lot on my mind."

"There's plenty of time."

"It's not that." She sighed and sat up, crossing her legs. "I'm wondering if I made a mistake asking Alex to be my maid of honor. It was a bit of an impulse. I hadn't seen her in a while, and I missed her. She's so full of energy and she can be … she brings out a different side of me and I missed that."

"What are you trying to say?"

"She's absolutely *obsessed* with the castle." She told him about Alex's inability to let go of the screaming, leaving out her own experience. She refused to believe it meant anything sinister, and so whatever she'd heard was irrelevant. She told him about the rumor. "Even if she doesn't irritate them to the point of canceling our contract, she's just … she's not focused. It feels as if the wedding is secondary to her."

"Is there something she's supposed to be doing that she's not?"

"No. She's always been self-absorbed. And a little secretive. I know that about her. She's a loner. I know all this, but maybe I forgot the reality of living with it."

He waited for her to continue.

"I do consider her my closest friend. I just wonder sometimes if it's a two-way street."

He leaned back in his chair. She half-expected him to turn and glance at his computer screen, but he didn't. Many men would. Almost every man she'd ever known, interrupted in the middle of work, would do that. Not Marcus. She loved that about him. When he was talking to someone, anyone, not just her, he gave his attention one hundred percent. "It's your call. You can rescind the offer."

"That's not usually done."

"Doesn't matter. It's still your call. But you should know your friends. You should know which friend is your closest. Besides me." He winked. He stood and crossed the room. He pushed her tangled bangs to the side and kissed her forehead.

She got to her feet and slid her arms around his waist. They held each other, then kissed for a while. Despite how it felt kissing him, a part of her held back. He was sympathetic. What he'd said had helped her clarify her thoughts, but so had speaking her thoughts out loud. He also seemed slightly detached. He could have been more sympathetic. Maybe. She wasn't sure what she wanted, or expected, from him.

She *should* know who her friends were. She did. Alex was absolutely the friend she enjoyed the most. She wasn't sure she could say Alex was her closest friend, because Alex revealed so little of herself. When it came right down to it, almost nothing.

Did Marcus see that? Or was that all in her mind because she wasn't sure herself?

Or was she overthinking everything?

CHAPTER 39

BEFORE: AMELIA

*I*n the stories my parents read to me when I was small, the children's playmates were animals or mythological creatures—fairies and elves, even ghosts. But when I started reading my own books, I was allowed to read more modern stories. In the pages of those books, I met children who had playmates. Other children the same age as they were. The idea shocked and fascinated and even scared me.

I wasn't sure why it scared me. There was something about it that made me think there might be something wrong with my life in the castle. Why weren't there any other children? Why didn't I have any brothers or sisters? There were no sisters when I had my real daddy and no brothers or sisters with my fake father.

When I asked my mother why I didn't have a sister, she said not all children do. When I asked her if I could get a sister or a brother, she said that's not a decision a child gets to make. I asked her if she wanted other children.

"No, sweetheart. I love you too much. Why would I want another child?"

"Will you change your mind and decide I can have a sister or brother?"

"No."

"Why?"

"Because I want to do the best job I can raising the one child I have. Raising a child is the most important job in the whole world. I want to do it right. That's why there are so many monsters and bad people in the world. Because a lot of people do it wrong."

"Why?"

"Because they aren't paying attention."

That confused me, so I didn't ask any more questions. Besides, what I really wanted to know was why there weren't any children for me to play with. I didn't care about bad people. They were only in books, and by the end of the story they were dead, or sent away, or they turned into good people because they were sorry for what they'd done.

"I want other children to play with."

"You have me. And Daddy."

I didn't have Daddy. It had been a long time since my daddy left, and he never came back. The man who came into our house and read stories in a different voice and smelled strange. The man I was supposed to call Daddy was not the daddy I knew when I was little, but I wasn't supposed to say that.

"I want other children. People my age who want to climb trees."

"I could climb a tree."

I laughed.

"I could. Let's go outside. I'll show you."

"It's not the same."

My mother looked like she wanted to cry.

"Why can't I have other children? All the children in books and movies have other children. They have so much fun. They play together. They go on adventures. It's not fair."

"It's not necessary. Besides, stories are make believe. They're fun to read, but that's not how life really is. You know that. Some stories have magic, and you know there isn't any magic, right? I've explained that."

"But there are children. I've seen them from my tower. Far away."

She sighed, a long sigh that made her sound tired. "Other people are disappointing. In stories, when they do mean or hurtful things, they learn lessons and say they're sorry. They change. That's not how it is in the real world. Life is full of heartbreak, and sadness and pain. Stories are entertaining, but the happy endings are lies."

I started crying. "Then why do we read them?"

"To make us feel better. To distract us and entertain us."

"It doesn't make me feel better if it's a lie."

"No one will ever love you like I do. Like your daddy does. Other children say mean things. They trick you and try to make you do bad things. They do awful, horrible, cruel, hurtful things that damage you forever. You could get in trouble. You could get hurt. You could get sick from doing awful things, drinking things. You could die. Lots of children die."

I was crying harder now.

She put her arms around me, but I pushed her away.

"I don't care! I want other children. I don't like being here all by myself!"

"You have us. That's all you need."

"It's not. I hate it!"

"Don't say that."

"I'm tired of being alone."

She tried to pull me onto her lap. I shoved her and she almost fell off the couch. "I'm too big to sit on your lap."

"You're not. You're still a little girl."

"I'm getting bigger."

She looked terrified.

I ran out of the room. I ran down the stairs, three flights to the ground floor. I ran out the door into my garden, but I still wasn't free. I was surrounded by the stone wall. I sat on the bench under the apple tree. I looked at my garden, but I hated it. I hated everything. All the beautiful rooms in my tower, even the castle that used to feel safe and strong.

I hated that man who lived there and pretended he was my father.

I hated my mother for thinking I was so stupid I would believe that man was my daddy. He was not. I might have been only five when my daddy left, but I remembered him. Even though that man looked like him a little, maybe, with the same color hair, he was *not* the same.

I stared at the stone wall and wondered if anyone in the whole world outside my wall knew that I was inside. I wondered if I would live there forever. I wondered what would happen to me.

Three days after that, my mother woke me as the sun was coming up. She stood in the doorway holding a tray with my breakfast on it. "A special treat today. Breakfast in bed!" She arranged the pillows behind me and placed the tray on my lap. There was a plate with two slices of buttered toast sprinkled with cinnamon sugar, my favorite. There was a mug of hot chocolate, and a bowl of sliced strawberries with cream poured over them.

While I ate, she told me there was a surprise for me in the garden. She tried to make me guess what it was, but I didn't feel like it.

After I was dressed, we walked slowly down the curving tower stairs.

As I stepped into the garden, I saw a beautiful white puppy. She was rolling on her back with her paws in the air. When she saw me, she flipped onto her feet and ran to me, wriggling her body against my leg. I knelt down and rubbed the back of her head between her ears.

"A playmate," my mother said. "Isn't she precious?"

She was. I loved her instantly. I called her Sugar. I loved her so much, but she wasn't a playmate. She was a puppy.

CHAPTER 40

NOW: ALEX

*I*t felt good to be tying my running shoes and stretching my shins. I planned to take it easy, starting with a slow jog and a short distance. I'd decided to go at dusk, using the pathways that criss-crossed the Black Mask vineyard. Because they were paved, they felt less treacherous than the shoulders of the roads that ran past vineyards and stately buildings featuring the names of well-known wines. I wouldn't have to deal with passing traffic.

I'd waited until the evening when everyone who worked at the winery was gone for the day. I planned to run to the winemaking and bottling building, then back to the house. Nothing strenuous. I wanted to be sure I didn't re-injure my ankle, just as it was getting better.

But as soon as I'd completed the short loop, my body began aching for more. My ankle felt absolutely normal, and my muscles cried out to be used, begging me not to sit them down once again on a soft couch when they were just getting warmed up. I jogged slowly past the house and down the long drive leading to the main road. A short jog from the gate up to the intersection with the highway wouldn't be too much if I was careful and took my time.

After about half a mile, I was aware that my ankle was feeling a little wobbly. I slowed, then turned and started back.

No cars had passed me since I'd turned, but after a few minutes, I became aware that a car was behind me, moving at a very slow speed because it hadn't come into my peripheral vision. I realized it had been there for a while. It was electric, so I hadn't noticed it right away. I wasn't even sure what made me conscious of its presence.

There was no reason for it to be going so slowly. It was traveling at less than five miles an hour in order to stay behind me. My first thought was that it might be Silas, but his car wasn't electric. I glanced over my shoulder to get a better look at it. A white compact sedan. I couldn't tell the make.

It wasn't a good idea to increase my speed, which was what I would have done under normal circumstances. I wasn't about to risk re-injuring my ankle. And it wasn't as if I had a chance of out-running a car. I couldn't very well hop over the fence and take off through the field, either.

I didn't think I was in danger, but I didn't like it creeping behind me. I didn't like it trying to intimidate me, or whatever the driver was trying to accomplish with their silent crawl.

Since I couldn't escape, I did the next best thing. I stopped. I faced the road and waited for it to come even with me, hoping for a good look at the driver, but the moment I turned to face the road, the car picked up speed, pulling ahead. The growing darkness and the speed it was now traveling prevented me from seeing through the side windows. I couldn't even tell if the driver was male or female. I couldn't see whether there were any others in the car.

It pulled ahead about thirty or forty yards, then slowed again, returning to its previous crawl.

I began walking. Once again, it maintained a pace too slow for the highway, but keeping ahead of me, maintaining a consistent gap so I couldn't catch up.

It continued tracking me in this way until I arrived at the gates to Black Mask. In the short time since I'd left the property, the gates had been closed and locked, no longer standing with open arms to welcome eager wine tasters. As I entered the security code, I watched the car pull away. I'd committed the license plate to memory, but I wasn't sure what good it would do me. I didn't know anyone who had access to a police officer willing to check a car registration for a civilian.

Back in my room, I stepped into the shower. As I scraped my fingertips across my scalp, rinsing shampoo out of my hair, I tried to scrape my thoughts in the same way, straining to figure out who might want to follow me while I ran. It made no sense because it wasn't as if someone needed to find out where I was staying. It wasn't a secret.

If the driver wasn't looking for the place I was staying, they must have wanted to unsettle me. But why? My first thought was Ella or Nolan. But Nolan had already delivered his threat.

Was it possible this had nothing to do with the castle? Had someone further back in my past come looking for me?

CHAPTER 41

BEFORE: TESS

*T*ess had thought she'd made a brilliant move getting herself hired as the CMO at Marcus's cyber security firm. What she'd failed to think through, in the heat of her passion to secure a place with guaranteed proximity to him, was how far her mindset as a consultant had drifted from the reality of corporate oversight.

After spending several years working first with a startup that consisted of four people, then working as an independent contractor, the rules and regulations of an HR department, backed by a rigorous legal team, were not at the top of her mind. Of course, she'd known it wasn't the height of propriety for a woman to start a relationship with her boss, but she'd brushed that thought aside in her obsessive belief that Marcus was the man she was meant to be with.

She wondered sometimes how someone with her education, her business savvy, her experience and intelligence could be so unbelievably stupid. Because that's what she was when it came to men. She either got into relationships with men she knew weren't right for her, or fell in love with men who were unavailable. Now, she'd managed to arrange a horribly inappropriate situation. One that would seriously damage her career while making her look weak and pathetic, even in her own eyes.

Why hadn't she stopped for two minutes to consider that?

It was almost as if some other force consumed all rational thinking. She'd *known* that Marcus and she had the potential for a deep, long-term, meaningful connection. A lifelong connection. She'd been overcome with certainty on that point. So overcome, all she could think about was how to ensure their paths were joined securely, so the inevitable had time to unfold naturally.

Maybe her behavior had been controlling. Yes, it was controlling, in the extreme. But that's how things got done. That's how she'd succeeded in her career—by taking control.

So she'd done what she always did when she had a project. She'd pushed objections and difficulties out of her thoughts entirely. She'd focused one hundred percent on accomplishing her objective—securing a permanent place at his side. She'd put all her energy into pitching her value to him as the CMO of his company, knowing that was the right path. As a result, she'd trapped herself. As surely as if she'd locked herself in a cage, turning the key with her own hand, then tossing that key through the bars into a crevice where it could never be recovered.

The situation was impossible.

The circumstances made it difficult for her to enjoy the unfolding of their relationship. Every conversation they had, every extended lunch, every meeting over coffee, and finally the dinners, was a delicate, fraught balance of the personal and the professional.

They both knew what they wanted and where they were headed, but neither one could say so.

She appreciated that about him, loved it, actually. He didn't place so much as the tip of his shoe over the line. She could feel that he wanted to start something, but he kept his thoughts to himself. They talked about everything, told each other their entire life stories. They shared hundreds of experiences from their careers—recounting wild successes, near failures, incredible travels, and experiences with people who had made an impact on their lives. They talked about their ambitions and their childhood dreams. They talked about their pranks in high school and their college romances.

Everything was said, but still, they kept the boundaries in place. He was the CEO. She was the CMO. Both executives, but not peers. He was the head of the company and she reported to him. As long as she worked there, speaking the words they both wanted to, would jeopardize those titles for both of them. More for him than for her.

How had she been so absolutely, blindly idiotic?

In the end, she'd decided this was her one shot at happiness. Careers could be re-imagined or re-built entirely. She could find a completely different path. She needed to be sure she didn't damage his career, but hers might have to be collateral damage.

She'd told Marcus how she felt and together they'd gone to the HR department, which in his fledgling company comprised three people. Tess had resigned five months into the revolution she'd pitched to him. She'd advised him as he recruited and hired her replacement, then worked as a consultant to bring her replacement up to speed.

They'd agreed with HR there would be no severance package, no stock award. It would be a clean exit that left Marcus unscathed.

She'd spent time traveling around Australia, taking weekend trips with Marcus and a few longer trips without him. When he'd begun talking about moving the headquarters of his company to San Francisco, they'd flown to California.

After a wine-tasting weekend in the Napa Valley, and a sales pitch about the mystery of wine from Silas Birch at the Black Mask Winery, which he'd whispered was going up for sale in the near future, she'd found herself filled with a vision for an entirely different career.

But was it really that different?

At the end of the day, nearly every career was about marketing. Every job involved presenting yourself and what you had to offer to the world in an enticing package. She'd done that with the circuit-filled boxes that were the backbone of the internet and she'd done it with a host of other products. She'd persuaded Marcus she could do it with the software that protected currency and data in the digital universe from bad actors. She could do it with wine. She could do it with anything.

CHAPTER 42

NOW: ALEX

*S*till feeling unsettled by the anonymous white car creeping beside me while I jogged, I drank two martinis after dinner and watched a movie by myself in the entertainment room. Marcus was working and Tess had gone to bed with a headache.

I should have slept deep and long after two martinis, not to mention the two glasses of wine with dinner, but I didn't. First, I had a dream where I was climbing the stone steps of the castle tower. In reality, I didn't know if they were stone, but in my dream, they were, and I was climbing in bare feet, feeling the cold seeping into my bones.

The stairs seemed to go on endlessly as I climbed ever higher, growing slightly dizzy. Unlike what I'd expected, there were no rooms along the way, simply a winding staircase curving up into the darkness. When I finally reached the top, I came to an ancient wooden door. I pushed it open, but before I could look into the room, I was back on the ground floor, starting my climb again.

When I woke, my legs were shivering with cold, although my bedroom wasn't particularly cold. The window was open, but the breeze felt pleasant on my face. The rest of me was covered with blankets. I couldn't recall how many times I'd climbed the stairs, but it felt like twenty or thirty, maybe more.

After that, I barely slept. When I closed my eyes, I saw the winding stone staircase and my mind refused to settle. My thoughts twisted around the car that had followed me, the rumor of a murder victim buried at the castle, and the memory of those screams. Around and around, as if my thoughts were still climbing the staircase.

Before the sun came up, when the light in my room was just starting to change to a dim gray, I got out of bed. I showered and dressed in yoga clothes. I went down to the workout room and closed the door. I told Tess's smart device to play nature sounds, rolled out a mat, and spent the next hour forcing myself to move as slowly and deliberately as possible through a series of poses. Forcing and yoga don't go hand-in-hand, but forcing was what was required. Even so, my mind screamed and reeled as I performed the warrior pose and tree pose and others. It chattered and speculated as I did forward stretches and backbends.

By the end of the hour, I felt only marginally calmer.

I ate breakfast and poured a second mug of coffee to take back to my room. I took a long shower, then stood at the window drinking my now slightly too cool coffee.

From where I stood, I could see the roof of the winery itself. It was after eight, so I assumed there must be people arriving, unlocking the doors. They might have been hard at it since sunrise for all I knew.

I put on a hoodie and went outside, taking a side door to be sure I didn't run into Tess or Marcus. It was best to avoid any questions about what I was up to.

I found Chuck outside the building smoking a cigarette, drinking from a travel mug. The aroma of the smoke made me crave one. I walked toward him, moving to his left so I was upwind. I took a deep breath and reminded myself about all the time I'd just spent focused on the purity of the air moving in and out of my lungs, flowing through my body. It helped, some.

I waved. "Hey."

He gave me a single nod and took a draw on his cigarette.

"I wanted to ask you some more about that murder at the castle," I said.

"I told you everything I know. I gotta get to work."

"Not until your cigarette's finished."

He pulled it from his lips as if he needed to check the status. He gave me a half smile and tapped the ash on the ground.

"Who told you about it?" I asked.

"I don't know. It's one of those things I've known for ages."

"You don't remember hearing people talk about it? Even if it wasn't the first time?"

"Not really."

"Not really? Or no?"

"Are you some kind of investigator?"

I laughed. "No."

"Then what's this about? I thought you were here to help Tess with her wedding."

"I am. But when someone tells me there's a dead body where my best friend is planning to have the party of her life, it bothers me." I gave him a sad, worried smile.

"Don't let it. I probably shouldn't have mentioned it."

"But you did."

"Put it out of your pretty little head."

"My pretty little head does not like the idea of knowing there might be a killer living in that castle."

"It's not like that."

"How do you know?"

He took a drag on his cigarette. "It was a long time ago."

"Are you sure?"

"I think so. Like I said, it was a rumor. I heard it years ago. And even then, I had the impression it was several years before that."

"But how many years? Two years? Or twenty?"

"You're very persistent."

"I want to know."

"Well, you're not going to find out from me. I told you every-thing I know. And I already told you, a couple of times, that's all I know." He dropped his cigarette on the ground and stepped on it. He took a sip from his mug.

"You can't tell me anything? You can't point me to anyone else who knows the story? Anyone you've ever discussed it with?"

"It's not like it gets discussed all the time. It's an old story. I rarely think about it."

"I'm not sure that's true, or you wouldn't have brought it up. You must remember someone else who's mentioned it."

He sighed deeply and loudly. He took another swallow from his mug. He bent down and picked up the cigarette butt. He went to a trashcan by the open door and dropped the butt into the trash. "The best I can tell you is to go to one of the bars downtown, where some of the local people hang out. Not the winery owners, but working people. Maybe you can find someone who knows more than I do."

I nodded. "Okay. Thanks."

"Do Tess and Marcus know you're so worried about this?"

I shrugged.

"Maybe they don't care. And maybe no one cares, which is why no one talks about it anymore. So it might not be a good idea to get things all stirred up."

"Thanks for the advice," I said.

"Any time."

He took another swallow from his mug and went into the build-ing. I stood there for a few minutes, then returned to the house. Another day stretched ahead of me. I had no plans to go to a bar in the middle of the day. It was unlikely I would find someone who could provide coherent information about an old rumor at nine in the morning.

CHAPTER 43

*M*y plans to go to the bar in search of details about a murder that may or may not have taken place, a murder that might not have anything at all to do with, *probably* had nothing at all to do with the screaming I'd heard, was deferred. I'd forgotten there was a champagne reception at the castle late that afternoon for the brides who had recently been accepted for the following spring.

Once again, Tess and I were decked out in high heels. I'd piled my hair on top of my head and put on long earrings with tiny gold balls at the ends of thin chains that danced around my jawbone. Tess liked them, but when I offered to let her wear them, she recoiled.

Other than that, she seemed warmer than she'd been after I'd told her about my confrontation with Nolan. She acted as if she'd let go of her irritation over my fascination with the towers. Maybe she'd decided she wasn't going to bow down to Ella anymore.

Ella needed to stop being so full of herself and start treating her customers with a little respect. At least that was my opinion, and I hoped Tess realized that. She shouldn't be cowering in fear as if we'd been transported back to a time when castle guards pointed their swords at a peasant woman, ready to slice off her head for displeasing the queen.

I laughed at the image inside my head.

"What's so funny?" Tess asked.

"Just picturing Ella trying to chop off the brides' heads if they do something wrong. Like the queen from Alice in Wonderland."

Tess stared at me as if I'd lost my own head.

"You don't think it's funny? Ella is a little like her."

"It's a story."

"She acts as if she's living in a story."

"Let's go," Tess said. "She's sending a car, but we're supposed to be waiting out front."

"That's nice of her, if not a little controlling."

"It's very nice. I can have all the champagne I want," Tess said.

"Absolutely."

"You too, but don't let it go to your head. No unauthorized tours of the towers."

"I can't get within fifty feet of those towers."

"Just so we're clear."

It amused me that Tess still, after all these years, after the events of my visit so far, thought she could tell me what to do. It was somewhat astonishing that she believed I would stifle my curiosity for the sake of pleasing the woman, who seemed to think she was the one who would decide what kind of wedding Tess and Marcus should have. If anything cast a shadow over her fantasy or disturbed her sense of control, Tess and Marcus would be kicked out the door. The gargoyle would glare at their disgraced backs as they slunk away from the castle walls, victorious that he'd cast out the bad energy.

I couldn't understand why Tess didn't see this facet of Ella. Or Nolan.

At the same time, I didn't want Tess to abandon her dream of getting married at the castle. That would mean I no longer had access.

And I would not be able to get a good night's sleep until I climbed the stairs into at least one, but ideally, both towers.

There were fifteen other brides attending the champagne reception. Each was accompanied by another woman. Some had invited their maid of honor, but others were joined by a sister or their mother. The terrace was dotted with small round tables for two. A serving table held buckets of champagne and an arrangement of flutes standing ready for service. A second table was filled with platters of pastries, charcuterie boards, and plates of thinly sliced fruit laid out in the shape of flowers.

A harpist sat at one corner of the terrace, running her fingers across the strings of her instrument, filling the air with the sounds of music that made it all feel like we'd stepped into another era.

Tess and I took our seats. After we'd finished our first glass of champagne and eaten a bit, Ella and Nolan spoiled it all by walking to the center of the terrace dressed in wedding clothes. Ella wore a gown that looked straight out of the 17th century. Nolan wore a top hat and tails, which was somewhat jarring because it was decidedly more modern. Making it worse, Nolan was holding a microphone.

The harp music stopped, and he spoke, telling us the story of how they'd met, matching the story Ella had told us word-for-word. When he was finished, they gave each other the most dispassionate kiss I'd ever witnessed. Then Ella took the microphone and stepped toward the bride-to-be at the table closest to where she stood.

"We're inviting all our brides to share their love stories today. It's an opportunity for each of you to show how very special you are and why you were chosen to celebrate your day at the Windy Hills Castle." She smiled as if this were the most delightful news any of the brides had heard all year.

I leaned close to Tess. "Did you know about this?"

Tess shook her head. She looked mildly concerned. I realized she hadn't been there when Marcus had told Nolan the story of how they'd met. She likely had no idea what he'd said. Was this some kind of test? Even if it wasn't, she probably wasn't thrilled about telling a bunch of strangers the intimate details of how they'd met. None of these women had even been introduced to each other.

The first bride began speaking. Her voice trembled as she stumbled through a story of meeting her fiancé through an online dating site. There was nothing magical or remarkable about her story, and I wondered how she'd made the cut. It didn't seem to fit Ella's idea of fairy-tale romance.

But then came the kicker.

"My fiancé's ex-girlfriend couldn't accept that he'd fallen in love with someone else. She broke into my apartment and attacked me with a meat cleaver." The woman held up her left hand. A diamond as large as a soy bean sparkled on her ring finger. "She cut off the tip of my thumb. But Stephen rescued me. He was my knight. He slayed the dragon and carried me out of the cave. I might have died."

She returned to her seat, crying softly. The woman at her table put her arm around the bride-to-be, pulling her head onto her shoulder.

I stared in fascinated horror. A meat cleaver. She was lucky she hadn't lost her whole hand. Then she wouldn't have a place to display that magnificent ring. Or a story to tell that had won her acceptance to the castle.

The next story was equally dramatic, but not as bloody—a woman who had been swept off her feet by a man who bought her coffee shop just as it was headed into bankruptcy. I wondered if she'd been carried away by his money or his love. Maybe it didn't matter.

I glanced at Tess. She was furiously texting, a terrified look on her face.

CHAPTER 44

*L*uckily for Tess, Marcus replied to her text before she was in the spotlight. Tess might have won the competition, if that's what the champagne reception fairy-tale hour was designed to be. She told a story that Marcus had indeed invented. I was surprised the story fit into Ella's somewhat distorted view of reality, but perhaps her distortion wasn't as rigid as I'd thought.

In Tess's story, she was the one who had done the rescuing.

Marcus had been the proverbial loner at the top, the CEO who had it all—a thousand colleagues, strong business relationships, and admirers, but no one who could see into his heart. The poor little rich boy with a bank account creeping up from the M's to the B's, but no one who loved him for himself.

Along came Tess Turner, freeing him from his isolated tower, giving meaning to his life, filling his days with beauty, and showing him what love was.

Every eye was damp with tears when Tess was finished with her fairy tale. Even Ella and Nolan were blinking and dabbing at their lashes.

I took advantage of all that blurred vision to slip away from my table. I hurried past the low walls of the vegetable garden outside the kitchen and around the corner toward the tower at the front left side of the castle. Both towers were surrounded by stone walls that were about twelve feet tall.

Walking up to the wall, I placed my hand on it. I could see the branches of a small tree that barely extended past the top edge. The long tendrils of vines planted on the other side hung over the wall as well.

As I walked along, dragging my fingers across the stones and mortar, I tried to imagine what might be inside. It looked as if there was a lot of space between the wall and the side of the tower, which made me think the garden must be quite large. All the other landscaping around the castle, and what I'd seen of the outlying cottages, were lush and carefully maintained by a crew of gardeners.

I paused. I moved my hand around, touching some of the smaller stones, checking to see if they might be loose. Nothing budged.

I let my hand fall to my side. Everything I did to try to get closer simply inflamed my curiosity. I felt further away than ever. I tipped my head back, looking up at the deep-set windows to see if anything was visible from this angle.

Just as I was about to turn away, I heard a woman's voice. It was faint, impossible for me to make out the words, but I could definitely hear a woman speaking on the other side of the wall.

Her voice was high, as if she might be calling out to a child. I had the irrational urge to press my ear against the stone, but of course, that would make it even more difficult to hear. I held my breath, straining to decipher the words she was saying. She seemed to be repeating something, but still I couldn't make it out.

"Hello?" I said, my voice raised slightly.

There was no answer. I waited, expecting to hear her speak again, but there was nothing.

"Hello? Is someone there? Can you hear me?" I asked.

Again, the response was silence. I walked along the wall, following it until it joined the castle wall. There was no gate or door, not even a small window or any kind of opening for passing through gardening tools or a hose. I walked back in the direction I'd come, still calling, asking if anyone was back there, if there was a way into the garden.

By the time I reached the other end of the wall, my shoulder was stiff from holding out my arm as my hand swept over the rocks. I let my hand fall to my side. I stared helplessly at the wall, wishing more than anything I had the shoes and equipment to scale it. I wanted to know what, and who, was back there almost as much as I wanted to go inside those towers.

I sighed. I needed to stop thinking about it. I needed to put it out of my head and stop spending every waking minute trying to claw my way through solid stone.

I returned to the terrace.

Surprisingly, my absence hadn't been noted. The brides had left their tables and were standing in the garden area, holding champagne flutes, talking to one another and their companions. Ella and Nolan were mingling with their guests. The disruption in the assigned seating had kept them from noticing the hole I'd left.

Grabbing a clean glass from the table, I held it out for a splash of champagne and slipped into the group of women, smiling and nodding as if I'd been with them the entire time.

As I wandered among the giddy brides, I asked questions about their weddings and did my best to make myself invisible to them. I felt the shadows of the towers, like daggers across the back garden.

CHAPTER 45

 was skeptical whether I would get any more information about the castle from Chuck, but I decided to give it one more try. After an easy jog around the property, one in which I kept my eye out for the arrival of his red Jeep Wrangler, I circled closer to the winemaking buildings and watched until I saw him light up his morning cigarette and take a sip from his travel mug.

When he saw me, he lowered his cigarette as if he was considering dropping it to the ground and putting it out before he'd even taken a second drag.

"I just wanted to ask a quick question," I said. "Don't look so worried."

"I'm not worried. But it's getting old being asked questions I've already answered."

"This is different."

"Did you go to the bar, as I suggested?"

"Not yet. I will. I was wondering if you know whether anyone else lives at the castle. Besides Ella and Nolan."

"How would I know that?"

"Because you knew the other thing."

"First, I don't *know* anything. I told you about a rumor I'd heard. I don't know it for a fact."

I ignored this.

He put the cigarette to his lips. He stared at the smoke curling off the tip, drew some into his lungs, then exhaled a few seconds later. "Second of all, I've never been there, as I told you. I've never met Ella or Nolan. Didn't know their names until you told me. I have no idea who else lives there. I don't know who works there. I'm a winemaker. They aren't a winery, so I have no association with them."

"Sure. But you must hear things, so I figured it didn't hurt to ask."

"No, it doesn't hurt, but as I also said, it's getting old. Why do you need to know so much about it?"

"Just curious."

"This seems like more than simple curiosity. Are you sure you're not an investigator of some kind?"

"I'm not an investigator."

"Well, one thing you should also know about this place. And not just Windy Hills, but about the Napa Valley in general. People here value their privacy. Some wineries are owned by families who have been here for generations. Even newer owners aren't gossips. They might have associations centered around the industry, but you need to understand that they're also competitors. So, being curious is one way to put it, but prying into other people's business is another thing, and it might not be looked upon very well. You might be seen as an industrial spy."

I laughed. "Seriously?"

"Yes. You call it curious. Other people would call it snooping."

"Good to know."

"You seem like an intelligent person. Maybe you should find something better to do with your time." As he'd done the last time I'd spoken to him, he dropped his half-finished cigarette on the ground, stomped it out, then picked up the broken stick and dropped it into the trash. "It's probably a good idea to focus on weddings." He gave me an awkward grin. He turned and went inside, disappearing into the darkness of the enormous building.

I stretched my calf muscles and began a slow jog back to the house.

As I rounded the bend in the path that led to the back garden and the tasting room, Silas was standing at the fork, blocking the path so I couldn't go in either direction without jogging off the path to go around him.

Conscious of my still-precarious ankle, I stopped. "Please move."

"I need to talk to you."

"I'm trying to finish my run."

"You've reached your destination, so your run is over. You can spare a few minutes to talk."

"You don't know that."

"You're quite the bitch."

"What do you want?" I asked.

"I want to know why you hate me. Tess won't like that. I don't think Marcus will be happy about it either."

"There's nothing I can do about it."

"You can explain why you took such an instant dislike to me. We need to be professional, and look for ways to establish a better relationship."

"I don't hate you."

"You're standoffish. And you're avoiding me."

"I don't have any reason to see you."

"You're Tess's best friend. We should get to know each other. Intimately."

"There's no reason for that."

"You're wrong. It's what Tess wants. So I have a list of questions to help me learn more about you."

"Not interested."

He narrowed his eyes and shoved his face closer to mine. "You think you're too good for me."

"I'm just not interested. It has nothing to do with—"

"There's a reason you're not interested."

Despite my ankle, I turned and started to cut through the garden toward the house.

"You think you're in a different class. Lady of the house and all that, and I'm just a worker on the estate. Right? Someone you can dismiss. Just walk away because you're done talking."

"You're making this into something it's not. I don't think I'm better than anyone."

He grabbed my wrist. "Maybe I haven't been clear. I want to get to know you. Are you free for dinner tonight?"

I yanked my wrist out of his hand. "No." It was an incomplete answer, because it left open the door that I might be available for dinner another night. "I don't want to have dinner with you."

"See!" His voice was triumphant. "You do think you're too good for me."

"I don't. But I don't want to have dinner." Again, I started walking toward the house. For a moment, he didn't follow.

I cut back onto the path and passed under an arched structure formed by iron bars set close together with ivy trained to grow over them. The passage connected the outside patio of the wine tasting room to the side garden of Tess's house. At the end was a gate that was kept locked when the tasting room was open.

The thick growth of ivy made the passage slightly dark. A bench stood on either side of the path. It was a pleasant area for escaping the afternoon heat with a glass of cold white wine, but right now, it felt a little like walking into a trap, because he was suddenly right beside me.

Somehow, he managed to scoot around me until he was standing between me and the gate, his legs spread wide, once again blocking the path. He wasn't a particularly tall man, but he looked like he had a feral strength in his long, thin muscles.

"Get out of my way," I said.

"I want to have dinner with you."

"I said, no."

"You haven't given me a chance. You don't even know me. How can you have any clue whether or not you would enjoy my company?"

"I have a very good idea I would not enjoy your company."

"You haven't spent more than ten minutes with me."

"It's been more than enough."

"So you're judging me on my looks and you don't like them? Isn't that what women hate about men? My looks and my job. I'm not a filthy rich, jet-setting CEO who can buy a winery with cash, so I'm no good?"

I laughed. "It has nothing to do with your looks or your job. You grabbed me. You're aggressive. And you're a liar. Any one of those is a reason."

Before I'd even finished talking, he'd grabbed my hair with one hand and pulled my head back slightly. "So that's a final no?"

I swung my good foot to the side, hoping my still weakened ankle would support me as I slammed the edge of my running shoe into his ankle bone.

He grunted, tightening his grip on my hair. He grabbed my neck and pulled me toward him. He put his mouth over mine, shoving his tongue at my lips, trying to force it past my clenched teeth. The hand on my neck pressed into my throat, then let go and slid down toward my armpit and around my breast.

I opened my mouth slightly, allowed his tongue to slide in, and bit down on the tip.

He let out a bellow and stumbled away from me. "You bitch." He clapped his hand over his mouth, took another step back, lost his balance and fell, sitting down hard on the ground. Taking his hand away from his mouth, he stared at his fingers as if he expected them to be coated with blood. There was none.

"That hurt, you stupid bitch."

"Next time, don't go where you're not wanted."

"You are so fucking full of yourself."

"Likewise."

I stepped over his splayed legs and walked toward the gate. Luckily for me, it hadn't yet been locked for the day. I opened it and stepped into the garden. I walked quickly toward the side door of the house, went inside, and locked the door behind me.

CHAPTER 46

PORTLAND, OREGON

*E*very night, after I heard my parents climb the stairs, walk down the hall, pause at my bedroom door to be sure I was sleeping, then continue down the hallway and close their door, I would slip out of bed. I took the mask from its hiding place inside a report I'd written about the United States Supreme Court when I was in sixth grade. I got a B+. The report was in the bottom drawer of my desk with all my other school reports that had not received A's. The A-reports were kept in a box in our living room where my parents could admire them.

I lifted my hair up and placed the elastic around my head, letting my hair fall over the strap. I positioned the mask so the holes were lined up perfectly with my eyes. I took my hand mirror to the window and opened the blinds, using the moonlight to see myself reflected in the mirror.

The glow of the moon made the mask look even more elegant and mysterious than the fluorescent lights in the Halloween store. I looked amazing. I looked like a supernatural being. I looked like a queen going to a masked ball. I would be the most eye-catching princess at the harvest festival.

Even so, I wanted more. I *always* wanted more. That was the entire problem with me, according to my father. It was the problem with the human race, he said, but it was especially pronounced in me. Wanting too much. Wanting things I shouldn't want.

There was a girl at my school who was in a musical theater program outside of school. Everyone knew this because she talked about it constantly. She never shut up about it. She went on and on about her amazing singing voice, her solos, the shows she was in, the practices she went to every day after school, the dress rehearsals on the weekends, the bouquets of flowers she was given for her performances, and the fabulous costumes. Her mother was in charge of costumes.

Gloria sang the songs to us. She handed out programs and flyers. She told us how people asked her to autograph their programs. She brought tiny photo albums to school and made us sit in a circle to look at the pictures of every production she was in.

I'd been to Gloria's house once when I was in elementary school. Now, I suggested to her that I would love to be invited over again. She'd told us a hundred times that her parents still made video recordings of every show she'd been in.

"If I came over, I could see you performing in Annie," I said.

"Oh! Really? That would be great. You'll love it." She seemed surprised that someone wanted to watch a recording of the entire show. She'd had several parties for all of us to see recordings of her shows when we were younger, but by sixth grade, no one wanted to go to the parties. Everyone was tired of sitting through the recorded musicals, listening to Gloria sing along with herself.

So I went to her house to suffer through the recording of Annie, singing about a hard knock life, which no child in our quiet, tree-lined suburban streets of Portland knew anything about. Then, after her mother made ice cream sundaes for us, I asked if I could see the sewing room where all the costumes were made.

While I encouraged Gloria to try on all her old costumes and model them for me, I watched her carefully. As each costume went over her head, blinding her for a few seconds, I grabbed pieces of silky fringe and strips of sequins, strings of shimmering beads and satin cord out of the trays of decorative items stacked beside her mother's sewing table. I shoved them into the pockets of my jacket that I'd insisted on wearing, telling her I was cold after eating the ice cream.

Finally, she modeled the last costume she was able to fit into. I thanked her mother for the ice cream. I told Gloria she had an amazing voice and reminded her that my mother was picking me up soon.

At home, I hid my stash in the shoebox with my Sunday shoes, knowing it would be safe for a few days.

On Friday night, while my parents indulged in the single night of TV watching they allowed themselves each week, I went into my mother's sewing room on the third floor of our Victorian house. It was a tiny room with a tiny window looking out at the trees just beyond our backyard. I took my princess dress, a needle and thread, a small pair of scissors, and returned to my room.

After all the decorations were sewn onto my dress, which took me several late nights of work, I was thrilled with the results. There was nothing about the dress that made it look ungodly or inappropriate. It actually looked beautiful.

I knew my father wouldn't like it, but at the same time, I was pretty sure my mother would be overwhelmed with how well I'd used my sewing skills. She would be touched that I'd taken up a sewing project on my own. There was a good chance, a better than usual chance, she would take my side. It didn't happen often, but sometimes.

She would tell my father he should be proud of how resourceful I was. She would show him the tiny, careful stitches. She would point out that I'd done everything she'd taught me, that I was well on my way to becoming an admirable seamstress. She would tell him I hadn't been sneaky or disobedient. I hadn't gone behind his back. Instead, I'd surprised him, both of them, with a creation of my own. I'd demonstrated how much I'd learned and how skilled I was at the womanly art of sewing.

He would consider what she said. He would recognize the effort and commitment required. He would be so pleased with my industriousness and with everything I'd learned from my mother, he would agree to let me wear the dress to the harvest festival, looking like a real princess.

Especially if I spoke to my mother ahead of time, if I reminded her that there was a lot of gold and silver mentioned in the bible, if I told her that descriptions of heaven talked about crowns and streets of gold. That the bible says very clearly the foundations of the heavenly city are made of sapphire and emerald and ruby and amethyst. Gems were in the bible. Gold was in the bible. Kings and queens were *in the bible*.

Kings and queens had children and the child would be a princess and that was me, and surely he could see that.

I was as confident as one of the four horsemen of the apocalypse in my belief that, finally, he would see my reasoning.

CHAPTER 47

NAPA VALLEY, CALIFORNIA

*A*lex walked into the kitchen with a look on her face that told Tess she was not going to enjoy her second cup of coffee. "How was your run?" Tess asked.

"Spoiled." Alex took a mug out of the cabinet.

Tess sipped her coffee and tapped on a headline offering an in-depth description of the El Niño weather pattern expected this winter. She'd never been so connected to the weather in her life as she was now. Every raindrop and every hint of smoke in the air from a forest fire, even if it was two hundred miles away, was now a critical part of her business. She wasn't sure if she liked this connection to the natural world or feared the utter lack of control.

"You have a serious problem," Alex said.

"I do?"

"Your tasting room PR manager or sommelier or savior, whatever he calls himself, is probably going to destroy you."

"That sounds dramatic."

"He assaulted me."

"Why does it seem like there are so many problematic men around here, yet you're the common denominator?"

"This is different from the situation at the castle. Much different.

And I'll just say this about Nolan, he lectured me about trespassing when I was running on a public road, so it didn't start off well. But I won't get into that."

Tess sipped her coffee. She was more concerned about El Niño than she was about Silas. For now. She'd had her problems with him, but he was a critical fixture she couldn't do anything about right now. She preferred to focus on things she could control. Not that El Niño fell into that category, but knowledge was power. If she knew what was coming, they could prepare.

"He grabbed me. He tried to shove his tongue in my mouth and grabbed my—"

"What did you do?"

"I bit his tongue."

"Oh, my god! Why?"

Alex stared at her. "Because it didn't belong in my mouth."

"But that's so … it must have been incredibly painful, and it's dangerous."

She shrugged. "Good."

"Alex. He's …" Tess pushed her coffee away. The situation with Silas was too complicated to explain. She couldn't fire him. Not now. Not anytime in the foreseeable future. His behavior toward Alex was awful. It was a fireable offense at any reputable company. She knew that. A sharp pain pierced her stomach. She straightened her back, reaching for her water glass, but neither the water nor the change in position eased the pain.

"I don't understand why you want someone like him working for you. He'll ruin your reputation, at best. He could destroy you financially, at worst. Don't you see that?"

Tess gritted her teeth. "I have it under control."

"You don't have anything under control. He assaulted me right outside your front door."

"Can you just stay away from him?"

"I have. Apparently, that's been upsetting for him. It's given him the impression I think I'm too good for him."

Tess covered her face with her hands. She couldn't explain it to Alex. She didn't have the words or the …

She pressed her fingertips into her forehead. She couldn't do this now. She needed to figure it out. Soon. But there were too many other things going on. Learning how to manage an operation the size of the Black Mask Winery was consuming nearly all her waking hours. And she wanted to plan the beautiful wedding she'd dreamed about, the wedding she and Marcus had spent hours imagining.

She wanted to enjoy the planning, she wanted to have fun, and relish every minute of it. She did not want to be dealing with the perversity of an employee who was currently essential to their success. Why couldn't Alex see that? Sometimes business was ugly. Occasionally, you had to do business with the devil. Hopefully, only for a while. Alex never understood that. For someone who was cynical in some ways, Alex could be wildly idealistic in her expectations of how things worked, in her expectations of how people should behave.

"I'm dealing with him. And I'm really sorry that happened."

"It's assault."

Tess slid off the bar stool. "Okay. It's not … he didn't …" She took a slow breath. "He made an unwanted advance, but it's not …" she sighed. "Do you want to cut your trip short?"

"No."

"Then what do you want me to do?"

"I told you. He should be fired."

Tess took her mug to the sink, dumped out the rest of her coffee, and rinsed the mug before putting it in the dishwasher. She spoke without turning to face Alex. "You don't get to tell us how to run our business."

"What kind of business welcomes predators? To allow them to walk around your property with easy access to your home? I don't understand you."

"The feeling is mutual," Tess said.

"I'm trying to protect you."

"I don't need protection. I need a friend." Tess felt her throat closing up, felt the tears pushing at the backs of her eyes, threatening to overwhelm her. But there was one thing she knew about Alex. She wasn't the sort of friend who wanted to have a good cry together.

Tess took a deep breath. "It's complicated, and I'm really sorry he behaved like that. We need him to help us get through this transition. There's a lot more to this than I ever realized. And to be honest, I wasn't prepared for it. I know I can do it. I'm going to make this brand one of the best, I'm going to make it wildly successful. But it's a steep learning curve. It's going to take time, and I have to do what I have to do."

"That sounds limp."

"I don't care how it sounds." Tess walked out of the room. She did need a good cry. She started up the stairs. As she began taking them two at a time, Damien, possibly sensing her distress, began squawking, then speaking in his sharp humorous tone. *Dangerous woman. Dangerous woman.*

For once, she didn't laugh. She wondered if Alex had heard him.

CHAPTER 48

*T*ess was impossible to understand, so I wasn't going to try. After our standoff over Silas, I decided we needed a break from each other. It wasn't as if we'd had too much time together. She'd been working all day most days. I'd been brooding and obsessing all day most days, but it seemed as if even more space was required.

I turned my attention back to murder, something I found much easier to get my head around.

Getting out of her house, putting several miles between Tess and me, as well as Silas and me, seemed like the best way to spend my day and my evening. I asked to borrow her car, which she quickly agreed to. Whether it was her guilt over what Silas had done and her refusal to deal with him, or an equal desire to be rid of me, I wasn't sure, but she was digging in her purse and handing over the key fob almost before I'd finished explaining my plans.

I decided to go for a drive to San Francisco, treat myself to a fabulous lunch and a little shopping. Then be back in Napa Valley in time to stop in at the bar Chuck had suggested that might put me close to people who would be eager to gossip about the murder at the castle.

While I was in San Francisco, I also needed to get myself a new cell phone. Diana was giving me the silent treatment over my resignation, but as soon as she acknowledged it, she would surely cut off my access to the phone I'd used since arriving in New York, aside from a burner or two along the way.

I texted Hunter a selfie, leaning against the hood of Tess's BMW. He didn't respond. I drove to the city, conscious the entire way that Tess did not know I didn't have a driver's license. I hadn't had one since I was a teenager because I never saw the point in the cost of owning a car. And I still liked minimizing my visibility in government documentation wherever I could, although that had grown increasingly difficult, and then close to impossible over the years.

But still, why invite more ways for them to keep tabs on what I was up to and what I looked like?

I wasn't going to do anything crazy with her car, so I didn't anticipate needing to show anyone a driver's license.

Sitting at a table covered with a pristine white cloth, a beautiful wine glass half-filled with Chardonnay in front of me, I posed for a picture that the server willingly snapped. I texted that to Hunter as well, but he still didn't reply. Not even a thumb.

I didn't want his cranky mood to infect my day, so I decided to stop the selfies and focus entirely on my delicious meal and shopping plans.

Five hours later, my belly was still pleasantly full, and the trunk of Tess's car was loaded with shopping bags, including a small bag with my new phone. I'd texted the number to Hunter, which was also greeted with silence.

I started the drive back to Napa as the sun was moving toward the horizon, casting a golden glow over the fields beside me, while the cars surrounding me on the freeway glittered like gems.

I parked in front of the bar Chuck had directed me to, locked the car, and went inside. In my high heels and short skirt, I was out of place and I could feel the atmosphere change as the door closed slowly behind me. The bar was decorated in the style of a British pub. I'd never been to Britain, but it was what I imagined a British pub might look like based on scenes in movies, which I had to trust were somewhat accurate.

I went to the bar, slid onto a stool next to a guy wearing a white shirt with the sleeves rolled up to just below his elbows. His longish hair was tucked behind his ears. He held his beer bottle with two hands as if he wanted to make sure it didn't slide away from him on the glossy surface of the bar. I smiled when he glanced my way. Nothing too flirty, just a friendly, *isn't it nice to relax after work* kind of smile.

I turned my attention to the bartender and ordered a vodka martini. "With three olives."

"Straight to the hard stuff, huh?" the guy in the white shirt said.

"Absolutely." I gave him a second friendly smile.

"Long day?"

"It was grueling," I said. "How about you?"

"Relentless." He took a sip of his beer.

"Where do you work?" I asked.

"For the local paper." He studied my expression. "You didn't think there were any reporting jobs left, did you?"

"I ... well, they aren't *all* gone, obviously."

"That's right. But those of us lucky enough. Whew." He laughed.

"Do you like it? Other than the ... I guess too much news and not enough people to cover it?"

"Yeah. Otherwise I wouldn't work for what I'm paid. You gotta love it."

"Why do you love it?"

"The adrenaline. Getting surprised every single day of every week, without fail. Trying to write stories to make people feel something. 'Cuz everyone's so numb." He took several long swallows from his beer bottle.

My martini arrived, and I took a sip to cover my smile, amused that he was sitting there trying to numb himself. "How long have you been doing it?"

"Eight years. What do you do?" he asked.

"I'm between jobs. I'm here on vacation."

"What jobs are you between?"

I told him, in as few words as I could manage, about Fly Higher. Even with my economical use of words, he still looked like most people did when I told them what Fly Higher did.

"Sounds a little ..." After a long pause, he finally said, "Fluffy."

"It does. But it's not."

"Give me the sales pitch."

"I'd rather not. As I said—done with all that."

"Now what?"

I shrugged.

"No idea at all?" He looked a little panicked at the thought. "You're just tasting wine from one end of the valley to the other?"

"I'm here helping my friend with her wedding plans, so I'm trying to focus on that."

He ordered another beer. I took a sip of my martini and ate one of the olives. I vowed I would ask about the murder before I ate the second olive. I would be out of there by the time the third olive was gone.

"Are you her photographer?" he asked.

I laughed. "No." I hadn't considered the idea. I wondered if Tess had. I guessed she would want someone who was a pro, the best in the business, all their experience in the wedding industry. She would want someone used to eliciting smiles and sleek poses, not a photographer who worked overtime to peel off the masks people wore by asking provocative questions.

"Why is that funny?"

"She's a perfectionist. She'll want someone who has experience with weddings." There was no graceful way to change the subject, so I ate my second olive and surged forward. "She's getting married at the Windy Hills Castle."

"Impressive," he said.

"I heard there's a rumor about a murder there."

He laughed softly and fiddled with the top of his beer bottle.

"Why is *that* funny?"

"Because it's a rumor that floats around all the time, but there are never any details. Everyone repeats it, but no one knows anything about it."

"Nothing? Not the year or who the victim was?"

"Zip. Sometimes I get the feeling it was manufactured to damage their reputation. Because all you hear is this persistent story about a murder, but that's it. No one knows anything."

"Have you ever checked your archives for a story about it?"

"Of course."

"And there's nothing?"

"Nope."

"How far back did you go?"

He laughed, sounding noticeably embarrassed. "You'll think I'm a nut job."

"No, I won't."

"I checked all the way back to when we first have records. The early 1900s, long before the castle was built. I wanted to see if there might have been a murder on the property at some point, thinking the story had been twisted somehow. There was nothing."

"Then why do people say that?"

"I have no idea. And it won't die. You can argue with some people and tell them there's no record and they'll tell you it doesn't matter. Someone was murdered, and it's a creepy, haunted place."

"Then why is it so popular for weddings?"

"I don't know. I've put it down to envy. People that can afford it don't believe the rumor, and people who get rejected by their weird acceptance process or who could never afford it, insist it's sinister because of the so-called murder."

I took a long sip of my drink. His theory made sense. But it also seemed like an urban legend that might have been disproved by now. It wasn't as if we were living in the 1950s and people held onto strange superstitions like that. Or maybe they did. Maybe superstitions change shape over time, but they never go away, no matter how sophisticated and educated the human race considers itself. "It makes sense," I said.

After that, he changed the subject, and I let him. There was nothing more to be found out, even from a reporter, which had been a lucky find on my part. If he didn't know, I couldn't imagine I would find anyone else who did.

The thing was, I still half-believed the rumor. Because those screams were very real. They sounded like someone staring at the tip of a sharp knife.

When my glass was empty and my stir stick bare, I told him I'd enjoyed talking to him. He asked for my card. I had one from the Black Mask Winery. I wrote my name and new number on the back and handed it to him. He gave me his card, and I left, wondering if we'd exchanged cards as business contacts, for further discussion of murder rumors, or a possible date. It wasn't entirely clear.

CHAPTER 49

*H*olding the steering wheel with my hands in the driving school position of ten and two p.m., keeping the speedometer at precisely two miles an hour below the speed limit, and using my turn signal religiously, I made my way back to Tess's estate.

I was fully aware that I should be dismissing the murder rumor. It was based on nothing. There wasn't even a name. There was no year. There was no story at all to add credibility. I was aligning myself with what the reporter had determined were envious, spiteful people who wanted to tarnish the reputation of a unique and fascinating structure because they were kept away. But I wasn't envious or spiteful. I was haunted by terrified screams.

I couldn't let go of it.

Rumors don't start out of nothing. If people wanted to throw mud at Ella and Nolan's enterprise, they could find other ways. A murder was a very specific story that had to have roots in something.

After my brain grew tired of turning the same tissue paper-thin fragments over and over until they dissolved into wispy fibers that clung to my mind like cobwebs, I pushed them away. I gripped the wheel with more force and pressed more firmly on the accelerator.

The extra focus on the forward momentum of the car made me realize the headlights in my rearview mirror had been steady for the past two miles or so. I was on a straight road. They hadn't grown larger or smaller, keeping perfectly matched to my speed. Was it possible someone was following me *again*?

I laughed. It wasn't possible. The lights were playing tricks on my eyes. Or my mind was playing tricks on me, unsettled by twisting thoughts and too much free time.

But when I turned onto the road leading to Black Mask and the headlights followed, I wondered if it *was* possible after all. Maybe it was one of the extra vehicles kept in the back, used by the workers for getting around the property or running business errands. Or maybe Silas owned two cars, the flashy Mini Cooper that he drove to work, and another that he used to harass women. Harassment certainly seemed to be his habit.

Was it possible this car had followed me all day? Into the city, then to the bar, but I hadn't noticed until the steady presence of the headlights captured my attention?

I stepped on the accelerator and shot forward, tossing aside my concern about getting pulled over without a driver's license. The lights were too close together, the car obviously too small for it to be a police car.

It immediately sped up, again keeping pace with me. I returned to my careful adherence to the speed limit.

A few minutes later, I drove through the gates at the entrance to Tess's property. The car followed. It was a risky move on their part since a security camera was mounted on the gate, although it was unlikely it would capture the driver.

I pulled up to the garage, hit the remote to open the door, eased Tess's car into its spot, and turned off the engine. The white car remained about twenty yards back, the headlights on bright, making it impossible to see the driver. I sat in Tess's car, waiting to see what would happen.

After two or three minutes had passed, I opened the car door and eased myself out. The moment I stood, my stalker turned quickly around the circular drive and sped back toward the entrance. A moment later, they disappeared from sight.

I gathered my shopping bags from the trunk and went into the house. Before I put my purchases away, I took a photo and texted it to Hunter with a witty comment about shopping. This also elicited silence from him.

After breakfast the next morning, I went to Marcus's office and knocked on his door.

He invited me in and leaned back in his chair.

"I just have a quick question about your security here."

He laughed. "That's the last thing I was expecting."

"What were you expecting?"

"I don't know … wedding plans? Sightseeing questions? Something about winemaking?"

I sat on the sofa and crossed my legs. I didn't want to tell him about Silas. I figured that was between him and Tess. Or maybe it wasn't. He was basically the investor here. The winery was her thing —she was the CEO. He had his own company. So whatever was going on with Silas, even though she made it sound like they both agreed he was essential to their success, I was pretty sure keeping him on was her decision alone.

"I went to the city yesterday, and someone followed me back."

"Followed you?"

"A car followed me into your driveway. It sat there for a few minutes, then left when I started to get out of the car."

"That's strange." He frowned. "Let me check the footage. I'll do it right after lunch."

"Thanks."

"Are you okay?"

"Sure. I was just curious about what you have set up."

"You've probably seen the cameras."

"I have. At the gate, and the doors to the house. Are there others?"

"There are several in the winery itself."

"What about the tasting room?"

"No. Why do you ask?"

"Just curious."

"Any reason?"

"No, I was just wondering if there were any other cameras that might have picked up the driver, in case the gate camera only got the car."

"Oh, I see. Probably not. But we'll get a license plate. Not that it will help much. If they left without doing anything, it might be harmless. People get lost around here all the time—tourists that are making the wine tasting rounds." He laughed and mimed sipping wine. "They make wrong turns."

"But it was almost nine. Don't all the wineries close by six?"

"True, but you never know."

I was thinking that for a cybersecurity expert, Marcus was awfully easygoing about physical threats. He attributed blood-curdling screams to unlikely natural phenomenon and strange cars driving onto his property to tipsy tourists.

I stood. "Thanks for checking the footage. Let me know." I paused, wondering if I should mention the other time I'd been followed. He would take it more seriously for sure, but I didn't really want him getting too interested in what was going on in my life, even though I wanted Silas dealt with.

This might not be Silas at all, and if it was someone I'd known before, someone who had followed me to California, I definitely didn't want Marcus interested in that.

"Thanks."

"You don't have to keep thanking me," he said.

"I know." I wasn't thanking him. I was covering up the fact that I'd entertained and discarded several other thoughts while I stood there. I gave him a grateful smile to put icing on my gushing appreciation.

CHAPTER 50

BEFORE: AMELIA

I loved my dog, Sugar. She was the best gift my mother had ever given me. She tried to convince me Sugar was also a gift from my fake father, but I knew better. Sugar was pure goodness, and that man was pretending to be someone he was not. There was no way he had anything to do with my precious, fun-loving, playful Sugar.

I won't lie and say Sugar didn't keep me company. I was still lonely, but Sugar helped a lot.

Some days, I loved my life. On other days, I hated it so much, I cried myself to sleep.

I knew it wasn't right to live this way. I'd read hundreds of books now that I was thirteen. I knew people lived with other people, not alone with their mother and fake father. I knew that the world was dangerous and bad things happened, but that didn't keep other people from going outside the castle walls and taking their chances.

My mother kept telling me I was a precious, fragile princess. I was pure and unspoiled, and I would stay that way forever. I was the most fabulous princess the world had ever seen.

But the world hadn't *seen* me. It never would.

I hated being a princess. I didn't care if I had a bed with a canopy and a room with sheer, colorful chiffon hanging from iron bars that drifted in the breeze, making it feel like I lived among the clouds. I didn't care that I had so many rooms in my tower and they all belonged to me. It didn't matter at all that no one had ever hit me or pushed me or said something cruel to me or left me alone or made me cry.

I cried almost every day.

"Please let me go out!"

"Don't talk like that, sweetheart," my mother said.

"You're breaking your mother's heart," my fake father said.

"I'm lonely," I wailed. "I'm all alone here!"

My mother put her arms around me and tried to hold me, but I shoved her away.

"You have us. You have Sugar."

"I want more."

"What's making you say these terrible things?" my mother cried. "You have everything any child has ever wanted. Everything."

"I have nothing! I want friends. I want …"

"There are bad people out there," my mother said.

"Very bad people," the man said. "You have no idea. We could tell you, but it would damage you and we don't want to fill your head with ugly things."

I picked up my dinner plate, shoved my chair away from the table, and hurled my plate at the wall behind me. The plate cracked into three pieces and crashed onto the floor. Peas and mashed potatoes, chicken and green salad with its Italian dressing clung to the wall and dripped down slowly.

"You need to clean that up," my fake father said.

I ran out of the dining room, along the hallway to the front of the castle, and down the long, low corridor to the tower entrance. I ran up the stone steps all the way to my room at the top. I threw myself onto the bed. I didn't even have tears for crying. A hot, dry rage burned in my eyes, so the tears sizzled and were gone.

Part of me wanted to throw myself out the tower window. I

wanted to feel myself falling to the ground. It would be a glorious feeling to fly through the air, just for those few seconds until I smashed into the earth.

Instead, I punched the post on my bed. The frame shuddered, and the canopy rippled above me. I punched it three more times until my knuckles ached, hoping it would crack, but it remained solid and strong.

There was nothing I could do to make them listen to me. No matter what I said, they replied with the same words.

There was only one way out. If they couldn't believe they were hurting me, maybe I could hurt them. The only way to do that was to hurt myself.

The next morning, when my mother placed my breakfast in front of me, I told her I wasn't hungry. She urged me to eat, she insisted I eat. Soon, she begged, then demanded that I eat. I refused.

I did the same at lunch and again at dinner. Even when the meal was over and my mother brought out her *treats for her sweets*, I declined.

Every night for as long as I could remember, she had served a fancy dessert she'd made specially for that evening—a cake decorated with fondant flowers, biscotti, chocolate eclairs, Russian teacakes, cream puffs, almond shortbread cookies filled with raspberry jam, macarons, and more.

Dessert was the grand finale of every evening meal. My mother and fake father gazed at each other across the table as they ate their sweets, a look of love in their eyes that sometimes made me wonder if they loved the sugar more than they loved me, despite the sugary words dripping off their tongues.

"Because every day is a celebration of our princess!" my mother said, giving me a smile brimming with devotion, her eyes sparkling with tears.

My fake father wasn't as patient with my refusal to eat. It didn't matter. No matter how much my stomach grumbled, no matter that the aroma of the food made me wild with desire, I refused to eat.

He locked me in my room. I still didn't eat. They took all the books out of my room and wouldn't let Sugar come in to see me. I still refused.

For five days, I didn't eat a single thing. I sipped water and lay in my bed.

My mother was crying every time I saw her. My fake father yelled every time he came into my room. He said I was going to die if I didn't eat. I said I didn't care. He yelled that I was breaking my mother's heart. I whispered that she had broken mine.

On the morning of the sixth day, my mother came into my room carrying a large basket. Inside were two kittens. One was black and one was white. She told me they would be mine if I would eat something.

"I want to leave the castle," I said. "I want friends, not kittens." My voice was so weak, it sounded hoarse, as if it were slipping out of my body.

"You can't leave the castle, Amelia. No matter how angry you are at me. Even if you sometimes feel lonely, I won't risk your safety. I know what's best for you. If you refuse to eat, you can't have the kittens. But you'll never leave the castle."

She turned and walked out of my room, taking the kittens with her.

When she returned that afternoon with buttered toast, a small piece of chocolate, and the basket with the kittens, I ate. I was too weak to play with the kittens, but I smiled, watching them roll around with each other. I wondered what it was like to have a friend.

My mother thought the chocolate and my willingness to eat it, my delight in the kittens meant I'd accepted her steely words that I would never leave the castle.

Never was a very long time. In all the days and months and years of *never* that stretched out ahead of me, there were hours and hours for me to think. And so, when I sat in my garden with my pets, I thought. And when I played games with my mother and that man, I thought. When I put a book on my lap and stared out the tower windows at the valley stretching as far as I could see, I thought. While I was crocheting blankets or knitting scarves, I thought.

Finally, one day, long after my kittens had become cats that slept on their pillows in puddles of sunlight more than they played, I took my knitting to the garden. When I smelled the aroma of my mother cooking dinner, I took a spare knitting needle and began scraping at the mortar around one of the small stones in the garden wall. The stone I chose was hidden behind a section of flowering shrubs planted close to the wall where no one would ever see it. A few flecks of mortar fell onto the ground. With the next rain, they would wash away.

It would take a while, but that was okay. Never was a very, *very* long time.

CHAPTER 51

NOW: ALEX

*M*arcus had texted me a clip from one of their security cameras. It struck me funny that we were in the same house and he texted me instead of trying to find me. I suppose it made sense since he was busy at his desk, but it was still funny. It reminded me of working in the corporate world, receiving emails from co-workers whose office doors were fifteen feet from mine.

The clip showed only what I'd expected. A white car, the same license plate I'd clocked when it followed me as I jogged along the main road, and the bottom section of the windshield, not even close to capturing anything identifying about the person driving. There wasn't even a flash of clothing that might indicate whether the driver was male or female.

I watched it three times and saw nothing. Less than nothing. Marcus sent a follow-up text assuring me it was most likely a confused tourist, as he'd suspected. In fact, they probably thought they were following a traveling companion and only realized their mistake when I got out of the car.

It seemed like a lot of explaining to make something fit around a situation that looked entirely different from my perspective. Of course, in fairness to Marcus, I'd left out half the information.

My question about security hadn't just been about getting a video clip of the car. I hadn't expected it to show more than what I'd seen with my own eyes in the darkness. What I'd really wanted to know was whether there was a security camera anywhere near the tasting room. Better yet, inside the tasting room.

Because I was working on a way to be rid of Silas.

Odds were good that he was the one who had followed me. He was definitely the type who wanted to intimidate. And following someone with a car when she's running, and then home from a bar in the dark, are both obvious attempts at intimidation.

Tess wasn't going to fire him for assaulting her house guest, her best friend, her maid of honor. She expected me to stay away from him. She expected me to brush it off. She expected me to understand. But what was I supposed to understand? That he was such an asset his predatory behavior should be overlooked?

Clearly, I couldn't resort to my normal method of dealing with problems of this nature. I wanted to. I absolutely wanted to rid this small section of the world of a slug like Silas, but Tess wouldn't have that at all. It would have been so satisfying to turn the tables on him. To let him kiss me, and more. To see the shock in his face, the utter victory in his eyes when I allowed myself to be swept away by him—for a single moment before that light went out forever. But Tess would know in a minute that I was involved.

Closing my eyes, I allowed myself to entertain the fantasy of slipping something into a glass of Black Mask Pinot Noir and handing it to Silas. I imagined his leering smile and his greedy sips, his lizard tongue licking his lips. I imagined his sagging smile when he realized he didn't have to put forth so much effort now that I was acting enthralled with him.

I imagined watching him drift to sleep as I got to work. I could see him taking his last breath as I walked away, feeling light and free, as I always did, the world a cleaner, less troubled place, if only for half a second, half a day, if only for one person for one moment in time.

But I wouldn't be able to walk away free.

Why, lately, did my life feel heavier and more tangled? As if the people I'd killed had their hands around my wrists, keeping me from breaking free, grabbing my ankles, preventing me from moving forward, and worst of all, their hands around my throat, squeezing the oxygen out of my lungs?

It was too much. I needed to focus my attention on the immediate problem. If I was going to stay indefinitely at Tess's, which it looked like I might, I needed Silas out of there. And it couldn't be in a body bag.

So my thoughts had drifted to cameras, to asking Marcus if they protected their tasting room with a carefully concealed camera. They did not, or so he'd said. With a camera of my own, I might catch Silas doing something unforgivable with a customer. I had no doubt he would do *something*. If he hadn't already, and surely he had, it was only a matter of time before he did something again.

I was annoyed with myself for not thinking this through when I'd been in San Francisco where a camera would have been easy to purchase. In Napa, it might be more challenging. I didn't want to take the chance of ordering one and having it shipped to the house. Any package was sure to invite Tess's curiosity. And Silas had a serious lack of boundaries. If the timing was wrong, he might encounter a delivery person and the package could end up in his aggressive, prying fingers.

My thoughts were interrupted by a text message. I picked up my phone, expecting that Hunter had finally responded to my selfies. He hadn't. It was from Diana. It had taken her long enough.

She'd received my email and had needed time to *process it*.

Controlling move number one.

She wanted to set up a video call to discuss what I'd written. Apparently, she couldn't graciously say goodbye. We needed to *talk* about it.

Controlling move number two.

CHAPTER 52

I replied to Diana's message that I would get back to her. I was prompt, she had not been. Now, she could wait—a controlling move of my own.

Rescuing Tess from the viper in her tasting room was at the top of my priority list. I couldn't find out whether or not there was a body hidden in the castle. I couldn't get access to the towers—yet. And I didn't have a clue who had been screaming in terror. I did not know why Hunter was ignoring me.

Well, maybe I had a small idea.

For now, one thing I could do, one thing I knew how to do, was to save Tess from Silas, and really, from herself.

It seemed like I'd had an experience of precognition rather than some weird manifestation of OCD when I'd spent my recuperation period writing down the times Silas arrived for work and when he left at the end of the day. Because of that exercise, I now had a detailed log telling me the best time to hover near the door of the tasting room in order to watch him enter the security code.

If I'd asked Tess for the code, she would have given it to me. But she also would have asked why I wanted it.

That evening I dressed in jeans, boots that resembled something a Harley owner might wear, a black T-shirt and my leather jacket. It was slightly warm for my leather jacket, even in the cool air just after sunset, but I wanted to look like I was dressed in a suit of armor. I wanted to look buckled and zipped up and unapproachable.

At six-twenty, I went out Tess's front door, knowing Silas would be leaving the tasting room in the next three to four minutes. I crossed the patio and walked past the front garden to the tasting room terrace. Just as my foot touched the flagstones of the terrace, the tasting room door opened and Silas came out, right on schedule.

Because I was behind the shrubbery that edged the left side of the terrace, he didn't see me. He pulled the door closed, and I approached quickly and stealthily just as his index finger touched the keypad to enter the code.

A moment later, I was directly behind him, my head tilted slightly as he entered the six digits—002864. It was an easy sequence to remember with the throwaway zeros at the start.

I spoke, certain that startling him before he saw me would make him less likely to realize what I was up to. "Hi, Silas." My voice dripped with honey.

He turned suddenly, a scowl on his face. "What do *you* want?"

"I wanted to browse the gift shop."

"Too late."

"Aww. I was really hoping to find a souvenir."

"Are you leaving California?"

"Not yet."

"Then it can wait."

He began walking toward the covered parking area and his sharp looking Mini Cooper. I followed, hoping to rattle him enough that it would never enter his mind that I'd been standing behind him when he entered the security code.

"Tess tells me you're the key to making the winery a success."

"It's already a success."

"An even greater success."

He shrugged.

"You don't seem very confident."

He gave me an outraged look. He was obviously upset that I would ever think he wasn't the smartest guy on the property, the only one here who knew how to market wine to eager drinkers, making them believe Black Mask offered the most complex and satisfying taste they could find in the entire Napa Valley, possibly in the state of California.

"Is there something you want?"

"A souvenir."

"As I already told you, but I guess you're a little thick, it's too late." He got into his car, slammed the door, and started the engine.

I moved out of the way, and he gunned the engine. He backed up fast as if he hoped to plow into me, then accelerated down the driveway and disappeared from sight.

Apparently, biting his tongue had done the trick. He was going to keep his distance from me.

Instead of risking another unlicensed drive in Tess's car, I called an Uber the following morning. I went to the computer store I'd researched—one that offered the type of security camera I needed. With Mr. Cybersecurity working from his home office, I couldn't risk getting a camera that connected to their Wi-Fi. Marcus would surely notice a new device sneaking onto his network, filming things he hadn't intended to film. Although he absolutely should have been filming more than he was.

For less than two hundred dollars, they set me up with a camera the size of my fist. It would connect to my phone's hotspot, which they were nice enough to walk me through. I would be able to watch Silas whenever I chose.

As women came through the tasting room, dropped off from limos to celebrate bachelorette parties and moms' getaways, and girls'-only day drinking, I would be watching him.

CHAPTER 53

$\mathcal{A}$t a little after one in the morning, I slipped out of bed, dressed in yoga clothes and running shoes, and picked up the camera and the small electric drill I'd bought. I went downstairs, dropping a large slice of mango between the bars of Damien's aviary to keep his mouth full, hoping he didn't need to comment on the mango itself. He didn't look completely awake and seemed happy to eat the mango in silence.

I went out the door that led from the pantry into the side garden. It was the only door without a security camera. I wasn't sure why, but the only reason I could figure out was that the area outside the door was fenced to contain their garbage and recycling bins, so maybe they assumed someone looking to break in wouldn't be aware it was even there. The door wasn't visible if you were walking around the house looking for points of access.

Getting the camera aligned so it captured the center of the bar where Silas spent the majority of his time when he was pouring wine, took longer than I'd planned. I wouldn't be able to capture everything because he often moved about the room, spent time on the terrace, and helped customers in the gift shop. I had to hope for the best. Besides, it wasn't as if he was an artist at discretion. He was aggressive and abundantly sure of himself. I suspected there wasn't a week that went by where he didn't hit on a woman in the tasting room, subtly or otherwise. I was genuinely surprised there hadn't been any complaints.

Of course, how many women out for a day of wine tasting assumed that it went with the territory, or they were so used to it, they never bothered to mention it? They didn't want to spoil their day by complaining about something that happened every damn day of their lives.

When my head finally sank peacefully into my fluffy pillow, it was after two thirty in the morning. Still, I was awake again at six, ready for a run. My ankle felt stronger every day, and I wanted to re-start my effort to work my way up to ten miles before I returned to New York to close out my life with Eileen, and decide what I planned to do about Hunter, if he hadn't already decided that for me.

Now, we'd reached the point that I was also playing the silence game. The ball, or rather, the selfies, was in his court. I was pretty sure he wasn't so petty he wanted to stop seeing each other because he'd had his feelings hurt. Sooner or later, he would be over it.

In the meantime, I had other things to occupy my mind.

I ran along the main road adjacent to Tess and Marcus's estate. I still wasn't ready to try the hill up to the castle again, although it called to me like a siren song.

After an easy jog for about a mile and a half, I turned back. As I ran, I began to feel the creeping sensation along my spine that someone was following me again. I tried to shake it off, certain it was simply becoming a habitual feeling because it had happened too often.

My mind flashed back to the sidewalks of New York when Ned had followed me to Hunter's apartment, not believing Hunter was real.

The feeling persisted, growing more intense. Finally, I yielded and turned my head. The shoulder of the road behind me was deserted. The fields were empty except for a tractor in the far distance. Cars were passing on the highway, but none were going at a slower than expected speed. They zipped by and were gone.

I faced forward and resumed my pace.

After the way Silas had behaved the day before, I wondered if I'd been wrong to think he was the one following me, trying to upset me because his ego had been bruised, or because he didn't like having me around. He'd reacted strangely from the moment we'd first met, but still. Maybe he wasn't the one following.

Maybe, thinking about Ned, this had nothing to do with California and the animosity I'd managed to stir up since I'd arrived. This might be about animosity I'd attracted in New York. And there'd been quite a lot of that. Starting with Ned Carter.

How difficult would it have been for him to guess that a random text on his phone from a woman who was found stabbed in an open grave might have been engineered by another woman he'd been harassing and harping at for months?

Surely, he would have wondered at the completely random nature of a message from a woman he'd never met, never even seen, that brought the police to his door. Once they realized there was no connection and stopped asking him questions about her death, he would have had plenty of time to brood over how that could have happened. He wasn't a stupid man.

Might he have guessed I had something to do with it?

Even if he hadn't guessed, might he wonder? And without a fiancée to keep him busy, what was to prevent him from hopping on a plane to California? He could have easily discovered the name of Tess's winery from Eileen.

Why not repeat his same, foolish, artless method of trying to disrupt my life as he had a month earlier?

It would explain the nondescript nature of the car—a rental. A man with time on his hands. Not doing anything to hurt me, simply following. Trying to scare me, *hoping* to scare me. He had no plan. But he thought he could upset my life with a silly game.

It also made me extremely concerned. If he had put those things together, he would wonder about my connection to Carolina's murder. This could turn into something far worse than a car trying to intimidate me while I was running, than someone trying to punish me for rejecting him.

I might have been too bold, trying to mess with Ned's life. There had been no need to involve him in Carolina's death. And now I might as well have dropped breadcrumbs from Carolina's grave across the continental United States to Tess's front door.

Without slowing my pace, I turned my head slightly, glancing behind. No one was there. I'd worked out an entire scenario of who might be following me, and right now, no one was, in fact, following me. I *felt* followed, but I was alone.

I ran for another half mile, but the feeling persisted. It was so strong, I slowed and came to a stop. I did a full 360-degree turn, scanning the field beside me, the road that seemed to stretch endlessly behind, shimmering with a mirage as it rose over a slight incline before appearing to fade into the sky. I looked at the modern concrete and glass winery across from me with a long, straight road lined with palm trees leading to the front. I scanned the road ahead of me.

Nothing suggested anyone was paying the slightest bit of attention to me.

All my physical senses told me that no one was following me. But my "spidey" sense insisted there was. It wasn't simply my experiences with Nolan. It wasn't only my disgust with Silas and the certainty he was going to engineer the failure of Tess's dreams for the winery. It wasn't even the memory of Ned and my too-late realization that my desire to punish him might have offered him a clue to what I did when no one was watching.

There was a physical sensation that wouldn't let go of me.

CHAPTER 54

I continued jogging, feeling as if something clung to my back. The desire to see the shadow I sensed with such certainty was overwhelming. I ran faster, mostly confident my ankle would hold. I hadn't felt even the slightest twinge of weakness the entire time I'd been jogging.

I turned onto the road which would take me to the castle. If someone was running behind me, maybe starting up the hill would force them to reveal their presence. If it was a car I hadn't noticed, there would be minimal traffic on the road up to the castle and a lone white car would stand out.

It felt good to push myself harder again, to feel my heart pounding and the sweat forming on the back of my neck. I took in deep breaths, making sure I hugged the edge of the road, finally moving onto the road itself. If a car came, I would hear it in time to move back onto the shoulder. I wasn't taking the chance of sliding into the gully again.

The closer I got to the castle, the less I thought about my follower and the more I thought about the rumored murder. What would happen if I asked Nolan or Ella about it? They wouldn't admit to knowing anything, but what might their expressions tell me? It wouldn't surprise me at all if one, or both of them, were killers. Their cold certainty suggested they had that capability. As they say, it takes one to know one.

Maybe the reason no one knew the details was because someone had whispered about a murder but was afraid to say more.

The gates at the entrance were locked, of course. I stopped before I entered the range of the security camera. I studied the razor wire fencing, trying to figure out whether I dared to slip between the wires. It looked like it wouldn't be that hard. But if it wasn't that hard, then it wasn't very effective, so it must be more difficult than it appeared.

I walked toward the wire and studied the fierce-looking barbs. One wrong step as I bent over and tried to creep through and I could rip a tear in my arm that would leave a scar for the rest of my life. If I lost my footing, I might end up tearing off the side of my face. I shuddered.

I turned back and studied the gate. It looked easy enough to climb over, if I could figure out a way to avoid the camera.

As I stood watching the camera move from side-to-side, sweeping its mechanical eye across the road, I saw how I could get the upper hand. Unless it was monitored live at all times, I only had to disable it for half an hour. That would allow me to climb over the gate, walk up to the castle, investigate the wall around that area where I'd heard someone's voice, and make my escape.

I was wearing capri jogging pants and a T-shirt over a sports bra. I pulled off my T-shirt and inched my way along the razor wire fence. I moved sideways with my back to the gate toward the camera, which was mounted on the gatepost where the two sides came together at the center. I tossed my shirt over the camera. It floated down over the lens. I climbed over the gate with its intricate ironwork that offered perfect footholds.

I was in.

Veering off the main drive, I followed the footpath that wound among the guest cottages toward the castle. Once I reached the gardens surrounding the castle, I let my mind spin out a dramatic story about how I'd been followed and the *fear that had gripped me* so that I could play the damsel in distress if I ran into Ella or Nolan.

I made my way to the wall surrounding the tower at the left where I'd heard the voice several days earlier. I leaned against the wall, straining for the sound of someone talking, for any suggestion of human activity on the other side. I heard nothing.

After standing there for ten or fifteen minutes, I began to walk slowly around, dragging my hand along the smooth stones and the grainy mortar holding them in place. It was almost mesmerizing, feeling the textures change as I walked around the entire enclosure. It surprised me there was no gate. The shape of it made me think the area inside was quite large and I couldn't understand why they wouldn't want a way in and out to the other gardens beyond.

When I reached the back, I reversed direction, once again trailing my hand across the stones.

About a third of the way around the wall, my index finger caught on something. I stopped and pulled my finger away. The mortar was loose and crumbling around a small stone, about the size of a white potato. I rubbed at it, brushing away the crumbling mortar. I wiggled the stone, and it came out in my hand. I put my face close to the wall, pressing my brow against the surrounding stones to see through the opening.

I could see enough to know that it went all the way through, that I was looking into a mass of greenery. Beyond, I could make out a lawn and the trunk of a tree. That was it.

Pulling away, I blinked to clear my eyes. I rubbed them gently, then put my face close to the wall again. It wasn't any better. I couldn't make out anything but green and possibly a glimpse of the tower wall on the opposite side.

I straightened. I replaced the stone, certain that it needed to be hidden from the vigilant attention of Nolan and Ella. I found a distinctive rock in the garden and placed it at the base of the wall so I would remember where the opening was. I had no idea how it would help me. It wasn't as if that absurdly small opening would give me access to the garden or to the tower itself, but I didn't want to forget where it was.

Continuing around the wall, I tried to think about what it meant. Someone had scraped away all that mortar. Laboriously. Who had put all that time and effort into making such a small, useless opening in the wall? And why?

Just as I reached the place where the garden wall joined the front of the castle, I came face-to-face with Nolan.

For several seconds, he stared at me with cold, dark eyes. He seemed unsurprised to see me. "I warned you," he said.

"It's not ..." I gulped, then breathed out all the air in my lungs so that my voice would find a tremor. "Someone was following me. It's the second time. He tried to run me off the road. I was scared so I—"

He took hold of my upper arm.

I leaned against him as if I were glad of the support. "I didn't know where to go."

"You don't have a phone?"

"I do but ..."

"But what?"

"I wasn't ... I was so scared." My voice trembled beautifully, like a songbird warbling in the garden.

"Of what?"

"I ... I don't know."

He seemed to relax slightly as I continued to lean into him, stumbling as he strode away from the castle. "You're trespassing. And I warned you."

"I know. But I—"

"Yes. You said. You were *so very scared*."

"Would it be asking too much to beg you for a ride? I'm afraid to continue my run. Tess owns the Black Mask Winery. I guess you know that."

"I do."

"Would you mind giving me a ride back? I'd be so, so grateful." I leaned harder into him, causing him to lose his balance and step to the side.

"Fine."

He went to the SUV parked beside his motorcycle, opened the passenger door, and walked around to the driver's side. He didn't speak until we were at the gates and they were opening. "Is that your shirt?" He put the car in park, got out, and grabbed my shirt off the camera.

He climbed back in, tossed the shirt at me, and drove through the gates. "For someone in fear for her life, you were awfully clever about sneaking onto our property."

"I wasn't sure what to do."

"It looks like the opposite—you were absolutely sure what to do."

"I didn't. Honestly, I was—"

"You do know that the motion of the shirt activated the camera? I received an alert."

We drove down the hill at a speed that felt somewhat unsafe. When he turned onto the main road, I asked him to tell me the story of how he and Ella had met.

He seemed unaware that I'd heard him tell the story at the champagne reception.

In a sharp, almost robotic tone, he repeated word-for-word the story Ella had rolled out for Tess and me. It had sounded silly when Ella told the story. Coming out of Nolan's mouth now, without the adoring eyes of Ella and her encouraging nods as she stood beside him in her old-fashioned bridal gown, hearing him try, once again, to turn a chance meeting into a fairy tale, sounded troubling in a way I couldn't put my finger on. Maybe it was hearing him describe the ray of sunlight breaking through thick clouds, circling him and causing his hair to shimmer like gold, transforming him into a Greek god. That was deeply disturbing coming from his own lips. Something felt off.

CHAPTER 55

The following morning, I checked what had been recorded so far on the camera I'd installed in the tasting room. I told myself I needed to keep on top of the recordings or they would pile up and I wouldn't have time to watch them all. I also told myself not to expect anything. It had been only twenty-four hours.

And yet, clearly I had expected something because I was irritated as I watched Silas pouring wine, making polite conversation, keeping a professional distance from all the women who entered the tasting room, even one who flirted with him for several minutes. When he didn't respond, she persisted, but he remained aloof.

I deleted what the camera had captured and told myself to be patient. A man who had behaved as badly as Silas had from the moment he first spoke to me was not going to avoid displaying his true nature on camera for long. In fact, it was possible he'd rejected the flirting because he preferred women who didn't respond to him. He had no interest in having any kind of normal, equal relationship. He wanted power. He was searching for a woman he believed he could dominate, or use for some other purpose.

It was possible his aggressive moves toward me had nothing to do with sex and everything to do with my relationship to Tess and Marcus.

I went downstairs to the workout room and spent an hour lifting weights and another thirty minutes doing yoga. When I was finished, there were three text messages from Hunter on my new phone.

Because it had been several days of silence, I decided I wanted time to read them with a clear head. I took a shower. I put on a black top with thin satin straps, jeans, and makeup in case we decided to video chat. I made a large salad with turkey and avocado, sliced almonds and bits of soft goat cheese. I took the salad and a glass of sparkling water out to the patio and settled down to read his messages.

Hunter: *You seem busy.*

Hunter: *I'm not into long-distance relationships.*

Hunter: *You didn't strike me as the passive-aggressive type.*

I laughed at the last one. I supposed I could be considered passive-aggressive. But I didn't think I was doing that with him. I wasn't even sure what he was referring to. Was it because I wouldn't tell him my plans? Was that passive aggressive? I didn't think so, but it was hard to say.

The screen went dark. Usually, responding to his messages didn't require a lot of thought. But this time, I wasn't sure what I wanted to say. And I wasn't sure which one to respond to first. Did the series of three mean the last one was the only one that really mattered? Did they indicate a change in the direction of his thoughts and the thing he really wanted to say, the thing he wanted to discuss most of all was my aggression?

I took a few bites of salad while I tried to figure it out. I sipped my water. Clearly, I could disregard the first message. The second one seemed to be feeling me out as to whether I was planning to return at all. I decided I could ignore it for now.

Alex: *Why do you think I'm passive aggressive?*

Hunter: *If you want to break up, just say so.*

So there it was. Message number two and message number three were the same, even though he'd already asked me that question. It seemed he'd been brooding about it.

Alex: *I don't want to break up.*

Hunter: *That's not the impression you're giving.*

Alex: *I wasn't aware I was giving an impression.*

There was no reply. I ate several more bites of salad, but there was still no reply. This was a conversation we should be having face-to-face, but I didn't see my phone burbling with a call, and I was busy eating. Sometimes, texting is more fun, because the forced delay sends things in an entirely different direction. So maybe, this time, it was better to leave it alone, despite my nice top and makeup.

My salad was gone, and the screen was still dark. I finished my water. I moved to a lounge chair, shifted one of the deck umbrellas to shade me, and settled back.

Alex: *It's really good to have a break from work. And I need to figure out my career.*

Hunter: *I get that.*

Alex: *Good.*

Hunter: *I just don't see the point in having a relationship if we aren't together. And if you don't plan to live in New York.*

Alex: *I haven't made any decisions yet.*

Hunter: *So I don't factor into your decisions?*

Alex: *I have to figure out what I want to do.*

Hunter: *You seem to have a chaotic decision-making process.*

I sent him the shrugging emoji.

Hunter: *I'm curious why you started a relationship with me if you weren't planning to stick around.*

Alex: *I wasn't planning to leave.*

Hunter: *Thinking back, you were very determined to go out with me.*

That was a strange thing to say. Why was he *thinking back*? What was he talking about?

Alex: *Was I? Determined?*

Hunter: *Yes.*

Alex: *I am that.*

He didn't respond again. But the ball was still definitely in his court. I just wasn't sure it would ever be returned.

CHAPTER 56

PORTLAND, OREGON

*M*y hopeful anticipation that my mother would be so pleased with my sewing skills she would eagerly persuade my father to view my dress with pride collapsed the moment she saw it.

"Your father won't be happy about this."

"I did it myself."

"Obviously."

"Aren't the stitches perfect? They're so tiny, just like—"

"Your father said you couldn't have glitter and flashy jewels. It's wrong to draw attention to yourself like that."

I reminded her of the gems and gold in the bible. She glared at me as if I were committing blasphemy. "It's not the same."

"Why not?" If I couldn't get her on my side, there was no hope with my father. She was the one who was supposed to convince him. She was the one who was supposed to tell him what a beautiful, womanly seamstress I was. She would point out how I'd learned so much, how I'd listened carefully and followed all the instructions.

"Those verses are talking about the new city where we'll live for eternity. This dress …" She held it away from her as if it smelled like something she'd pulled from the bottom of last week's rotting garbage. "This is to make yourself look wealthy and important. It's to make yourself look like you're in a higher position than everyone else. We're told to humble ourselves."

"There are kings in the bible!"

"God appoints rulers. We don't make ourselves into kings."

"It says we're—"

"I'm not going to argue about it with you." She rolled the dress into a tight ball. "Not only did you disobey your father's clear instructions, you went sneaking around behind our backs. I'm so disappointed. You make my heart hurt." She closed her eyes. Without opening them, she whispered, "Where did you get these things? They're cheap and tawdry." She let out a half-choked sob. "This dress looks like it belongs to a whore now." She clapped her hand over her mouth, then let it fall away slowly. "I mean a—"

"I know what a whore is," I said.

"You don't."

I stared at her.

She blinked back tears and turned away.

I knew they would both be startled by all the things I'd learned at the library. It truly was a treasure house. I also knew she was not on my side. This was worse than ever. I couldn't understand why she was doing this. But I was never sure with her. Sometimes she was on my side, sometimes she was on his. It was confusing and I couldn't always figure out what it was that tipped her one way or the other.

Clenching the dress, she walked out of the room.

I thought she was throwing it in the trash and that would be the end of my chance to attend the harvest festival. I thought about my beautiful mask hiding inside my B+ report. But she had another punishment in mind. She'd spent too much time around my father to let me off so easily.

That evening, when I walked into the dining room, my parents were already seated at the table. Tom had gone to a friend's house for dinner. Since my two older brothers were away at college now, I was alone with my parents. My princess dress was on a hanger, hooked to the light fixture above the table, the skirt pooled at the center of the table, the bowls of food arranged around it like some kind of offering to a headless goddess.

"Please take your seat," my father said.

I did.

My father began praying. Although I expected the prayer to include a detailed description of my sins, it didn't. He focused on gratitude for our food. When he was finished, my mother served our food. We ate in silence for several minutes.

Finally, my father spoke. "You disobeyed me."

I explained to him about the sapphires and rubies and amethysts in the heavenly city.

He stared at me as if I were letting a string of curse words roll off my tongue.

"Are you finished?"

"Do you remember that part? And the streets of gold? And all the kings and the—"

"That's enough." He put down his utensils. "I told you there would be no glorifying yourself with worldly ideas. I told you what kind of dress you would wear. I told you no crown."

"But I don't have a—"

"No jewels. This is not a party where you'll be dancing with the devil!" His voice rose a touch. "It's a harvest festival. To celebrate the food provided in god's creation. Which I already feared was a misguided idea, but we'll see. Now ..." He wiped his mouth with his napkin and placed it on the table.

He stood and unhooked the dress from the light fixture. He turned to the sideboard and pulled open the drawer. He took out a tiny pair of scissors and handed them to me. "I want all these cheap, flashy stones and fringe cut off. If you cut the fabric while you're removing them, your mother will make patches you can sew on. That is the dress you'll wear to the harvest festival. There will be no crown, no jewels. And certainly no mask to hide behind. You will go as a humble servant girl. Your mother has a scarf you can wear over your hair." He left the room.

I spent the rest of the evening cutting off all the things I'd sewn onto my beautiful dress. I didn't make any cuts in the fabric, so there was no need for patches, but it still looked strange. There were little puckered spots and tiny holes where the stitches had been pulled out, and a few knots remaining where I'd tied the ends of the thread. Those had been hidden beneath the gems, but now they were exposed.

The dress looked limp and tired.

While I cut, I considered my options.

As the last piece of fringe fell off the dress, an idea came to me. I still had my mask, and I still had a way to look like a princess. I took the largest ruby and tucked it into my sock. I threw the rest of the gems and fringe into the trash while my parents watched.

CHAPTER 57

BEFORE: AMELIA

J was fifteen years old, but in some ways, I only knew this because I'd been told. I had a calendar in my classroom, but sometimes I didn't look at it for days, maybe weeks. My mother reminded me what day it was. She instructed me to include the date on the papers I had to write about history and the book reports I produced for her and my fake father. But the dates meant nothing to me.

We celebrated holidays and birthdays. Aside from those, the rest of the days ran together like melting ice cream. Even the birthday cake with the candles every year felt like something that appeared without a clear mark in time. There was no time. There was sunrise and sunset. There was schoolwork. There were books. There were movies and games. There was sitting in the garden and knitting. There was dreaming and playing with my pets.

But time was like water flowing around me, never taking shape because it didn't fit into anything. It felt slippery and unreal.

So yes, I was fifteen. But if you never think about your age or who you are and there are no other people around, maybe you forget who you are.

My life felt like something very different from the lives of people who lived in books and movies. I felt as if I lived in another sort of universe. I wondered if someone would travel through time, like I saw in some movies. They would step through a rip in the fabric of the universe and find me existing in this castle. They would take me with them to the future, or the past. Anywhere but now.

There were others. I knew that.

Lots of others.

Almost every weekend, there were big parties at the castle. Weddings, my mother said. But I couldn't see the people on the terrace. The windows on my tower faced toward the front of the castle and the valley. I saw people walking around the cottages on the castle property. I heard music, but whatever happened on the back terrace was a mystery. Whatever happened in the grand hall or the dining room was invisible to me. Sometimes I heard cheers. I heard music and talking. I saw cars coming and going. I saw people enter the castle. I bakery vans arrive. I saw chairs and tables and boxes, but I couldn't know what was inside.

After a while, I stopped watching. It was too hard. And they couldn't see me. People looked up at the towers, but the walls were thick and they couldn't see me behind the window. Even if the windows were open, I couldn't lean out.

I was tired. The only things that made me happy were Sugar and my cats—Salt and Pepper. I don't know why my pets were named after condiments, but that's how it turned out. I loved them with all my heart. Because there was no one else, all the love that existed in me flowed out to them.

My mother—I couldn't say anymore how I felt about her. I needed her, I suppose, to keep me alive. To have someone to talk to. Otherwise I might lose my mind.

My fake father? When I was fifteen, I was suddenly tired of listening to him lie about being my father. Just sick of it. Sick, sick, sick. How many years can someone tell the same lie when it's so obvious it's a lie? Did he think I was stupid? I guess he did. I guess she did too.

I was so tired of not saying I knew they were lying, because they became so furious when I said it was a lie.

But by the time I was fifteen, I had spent years thinking about something else. My real father and I had the same red hair. This finally made me realize something else that was wrong with my fake father.

The inside of our castle was filled with shadows. And my mother liked to use candles instead of turning on all the lights, so it had taken me a long time to notice that the color of my fake father's hair changed from time to time. Every so often, it looked a little brighter. It shimmered more. And then it faded. Then it would get bright again.

I knew about hair dye. I think my mother and that man weren't always aware that I knew some things. Maybe they forgot how many things about the world that I wasn't allowed to visit were written in stories. I knew people could change the color of their hair.

Once I recognized he was dying his hair to make himself look like my father, that he thought I was such a stupid little girl when he moved in that all I would notice was his red hair, I couldn't look at him at all anymore.

I stopped looking at him. I stopped speaking to him.

When we ate dinner, my mother talked. I answered her questions. She talked some more. Sometimes they talked to each other. It was very strange. Some nights, we all ate and no one said a single word. It was eerie.

After dinner, in the summer, they would go out to the terrace with a glass of wine.

I went into my garden with Sugar and Salt and Pepper. I took my knitting project. I removed one of the needles and went to work on my more important project. She never saw how the needles got damaged. She was in the habit of buying me so many craft projects over the years. Whatever I wanted, she ordered for me. My rooms were filled with paints and paper, modeling clay and fabric and needles and yarn and embroidery floss. When you're locked in a tower alone, you need things to keep you busy. I guess she realized that.

I took the damaged needles and hid them in the trash. She didn't seem to notice.

I had to be careful not to get scratched up when I worked on my project or she would notice. I scraped carefully, knowing that one day, it might be a very long time, but one day, the rock would come loose.

I wasn't really sure what would happen once I removed the rock, but maybe … maybe I could find someone to talk to outside the wall.

CHAPTER 58

NOW: ALEX

*D*espite never having seen a single hint of anyone following me before I'd snuck onto the grounds of the Windy Hills Castle, I was absolutely certain I *had* been followed. Maybe my stalker, or whatever he or she should rightfully be called, had gotten more clever. Maybe I'd missed something.

It didn't matter. I wasn't going to doubt my intuition. I'd felt someone noticing me and that was not a feeling I had without some basis in reality. It wasn't that paranoia never crept into my mind, but it wasn't running wild in there.

I'd definitely discarded the possibility of Silas, and had settled on Ned. I didn't like thinking about what that might mean, but the first step was to find out if I was right.

I sent a text to Eileen asking how she was doing in the apartment on her own. I told her I was up for a video chat if she wanted a mini virtual tour of the garden at a Napa Valley Winery. She'd never been out of New York City. For someone who lived in one of the most thrilling cities in the world, her life had been sheltered. I figured she would be excited to see a winery up close, even if it didn't include vines or the bottling facility.

While I waited for her to reply, I checked out Tess's Pinterest board for her wedding. She'd been reminding me every other day since I'd arrived to look at it so I could see her colors and themes, moods and dreams. It was entertaining scrolling through her pinned images, but it also made my brain feel like it might explode because it seemed as if she might have enough ideas for three or four weddings. I wondered if she was aware of that.

Looking at pictures of women in matching dresses from strangers' weddings made me curious about the others who would be standing around beside me, holding flowers while Tess and Marcus promised to love each other right into their graves.

I laughed at my morbid thought. I shouldn't have pictured it that way, but it had always seemed strange that death was there front and center in a marriage ceremony. Couldn't couples simply promise to love each other forever and leave it at that? Why did they find it necessary to be so specific? It was almost as if they wanted to be clear that they had the option of finding someone else if the other one dropped dead.

It was an open invitation to dispose of the other early if married life wasn't to your liking after all.

A message from Eileen appeared on the screen, blocking out seven women in silver, off-the-shoulder dresses.

Eileen: *I'd love to talk and see Tess's garden!*

I closed Pinterest and called her.

She looked more relaxed than she had when I'd last seen her. I wondered if she appreciated me for removing Ned from her life.

"How's California?" Eileen asked.

"Sunny and warm. I've been hanging out in a castle."

She laughed. "Seriously?"

I told her about the castle, leaving out the murder and the screaming, the strange owners and the small hole in the garden wall.

"Ready for your tour? I can walk out to the vineyard and show you a real live grapevine, if you've never seen one."

"I haven't. That would be amazing."

I put in my earbuds and walked down the stairs while she told me what she'd been up to.

Once I reached the back patio, I removed the earbuds and slipped them into my pocket. I flipped the camera to show her the back of the house, the patio, and then slowly scanned the garden. She made appreciative sounds at everything I showed her.

I stepped off the patio and began walking along the path toward the first vineyard. It was surprisingly close to the house, less than a hundred yards from the low fence that surrounded the garden. As I showed her the vines, she asked me all kinds of questions about wine making, none of which I could answer.

"I should probably take a tour, but I haven't had a chance yet." I began walking back to the patio.

"What have you been *doing*?" she asked. "It's been weeks."

I settled on the lounge chair and told her about my sprained ankle, the champagne reception, the cake tasting. It seemed to satisfy her, even though those things had taken a fraction of my time.

I flipped the camera back so she could see my face. "Has Ned left you alone?"

"Don't be like that," she said.

"Like what?"

"Just because he … I know he was creepy, but he's still …"

"Still what? A good guy?" I laughed.

"No. But I don't want to talk trash about him."

"Have you heard from him?"

"Actually, yes. It was really weird. He was upset. Some woman he'd never heard of sent him a text message about getting together. Then the police showed up and said she'd been murdered, so they were asking him all these questions."

"Wow. That's … he didn't know her at all?"

"No. He'd never even seen her, never heard her name. Nothing."

"How did he know he'd never seen her? Did he see her body?"

"You're awful, sometimes." She made a face. "They showed him pictures of her."

"Dead?"

"No! Of course not."

"What ended up happening?"

"Nothing. They decided it was a wrong number."

"And he's still in New York?"

"Of course. Why would you ask that?"

"When was the last time you saw him?"

"I haven't seen him since we broke up. Why do you want to know?"

"Just curious."

She tilted her head and looked at me in disbelief. "Curious, why?"

"I just wondered if he was trying to get back with you."

"No, you weren't wondering that. Why are you asking? Did you hear from him?"

"No."

"Then why are you asking about him? I thought you wanted nothing to do with him? Why do you care?"

"I don't. I was just checking on how things are going."

"It feels like you want to know something, but I'm not sure what."

I laughed. "You know me. If I wanted to know something, I'd ask."

She laughed, but she looked unsure.

I changed the subject to Tess's wedding. I told her more about the castle and how curious I was about the towers. She agreed it was a waste of the best part of the castle to keep them off limits.

We said goodbye without mentioning Ned's name again.

If she hadn't seen him since he'd left her apartment, there was no proof at all he was in New York. Once he'd finished talking to the police, he might have hopped on a plane to come bother me just as he had before, following me in his clumsy way, trying to find out more about me. Now, he might be more determined than ever.

CHAPTER 59

*a*fter I'd shown Eileen the grapevines, while I was interrogating her about Ned, I sat on the lounge chair, letting the umbrella shade me. I'd kept my attention focused solely on Eileen's face, trying to read every flicker of her eyelids and every twitch in her lips.

As a result, I hadn't noticed that Tess had come out onto the patio.

I don't think she planted herself there intending to listen to my conversation, but who can say? She stood there longer than necessary. And she hadn't moved around enough to catch my peripheral vision. She didn't make any sounds loud enough for me to notice. Had she closed the kitchen door? I couldn't be sure.

But suddenly, when my call ended, she was beside me. She was dragging a lounge chair closer, holding a tall glass with ice and sparkling water. Then, she was sitting on the edge of the chair, leaning forward, her sunglasses pushed up through her hair, spikes of her bangs escaping, staring at me with those dark, penetrating eyes.

"Who is Ned?" she asked.

"My roommate's former fiancé."

"Former? Oh, that's sad."

"Not really."

"Why not?"

"He's a creep. Very controlling. And the minute Eileen was out of sight, he tried to hit on me."

She laughed sharply. "Why is every guy always *hitting on you?*"

"They aren't. All women experience guys who can't read the signals hitting on them."

"Okay, that's true. Maybe it's just ... that is really creepy."

"It shouldn't have surprised me. Like all guys who do that, it was more about him just wanting what he wanted than actually being interested in me, right?"

"I suppose. Why were you talking about a dead woman?"

I told her about the text message with as few words as I could manage, then tried to change the subject to something, anything. It didn't work.

"I guess it's good that she found out who he really was before they got married," Tess said.

"Yes."

"Why were you asking about him?"

"I was just checking in to see how she was."

She sipped her water. "You sounded very interested in him, not her."

I laughed. "I think you misread me. She's a little gullible. Too nice, sometimes. So I just wanted to be sure she was doing okay. I could see him trying to turn the situation around into something that was my fault, now that I'm not around. And she always tended to believe him, even when it was obvious he was lying."

Tess took another sip of her drink. She put her glass on the table and settled back on her lounge chair, stretching out her legs and kicking off her sandals. "It feels good to take a break in the middle of the day."

"You work long hours."

"I do, but I'm loving it. As much as I loved my career, having something to call my own is a whole new level of awesome. It feels amazing to know that I own this, and I can build it into something that reflects me. That I can make it great, or I can cause its failure."

"Except for the weather."

She laughed. "There are always forces you can't control. But it's still mine. Even when I was a consultant, the business was mine, but the work I was doing was all about executing other peoples' visions, and helping their companies be successful."

We were quiet while I wondered if it was possible for me to live a life like that. Maybe it wasn't in my DNA, as they say.

I had no idea what Tess was thinking about. I thought she was basking in the delight of making wine until she spoke. "It's really weird for someone to risk his relationship by hitting on his fiancée's roommate."

"It is."

"Are you sure you didn't set him up?"

"Is that what you think I'd do?"

"If you thought he was controlling and she shouldn't be with him, it wouldn't surprise me." She laughed.

"I didn't set him up." Maybe Tess wouldn't be surprised, but I was a little surprised she could see that in me.

"It's almost as if he sabotaged himself. He must have known you would tell Eileen. So why would he do that? Did he want her to break up with him? Or is he so full of himself he thought she would forgive him?"

"Because he's full of himself."

"That's some first-class arrogance or …" She picked up her glass and took a few sips of water. "And you absolutely didn't set him up?"

"No, Tess. I did not set him up. He forced his way into my room a few times, and the last time, he came in wearing nothing but a bath towel, and then he lost that and was all over me."

"Wow." She sipped her drink. "And you never saw it coming?"

I sighed. "He'd been talking to a guy I used to see and found out I didn't mind sex without strings. So he thought it would be easy. Maybe he thought I wouldn't tell Eileen. I don't know. It doesn't matter. Let's talk about something else. Like, why were you listening to my phone call?"

She grinned. "I wasn't aware it was private, since you were on the patio."

I couldn't argue with that. I swung my legs over the side of the chair. "I'm thirsty."

"I'll get us some wine."

She left and returned a moment later with two glasses of Pinot Grigio and a glass of water for me. We clicked our wineglasses together without making a toast. We each took a sip.

Tess held her glass out in front of her, tipping it slightly, watching the wine sway from side to side, the sunlight shining through the pale liquid. She lifted the glass higher, then turned to me and tapped her glass against mine again. "To loyalty. I just hope you don't break up my engagement." She laughed. "It's a joke."

"I assumed it was." I took a sip of my wine. "If it can't be broken up, then I wouldn't be able to, right?"

She smiled. She looked supremely confident, but I had a burning curiosity to know what she was thinking.

CHAPTER 60

*a*fter listening to Alex's phone call, which she knew she shouldn't have, but at the same time, the call had been wide open for public consumption, Tess decided she and Alex needed to have a deeper discussion. She was also fully aware that might be an exercise in futility. Alex discussed what she wanted to discuss, and Tess could ask direct, probing questions all she wanted. It didn't mean she would get any more insight or feel any closer to her wildly fun, exciting, enthralling, complex, and often infuriating friend.

She was drinking coffee at the kitchen bar, eating a bagel with whipped cream cheese and smoked salmon.

The front door opened and closed. She heard Damien's hopeful voice—*Delicious mango! Delicious mango!*

A moment later, Alex was in the kitchen.

"That looks good," Alex said.

"Help yourself." Tess sipped her coffee. "Do you have plans today?"

Alex filled a mug with coffee. "I think I'll shower before I eat breakfast."

"After that?"

"I need to arrange a video call with Diana. One of these days."
She grinned. "But no rush."

"I booked a spa day for us."

"Again?"

"Why not?"

Alex shrugged. "I've had about six spa days in my entire life. And
one of them was ten days ago. Also with you."

"You don't want to go?"

"It sounds great. The massage was awesome. I'm just surprised."

"Working all day at the computer makes me need massages a
lot." Tess laughed. "I know … I'm a spoiled brat."

"You've always worked at computers. Were you always sneaking
away for spa days?"

"Living close to Calistoga makes it easy. When I was in the
corporate world, it was all face-to-face meetings. You don't realize
you're moving around more. Staring at a computer, participating in
virtual meetings locks up your entire body. I don't want to turn into
that gargoyle." She twisted her face and arms into a hideous pose.

Alex laughed.

As they walked through the entryway into the spa, Tess felt her
shoulders relax in pure anticipation. The cool gray tones of the tile
floor and the walls and furnishings, the sound of water trickling
over stones that wasn't piped in through speakers but came from an
actual stream running through the building, and the faint scent of
gardenia was all it took.

After their massages, they sat in the steam room. Two other
women were soaking in the warm, moist air, so Tess kept her
thoughts to herself. The other women whispered quietly about their
children. After a while, they left. Tess stretched out her legs on the
bench, crossing her ankles, leaning back against the smooth oak
wall behind her.

She wasn't sure how to begin the conversation. Bringing up the
roommate and this Ned guy was combative. It wasn't as if she
blamed Alex for a man's creepy behavior. And it wasn't as if she had

any doubts whatsoever about her relationship with Marcus. Or about whether Alex had the potential to betray her.

There was just something upsetting about the story.

It was upsetting to think that an engagement had ended in the way it had. All the pieces fit when Alex had described it. Eileen was lucky to have discovered what the man she had loved was really like. But the story had nagged at Tess all afternoon and evening. She couldn't fully explain why. It was making her feel as if she was deeply insecure. She wasn't. She had nothing to worry about where Marcus was concerned.

Maybe it was because Alex didn't seem to feel any sadness or regret over what Eileen might be going through. Her sole focus was on how good it was that Eileen had escaped a terrible mistake. But knowing you'd escaped something didn't make the hurt go away. It must have been devastating for Eileen. And none of that pain was evident, not even a thread, in the story Alex had told.

It was as if she'd clapped her hands together, smacked away the dust, and carried on. Nothing but relief.

If, for some unfathomable reason ,Tess and Marcus broke off their engagement, Tess couldn't imagine the pain she would feel. Her life would be gutted, at least for a while. Eileen's life must have been the same, but Tess hadn't heard Alex ask anything about how Eileen was feeling, how she was coping.

Alex seemed absolutely delighted to have been proven right. That was the end of the story for her. A happily ever after that was a pure tragedy in Tess's mind.

"How is Eileen doing since her breakup?" Tess asked.

"Fine."

"Are you sure? How long ago was it?"

"Right before I came out here."

"That's quite recent."

Alex looked at her with a blank expression, as if she were waiting for Tess to say more.

"It must have been really painful for her."

"Why do you want to talk about that? Shouldn't we be talking about your wedding?"

Tess took a deep breath. She was feeling overheated. Maybe it was time to get out of the sauna. "We could. Sure." She smiled. "How much longer do you think you'll be here? Maybe I could invite the rest of my attendants for a weekend and we could take a look at dresses."

"I'm not sure. How long am I invited?"

"However long you'd like."

"Honestly, it's hard to think about going back to New York. I'm a little stuck in figuring out my new career."

Tess nodded. She couldn't stop thinking about Eileen. "We have plenty of room. We hardly even know you're here, so make yourself at home as long as you'd like. You can invite Hunter to visit. We'd love to meet him."

"Hmm."

"Should we plan on at least another month?"

Alex smiled. "That would be awesome."

Tess wasn't sure another month would bring them any closer, but maybe if she stopped pushing, Alex would relax and open up more. Maybe she should just let Alex be Alex. It wasn't as if she was worried about her connection to Marcus.

"We should go by the castle on the way back to your place," Alex said.

"Why?"

"To keep it fresh in our minds."

"Why do we need it fresh in our minds?"

"When I looked at your design ideas on Pinterest—"

"You finally looked?" Tess gave her a lazy smile. The hot, moist air was making her thirsty. And sleepy.

"I found myself forgetting little details about the castle."

"We can't just drop by any time we feel like it," Tess said.

"Call Ella. I'm sure she'll say yes."

"They don't want people dropping by every week to look

around. They schedule events for that sort of thing. And we'll have periodic meetings there with the planner."

"Just try."

"We're not supposed to have an agenda today. We're going to have a nice lunch, a glass of wine, a heart-to-heart talk, maybe."

"A talk about what?"

"The point is, we're spending the day relaxing. I don't want to rush off to the castle. We have months before the wedding."

"It won't interfere with our day. We can just stop by on the way back to your place."

"Why do you want to go today?"

"I feel like we've been rushed every time we've been there. I don't have a good sense of what it feels like."

"You just want to snoop around and see if you can get into the towers."

"I can't get into the towers," Alex said. "I think that's clear."

"Then what do you want?"

"I just want to see it again."

"You're popping my tranquility bubble," Tess said.

Alex laughed. "By going to the castle where you're dying to have your fantasy wedding? How does that pop your bubble?"

"I want to relax. I don't want to think about going home. I don't want to think about what time it is. I don't want to make a phone call and schedule an appointment."

"You can call when we're on our way."

Tess closed her eyes. The bubble had already been punctured. Alex wasn't going to stop talking about it. "Fine. I'll call when we're on our way. But if she says no, I'm not pestering her."

Alex smiled.

CHAPTER 61

*D*espite pushing Tess to ask for an unplanned visit, it surprised me that Ella agreed to let Tess and me stop by for a walk around the interior of the castle. It surprised me even more that she allowed us to go unaccompanied. Dragging Tess after me, but without telling her what I was really looking for, I located an interior door that looked like it might be near the area where the garden wall connected to the left side of the castle.

Now that I'd walked around the exterior, and had toured each of the downstairs rooms several times, I had a better sense of the layout. Both towers were accessed by the long low-ceilinged corridors I'd seen before, but this one, and presumably the other, also had a narrow, nondescript door that looked as if it also provided access. The door was easy to miss because it was tucked inside an alcove that contained a small sofa and end table, so at first glance, it looked like a quiet sitting area. The door itself was hardly noticeable because it was partially concealed by chiffon draperies hung from iron bars—Ella and Nolan's go-to decorating feature.

The door was locked, which was not at all surprising.

So our impromptu visit yielded nothing. Although I suppose

new information is always something, even if it didn't get me any closer to finding out what, or who, was inside.

When we arrived home, Tess took hold of my wrist before I got out of the car. "Now I have a favor," she said. "There's a VIP group in the tasting room. It's for the owner of a local restaurant who has a lot of influence around here recommending wines. I want to stop in to say a quick hi. Come with me."

I followed her into the tasting room.

She introduced me to the restaurant owner and the group of women who were with her. They appeared to have had quite a few generous pours, maybe more than the allocated amount, because the conversation was loud, the laughter louder and somewhat frantic.

After being charming on Tess's behalf, I drifted away from the group. I wandered through the gift shop, keeping one ear focused on Silas. I moved out of his line of sight, standing behind a rack of hats, watching him. He seemed to be enjoying the tipsy women and was eagerly refilling their glasses.

Tess was now deeply engaged in a quiet conversation with the restaurant owner. They'd moved away from the rest of the group and stood with their heads close together.

Silas was leaning on the bar, talking to the youngest woman in the group. She looked much younger than the others, barely twenty-one.

He straightened, picked up a bottle, and poured wine into her glass. He handed it to her and as she took the glass from him, he let his hand trail across the tops of her breasts near the base of the glass. I glanced at Tess. Her head was still bent close to the restaurant owner's, and they were talking a mile a minute. I considered stepping out from behind the hat rack, alerting Tess, but I was also confident the camera should be capturing this.

Tess and the other woman turned. Tess opened the door, and they went outside to the terrace.

Silas looked up and surveyed the room. His gaze passed over the hat rack. He didn't seem to notice me, but he clearly seemed to be looking for Tess. I took a few steps back, then moved quickly toward the entrance to the gift shop area. I stepped out and walked as fast as I could toward the house.

Inside, I ran up the stairs, listening to Damien chortle as I went.

I flopped on my bed, kicked off my shoes, and pulled out my phone. I brought up the app, wondering what Silas might do now that he knew it was only himself, the tipsy twenty-one-year-old, and three other women. As I studied the view through the camera, I saw that the other women had also gone outside.

Then, as if he knew the camera was there, Silas gestured to the young woman. He began walking to the end of the bar. She followed on her side of the bar, sipping from her wineglass as she walked carefully, obviously aware she was tipsy and more unstable in her high heels.

At the end of the bar, he took her hand and led her into the wine storage room. Just before they disappeared out of camera range, I saw his hand slide up her leg under the hem of her dress. And then they were gone.

I stared at my phone in disbelief. He wasn't stupid. In some ways, I suppose he was. He was taking an enormous risk, with the other women still close by.

The camera wasn't even picking up the audio from whatever was happening.

Trying to be optimistic, I continued staring at the vacant tasting room, the bar with a few wineglasses and several half-empty bottles of wine.

The door opened and the restaurant owner came inside. "Tanya?"

The girl appeared. She looked calm, but a bit unsettled. She hurried out with her companion, and the room was quiet again.

Still, I watched, wondering if Tanya would say something and they would return. Maybe she would complain to Tess and Tess would come back in, her dark hair flying behind her, dark eyes flashing with rage. But there was nothing. I continued watching until Silas came out and began picking up the empty glasses.

And still I watched.

I heard the faint sound of a door, but no one entered the tasting room. Silas looked up, then walked out from behind the bar and out of camera range. I realized someone had come into the gift shop area. I heard voices but couldn't make out what they were saying, couldn't even make out if it was a man or woman, just the hum of people talking in another room.

After another minute or two, Silas returned to the tasting area. With his back to the camera, his head turned toward the gift shop, he said, "Like I told you, I don't know why she's still here. Can't help you."

The door opened and closed. Silas began cleaning up the bar.

I stared at my phone. It sounded very much like someone had been asking about me. I'd heard Tess come into the house twenty minutes ago. The wine tasting group was gone. What other *she* could he be referring to who was *still here* besides me?

CHAPTER 62

BEFORE: AMELIA

Sometimes I wondered if I'd lost my mind a long time ago.

I didn't know. I had no reference point besides my mother and that man and the hundreds of books I'd read. How did a person know if they were sane, or normal, or anything at all? I'd been living alone in my tower my entire life.

At seventeen years old, I was almost an adult. I'd asked my mother what would happen when I was an adult.

"You are not almost an adult," she said. "Eighteen years old is not an adult by any stretch of the imagination."

"But I read this story about—"

"How many times do I have to tell you that stories mimic life? They are not *real* life? You are not an adult until you're twenty-one."

"What will happen then?"

"We don't need to talk about that yet."

"I want to."

"It's years away."

"But what will happen to me?"

"Nothing is going to happen to you, sweetie." She tried to hug me. I pushed her away. I did that a lot. She didn't like it. Most of the time when I shoved her away from me, when I peeled her arms off my body, she looked like she might cry. Sometimes, she looked scared.

"I think something will happen."

"Nothing can happen. You're safe here."

"Safe from *what?!*" I screamed this so loudly she jumped.

She slapped her hands over her ears, pressing them against her head. "Stop screaming."

I screamed as loud as I could, for as long as I could manage before I was gasping and choking for air.

"Stop it!"

"I'm not safe! I'm losing my mind."

Her face was twisted, almost cruel. "You don't even know what that means. There's nothing wrong with your mind. You need to calm down and appreciate all the things you have. You need to be grateful for everything that your father and I have—"

"He is *not* my father."

"Stop saying these things. Just stop."

"Okay. That's a good idea. I think I will just stop."

And after that, I stopped talking to her as I had to him. If she asked me a question I could answer with a nod or shake of my head, I did. But other than that, I didn't communicate. I didn't ask for a second serving at meals and I didn't express any preference for food. I ate what was given to me. I stopped playing board games with them.

If I was on my way to losing my mind, I might as well let it go completely. It couldn't be any worse than what I was feeling already. Maybe it would be better.

When I was a little girl and I still believed I was a princess, I'd written letters to my fairy godmother. I stopped writing them after my fake father came to live with us. Since she'd sent me a fake father, it didn't seem as if my fairy godmother was real after all. I *knew* she wasn't real. If she could do magic like the fairy godmother in the story of Cinderella, there wouldn't be a man in our house pretending he was my father.

Now, I went digging through years of notebooks and school papers, looking for the pink spiral notebook that I remembered. There was a sticker of a fairy godmother that I'd put on the cover, along with a sticker of Cinderella's pumpkin coach.

Even then, I'd known I wanted to escape. I wondered if I'd written about that in any of my letters. I also wondered if my mother had read those letters. She was very inquisitive and liked to read all of my notebooks. I'd never dared to write things I didn't want her to see. I was sure that, somehow, they would be found.

Now that I was almost an adult. I was certain I'd read more books than she had. Maybe I didn't know much about life and the world, but I knew a lot from books, possibly more than both of them realized.

The notebook filled with letters to my fairy godmother turned up at the bottom of my toy box in the playroom. I took the notebook and climbed the stone steps to my room at the top of the tower. I stood in the center of my room and looked around.

It took me almost an hour to figure it out, but I finally found a safe place. I made a pouch by taping several sheets of paper to the back of the mirror that hung above my chest of drawers. I slid the notebook inside and rested the mirror back against the wall. I knew my mother would sometimes sweep her hand between my mattress and box spring or look through my drawers, but I was quite sure she'd never moved the mirror away from the wall.

And if she did, what else could she do to me?

Was there any punishment left?

I wanted to keep my letters safe, my thoughts away from her prying eyes. But I also knew I had to get those thoughts out of my head or I would lose my mind. It was twisting into something so strange, I was afraid it might turn into something I didn't recognize. I might get lost inside and never find my way out.

That night, when the castle was dark and the door to my tower was locked because my mother and that man were asleep in their tower on the opposite side, I took the notebook out of its pouch.

It was possible to see the light in my room from their tower, so I didn't turn on the lamp or use a candle. I sat near my window in the light of the moon. I'd chosen a green pen because the ink was easier to see in the dim glow. I opened to the first blank page after the one with my childish printing where I'd told my fairy godmother I wanted to ride in a carriage. I'd told her I wanted to go to a beach and put my feet in the ocean. I wanted to go to an amusement park and ride on a merry-go-round and a Ferris wheel. I also wanted cotton candy. And I wanted a friend. I didn't care if it was a boy or a girl, just someone to play with—someone my age.

This time, my requests were darker. I told my fairy godmother that I was certain I was losing my mind because I believed she existed even though I knew fairy godmothers weren't real. I had to believe she was real or I might jump out the tower window. I told her I was going to explain what my life was like, every detail, as far back as I could remember. She needed to understand that if she didn't show up soon with her magic wand, I would die.

And then I told her I still wanted a friend. I needed a friend. I was desperate. I told her I needed someone to rescue me from the tower.

CHAPTER 63

NOW: ALEX

*I*t was going to be a challenge finding out who Silas had been talking to without him becoming aware I knew he'd been talking to anyone.

I was lying on the king-sized bed in the guest room. I was watching the white ceiling fan turn slowly and silently, trying to decide whether I believed it was true what Tess had said—if you moved the switch, the fan would push the air up instead of down. It didn't seem worth experimenting with because I wasn't sure I would be able to feel the difference.

Besides, I shouldn't be thinking about air flow direction.

I was supposed to be deciding what to wear when I went into the tasting room to communicate the right sort of message to Silas. I didn't have the stomach to flirt with him, even though it was almost always the easiest solution. This time, it felt like too much work. It seemed like something that would cause too many problems down the road. That approach was fine with a stranger, or with someone I wasn't likely to encounter again, with someone I knew for a fact I would never encounter again.

The best approach was professional—I was Tess's friend. He was her employee. We should have a cordial relationship. As long as I didn't put too fine a point on him being her employee, which would rouse his need for power that lurked so close to the surface.

I sat up. Jeans and a silky button-down shirt with the sleeves rolled up. And ankle boots. It was warm for boots, so I discarded the idea of the button-down shirt and chose a navy blue top with cap sleeves. I put my hair up and wore minimal makeup.

As I walked past the kitchen, I saw Tess in front of the fridge, filling a glass with water. "Where are you going all dressed up?"

"I'm not dressed up."

"Boots? It's—"

"Just headed to the gift shop to pick out a few things. I should look decent in case any customers are there, right?"

She laughed. "I thought you were staying for a while longer. What's the rush with souvenirs?"

"I might ship something to Eileen."

She gave me a puzzled look but didn't say anything more.

Inside the tasting room, a couple stood at the bar. They were drinking red, so they were at least midway through their tasting. I wandered around the gift shop. Now that I'd told Tess what I was after, I needed to find something for Eileen.

By the time I'd picked out a T-shirt, a set of coasters, and a Black Mask shot glass, which seemed odd at a winery, the couple had left. I walked into the tasting area.

"Hi."

"You can work out your purchases with Tess," Silas said. "I'm sure she'll give them to you at cost."

"I don't need a discount. I'd rather pay for them now."

"I can't help you. I'm busy."

I carried my purchases into the gift shop, left them on the counter, and returned to the tasting area. "I thought we could start over."

He let out a laugh that sounded like a small dog's bark.

"I'm going to be around for a while," I said. "And for Tess and Marcus's sake—"

"There's no reason for you to be anywhere near the tasting room."

"I'd rather we have a professional relationship."

"I don't give a fuck what you'd *rather have*."

For some reason, I was suddenly aware of the camera. This wasn't what I'd planned. I'd wanted to capture the details of him harassing a customer, not arguing with me. But maybe having this recorded would be useful as well. I smiled.

"What are you laughing at?"

"I'm not laughing."

"You're grinning like an idiot."

"I think Tess would appreciate it if we can be polite and at least superficially friendly."

"I'm not friendly to a bitch who bites my tongue."

"You assaulted me."

"I didn't *assault* you. I tried to kiss you. If you weren't interested, you should have said no."

"I told you I wasn't interested."

"Whatever." He turned his back to me and began unnecessarily arranging the wine bottles displayed on the shelves behind the bar.

I waited for him to turn around. The minutes stretched around us. The only sound was the tap of the heavy glass bottles on wood.

"You can leave now," he said.

"I haven't paid for my gifts."

"Work it out with Tess."

I opened my purse and took out my wallet. I removed my credit card.

He turned.

"What's wrong with you?" he asked.

"Nothing."

"No wonder you're in trouble."

"I'm not in trouble."

He smirked.

I held out my credit card.

"I wouldn't be so sure about that," he said.

"What do you mean?"

"Someone's looking for you."

"Oh? Who's looking for me?"

He stared at me. "No idea."

"Then how do you know someone is looking for me?"

"Someone came into the gift shop asking questions about you."

"What questions?"

He laughed. "Are you worried? Did you bite someone else's tongue? Or worse?"

"A man was looking for me?"

"I didn't say it was a man."

"Okay. A man or a woman. Did they give you a name?"

"I don't owe you anything after the way you treated me. I'm not some creep you met in a nightclub that you have to pull the pepper spray on. So you can—"

"I didn't pepper spray you."

"I think you piss off a lot of people if you go around biting tongues just because you send a guy mixed signals and he tries to kiss you. So fuck off. I have work to do."

"Who was looking for me?"

"I have no idea."

It was clear I could keep asking the same question and keep getting the same answer. All I was doing was making myself look desperate. It was possible he didn't even have a name. A description might help, but if he was too vague, it might not.

I walked out, validated that my sense of being watched had been accurate. Concerned that I had bigger problems than satiating my curiosity at the castle.

CHAPTER 64

*E*ven though it was mid-day and the odds were high that Eileen was working, I called her. The call went to voicemail. I left a message telling her to call me. I sent her a text telling her to call me.

I changed into workout clothes, spent an hour lifting the heaviest weights my body could bear, avoiding squats because I wasn't sure about my ankle. I rolled out a yoga mat, but then I stretched out on my back, my arms out to my sides, eyes closed, and ran through a list of all the people who might have come to California looking for me.

Why would someone do that? Why would they follow me—hiding who they were—then expose themselves to Silas? Had this person asked Silas not to reveal their identity? Or was that his own game? It was impossible to know.

If it was someone from law enforcement, they would have identified themselves right away, so I didn't think I had to be concerned about that kind of exposure.

I considered relatives of James. I thought about Victoria. I wondered if Ned's constant pestering of Kent had stirred up his lingering questions about me. All of them were possibilities, but none of them pointed to clear danger. None of them screamed that someone knew what I'd done. Each one of those people definitely had questions about me. They wondered about me. They might be aware that I'd said things that didn't quite add up. But no one had *seen* anything. No one *knew* anything. Did they?

At the end of the day, no one had the imagination to actually come to the conclusion that I'd committed murder. There just wasn't enough information to put all the pieces together. Each one might have a nagging sense of unease at the back of their mind, but that was it.

All of it added up to one big warning—I had become less cautious.

I sent Eileen another text.

Eileen: *I got your messages. What's the emergency?*

I peeled myself off the floor, rolled up the mat, and went upstairs to take a shower. I took my tablet to the living room. I texted Diana, asking her to send me some dates when she was available for our totally unnecessary video chat. I did a Google search for interesting careers that might be a good fit for my eclectic set of skills.

My phone buzzed and the avatar I used for Eileen fill the screen. When her face appeared, she looked anxious. "Are you okay?"

"Yes."

"Oh, I thought something happened."

"I need you to—"

"You're not in the hospital or anything?"

"No, I—"

"Then why the voicemail and all the text messages?"

"I only sent two."

She sighed. "It felt urgent. What's going on?"

"Will you find out if Ned is actually *in* New York?"

"What? Why?"

"Because someone who refused to identify himself was here asking questions about me."

She laughed. "Are you serious?"

"Yes."

"Someone where?"

"That's not important."

"I think it is," she said.

"It's not that hard. Just go by his office or his apartment and see if he's around."

She laughed, but she sounded angry this time. "I'm not doing that. I'm not stalking my ex-fiancé. I'm not stalking anyone. No."

"I need to know if it's him."

"First of all, why do you need to know? And actually, this should be my first question, why on earth would you assume it's him? Why would he fly to California to *ask questions* about you? What kind of questions?"

"Look, you know I got under his skin. He blames me for the end of your relationship. And—"

"So what? Why would he fly all the way to California to ask questions about you? That makes no sense. He knows you. He doesn't have any questions." She laughed. "You sound like a narcissist. You think he's just sitting around thinking about *you*? This is insane. I need to get back to work."

What she was saying made sense. But she didn't know the whole story. And of course, he wasn't really asking questions about me. I had no idea what he wanted. The only thing I was aware of him asking was why I was still in California. It didn't seem important. Unless he'd gotten it into his head that I was hiding from the New York police so I wouldn't be questioned in Carolina's murder.

"It's just that now that he's had time to brood about things, he probably thinks it's my fault you broke up."

"I doubt that. He knows what he did," Eileen said.

Ned was fairly intelligent. Could he have guessed that his number showed up on Carolina's phone because I'd put it there? I'd been so obsessed with punishing him, doing something to make his life uncomfortable. It had seemed like such a clever idea at the time. I'd known it wouldn't stick, but I'd enjoyed thinking about a few days, maybe a week in which he would squirm under the scrutiny of a detective trying to decide whether he'd stabbed Carolina Scott.

The sheer odds against the coincidence of this total stranger having his phone number might have started Ned wondering how that might have happened. It was equally possible my involvement had never crossed his mind.

I didn't know. And I didn't like not knowing.

Just as I didn't like not knowing who Silas had spoken to. Even a vague description from him would have told me whether or not it was Ned. Over or under forty years old, for example. He wouldn't even tell me if the visitor was male or female.

"Please." The word sounded thick and unfamiliar on my tongue. It sounded stiff and insincere, but apparently it struck Eileen's eardrums much differently than it did mine.

"You sound desperate," she said.

I grabbed the word out of her lips. "I'm really, truly desperate."

"It doesn't even sound like you." She laughed, but stopped suddenly, as if she wasn't sure it was all that funny.

"I don't know what to tell you."

"I don't like the idea of stalking him," she said.

"You're not stalking him. That's only if you harass someone or continue bothering them. You just need to check out his apartment or his office a few times until you see him. Or not."

"How many times?"

"I think his office is the easiest. If you watch for him two or three days and you don't see him leaving, that's probably enough."

"Probably? You won't start asking for more?"

"I don't think so." I'd thought about placing a call to his company, asking to speak to him. But that had its own risks. Maybe Eileen would see him on the first day and the question would be answered. At least one question would be answered.

She promised to look for him, even though she still thought I was behaving strangely.

If she was able to verify he was in New York, then what?

CHAPTER 65

BEFORE: AMELIA

There were so many places in the castle to explore, but some were off-limits to me. I'd never been inside the second tower at all. Because I'd never seen it, I spent a fair amount of time wondering what it was like, wondering if it was identical to mine, imagining how many rooms there were and what they were used for.

I rarely even saw their tower because it wasn't visible from my walled garden. The only window in my tower that looked in that direction was in my classroom and I was only in my classroom with my mother, so I never spent time looking out. It's hard to gaze at something and let your thoughts run freely when your mother is right beside you, staring at the side of your face. Your mother, who is familiar with all your expressions, who sometimes acts as if she can read your mind. Even if she can't.

It felt as if she could read my mind because she knew me so well. She knew everything about me. There was no part of my life that she hadn't observed or been part of. The only thing I had that didn't belong to my mother were the things inside my head. Even many of the books I'd read had already been read by her.

Nothing was all mine.

Except my thoughts. My dreams. My plans.

So although I didn't spend much time looking at their tower, I did think about it. A lot.

I also wasn't allowed on the other floors where the wedding guests spent the night. My mother and that man never gave me a reason for keeping me confined to the ground floor of the castle. The doors leading to the staircases were locked, as were many of the doors. All the keys were kept in a single cabinet in a small room off the kitchen. My mother had the key to this cabinet. It was a tiny key for something so important. She wore it on a long black ribbon around her neck.

They thought they had me locked up forever, but I don't think they ever considered that my mind kept growing outside their control, beyond what they could see, all on its own. It grew up and over the castle walls and there was nothing they could do to stop that. They could lock up my body, but they couldn't keep my thoughts from growing. They couldn't keep them from escaping.

Even though I eventually managed to scrape one small stone out of the wall, I knew it wasn't enough. The opening was barely large enough to slide my hand through. Still, I liked to sit in the garden when I knew they were busy with their wedding guests. I removed the stone, lay on the grass, and looked out. It felt amazing to have a secret view they didn't know about. I couldn't see much, but I could see things they didn't know I could see.

I knew that even if my hair grew long enough, no prince would ever climb up my braided hair to rescue me because the garden wall prevented anyone from getting close to the tower. Besides, that was a fairy tale. Even I knew that.

I knew the loose stone wouldn't help me escape. I couldn't fit through it. Not even Salt and Pepper could squeeze through that tiny opening.

But when I peered through that small space, I liked to imagine my thoughts escaping. I imagined them racing across the gardens and weaving among the trees surrounding the castle, over the fence and down the hill, across the valley and out into the world.

At night, when the moon was only a thin sliver and there wasn't enough light for me to write the fairy tale of my life, I thought about the ribbon around my mother's neck. I thought about the tiny key. I wondered if there was a way for me to get it without her knowing.

I had all the time in the world to think about that ribbon and the tiny key and my mother's habits, which I knew almost as well as I knew my own. I knew the details of her life almost as intimately as she knew mine. Did she ever wonder if I could read her mind as she believed she could read mine?

One night, while I was staring at the moon, I saw how it looked a lot like the curved needles I used for stringing beads into bracelets and necklaces. I thought about hooking that needle around the ribbon and slowly pulling it away from my mother's neck. The ribbon would move closer to her throat, bringing the key with it. If I pulled it tightly enough, it would cut off her breathing.

I didn't want to kill her. Did I?

Sometimes, I wondered if I did want to kill her, because she was killing me. I was sure of it, and I wondered if other people might also see it that way. I couldn't breathe. Why should she?

But for now, what I wanted was that key. I wanted to hook my needle around the ribbon and pull the key out of her dress. She would feel it moving, feel the metal sliding across her skin, the ribbon grazing her neck. I didn't know how I would do it without her noticing.

But finally, one night, my thoughts produced an idea.

A few days later, I offered to braid her long blonde hair, as she had always done with mine. I did this for several weeks, so she wouldn't think it was strange. I wove ribbons into her braid, as she'd always done with mine. Then I asked her to do mine to match. I could see her eyes soften when she looked at me, thinking that somehow, in a magical way she couldn't quite understand, she had won me back.

Then, one day when it was dark outside because it was raining hard, I placed my bead project on the table beside us. I began to braid a red ribbon into her hair. As I wove it through the strands, I fumbled and stopped. "Oh!" I said.

"What's wrong?"

"The ribbon is twisted." I yanked it out, pulling sharply on the fine hairs at the base of her skull.

"Ow!"

"I'm sorry."

"It's okay. Sometimes the hair doesn't cooperate." She reached back and patted my hand.

I started over. Once again, I yanked out the ribbon, pulling on the tiny hairs. I felt her shoulders tighten and heard the suppressed cry of pain. I started over yet again.

Holding the partially finished braid in my left hand, I tugged on the ribbon. "Oh, no. It's tangled again. It's really a mess this time." I reached for my curved needle. Fumbling around at the back of her neck, pulling on the hairs, listening to her try, and fail, to suppress her cries of pain, I hooked the needle under the ribbon holding the key.

As I'd practiced for days on one of my dolls, with four swift, sharp, simultaneous movements, I scraped the needle down my mother's neck, pulled the ribbon holding the key away from her body, cut it, and reached around to grab the exposed key. She hardly noticed what I was doing as she screamed at the pain from the needle, placing her splayed hand on the back of her neck.

"What did you do?" She cried and twisted away.

I dropped the key and tiny sewing scissors into my pocket. "Oh! I'm so sorry. So, so sorry. I tried to use my needle to get the ribbon out because it was tangled. I thought I could use that and it wouldn't keep pulling on your hair, but it slipped."

I knelt in front of her, tears in my eyes. "Let me clean it up and bandage you." I handed her tissues from my other pocket to stop the trickle of blood.

I raced to the pantry, unlocked the key cabinet, and removed the key to the tower I'd never been allowed to enter. I slipped a new length of ribbon through the tiny key she wore around her neck, went to the bathroom behind the kitchen where I gathered first aid supplies, and ran back to the sitting room where my mother was staring at her palm, covered with blood.

I cleaned her up and replaced the key around her neck.

When she was lying down after taking ibuprofen and drinking a glass of water, I ran down the corridor, my bare feet slapping the stone floor. When I reached the door, I shoved the key into the lock.

The stone staircase was identical to the one inside my tower. As I climbed, I saw that all the rooms were the same in their layout, but entirely different in their contents, which I'd expected. There was an office with desks holding two huge computer screens, a sitting room, and a library. The library looked very different from mine, but I couldn't say why. I didn't want to waste time figuring it out, so I kept climbing.

The most surprising part of their tower was the top two floors—two bedrooms. My fake father's came first. It obviously belonged to him because the walls were decorated with posters from the action movies he loved.

I climbed the rest of the stairs.

The bedroom at the top of this tower was decorated in purple—a purple canopy on the bed, a satin purple comforter and pillows in different shades of purple. Purple chiffon hung from iron bars and the sofa and chairs were upholstered in purple. The circular wall was lined with framed photographs of me, from infancy to one taken just a few months earlier.

On the nightstand was a lamp with purple fringe and a framed photograph of my mother holding me when I was a newborn. Standing beside her was a man. I didn't even have to enter the room to know it was my father—my real father, my father who had gone away and never returned.

Across from the foot of the bed was a bookcase. The bottom

shelf held a shimmering glass figurine of a princess that caught my eye. Beside it was a white leather photograph album.

I sat on the floor beside the shelf, pulled the album onto my lap, and opened it.

The first pages contained pictures of my mother when she was a little girl. I knew almost nothing about her childhood. I'd never met my grandparents because they'd died before I was born. As far as I knew, I had no aunts or uncles, no cousins.

But now, I saw a different story.

It looked as if my life had been even more of a fairy tale than I'd realized.

The first pages of the album were filled with pictures of my real father, with his flaming red hair, when he was a little boy. When my father was about twelve or thirteen, a baby sister appeared in the family photos. The last picture of them together showed my father, close to my age now, holding his little sister with her long wavy red hair on his shoulders, both of them smiling their hearts out.

Somewhere out in the world I'd never experienced, there was a girl with red hair, just like mine. She didn't know I existed and looking at her small little face, I wondered—even if I found a way to escape one day, would it ever be possible to find her? Would his sister wander the earth, never knowing about me?

The next pages held pictures of my mother. She also had a sibling. In the photographs of her, there was a brother who appeared to have been born a year or two after she was. As I flipped through the years, watching the two of them grow older, the boy looked more and more familiar to me. By the time I saw pictures of my mother when she was marrying my father, I realized why her brother looked so familiar—he was my fake father.

My fingers were icy cold and stiff as I closed the thick, heavy cover over the pictures of the past with all its secrets.

My father had gone away and never come home. My uncle took his place and pretended he was my father. *Why?* Why had they done that?

I wanted to cry, but I couldn't find any tears inside me. Instead, I felt as if there was a deep, bottomless chasm in my heart. I felt hollow.

I put the album on the shelf, walked out of the purple room, and moved slowly down the stairs. Because I was numb and I no longer felt like time was pushing me to hurry out of their tower before I was caught, I stopped halfway down and entered the library.

Now I understood why this room full of books was different from mine, different from the one in the main part of the castle that they showed to guests.

CHAPTER 66

PORTLAND, OREGON

y father drove me to the harvest festival and walked me to the doors of the church hall to be sure I was safely handed off to the responsible adults in charge of my decorum.

He was proud of how demure I looked in my tattered dress and the cotton scarf covering my hair, tied securely under my chin. It was so secure and so thick across my scalp, he wasn't aware of the mask pinned to the bottom layers of the scarf, resting against my hair. Because my dress was loose, with long sleeves and a modest neckline, he didn't notice it looked a little fluffy on me.

Once I was inside the building, I scurried across the linoleum floor in my Sunday shoes, the only concession to princess-hood, and into the girls' bathroom. I locked myself in a stall and began to create a costume that was a little closer to the one that still lived inside my imagination.

Holding the back of my head so the mask wouldn't fall out, I untied the scarf. I hung it and the mask on the hook on the back of the door. I unzipped the hideous dress and wriggled out of it. I placed it over the door. Underneath, I was wearing a green satin dress that Gloria had let me borrow.

I didn't really look like a princess in it. I looked more like a mermaid. The only problem was, there were no mermaids in the bible, and magical creatures were not something we were supposed to aspire to, so I'd needed to think of someone else to be. The adults, who were sure to be interested in my costume because it was pushing the boundaries of biblical heroines, were going to want a good explanation for green satin and a black feather mask with shimmering diamonds.

I'd thought about announcing I was Bathsheba. This was the trouble with church rules, and my father's rules. They didn't think things through, but they would be angry with me for pointing that out. Bathsheba was front and center in the bible. Everyone knew who she was. King David wouldn't be who he was without her. But I knew, and they knew I knew, she was not someone we should aspire to be. Even though *she* did nothing *wrong*.

She was minding her own business, taking a bath on her own rooftop. King David was the Peeping Tom. It's possible she was being an exhibitionist. Who knows? When they read the bible story to us, they never mentioned whether it was common to take a bath on the roof in ancient times. Maybe it was like a hot tub. No one delves into those details.

But David was the king, and he ordered her husband sent to the front lines. When the poor man was inevitably killed in battle, David moved in on Bathsheba. There's no doubt who the *evildoer* was in that story.

A pawn. That's all she was. A pawn for the king. But I could imagine the looks on their faces if I announced I'd come to the harvest party dressed as the woman who *tempted* god's chosen king.

Queen Esther was the character I'd decided upon. She'd been told to conceal the fact that she was Jewish when she was chosen to marry the king of Persia. For this reason, I was wearing a mask, to symbolize that I was concealing my identity. The dress was green because when Esther advanced to the highest position in the king's harem, before she saved her people from annihilation, she was covered in gold jewelry and perfumed with myrrh. I would inform my inquisitors that the green represented the tree from which myrrh was made.

My symbolic costume was a massive hit among the adults. They approached me with concern, none of them having considered whether masks should be allowed. The majority of the kids had opted for makeup over masks, because it was more fun to play with, and less of a commitment to discomfort for a three-hour party. But when they heard my story, they cooed over the symbolism of the mask. They thought it was brilliant. They ignored the flamboyant feathers and diamonds. They looked past the shimmery quality of the dress and the way it clung to my body, perhaps more than it should have.

Most shocking of all, no one asked about my identity. Once they were captivated by details from the story of Esther, which they'd frankly forgotten, or never taken the trouble to read much about, they didn't think to inquire who was behind the mask. They were too busy turning to the other chaperones to marvel over my clever choice and my biblical knowledge.

And so I left the party the same way I'd come—via the girls' bathroom and back to my father's waiting car.

A masked woman who was now enthralled by the possibilities that came with concealing her identity.

CHAPTER 67

NAPA VALLEY, CALIFORNIA

For two days, I'd spent over three hours in my room at night watching the recorded feed from the camera in the tasting room. Silas had flirted and poured wine. He'd given impressive sales pitches to customers, enticing them to join the Black Mask wine club. It was a rare person who didn't sign up to receive three bottles of wine every two months. Part of his skill lay in the fact that he seemed to know instinctively who was inclined to join and only spent his time and effort pitching to those who would be easy to close.

I wondered how his success compared with other wineries. Did this many casual wine tasters sign up to be members of a club? He made it sound as if he were doing them a favor, getting them into this *exclusive* group of people called the members of the Black Mask Winery. I wanted to laugh.

Tess had been right. He was good at what he did. At least this aspect.

Everyone who walked out of that tasting room had smiles on their faces as they passed the camera on the way to the door, bags full of wine in their hands, membership cards in their wallets, or nothing but a nice haze of alcohol in their veins, they all looked as if they'd had a marvelous afternoon.

I skimmed forward, watching at 10x speed to see if anything caught my eye that was worth slowing down for. I was starting to think he assumed Tess had a camera hidden somewhere in the room. Because there were others on the property, maybe he'd guessed there was a good chance he was being watched. Maybe he was cautious about what he did, or so subtle, I was missing things.

Something flashed across the screen. I hit pause, then reverse. Tess was in the tasting room, leaning over the bar, her face close to Silas. She seemed very intense and upset. It almost looked as if she were shouting at him.

I tapped play.

"What's wrong with you?!" She wasn't shouting, as her posture suggested, but her voice was loud and sharp. I'd never heard her sound so angry.

"Nothing."

"You're supposed to be a professional."

"So are you."

"This is entirely different. And don't—"

"How is it different?" he sneered.

"I don't want to—"

"I wasn't unprofessional."

"There are boundaries. You crossed one and you know it. I need to trust you."

"Scared?" His tone was mocking, condescending.

"No."

"Maybe you should be."

"I'm not scared. She's angry. And if she goes to Marcus about this, she ..."

Now I realized she was talking about me. And Silas. I wondered why it had taken her so long to confront him. But finally, she was. I moved the phone closer, even though it wasn't necessary. I felt as if I were watching a gripping, must-see reality show.

"She won't."

"You don't know her. At all. You are completely underestimating her."

"I don't think so."

"She doesn't understand why I'm not doing anything, and if she decides that's unacceptable, I guarantee you, she'll talk to Marcus about it. And then—"

"Calm down. That's your fear talking. You brought this on yourself." Silas laughed. "Scared little Tess. In over your head?"

"Stop."

"What do you want me to do? That bitch—"

"I don't need to hear it again. I'm just telling you, stay away from her. And if you do see her, you better act like …"

"Like what?"

"Like a man who respects women. Like most men, I'd like to believe. Do you hear what I'm saying?"

"How can I not? You're shouting."

"You need to be exemplary for the rest of her stay."

"And how long is that?" He backed away from her, folding his arms across his chest.

"I don't know."

"That sounds about right. Pretty much how you deal with everything—changing your mind … *not sure … you don't know.*"

Tess moved away from the bar. She was silent for a long time.

I couldn't believe she was letting him talk to her like this. Why wouldn't she *fire* him? Surely he couldn't be that valuable. I didn't care how many club memberships he sold or how much he supposedly knew about wine. There were thousands, hundreds of thousands of good salespeople in the world. We were in the outer rim of the San Francisco Bay Area, in the heart of the Napa Valley—one of the premier wine regions in the world. Silas was not the only wine expert who knew how to sell. It was beyond belief that she thought she was stuck with this guy.

"Watch out, Silas." Tess turned and walked toward the door.

Silas laughed. He didn't sound at all concerned. In fact, he sounded as if he felt sorry for her. He laughed harder, continuing even after the door had closed behind her.

CHAPTER 68

*A*fter they'd eaten dinner, Marcus returned to his office for a conference call with part of his team located in India. Tess sat on the patio sipping a glass of Malbec, scrolling mindlessly through one social media app after the other. Alex was beside her, holding a glass of wine, but it didn't look as if she'd taken a single sip.

Tess took a sip from her own glass. She was well on her way to slipping over the edge into feeling tipsy, her thoughts going sideways as if they'd spilled out on the ground and were running along the spaces between the flagstones. She'd felt more unsettled than ever since her conversation with Silas.

Owning the winery was supposed to be a dream come true, something that would take her to new heights and satisfy her ambitions. Instead, she felt utterly trapped. She felt as if she'd fallen into a hole that had been covered with branches and leaves, designed to capture an unsuspecting wild animal. Now she was at the bottom of a deep pit, staring up at her predator. There was no way out. Ever.

She wanted to cry.

She was wondering if it might be better to sell the place. Would that get her free of him? But how would she explain that to Marcus?

He would think she'd lost her mind. Worse, he would question her judgment, and she valued his respect as much as anything.

"Dinner was amazing," Alex said.

"It always is."

"It's like you have your own personal chef."

Tess gave her a weak smile. "I don't think of him like that."

"But that's how it is."

"I love him. And he cooks because he enjoys it. He loves feeding me." Just saying the words gave her a warm, comforting feeling, as if she were tasting his food that very moment. It left her in a constant state of awe, seeing how Marcus took such absolute delight in watching her eat, his eyes shining as she put each forkful into her mouth. He spent hours poring over cookbooks, considering her tastes, looking for new ways to surprise her.

Alex sipped her wine.

Finally. Tess had felt like Alex was waiting for something, that she had something she wanted to say and she'd been refusing to drink her wine until she said it. Maybe it had only been about the food.

"I heard you and Silas talking about me," Alex said.

And there it was. Tess felt as if she'd swallowed an ice cube whole. "What?"

"I appreciate you telling him to back off, but it's a little late. And I don't understand why you allow him to talk to you the way he does."

Tess sat up quickly. Her phone slid off her lap onto the chair. She grabbed it before it fell to the ground, splashing wine onto her jeans in the process. "How do you know that? Were you ... where were you?"

"I installed a camera."

Tess put her glass on the table, swung her legs over the side of the lounge chair, and sat up, facing Alex. "You installed a *camera*? Where?"

"In the tasting room."

"You had no right to do that. You need to—"

"He has no right to talk to you that way. You're his boss."

"That's illegal, Alex. You can't record someone without their permission."

"I thought I should keep an eye on him."

"No." Tess shook her head. "What if customers found out? No. And even Silas. No. Absolutely not." She stood. "You need to show me where it is right now. You need to get rid of it. Immediately."

"Calm down." Alex took a sip of wine.

Tess reached over and removed the wineglass from Alex's hand. "We need to get it out of there right now."

Alex sighed. "It's so nice out here. Let's enjoy our wine. There's plenty of time tomorrow."

"Silas gets in early. I want it gone."

"Can we finish talking about—"

"No." Tess went into the house and got a small toolbox they kept in the pantry for minor repairs. She returned to the patio and started along the path toward the tasting room. She called over her shoulder. "Now! Come on." A moment later, she heard Alex's footsteps behind her.

When the camera had been removed from the wall and placed in an empty wine bottle carton, they returned to the house.

Settled once again on the lounge chairs, she saw that Alex had brought out the bottle of Malbec.

"Now," Alex said, topping off their glasses, "I want you to explain what the deal is with Silas."

"I've already explained. You need to apologize for violating my trust like that."

Alex laughed. "That guy could ruin you. Why can't you see what a risk he is?"

"That's my business."

"You're not managing it very well."

"You have no idea what you're talking about. You've never managed anything."

"True."

"You can barely manage yourself."

Alex laughed. "I think I do alright."

"Do you?"

"I know you're annoyed about the camera, but I am actually trying to protect you."

"I don't need that kind of protection. I could get in a lot of trouble."

"Why won't you tell me what's going on with him?"

"There's nothing going on." Tess dribbled more wine into her glass. She shouldn't. She was drinking it too fast, especially given how she was already feeling, but the conversation with Silas had pushed her close to the edge. She wanted to tell Alex, she really did, but once she opened her mouth, that would be it.

Alex hadn't actually *caused* the destruction of her roommate's engagement, but it felt that way—because she'd been there, and because she was unsympathetic about it. Because she almost seemed pleased, as if she'd done Eileen a favor. Tess could see that was the truth. Still, it felt … uncomfortable.

There were zero similarities to Tess's relationship with Marcus. In fact, you could almost say the roles were reversed. If anything happened to her and Marcus now, it would be Tess's fault entirely.

She shouldn't be afraid to tell Alex what had happened. She needed to tell *someone*, or she would lose her mind. She needed a second opinion, some input from outside her own constantly circling, anxious, terrified, worst-case-scenario thoughts.

But she wasn't always sure she trusted Alex. It wasn't as if Alex was the type of person who chattered all the time, talking about things other people had said. She rarely gossiped. Even though she seemed to have an insatiable, almost blood-thirsty need to know other people's business, she didn't go around broadcasting that information.

At the same time, telling her about this could destroy Tess's life. And she wasn't ready to place her life in Alex's hands. A significant role in her wedding, sure. Free run of her house? No problem. Hiring her again? Absolutely.

But this. It was—

"You're thinking about it. I can see your brain whirling." Alex laughed softly. "I won't tell anyone. You know I won't. Who would I tell?"

"It's just ..." Tess took a long swallow of wine. Maybe Alex would have some insight. But there was no insight to be had. It was a hopeless situation. She was absolutely, utterly trapped. A pit that was twenty feet deep, with concrete walls, smooth as steel. In fact, walls *made* of steel. Escape was impossible. Alex would not have any ideas. Not even one.

"You look really stressed," Alex said.

"I'm not stressed."

"You sounded frantic when you were talking to him, not at all as if you're in charge. You sounded as if you wanted to fire him, but you ... almost as if you couldn't. Your threats sounded empty."

"You don't understand the situation, so let's talk about something else." Tess could hear that her words sounded loose, not as articulated as they should. No more wine, she told herself. Then she took a sip. It was so good, and it soothed her racing thoughts. She *was* stressed. She'd never been so stressed in her entire life.

They sipped their wine. Alex didn't speak. Tess almost wished Alex would continue pestering her because at least the effort of telling Alex she didn't understand and making up excuses for not revealing what had happened gave her mind something to work on. In the silence, she found herself taking more frequent sips of wine. She found her thoughts slipping toward panic. Imagined scenarios of what Silas might do, even if she didn't disrupt the precarious status quo, provoking him to anger, began gnawing at the back of her mind with an increasing frenzy.

She took another long swallow, then topped off her glass yet again.

"I know you want to tell me," Alex said. "You're slamming down expensive wine like a college girl chugging beer at her first frat party—hell bent on getting drunk as fast as you can."

"No, I'm not."

Alex was silent, but Tess could feel that she was smiling in the darkness, knowing she'd read Tess's mood. It was obvious. She'd been pushed to her limit and maybe if she didn't tell someone what was going on, she was going to be in worse trouble. She needed to find a way out of this situation, and all her own efforts at circling around the problem had done nothing but wear a deep groove in her mind that prevented her from sleeping, interfered with her work, and now, was causing her to drink too much—the entire root of the problem to begin with.

She'd noticed it even before Alex had arrived. Every night, opening a second bottle, topping off her own glass more often than she refilled Marcus's. He hadn't seemed to notice, but how long until he did? How long until he asked her what was going on? And that would be so much worse than Alex prying into her agitated behavior.

She touched her cheek, suddenly aware that it was damp with tears that had been making their way out of the corners of her eyes, hovering in her lashes, then sliding across her skin. She blinked hard.

"I really fucked up," she whispered.

"It happens," Alex said.

"Not like this." She put her wineglass on the table. Then, just as quickly, she picked it up again, took a long swallow, and returned her glass to the table. She needed false courage to tell Alex what she had to say. "When we first took over the winery, Silas gave me a tasting to teach me about the wines."

"Sure," Alex said.

"Don't give me attitude."

"I'm not. It makes sense you would have a tasting."

"It was very detailed. We went through all the wines from Black Mask. Comparing them with each other, and with the same varieties from other wineries. And of course, I should have realized this would have been better spread out over several different sessions. I know my limits. But I was so damn eager to get fully immersed. I wanted to learn everything. I wanted to be on top of everything, to get up to speed *fast*, to hit the ground running, all that stuff. So I dove in. And of course I had way too much."

"I can imagine."

"I thought I was pacing myself. Even tipping extra pours into the dump bucket. But those tiny sips add up."

"They do." Alex took a sip of her wine.

Tess felt a longing for another sip, but forced herself to leave her glass on the table. She wanted to get the words out as quickly as possible. She couldn't stop now. "I got ripped. More than I have in a long time. It was so bad. And he started touching me and I just ..." She was sobbing now. "I don't know what's wrong with me! I love Marcus. He is absolutely my soul mate. I know you don't believe that's a real thing, but I do, and he is. And no one else even interests me. I want to stay with Marcus until the day I die. When he gets old, if he gets sick, I will absolutely be there for him. I don't care what happens, I don't care if we lose everything. He's my one and only."

"I get it. That's why you want the castle."

"God, Alex. Forget the castle for two seconds, okay?"

"Sure."

"Anyway. We ..." She couldn't say it. Surely, she didn't have to say it.

"Oh."

"Do you think I'm the most stupid woman alive?"

"No."

"What do you think?"

"You were drunk," Alex said.

"It's not an excuse."

"But it happens. It makes us stupid."

Tess sighed. This was why Alex was a friend. Truly, she was her best friend. There was no one like her. She wanted to fling herself onto the other lounge chair and hug Alex, she wanted to cling to her and beg her—*Tell me what to do!*

"He's blackmailing you," Alex said.

"Yes. He took pictures."

"He's scum."

"I love Marcus with all my heart."

"But you don't think he could get past it?"

"I don't know!"

Alex splashed wine into her glass and took a sip.

Despite Alex's proclamation, sounding like it came from experience, that alcohol made people stupid, Alex seemed to be able to absorb endless quantities without showing any effect. It was surreal. Tess pushed the thought aside. "He's helped the winery a lot. He still does. He truly is invaluable."

"But you want him gone."

"Absolutely. Out of my life forever."

Alex took a long sip of wine. She placed her glass on the table. "Well, maybe you're underestimating Marcus."

"I can't take that risk."

"Let's see what happens," Alex said.

"That's all you have to say?" Tess felt as if she sounded pathetic. Weak and childish and helpless.

"He's not doing anything right now. And it's good that I know. And …" She sipped her wine. "He doesn't know that I know. That gives you power."

"It doesn't feel like it," Tess said.

"It does."

Tess no longer felt like crying. She felt less tipsy, and surprisingly, her panic had subsided, for now.

CHAPTER 69

NOW: AMELIA

The library in my mother's tower didn't have nearly as many books as mine. I hadn't noticed when I'd glanced at it as I first passed the doorway. Standing inside now, it struck me that the shelves were much higher. Many of them were filled with decorative objects and held only a few leather-bound books. They seemed to be there for show because when I picked one up, the gold-leaf edges were stuck together as if I were the first person to turn the pages.

The room was much colder than any other room in the castle, and I shivered as I stood in the center, turning slowly, wondering why it gave me such a strange feeling. I rubbed my arms and studied the objects on the shelves, the things I'd never seen before—bronze statues of figures from fairy tales and bottles that looked like they might contain genies.

Directly across from the entrance was a cabinet built into the wall. It had a glass door and inside was an urn that looked like one I'd seen when I was doing research for a report on funeral customs. The only difference was the urns I'd seen were about twelve to eighteen inches tall. This was at least three feet tall. It was painted turquoise and gold.

I opened the glass door and ran my fingers over the glossy paint.

A chill ran through my body. Despite its size, I was even more certain that this was an urn containing someone's ashes.

And then the horrible thought came to me. It descended like a heavy blanket had fallen over me, making it difficult to breathe. Was this where my father had disappeared to?

My hands shook, seeming to move toward it of their own free will. I wanted to remove the lid. At the same time, I couldn't imagine doing something so awful. I didn't want to see what was inside. I didn't want to see ash and bits of bone. Just because it was an urn didn't mean it was him. And how would I know? Still, I wanted to open it, even knowing a pile of ashes would tell me nothing. I wouldn't see his red hair, reflecting the color of mine. I wouldn't look into his eyes or hear his voice.

But I couldn't stop myself. I lifted the lid. It came off easily.

When I saw what was inside, I gagged. I felt my fingers start to lose their grip on the top. I grabbed it with my other hand so I didn't drop it.

Inside were not only ashes, but a skull and several long bones. I shoved the top on the urn, closed the cabinet door, and ran out of the room. I rushed down the stairs as fast as I could, keeping my hand flat against the stone wall, feeling as if the railing wasn't enough to keep me steady, that I needed the solid feel of stone to keep me from tumbling head over heels down the curving staircase to the bottom.

My mother never mentioned finding the cabinet full of keys that I'd left unlocked because I'd had to return the key to the ribbon around her neck. Maybe she thought she'd forgotten to lock it. Maybe she knew what I'd done. Maybe she knew, deep inside, that the end of her fairy tale was inevitable. I was nineteen.

After that horrifying moment, I began screaming every time I was aware of strangers entering the castle. I spent most of my time in my bedroom, looking out the tower window, watching for visitors coming up the drive toward the entrance. When I knew they were inside, I would scream as loudly as I could, hoping the sound might carry down the tower stairs, past the locked door, into the other rooms. I didn't know. I could only hope.

I began to think my screaming was futile.

Then, one night, Nolan came into my room. He woke me by turning on the light and shouting my name. He spoke in a low, calm voice. "If you scream again, one of your pets will die. Each time you scream, a pet will lose its life. Your choice."

A moment later, the light was off. He spoke into the darkness. "You've been warned."

And there was nothing left for me to do. I had been warned.

Until the day I heard a woman calling from outside the wall, asking if someone was there, asking if I could hear her.

I froze.

Who was she? A friend of my mother's? I wasn't sure she had any friends. Was she someone who worked at the castle? Or one of the brides who came there to live her fairy tale? I didn't answer because I didn't know if she was there to trick me. Nolan might have sent her to see what I would do.

He was so cruel he would kill my precious animals, the only friends I had in the entire world. Sweet, blameless creatures who never did anything wrong. Who did nothing but give love.

If I spoke to her, what would happen? What did she want? Why was she calling out to me? No one had ever done that before. Thousands of people had visited the castle over the years of my life, and no one had ever come up to the wall around my garden. No one had ever tried to speak to me.

Maybe she wasn't even real. I might be imagining her. This might be a waking dream. I might be hallucinating. It could be anything. She could be anything.

After a long time, I whispered, "Hello?"

There was no answer.

I spoke in a slightly louder voice. "Hello? Who are you?"

There was still no answer.

It was too late. She was gone.

CHAPTER 70

NOW: ALEX

There was nothing to be done about Tess's blackmail situation. Not right away.

I had rules about how many martinis I would drink in certain circumstances. I didn't have such strict rules with wine, but I had a general idea. It surprised me that Tess didn't have rules of her own. Maybe she did, and she'd tossed them aside in her rush to become familiar with the wine she was producing and bottling.

Even with that, it was difficult for me to imagine how she'd gotten herself into the mess she was in. She'd said nothing about Silas assaulting her, so it was obviously her own mistake. But she certainly wasn't to blame for the photographs and the blackmail, so my opinion of Silas had only grown worse.

For now, she would have to wait. So would Silas. So would I.

I wondered what he really wanted from her. He'd threatened to tell Marcus, but there had to be more to it since he hadn't asked for money or anything else. He would gain nothing by telling Marcus what she'd done, so he was playing a longer game we couldn't see. And although I think a part of her hated me for it, because there was nothing she could do with it, she did have a little more power. It would just take time.

Now, I was waiting for Diana and our long-postponed video call. I sat at the desk in the guest room, my tablet propped up, and my face made up as if I were going to work.

Diana came onto the screen and for half a second, I was thrown back to the first time I'd met her. She looked more like her old self when she gave me a little wave hello. She was wearing the wrist full of bangle bracelets that used to clatter up and down her forearm until she became my boss and tossed away all the fun aspects of herself.

She got right to the point. "Your resignation was abrupt and somewhat unprofessional. And delaying this meeting has been really annoying. I think I deserve more respect than this. As your employer, your former colleague, and as a friend."

I stared at her. "Normally, it's not possible to be friends with your boss."

"We were friends before I was your boss," she said.

I didn't want to get into a debate about friendships or relationships at all. I'd resigned. What I wanted to know was why we were even doing this. "Why did you want this call? So you can tell me what I'm doing wrong? Again?"

"Is that why you resigned? Because you can't take direction or do anything to be part of a team?"

"No."

"You seem to have significant issues with authority."

"Maybe."

"Why is that?"

"I didn't agree to this call because I need therapy. I'm resigning. Do you have questions about the handoff? It sounded like Dean had a good grip on everything before I left."

"It was so abrupt. It's hurtful. I don't understand why you're leaving."

I laughed.

"You think that's funny?"

"I think work shouldn't have anything to do with hurt feelings.

The job isn't satisfying anymore. I need freedom in how I interact with clients. I can't accomplish what I did when I'm sharing the clients with another photographer. I told you that. And you and I have been disagreeing about everything. It's time to move on."

"So that's it?"

"What else is there?"

"Don't you feel any connection to our vision? To me?"

"I liked what I was doing. Things changed, and now it's not as much fun. So I need something new. It's not personal."

"Work isn't always *fun*."

"I know that."

"You're being childish."

I gave her a tiny smile, one that I thought might look sympathetic, or it might be interpreted any way she chose.

"I feel like I deserve an explanation," she said.

"I told you, it's time to move on. I need a change."

"That's all you're going to say?"

"That's all there is."

"I don't feel good about how this is ending."

"Dean will fit in great. I'm sure you'll feel really good about that."

"But—"

"There's nothing more to say."

"I'm really sorry to see you go, Alex."

I stared at her for a moment, trying to think about what I should say. It was confusing that she hadn't seen this coming. She'd been annoyed with me constantly since the moment Trystan died. She complained about everything I did. I really didn't understand why she was suddenly so interested in getting along. It kind of made my head ache. I smiled as the words popped into my head. "I hope you Fly Higher."

"Are you mocking me?"

"Not at all." I kept smiling and gave her a little wave. "Bye." I ended the call, mesmerized for a moment as she stared at me, her eyes wide with shock, and then, in a blink, she was gone—from the screen and my life.

Now I could focus on what interested me, and oddly enough, it had to do with photography.

I'd thought of another plausible reason to request a visit to the castle. I would explain to Ella that we needed more detailed photographs for the wedding planner and designer. I would tell her that the photographs Julia had taken weren't enough. We needed some detailed close-ups.

I would come alone because Tess didn't need to be involved with such minutiae. I would tell her Kate was swamped, but she knew that I understood Tess's vision, so she'd asked me to do her a favor and take care of it.

Because of my encounters with Nolan, I wasn't sure Ella would swallow my story. At the same time, I had no doubt she would handcuff me to her wrist, so what was there to worry about? And she wanted to keep Tess, the bride with the most moving fairy tale of all, in a state of anticipatory bliss.

Ella said yes. Perhaps my sales skills rivaled those of Silas.

Instead of borrowing Tess's car and stirring up her concern about my obsession with the castle yet again, I called an Uber.

Once I was inside, Ella indeed kept herself as close as my shadow. Not only that, she insisted I keep my phone in my purse. "I'll take whatever photographs you need."

"I'm a professional photographer. Did you know that?"

"Tess mentioned it."

"I should take the pictures."

She smiled. "These aren't publicity shots. They're working photos for planning purposes only. In fact, the contract Tess signed forbids you from using any photographs taken here that haven't been reviewed by myself or Nolan."

"I was asked to—"

"I'll take the photographs, Alexandra. You won't be getting professional shots on a cell phone." She laughed. "Just tell me what you need, and I'm happy to capture whatever is necessary. Anything you need. Anything at all."

We covered every square foot of the great hall, the terrace, the dining room, even the dressing rooms for the bride and groom.

"I'd like to see the second floor as well," I said.

"No."

"But we want to add some welcoming touches for the bridal party's overnight stay."

"Our staff will provide flowers and hand towels to match the wedding colors. Nothing else is allowed."

"But Tess—"

"Tess knows the rules."

"Then I guess all that's left is the kitchen."

"I *guess* so." She smiled.

"First, I need to use your restroom."

She heaved a deep sigh, following me down the hall to the nearest restroom. I locked the door behind me and took out my phone. I set it to record a video, placed it in the front pocket of my jeans in a way that the camera was exposed, flushed the toilet, ran the water in the sink, then waited a few seconds before re-joining Ella in the hallway.

"After a few quick shots of the kitchen, I'd like some photos of the garden."

"This is getting out of hand," Ella said.

"Is it?"

"I don't understand why your planner needs so many photographs."

"She's very thorough."

"She has the floor plans. She already saw the place. Her follow-up visits are already on the schedule."

"She's one of the best," I said.

"So I've heard." Ella turned and hurried toward the kitchen.

I rushed her through the kitchen photos, which were just a

distraction on the way to photographing the opening in the garden wall surrounding the tower.

"Now some shots of the terrace and the gardens and we'll be finished."

"Will we?" Ella asked, her tone sharp with sarcasm.

"I think so." I gave her a charming smile.

She walked quickly back toward the great hall and out to the terrace. She took the photos as I directed, brushing her slightly as I moved toward the path that circled the entire castle.

"I don't understand why you need all these."

"I told you, Kate is very thorough, and Tess is a perfectionist. She wants her wedding to be the most incredible one you've ever had here."

"It's not a competition."

"Isn't it?"

Ella smiled. At least we understood each other on that front now.

As we approached the wall surrounding the tower, I slowed my pace, wanting to be sure I got a good long video of the opening in the wall. I hoped my phone was angled correctly to capture it. Trying to walk slowly, focusing on Ella, directing her photographs, and thinking about the phone in my pocket was challenging.

A few steps before I reached the spot where the missing stone was, something caught my eye.

Nestled in the curve of the mortar where the rock had been removed was a tiny crocheted bag. It was gray, almost the same color as the mortar.

CHAPTER 71

$\mathcal{W}$ ithout hesitating, I let out a tiny cry and threw myself sideways as hard as I could onto the decorative rock and rose bushes that lined the path. I cried out again, louder and with genuine pain this time. As I lay there, I shoved my phone deep into my pocket, then flung my arm across one of the rose bushes, letting the thorns tear the skin on the back of my forearm. I whimpered as the thorns dug into my flesh. I turned away, unable to bear looking at the blood oozing up from the wounds.

Ella suddenly stopped, stumbling off the path as she did. "What happened? Are you okay?" She moved toward me and extended her hand.

"I don't know." I placed my hand over my bleeding arm, then took it away, staring in horror at the smears of red across my palm.

"Don't touch it!" Ella said. "Take my hand."

"I don't know if I can get up."

She bent over and put her hands under my armpits.

"No. Wait. I can't …"

"What's wrong?"

"I don't know if I can stand right away. I sprained my ankle a few weeks ago. I think that's why I fell. It's still weak and I … will you get me some bandages? And antiseptic? I think I need to rest for a minute before I ..."

She heaved a pained sigh, so heavy you'd have thought she was the one who was injured. "I'll be right back. Don't go anywhere."

"Not to worry." I pointed at the dripping blood and the ankle I was holding with my other hand, as if it were throbbing more than it was.

When she rounded the corner toward the back terrace, I scrambled across the path, grabbed the crocheted bag, and stuffed it into my bag. I stumbled back to where I'd been and sprawled beside the rosebush. I pulled my phone out of my pocket, stopped the recording, and dropped it into my bag.

By the time she returned, I'd arranged myself in a more comfortable sitting position. Blood was still dripping off my arm, but I wasn't looking at the wounds, only the occasional drop as it fell onto the path. The scratches weren't deep and already the bleeding seemed to slow.

Ella patched me up with more expertise than I would have expected. She was clearly annoyed and didn't speak the entire time. Finally, she stood. "Are you going to be able to walk?"

"I think so. It feels a little better now. Like I said, it's still weak from my sprain."

She looked like she didn't believe me, but at the same time, she couldn't quite put her finger on exactly what was unbelievable about the situation.

She waited in front of the castle with me, making anxious small talk until my Uber arrived.

The minute the driver rounded the first curve headed away from the castle, I pulled the tiny crocheted bag out of my purse. Inside was a scrap of paper. It read—*Please come back. Rescue me. ~Amelia*

During the rest of the drive back to Tess's, my mind ticked through a plan. By the time we reached the gates of the Black Mask Winery, I told the driver I needed to run a quick errand. I asked her to take me into the town of Napa first. While she waited, I went into a discount store and bought several towels of varying sizes, a roll of duct tape, and a good pair of scissors.

I took a nap before dinner. It was going to be a late night, possibly an all-nighter.

I left Tess's house at one o'clock in the morning, using the unmonitored kitchen door. I was carrying a backpack stuffed with the towels, scissors, and duct tape. I'd written a note to Amelia telling her I might be able to help, but I needed to know how far she was willing to go in her desire to escape.

I walked across the garden and through the edge of the vineyard. I wrapped the towels around the razor wire, taped them in place, and climbed through, safely avoiding the security cameras at all the entrance points. I cut the tape, packed up my towels, and began an easy jog back to the main entrance. I'd pre-arranged an Uber, paying a hefty fee to have the driver pick me up at that time of night and wait for me once I was dropped a few hundred yards from the castle gates.

At the castle, I wrapped the razor wire again and crawled through. I hiked up the incline and went to the garden wall. I placed the tiny crocheted bag containing my note into the opening in the garden wall. By three-thirty, I was in bed, my muscles relaxed, although my heart continued to pound with adrenaline. It was nearly five by the time I fell asleep.

The following night, I did the same thing again, knowing I would find another note in the little bag.

Instead, Amelia had a different surprise for me.

A piece of dark gray yarn tied around a small stone lay in the opening. I pulled on it. At first, the yarn grew taut and seemed stuck. Then I felt something heavy start to move. The object hit the side of the wall and stopped. I held the yarn with one hand and wriggled my hand through the narrow opening. A cardboard tube was tied to the other end.

After a lot of maneuvering, I could position the tube so the end fit into the opening. I poked my fingers inside and worked the tube through to my side of the wall. It turned out to be an empty paper towel roll. It was filled with rolled up sheets of paper that had been curled to fit around the inside.

I waited until I was back at Tess's to start reading.

The exquisite handwriting, perfect penmanship that might have come from the hand of a young woman in the 1940s, was a sharp contrast with the lined paper torn roughly from a spiral-bound notebook. The pages contained passionate, desperate-sounding letters written to a *fairy godmother*. They told the story of a little girl who was raised to believe she was a princess, growing up all alone, held captive in the castle tower.

I read about the disappearance of her father and her increasing realization that there was a world beyond the castle walls she would never experience because her mother and the man who was pretending to be her father believed they were somehow keeping her safe inside the castle.

Turning the last page, I read this:

I finally found my father. His bones are in the other tower. So now I know what they did. And I'll do anything to get out of here. Anything. If I don't, I'll die here, and my bones will remain in this tower forever.

CHAPTER 72

*W*hile I'd waited for midnight to come and go before making my trips to the castle, I'd formed an escape plan for Amelia. One that would free her from the castle tower, from Ella and Nolan, and would conceal my identity from her, just in case she had some regrets down the road.

After all, these people were the only ones she'd ever known. Their horrific deaths might weigh on her more than they did on me, even though it would mostly be by my hand. Now, all she wanted was her freedom. But I couldn't predict how she might feel when they were removed from her life permanently. She'd never experienced freedom. Maybe it would turn out to be something she didn't want after all. For some people, freedom is too much. They prefer safety.

I couldn't comprehend spending my entire life knowing only three human beings. I couldn't imagine what it would be like to live, not inside four walls, but inside a single circular wall, built around a spiral of stone steps, every day of your life. She could see the valley beyond, she could hear the voices of other human beings, but she saw no one who was more than a miniature figure walking across their property. She never spoke to anyone but her mother, father, and Nolan.

What would her life be like once she escaped?

But that had nothing to do with me.

Still, she seemed clever. Despite the walls they'd built around her, they couldn't construct a stone fortress around her mind. That had escaped years ago.

First, I needed a way into the castle that didn't involve constant excuses for preparing for Tess and Marcus's wedding. I'd run out of those. The idea formed in my mind when I read what Amelia had written about Ella and Nolan drooling over their freshly baked sweets every night after dinner, and recalled the elaborate cake tasting that had been set up for Tess so far in advance of the wedding. These people valued their desserts.

For the third time, I knocked on Marcus's door and interrupted his work. I made myself comfortable on the sofa across from his desk and gave him a needy, worried smile.

"I don't know if Tess mentioned, but I had to quit my job. It was premature, I realize that, because I don't have anything else lined up. But the environment had become really toxic." I gave him a sad smile. "Staying here has given me a lot of clarity." I took a deep breath. "But I'm still figuring things out, and while I do that, I need to keep myself busy."

He looked slightly worried.

I laughed. "I'm not asking you for a job."

He didn't look any less worried. I wondered what he thought I wanted. "Tess said you have a lot of connections in the community here."

He nodded once. The worried look was gone, replaced by neutrality.

"It's kind of silly," I laughed in what I was fairly confident was a lighthearted tone. "I'm really taken with the castle, and—"

"So I've heard."

I laughed. "I was thinking it would be fun to get a job with the bakery that supplies the wedding cakes for them. I could work at the weddings, keep myself busy, indulge my castle love, and earn some extra cash."

"You've given a lot of thought to this."

I smiled.

"Still thinking you heard someone screaming and you're determined to figure that out?"

I laughed. "No. I think you're probably right."

"Do you?"

"Absolutely."

He laughed.

I couldn't tell if he didn't believe me, or he didn't believe it himself and he'd come up with that story to make Tess feel comfortable. "I just think the castle is really cool. And I do need to keep busy. I've always worked and I'm going kind of crazy."

"Wouldn't it make more sense to find an apprenticeship with a photographer?"

"I'm thinking about a significant change. I want to do something that will put me in a completely different environment so that my mind isn't locked into thinking about what I've done in the past. I want to be completely open to new ideas."

He nodded. He actually looked interested.

"Anyway, I'm sure they need people to help with serving, clean up. Anything, really."

"I have met her, and of course now she knows both of us because of the wedding ... I'll ask."

He did, and within four days, I had a minimum wage position serving wedding cake. I wouldn't be allowed to plate the cake. That was another job entirely—a specialty, with higher hourly pay— which made me laugh. Not being able to put slices of cake on a plate was a slight upset to my plan, but I would figure out a way around it. I had my foot in the door.

Next, I took an Uber to Vallejo, about fifteen miles south of Napa. It offered more shopping choices for the things I needed, not to mention greater anonymity. I didn't need anyone in the some-what small town of Napa remembering a woman with flaming red hair buying one of the more unusual items I needed in order to help Amelia be rid of her mother and the man who was not only a fake father, but was pretending to be part of a fairy tale with his sister, repeating a story of a romantic love that didn't ring true for reasons that were now quite obvious.

Amelia's fairy tale had also helped me understand why Ella reacted with visceral fear when she'd first met me. The color of my hair must have given her a moment of panic that the sister of her murdered husband had come looking for him.

During my shopping trip I bought several butane lighters. I also bought a pair of nice-fitting leather gloves, just in case. I bought several rope ladders, an extra coil of rope, a fishing knife, a large, sturdy basket that would hold a small dog and two cats, and the item that was sure to arouse the most interest if I'd purchased it in Napa—a box of syringes with long, blunt-nosed metal tips.

Then, I tucked my hair inside a knitted hat, put on jeans and a hoodie, and waited for dusk. I found one of the bars, of which there's always one and usually more than one in every city, identi-fied a guy who was conducting business on the side, and bought some roofies.

Back at Tess's house, I wrote a list of instructions for Amelia.

This was the biggest risk. Although she had never seen me, and never would, if someone else—namely Ella or Nolan—happened to get to the rolled sheet of paper before she did, there was an extremely good chance that their thoughts would turn quickly, if not immediately to me.

I'd considered splitting my instructions into six or seven different pieces, but even on their own, most of the segments would be incriminating. And every trip to the small opening in the wall, every item left in that hollowed out space, increased the risk of discovery.

At first, I'd thought my plan was so perfect. Amelia would never see me. Nolan and Ella would die with no one ever knowing I had anything to do with it. I would be sitting in Tess's living room sipping a martini with her when it happened. It was brilliant. Until I realized this point of vulnerability.

I lay awake for two entire nights considering all the possibilities, all the choices, trying to find ways around it.

Finally, I decided there was no actual proof. I was using my gloves to be sure I didn't leave fingerprints on the paper. Besides, it was unlikely that two people who were holding a woman prisoner in one tower of their castle and the bones of a man in the other tower were going to run to the police with a handwritten sheet of paper outlining a murder scheme. They were much more likely to come after me themselves, and that was a threat I could manage.

So I outlined the things Amelia needed to do and explained what I would be doing to assist her.

I would be working at a wedding on the following Saturday, which would give me a chance to mentally work through the logistics of what I was planning. The weekend after that, there was another wedding, as there were most weekends. I told Amelia to be ready.

CHAPTER 73

A text message from Eileen woke me at seven in the morning.

Although I'd been hyper-alert to anyone noticing what I was up to, Ned had not been the person on my mind.

My thoughts were focused on ensuring that Marcus and Tess didn't notice me coming and going from their estate. Even more, I was consumed with wondering how attentive Nolan and Ella were to their security camera, wondering how many other cameras there were on the property that I hadn't seen. The others on their staff arrived in the morning and left at dusk, so I only needed to watch out for those two—monsters far more hideous than the gargoyle standing in their entryway. At least gargoyles served a worthy purpose.

I longed to know what they thought they were protecting Amelia from. I wanted to ask them why they'd kept her locked in that tower her entire life. I wanted to hear them explain themselves.

If I'd thought my father had twisted ideas about protecting his family from what he believed were the evil influences of the society surrounding us, Ella and Nolan had transformed that desire to escape the world into something so extreme I wondered if even my father might be shocked. But my father would never know.

Ella's reasoning for the near-destruction of her daughter's life would die with her. Nolan's reasons for trying to pass himself off as Amelia's father would also perish. All I could do was speculate. My guess was that her father had reached a point where he could no longer stomach the idea of keeping his little girl in a cage. Unwilling to give up the fantasy of a child who would never be *damaged* by life, Ella, alone, or with the help of her brother, had murdered her husband. From that point, nothing was too bizarre—even making believe they had a fairy tale romance so they could host weddings at the castle.

Whatever their strange, distorted thoughts had been, they would all be burned to ash.

Eileen's text told me she'd seen Ned leaving his office building two days earlier. Now, I realized her effort hadn't helped me at all. There'd been plenty of time for Ned to spend over a week in California, checking on me, then fly home in time for Eileen to verify his presence. I still couldn't definitively cross Ned off my list of people to be concerned about.

Another text promptly followed the first.

Eileen: *When are you coming home?*

That was a disturbing choice of words. The apartment was certainly my home when I lived there, but it was strange that she thought of herself and the apartment as a home I might return to.

Those five simple words clarified everything.

I'd had enough of New York City. At least for now.

Which, of course, created an even bigger problem with Hunter, but I would figure out how to fix that later. After Amelia.

I took a shower and dried my hair. I put on makeup and jeans and a white tank top and my necklace with the single pearl. There were three more text messages from Eileen, asking me why I wasn't responding, asking me if I'd received her message about Ned, asking me if there was something I wasn't telling her.

Shoving my phone into my pocket, I went downstairs and made a fresh pot of coffee. I filled a mug, grabbed a banana, and went out to the back patio.

My phone buzzed with a video call from Eileen. I took a sip of coffee and answered.

"Hi," she said. "Why are you ignoring my messages?"

"Do you know what time it is here?"

"Yes. But I thought this was a big emergency to know what Ned is up to."

"You said you saw him two days ago."

Her face turned faintly pink. "I got distracted. Actually, I met someone ..."

"That's great." It made things easier. I took a few sips of coffee and waited for her to say more.

"When are you coming home? It's been almost a month."

"I'm not coming back to New York."

She stared at me. "You're not ... what? Not *ever*?"

"I doubt that. It's an amazing city. I really like it. But not in the foreseeable future."

"But your room. The ... our agreement. I thought we ... we're roommates."

"You can find another roommate."

"That's it?" Her face was no longer pink. It was as white as a glass of milk. "You're just walking away? I thought we were friends? We agreed to ... I don't even know what to say." Her eyes filled with tears. "This is so, so hurtful. I can't believe you're doing this to me. Did I do something?"

"No. Of course not. I just need a change of scenery."

"What will I do?"

"You know so many models. It should be easy to find another roommate."

"That's not the point!"

"I'll make sure to get my stuff out of there."

"How?"

"I'll ask Hunter."

"You can't even come back to say goodbye?" Her voice was shrill.

"I have a lot going on."

"Like what? Someone following you?"

"Yes, that. And the wedding. And figuring out my career."

"You can do that here! You can talk to me. I'm your friend. I could help you figure things out."

"I enjoy being here. I like having more space. I love the excitement of New York, all the restaurants, the people. But I need a change, and this is perfect for now."

"The only thing you like about New York is the food? What about me?"

"Not just the food. That's not what I said. You and I had some fun times, but now I need a change."

She shook her head, then looked away from the screen. "I can't even ..." A moment later, the screen went dark.

I bit my lower lip. I placed the phone on the table and peeled the banana. I ate it and sipped my coffee. She didn't call back. I hadn't expected her to, but I'd wondered.

We needed to work out arrangements for getting my clothes and moving out my furniture if her new roommate didn't want it. But since Hunter wasn't being chatty and attentive, I wasn't sure he would leap at the chance to pack all my clothes and shoes and makeup. The job could probably be done in less than three hours, but still.

For now, I needed to focus on Amelia. Hopefully Eileen wouldn't toss all my things in the dumpster.

CHAPTER 74

$\mathcal{T}$he wedding was right out of Cinderella, including a horse-drawn carriage that brought the bridal couple up the winding road to the castle doors. The female guests were all dressed in teal, per the bride's *request*—meaning requirement. Their dates wore tuxes with teal bow-ties. The attendants wore pale pink and the groom's attendants wore pale pink jackets and bow-ties.

It was a festival of blandness, despite the brilliant teal.

I didn't spend a lot of time paying attention to the wedding or the partying after. I had a lot to do in a very short time period. This was far more challenging than anything I'd ever done. Luring a man to a hotel room and slipping a roofie into a martini is easy. I could have done it when I was fifteen years old.

What I'd done with Carolina had been considerably more complicated.

This was like walking a tightrope between two skyscrapers versus trying to walk along the edge of a concrete planter three feet off the ground. My timing had to be perfect, my nerves like steel, which they generally were, but then there was that tightrope …

I stood at my assigned post near the cake table. This wasn't a job in which employees were allowed to stand around gossiping while they waited for customers to show up. We were pointed to a spot and told to remain there, hands clasped demurely behind our backs, until the cake was cut. Permission had to be requested even for a bio break.

The syringe filled with crushed up roofies blended into olive oil was in my pocket.

Once Ella and Nolan told their fairy tale to the guests, offered a champagne toast, and ate their cake, I had about thirty minutes before the roofie-infused dessert hit their bloodstream. In that time, I had to guide them off the terrace and into the small room with the nearly hidden door leading to Amelia's tower.

Their toast was always done toward the end of the festivities. The guests ate their cake, the couple left for their honeymoon, and cars would begin arriving to usher the guests away from the castle.

I was ready. I hoped Amelia was as well.

Nolan raised his champagne flute and looked down at Ella with an adoring gaze. They began telling their fantastical story. Every face was turned toward them, everyone caught up in the spell of an expert conman and his even more talented partner. I pulled the first syringe out of my pocket and injected it into the slice of cake closest to me. I did the same with the second syringe, wrapped them both neatly inside a paper napkin, and returned them to my pocket.

As their story unfolded, I felt the adrenaline in my veins ease a little now that the cake was ready. I smiled up at the darkening sky. The stars were glittering, and the moon formed a perfect crescent.

I positioned myself to ensure I was the one who would serve the cake to Nolan and Ella.

By the time all the guests were eating cake, Ella and Nolan were looking mildly disoriented. I walked over to where they stood and took both their arms. "You look tired. Why don't you sit down for a moment?"

"We can't." Ella tried to pull away from me. "There's too much to do." She didn't put much effort into her resistance, as if, half a step into it, she'd forgotten why she wanted to remain where she was.

"Come on. You've done so much already," I cooed. I began leading them into the castle, through the great hall, and around the corner past the dining room.

"Where we goin'?" Nolan asked.

"To have a rest," I said.

I hurried them to the alcove outside the tower where Amelia lived. I didn't have to urge them to sit as I'd expected to. They collapsed onto the sofa, leaning against each other like the lovers they pretended to be.

For another ten minutes, I stood watching them. Steadily, their breathing grew deeper. I saw them relax more fully into each other, their heads lolling back toward the wall behind them.

I'd cut things very close. Another five minutes and they might have passed out on the terrace. I hadn't been sure how the roofies would behave in the cake since I'd always used them in alcohol, so I'd used a bit extra. I had nothing to guide me. It'd been a wild guess. A lucky guess. A *very* lucky guess.

When it was clear they were not going to wake up, I untied the ribbon from around Ella's neck. I went into the pantry and got the key to Amelia's tower from the location she'd noted. I hurried back to the alcove and unlocked the tower door.

With my hands under Ella's armpits, I dragged her off the sofa, across the short distance to the doorway, and into the ground floor room of the tower. Nolan was more difficult. As I pulled him off the sofa, his hips hit the floor hard, and he groaned. I paused, staring at his face, hoping the pain wasn't enough to wake him.

I glanced at the doorway. It was open to the corridor, nothing but a chiffon drapery to conceal what I was doing. The work of cleaning up from the wedding reception was loud, but that didn't mean someone wouldn't hear if I hurt him again, and he cried out with more force.

Clenching my jaw, I struggled to lift his shoulders off the ground, letting his head rest against my shin, then dragged him into the tower. By the time I had him fully inside, lying beside his sister, sweat was pooling on the back of my neck and making my face wet. I wiped my forehead with the back of my hand, then pulled my ponytail away from my neck to cool my skin.

I returned to the alcove and picked up some of the chiffon draperies that were hung from the iron bars that were mounted over doorways and windows throughout the first floor of the castle. I'd gathered as many as I could while the guests were dancing and drinking in the great hall. I added them to the bars that decorated the lower level of the tower.

I placed the butane lighter on a small table near the foot of the staircase. Beside the table, I placed the basket containing the rope ladders, the additional rope, and the knife.

For a moment, I stood looking up the staircase, longing to climb to the top as I had for weeks now. But there wasn't time. Meeting Amelia was not part of my plan. Sometime after, I would meet her, but I would be one of a host of others she encountered in her new life. She would never know I was her fairy godmother.

After everything was in place, I decided not to return the key on its ribbon to Ella's neck. When her body was found, it would simply raise questions about the key cabinet. If it disappeared, the unlocked cabinet would most likely go unnoticed. I left it in my pocket. I placed the key to the tower door in Ella's hand, then closed the tower door, leaving it unlocked.

I continued with my cleanup duties, offering my apologies, and accepting the criticism for *disappearing* and leaving the others with extra work.

When all the cleanup was finished and the catering and bakery staff were getting ready to go, I left alone in an Uber. No one asked where Ella and Nolan were. No one cared. They'd done their jobs and to Ella and Nolan's credit, I suppose, they'd been well paid. Now they were tired and ready to relax.

I was eager to enjoy a martini with Tess in her living room, as we'd agreed earlier. I'd gathered lots of colorful stories from the wedding, stories that I could embellish long into the night to ensure she remembered that I'd been sitting right beside her when the castle tower went up in flames.

CHAPTER 75

NOW: AMELIA

*T*he notes that were passed to me through the hole I'd created by removing one small stone from the garden wall were filled with detailed instructions for starting a fire that would turn quickly into an inferno. The instructions were horrible because they were so precise, so cold, but clear, so very, terrifyingly clear.

I cried when I read them.

First, my tears were for my mother.

I loved her. Rather, I *had* loved her.

Once upon a time ...

With all my heart. She was my everything. She was my playmate, my mother, my goddess, my storyteller, my teacher. She was the sunlight in the morning and the moon at night. Her smile made me happy. I loved to do things that made her smile. I loved to cuddle beside her while she read stories to me. I loved the feel of her brushing my hair and weaving it into braids. I loved telling her about the thoughts in my head.

We played hopscotch and board games. She played make-believe games with me and hide-n-seek in the garden and inside the countless rooms of the castle. When I was little, I thought the corridors were endless. The entire world existed inside our castle.

But then I found out she lied to me. About the castle. About my father. About the world.

And slowly, she turned into a monster. Day by day, my love for her died. She killed it every moment of every day when I sat at my window and looked out across the valley, knowing I would be locked up there forever. I would never speak to another human being. I would never have a friend. I would never find love. I would never live.

My tears turned to tears of rage.

The instructions had been written by my fairy godmother. She answered my letters, even though it didn't seem magical. It hadn't happened the way I'd expected, although I couldn't say what that way *should* have been. But that woman's voice called through the wall, and then she took my note, and then she took my letters, and then she wrote back.

When I saw the horse-drawn carriage arrive at the castle, I knew it was the day of the wedding. It was the day I would find my mother and Nolan on the first floor of my tower after the wedding guests had gone home. They would be unconscious, as if they'd pricked their fingers on a spindle like Sleeping Beauty. I didn't have to touch them.

All I had to do was start the fire.

I watched from my tower window as the carriage and horses started down the road. I heard the clop of the horses' hooves on the pavement. The cars waited for quite a while before they followed because they knew the carriage would be slow.

Soon, the cars began to leave, following each other closely like a long caterpillar. Finally, the vans with the catering staff and the bakery people and everyone from the neighboring winery who had served the champagne and wine left, too.

When they were all gone, I knew I only had a few hours before the drugs in my captors' bodies would start to wear off. I walked slowly down the stone staircase.

I was scared. My hand was freezing cold, I could barely curve my fingers around the railing. Starting a fire and leaving a man and woman to die didn't seem like something a fairy godmother would tell someone to do. But she knew I wanted to be free. She said they had no right to lock me up. She told me they might go to prison for murdering my father, but they might not. It could be hard to prove.

On the first floor, I found the lighters. I saw all the chiffon, just like she'd told me. I looked up into the stairwell and saw the stone walls draped with it—pink and white. The colors my mother had chosen for me. *It softens the stone*, she said.

I carried the basket up to my bedroom at the top. I cut the extra rope she'd given me and tied the rope ladders together to form one long ladder that would reach from my window to the ground. When I was a child, my mother gave me all kinds of toys for make believe. That's what I was supposed to tell the firefighters when they came to put out the fire, when they asked how I'd had so many ladders to escape the flames that killed Ella and Nolan.

I dropped the ladder out the window that faced toward the front of the castle, outside the enclosure of the garden wall. I stood on a chair and secured the ladder to the iron bar above the window.

When everything was ready, I closed my bedroom door, leaving Sugar and Salt and Pepper inside. I hadn't fed them their dinners. They would be hungry and eager to jump into the basket when I put their food inside.

Feeling colder than ever, as if I'd turned to ice, I walked even more slowly back down to the ground floor. I saw them lying there and thought about kissing my mother goodbye, but decided against it. I'd kissed her goodbye a long time ago—the day she told me Nolan was my father.

I picked up the butane lighter and pressed the switch. The flame shot out. I touched it to the first piece of chiffon. It burned so fast, I shrieked. I hurried around the room, lighting the chiffon. Then, I ran up the stairs as fast as I could. I put the animals' food into the basket.

As I'd known they would, they scrambled inside. I used a piece of rope to hang the basket over my shoulders and began climbing down the ladder. My hands ached and burned from gripping the rope so hard. Sugar barked, then went back to eating her dinner. The rope from the basket cut into my neck. They were heavier than I'd guessed. I wanted to go faster, but I was afraid my feet would slip. It was dark, and I hadn't brought a flashlight.

It seemed like forever before my feet touched the ground.

When I turned, I could see the flames through the windows, already on the third floor of the tower. They raced up the staircase, grabbing at the chiffon draperies as they went. They engulfed each room, consuming my craft room filled with yarn and fabric, my playroom with so many wooden toys, my classroom with maps and posters, and the sitting room where my mother used to read stories to me. They devoured the books—so many books it made the tears run down my hot, burning face. But the books were alive inside my mind where they would remain forever.

After a long time, when the flames were shooting out the windows I'd left open in my bedroom, I heard sirens. And then, a while after that, fire trucks were pulling up to the doors of the castle.

My fairy godmother had told me there would be a lot of story-telling for me to do. I would have to tell truthful stories about being held captive, and how my mother and her brother had pretended to be blissfully married lovers. I would have to tell about my father's bones, although those would be found to confirm my story, if the fire trucks arrived in time, which they had.

After that, I would have to tell a fairy tale of my own.

I would tell them I was sleeping with my pets when I smelled the smoke. I would tell them about running down to my childhood playroom and seeing the flames racing up the staircase. I would tell them about grabbing the rope ladders. I would tell them about the games my mother and I had played, for which she'd bought rope—camp-outs and adventures in the woods surrounding the castle.

Then, I would cry my heart out for the loss of my mother. And my uncle.

The tears for my mother would be real and the pain would stay with me forever.

I would hold Sugar close to my heart. I would rub my face in the soft fur of Salt and Pepper. If the firefighters and later, the police, believed my stories, the castle would belong to me. Eventually, the fire damage would be repaired. If I wanted it that way, the weddings could resume, and I would become the queen of the castle.

CHAPTER 76

NOW: ALEX

*T*ess and I drank three martinis the night of the fire at the
Windy Hills Castle. We did not hear the sirens. We were
listening to demo playlists from bands she was planning to audition
for their wedding. It wasn't even my idea, but I couldn't have
arranged it any better.

Not knowing about the fire at the castle until the following day
made it even less likely to cross her mind that it had anything to do
with me. I'd been home for hours after the wedding. She was sitting
across from me as we sipped our first drink.

Halfway into our second drink, we were up, dancing to the
music.

By our third drinks, the bifold doors were open, and we were
dancing in and out of the living room, onto the patio, and back for
another sip. We laughed a lot and as we nibbled our olives, Tess said,
"I'm going to have to listen to these all over again because all I'm
thinking about is dancing and I'm not comparing them at all. I can't
even remember which songs go with which group."

I laughed.

She laughed.

"Marcus needs to hear them anyway," I said. "Right?"

"But I was supposed to narrow it down for him. He thinks I have a more discerning ear." She giggled. "Right now, I can't discern a damn thing." She whirled around with her arms outstretched, almost falling sideways.

"The music is making its way into your subconscious. When you listen again, you'll be able to decide faster because your instinct will be sharper."

She laughed as if it were the funniest thing she'd heard all year. "If you say so."

"I'm sure that's true. It sounds true."

"You think that anything you think is true."

"That sounds like a riddle," I said.

She laughed again. "You make it all up as you go along."

I laughed as if that were the funniest thing I'd heard all year. Maybe it was.

We finished our drinks. We sat sideways on the sectional, our legs tucked up, facing each other, sipping water. "Should we have another?" Tess asked.

"Absolutely not."

She nodded. "That would be stupid."

"You would regret it all day tomorrow. And maybe the next."

We finished our water and went upstairs to bed, gripping the railing on the stairs as if our lives depended on it. Which they probably did. The stairs were long, curved, and treacherous.

When I came down for coffee the next day, knowing I wouldn't be going for a run, not because of the three martinis necessarily, but because I was waiting to see how, and when, Tess would hear the news, waiting to hear how it would all play out, Tess was already seated at the kitchen bar.

She'd made espresso.

I let her pour me a tiny cup and sat beside her. The jolt of caffeine made my blood feel cleaner, somehow. It was an illusion. I knew that, but still, it felt good.

"There was a fire at the castle." She sounded calm and strangely unconcerned.

That concerned me. I didn't want to hear news of a minor fire, something easily extinguished. I didn't want to hear news of an enraged Nolan and Ella, wondering why they'd woken in a stupor, choking on smoke and the ash of burned chiffon in the bottom room of Amelia's tower.

I took a sip of espresso.

"Where did you hear that?"

"It's on Instagram. A guest from yesterday's wedding posted it."

"Was it bad?"

"One of the towers burned." Without moving her head, she looked up at me to gauge my reaction to the destruction of my obsession.

"I guess with all the candles and torches, and all those unnecessary draperies ..."

"It is dangerous. I mentioned it to Ella, because I want a long veil and a train that drags on the floor." She grinned.

"A princess through and through."

She shrugged. "I asked her if we could use electric candles in the main hall."

"What did she say?"

"She wouldn't give me a straight answer."

"What happened with the fire? Was the tower the only part that was damaged? It won't affect your wedding, will it?"

"I doubt it. There's plenty of time for repairs." She scrolled through her phone. A moment later, she gasped. "Oh, my god! Oh god. This is ... oh, how awful!" She whimpered softly.

"What's wrong?"

"They ... they're ... oh, my *GOD*!"

"What?"

She dropped her phone onto the counter and put her hands over her face.

I felt a sense of satisfaction spread through me, although I hoped it wasn't premature. I wondered how long it would take for the story of Amelia to emerge. She seemed capable. She … I knew nothing about her. I would have to wait because I couldn't begin to guess how she might have handled things. Although it sounded as if she might have set a blaze fierce enough to consume the tower entirely.

"They're *dead!*"

I waited for her to tell me more.

"Ella and Nolan burned to death in the fire. That's so awful! It's … what a tragedy. It's so … I can't believe this." She picked up her phone again. She scrolled and tapped, lowering her head over her phone.

I wondered if she felt a loss or if she was thinking about her wedding.

"It's so awful. They were dead when the first responders got inside. Burned … almost …" She put her hand over her mouth and turned her phone face down on the counter again. "I can't read this. Why are people posting these things?"

"What happened?"

"It was an inferno," Tess said softly. "The fire started on the ground floor. There's a staircase … the fire just raced up. They must have had those draperies everywhere. You know they did. And someone was *living* there." She stared at me, but didn't seem to be focused on me. Her eyes were wide, and she hardly blinked. "In the tower. She's a teenager … or a young woman, I guess, living there. She climbed out of the tower on a rope ladder. So strange." She put her hand to her throat. "I feel a little …" She got up and hurried out of the room.

I wondered if it was the martinis or the thought of the burned bodies, or someone hidden in the tower she hadn't known about. Maybe all three.

Whatever it was, I'd escaped the spotlight for now and wouldn't need to express horror and disgust and all those other things that would be expected of me in the coming days.

For the next three evenings, during dinner, and sipping wine on the patio after, Tess and Marcus talked about nothing else. They pored over news articles. They texted neighbors and colleagues. Tess was on the phone half the day. She spoke to other brides who had weddings booked at the castle. She made me call the bakery and find out everything I could.

She was like an information clearinghouse, gathering every bit of gossip and data and local news she could get her hands on. When I mentioned I'd met a reporter a few weeks earlier, I thought she was going to grab my phone out of my hand and try to call him herself.

For a while, she became as obsessed with the woman locked in the castle tower as I had been.

CHAPTER 77

*I*n the weeks following the fire, everyone who came into the tasting room, visitors who stayed for tours of the winery, people in restaurants and the shops in Napa, and in places where locals hung out, talked about the woman who had lived her entire life hidden inside the castle tower. They were mesmerized by her and her story.

When Amelia appeared at the Farmer's Market with Sugar on a leash, a crowd formed around her. Five or six attorneys had offered to handle the settling of her mother's estate for her without charge.

The local paper ran a four-page story about her, including lavish photographs of Amelia and her pets, the garden outside her tower, and pictures she'd given them of the lavish rooms inside her tower.

Contractors offered discounts to restore the burned tower. It was quickly determined that the stone had survived the fire with minimal damage.

After the curiosity had been satiated, mine included, with a tour of the tower that remained in-tact, Tess informed me she and Marcus had decided their wedding would take place at their own, absolutely gorgeous winery. There was no great hall, and they weren't sitting on top of a hill. There were no towers, and it was possible some of the mystique was missing—the aura of a fairy tale. Instead of a gargoyle greeting their guests, Damien would welcome them with an offer of Chardonnay. The Black Mask Chardonnay was quite good.

"I don't like the feeling of getting married in a place where people were burned alive," Tess said.

"It does seem a little creepy."

"Marcus doesn't like it at all."

"Your patio is beautiful. And if you move the furniture out of your living room, it would be great for dancing."

"It's not as if we'll be having five hundred guests." She laughed. "I'd discussed it with Ella ..." She shivered. "I wanted to know if there were ways to arrange the hall so it didn't appear so massive. Ella wasn't very cooperative, though."

"You don't really need a fairy-tale wedding," I said. "There's a lot of death in fairy tales."

She gave me a somewhat frightened look, but didn't say anything. She took a sip of her sparkling water. "I was thinking ..." She got up from the chair where she'd been sitting and moved across to sit beside me. She scooted close until our thighs were touching.

I inched away, but she put her hand on my leg to stop me. She leaned over, putting her lips close to my ear. "I was thinking about my other problem. Him." She nodded her head in a vague direction, which I could only guess was supposed to be toward the tasting room. "And your situation. I was thinking we might come up with something that's, well, I guess the best way to say it is, we could have a mutually beneficial arrangement."

I wished she wouldn't sit so close, but she obviously didn't want anyone to overhear. Not even Damien. He was far enough away, but that bird had sharp ears. And he made his own choices about what phrases he adopted. Once or twice, when I'd tried to teach him a phrase, he'd looked at me with a clear, steady gaze and stubbornly refused to even try repeating my words. Other times, someone let a word slip in passing, and he was all over it. Maybe she was concerned he would pick up on an unfortunate phrase and make it part of his repertoire.

"Since you're between jobs," Tess said, her voice low and somewhat conspiratorial, "I have an idea."

"I don't think you can say I'm between jobs, because that implies I have another job on the horizon."

"I'm thinking of promoting Silas."

"That's a brilliant idea. Reward the man who's blackmailing you."

"It's not a reward. It's a tactic. I'll promote him to something fluffy. It will put some space between him and our customers. If you're interested, you could become the manager of the tasting room and gift shop. At the same time, you could keep an eye on him."

I could not imagine anything more perfect. Keeping an eye on Silas … it was a job made for me. I could watch him until I found a way to lead him right into his grave. It sounded as if Tess knew me better than I knew myself.

Did she *know*? Did she *really* know in some deep part of herself that wasn't aware of what she knew? That wasn't possible. But it was so absolutely perfect it was one of those things of which many people would say—It's a gift from heaven.

"I would be honored to work for the Black Mask Winery." I scooted away from her.

"Don't mock me."

"I'm not."

"It sounds like you are."

"Not at all. Not even a little. It's perfect. I love wine. I want to keep an eye on Silas."

She nodded, her eyes widening, gazing at something I couldn't see, staring past me. Perhaps she was imagining all sorts of unpleasant outcomes.

"I think I can get Hunter to go to my apartment and pack my things for me."

She laughed. "God, Alex, he's not your lackey."

"I know. But he'll be glad to—"

"Then maybe you should invite him to deliver them to you. I want to meet this guy. Don't you think he deserves a trip out here? As a thank you? If he agrees to pack up all your crap?" She laughed. "I mean, why is this guy so devoted to you? You act like you hardly think about him. You haven't mentioned his name for ages, and now, the first time I hear you talk about him, it's because you want him to be your PA."

"He's more of a beer drinker."

This time, she moved farther away from me on the sofa. "That's why you haven't invited him? Because I own a winery? Are you ... I don't even know what to say." She laughed, but it was a strange sound, as if she didn't think it was very funny at all, as if she were a bit frightened.

"I'll invite him. But he's also not speaking to me. So, we'll see how that goes."

She stared at me. After a few minutes, she stood. She extended her hand. "Welcome to the Black Mask Winery."

"What's my salary?"

"Something along the lines of what you earned when we worked on the TruthTeller app. I'll write up an offer. So we can be formal. I need to figure out the offer for Silas first."

"Sure."

Our voices had risen as we talked. Because at that moment, Damien's sharp hearing made itself evident.

What's my salary? What's my salary?

The word salary wasn't as crisp as some of his words. The casual listener might not pick up on it. But Tess and I laughed. I hoped he would forget the conversation before he perfected his pronunciation.

CHAPTER 78

*S*ince his strange text message telling me I'd been very *determined* to go out with him, Hunter's messages had been even stranger. Not in the same way that message had been strange, but in a new way. As if we were now friends who kept in touch once in a while. Two people who used to be together and now weren't. A couple who didn't have a lot of passion, so things had ended with a whimper. Or dissolved into nothing.

Every few days, he asked how I was doing. In between, I asked what he was up to and what was happening in New York. He told me weird stories about his job and things he'd seen in Central Park, which were the things you always saw in Central Park, so they weren't all that interesting.

I told him about the castle. He'd continued to accuse me of being obsessed, which I was used to. I was also tired of it because that's a word that gets thrown around a little too much, especially at me.

We exchanged only a few brief messages at a time, and some of our exchanges were close to wordless. There were a lot of weather reports, lots of emojis of the sun and clouds with the sun peeking out, a few with rain. I'd sent far too many photos of grapes on vines and he'd sent far too many pictures of beer bottles. I'd sent photos of practically every glass of wine, telling him how delicious the Black Mask wines were.

Now, I realized I was going to have to learn a whole lot more than how much I enjoyed drinking it. I knew nothing about bouquet and body, complexity and tannins. I didn't know fruit forward from jammy. Things were going to get interesting.

I sent him a text telling him that Tess had offered me a job.

Hunter: *Selling wine sounds perfect for you.*

Alex: *I agree.*

Hunter: *Good luck.*

Alex: *Thanks.*

I waited for him to say more. The screen went dark. I waited for fifteen minutes. There was nothing. The conversation seemed unfinished, but it was his turn. Wasn't it?

An hour passed and there were no more text messages.

I took a shower, put on a turquoise top that slid off one shoulder, lots of makeup, and waited for my hair to dry naturally. I went into the sitting room where I'd spent so much time with my sprained ankle. I sat with my legs up on the love seat and took a few selfies with the windows behind me so he could get a glimpse of the view.

After picking the best one, I sent it to him.

Alex: *It's an amazing house.*

It was ten minutes before he replied.

Hunter: *I know.*

Alex: *Want to join me?*

Seven minutes passed. He was starting to annoy me. I wasn't sure if he was busy or playing games. Unless he was in a meeting, I doubted he was that busy. And if he was in a meeting, he wouldn't be texting at all.

Hunter: *It's a little late for that, don't you think?*

Alex: *Why?*

Hunter: *I'm not sure if this is a game or what.*

Alex: *No game.*

Hunter: *It feels like one.*

Alex: *It's not.*

Hunter: *Why now?*

Alex: *Why not?*

He didn't respond for two hours.

Hunter: *Okay. Sure. When?*

Alex: *Whenever you can get away. Tess offered to get you a first-class ticket.*

Hunter: *No thanks. I'll take care of it.*

Alex: *I do have a favor.*

He sent the cynical emoji with the raised eyebrow.

Alex: *Do you mind packing my stuff for shipping? In my apartment. I'll arrange it with Eileen. I'm leaving the furniture. Just my clothes and stuff.*

Hunter: *I can't.*

Alex: *You can't?*

Hunter: *I'm traveling right now. So I won't be flying from New York.*

Alex: *Where are you?*

Hunter: *Not in New York. I'll explain when I see you.*

I didn't think Eileen was going to be willing to pack my things. I closed my eyes and pictured all my beautiful clothes, all the makeup I'd invested in over the years—makeup for fun and makeup for altering my appearance. I could walk away from it. I was sure my new salary would be nice. It might be time for a wardrobe refresh, although astronomically expensive when I thought of some of my nice boots and high heels, coats, and dresses.

Maybe Eileen would do it. She had to get it out of the apartment anyway.

Maybe I should fly back. I sighed. I wanted a clean break. I was settled and comfortable.

I would decide later. For now, I found myself suddenly excited to see Hunter. And very curious about where he was, and why. But mostly, eager to see him.

CHAPTER 79

NOW: HUNTER

*H*unter closed his laptop.

He'd been texting Alex from the laptop app rather than from his phone because he'd wanted to read each message carefully. He didn't want a slip of the thumb to send a message before he'd reviewed it three times. The extra caution was extreme, but he couldn't afford to make a mistake.

The invitation to visit her, with no end date mentioned, had caught him off guard. Of course, everything she did caught him off guard. It had been that way from the moment he'd seen her standing outside his office building at six-thirty in the morning, waiting for him like a clumsy stalker who didn't know how to conceal herself. Although he'd since learned there was nothing clumsy about her. It was the reverse—she always seemed to know exactly what she was doing.

He worried about her all the time, but not about her wellbeing.

He'd spent countless hours trying to work out her motives. Was she just an assertive woman who knew her own mind? A girl who was sure of what she wanted and went after it without hesitation or concern for what anyone might think? Was she socially awkward? She didn't seem that way in most situations. In fact, it was just the opposite in that case as well. And yet, she didn't care, she hardly seemed to notice when she disrupted someone else's plans or expectations.

But those weren't the things that genuinely concerned him.

He worried she was setting him up. That was the fear that consumed him.

There was something so unconventional about her. He felt that every time he saw her, she had a plan he wasn't aware of. Every message exchange, every phone call, every conversation. She appeared to control the direction or have the end point in mind.

Even those thoughts made his head hurt because he wasn't sure those were accurate either.

But something constantly wiggled at the base of his skull as if a tiny group of larvae nested there, squirming and eating their fill, growing into something he couldn't foresee.

What worried him was that Alex wasn't at all who she said she was.

What terrified him was that she was part of some grandiose plan to gradually suck him into a place where he was so obsessed with her that he lost all awareness of anything else. And then, they would come for him. They'd been watching him all this time. For years.

They'd sent her, and she'd ripped him open. He'd let down his guard. She was going to worm her way further into his life, and then they would take everything and everyone he loved. When they were done, they would also kill him, in the most brutal way possible.

It sounded paranoid. It sounded, when he actually allowed the thoughts to play out like that, irrational. He felt as if he was completely unbalanced. But that was what he feared, and he couldn't stop those thoughts from creeping up on him at the most unwelcome times.

So he'd decided he needed to find out. He needed to know more about her.

Looking into her company had given him nothing. There was very little information about her online, at least not for the casual searcher. Despite his somewhat serious suggestion that he should hire a private investigator, he wasn't sure that was the right approach. It might cause more problems than it would solve.

Instead, he'd flown to California himself and followed her. He'd been rather clumsy himself, it turned out.

He knew that she'd seen him the first time he'd tried to follow her in his rental car. After that, his technique had become even more sloppy. As a result, he'd learned nothing. Researching the background of the Black Mask Winery and the new owners had also yielded nothing useful.

Now he had an invitation to live in the same house with her indefinitely. Would that kind of twenty-four-seven proximity allow him to learn anything new? If she was setting him up, inviting him to live with her seemed like a risky move. Or was it another method for subduing his instincts?

Because he'd spent enough time with her to understand that no matter what he did, she always seemed to keep one step ahead of him.

A NOTE FROM CATHRYN

I hope you enjoyed reading *The Woman In the Castle* as much as I loved writing it. This book was a lot of fun to write because Alex did things a little differently than usual! I thoroughly enjoyed finding out what she thought about fairy tales and fantasy, and I loved seeing how she found a way to deliver her form of justice without revealing her identity.

When I first started writing about Alexandra Mallory, I thought she would be a character threatened by a strange roommate in a standalone psychological thriller—*The Woman In the Mirror*. Within a few chapters of starting that novel, Alex took on a life of her own. Her voice came into my head in a way I had never experienced with other characters. By the time I finished writing that book, I knew she would have a few more stories ... and here we are, with the fifteenth book and no end in sight. Yet.

The response to this woman with clear sociopathic tendencies and deeply held opinions on everything from olives to the place of religion in the world has overwhelmed me at times. Readers have told me she scares them. They see a small piece of themselves in her, and they've felt empowered by her. The greatest thrill for me is that I've experienced all of those reactions myself.

There are no words to express the gratitude I feel in knowing people enjoy reading my books and find a few hours of escape through the stories I tell. Knowing that you've enjoyed this character through so many books is humbling, and an honor that I don't take lightly.

Thank you so much for reading. It means the world to me.

ABOUT THE AUTHOR

Cathryn is the author of over thirty psychological suspense novels, including the ALEXANDRA MALLORY series featuring a sociopath you can't help but love. Readers have called the series "addictive".

The things that torment us in real life—obsession and revenge, guilt and envy and longing—are endlessly fascinating in fiction and she never grows tired of writing stories about characters struggling to overcome the worst.

Cathryn also writes ghost stories because who knows what lies beyond our senses—The Haunted Ship Trilogy and the Madison Keith series of novellas.

When she's not writing, she's usually reading, walking on the beach, or playing golf, going way out of her way to avoid hitting her ball in the sand or the water. She lives on the Central California Coast with her husband and her cat, Cleopatra.

You can get in touch with her by email, find her social media links, or sign up for her monthly newsletter at cathryngrant.-com/contact. As a thank you for signing up, you'll receive a free short story about Alexandra Mallory.